Midnight Fear

by

Evelyn Silver

The Bloodline Chronicles, Book 2

Midnight Fear

Cover Art by *Lisa Dawn MacDonald*

The Wild Rose Press, Inc.
PO Box 708
Adams Basin, NY 14410-0708
Visit us at www.thewildrosepress.com

Publishing History
First Edition, 2024
Trade Paperback ISBN 978-1-5092-5360-9
Digital ISBN 978-1-5092-5361-6

The Bloodline Chronicles, Book 2
Published in the United States of America

A cold, soft hand caressed her cheek, and Sarai melted against it.

"Don't worry," Marcelle said in her ear. "We won't bite." She whirled the witch around, their lips inches apart, and Sarai felt her body flushed with heat at the sight of Marcelle's blue eyes turning red with lust.

The first few cords of string instrumentals played and introduced a tango. Marcelle's body undulated in response. Setanta grabbed his lover's hand and pulled her towards him, then spun her out towards Sarai. They began a duet in those first bars of music, Marcelle's leg sweeping out sensually from the slit in her dress. Setanta's movements were more powerful, demanding, and full of purpose as he manipulated her body to press against him. He commanded, she responded. Her fangs slipped from her mouth, and he smirked just enough to reveal his own.

It looked like foreplay and Sarai wanted to participate in the celebration of sex and power. Setanta maneuvered Marcelle closer towards her. They made eye contact before Marcelle let go of her sire and circled Sarai, a hand trailing across Sarai's collarbone, just above her breasts.

Sarai felt her heart nearly stop as she was tilted back, then spun around to face Marcelle.

"Ready to dance?" the woman said.

Author's Note

Dedication

To Ashley, Rachel, and Evan

I'd also say to Mom, Dad, Joshua, my boys, and the in-laws… but there's sexy things in this book so maybe next time!

Chapter One: Marcelle's Pain

"Forty-nine." Marcelle's voice trembled as she spoke the number. She took a few moments to linger in the pain she had counted, waiting for the next strike she was meant to count. There was a long pause, letting her rest, then it began again.

Setanta brought the whip down gloriously on her skin: her lower thighs this time. The target came as a surprise. She'd expected another blow to her naked bottom. Marcelle arched and cried out, gripping the chains that held her cuffed hands spread between bed posts. There was just the thinnest sliver of silver in the shackles, made to cause minimal burning, but to keep her from being able to break out with her unnatural vampire strength. It thrilled her to pull against the restraints and feel no give. To be at her master's mercy. The mercy of an ancient and powerful pureblood prince and soon to be king.

"Fifty."

"Are we going past fifty today?" Setanta mused and closed the space between them so that he could run his hand against her willing body.

"Unless you're not up to it?" Marcelle leaned back against him, feeling his need pressing back. "Stop holding back."

She heard his breath flutter in amusement near her ear, and he caressed her waist with the adoration of a love centuries in the making.

"As you wish, *mo anam cara*."

He let her linger in the moment of anticipation before he stepped back and lashed across her back again. She trembled, aching for more of his skill.

"Fifty-one."

Next, he hit her bottom, and it felt different. It was bone deep, the way it felt when he didn't hold back as much. The pain was more intense, and Marcelle screamed, letting her body hang in the chains as she absorbed the shock.

"*Jaune*," she whispered instead of counting. Yellow, in French. It was their safe word, their code if something became too much and she needed him to slow down. Rouge meant she needed to stop.

The whip was thrown aside without hesitation, and her lover stood behind her, holding her up, gently pressing against her.

"How do you feel?" he asked. She shook against him. A switch had flipped in her mind, and she wanted no more.

"*Rouge*," she said. "Let me out."

Setanta's expert hands unfastened her restraints, and he swept her off her feet, cradling her in his arms. It felt good, the sensation of vulnerability and protection. She was strong and her body healed from everything done to it, but for a moment she could pretend to be delicate. She wanted to be delicate, a flower tended to by loving hands. It reminded her of the night he'd turned her, when he'd plucked her from the filth of the gutters and whisked her away to a new, better life.

He laid her on the bed and kept her close, a warm hand running through her hair.

"Are you all right?"

"I, I'm sorry, that last one just…" She buried her face against his chest.

"Don't be sorry. You don't have to push yourself into our regular play so soon after what happened. If you're not ready—"

"I'm ready!" she said. She couldn't let a little bit of torture at the hands of a psychopathic witch taint the enjoyment she found in her own masochism, in the pleasure of Setanta's sadism. But the usual pleasure just wasn't there the way it had been before. And it infuriated Marcelle that an amateur torturer such as Sarai's older half-sister, Alma, had such a lingering effect. Something as simple as the feel of a wooden chair dragged Marcelle's mind back to being trapped, having her skin flayed, burnt, and cut from her body. How did someone as good as her lover, the beautiful and kind witch Sarai, have a sister who was so cruel?

"You haven't said *rouge* in years. When was the last time, the twenties? That's eighty years ago, Marcelle."

"I don't know why…" Marcelle shut her eyes. "It feels good here, with you. I'm in control of the pain. I know you'll stop when I tell you to. I need that. I need to be able to tell you to stop."

Setanta held her close, and she basked in the light warmth of his body, listening to his slow heartbeat. It wasn't the burning heat of a true mortal, but his lukewarm body temperature felt like a hearth to her cold touch.

"This shouldn't be about pain for the sake of pain. You usually enjoy it." His hand slipped down between her legs. "You're not even wet. I like beating you because you enjoy it. I don't want to be your torturer,

3

Marcelle."

"It's not torture... I just need the kink for not-sex reasons this time." They were silent for a while. Marcelle felt he understood, felt it in the way he held her close against his naked body.

"Any plans for today?" she asked, feeling sufficiently soothed.

"An ambassador from Kemet should be arriving around midnight," Setanta said.

"I should be there."

He shook his head. "Take the night off, Marcelle. Tomorrow too."

"I've taken the whole week off."

"Yes, and it's the first week you've taken off in ages. You deserve a break." He pressed a soft kiss to her forehead, making her almost feel warmth in her cold, unbeating heart. "That's an order, by the way."

"From my Master or my Prince?"

"Both."

Marcelle sighed.

"I suppose I did tell Sarai I'd teach her some hand-to-hand combat." She could almost feel Setanta roll his eyes, and added before he could object, "Spending time with her doesn't count as work anymore. I like her."

"You should get back to her then," Setanta said as he sat up and offered her a robe. "It's getting late, she might wake up and wonder where you are."

Marcelle let him help her into the silk robe and gave him a quick peck on the lips. "Thanks, for all this. I'll be by again soon."

He returned a more passionate kiss, lingering against her and taking his time. She melted into the affection, realizing she was starved for it. As usual, he knew exactly what she needed. When they parted, he said, "I look forward to it."

Chapter Two: Sparring

"If I could just crawl into your skin and have all those good things, my life would be perfect."
"You made me miserable."
"You were that extra sister I didn't need around, and I got rid of you."
"Fuck you, Sarai."

The cruel words echoed like a masochistic broken record in the twenty-four-year-old witch Sarai's head. She sat curled up on her vampire lover Marcelle's ornate French bed, watching the sunset as it descended along a thin line in the closed curtains. She'd spent a week trying to adjust her sleep cycle to the vampires' preferred schedule, but it was so difficult to make the change. And every time she tried to sleep, she seemed to find herself staring wide-eyed for hours at nothing, hearing her half-sister Alma's words echoing in her mind.

Constant battles took place in her head. Did Alma ever care for her, or had she always been trying to get something from her? When had life become a competition between them, and how had Sarai been oblivious to it? Sarai had to believe there had once been authentic love there. But now... if they came head-to-head again, would it be to the death? When Alma channeled her necromancy through her whip and attempted to kill Setanta, Sarai had reflected it back at her to save him. If it ever came down to a choice between

Marcelle and Setanta or Alma…

The idea of seeing her sister dead was unthinkable. But so was seeing either Marcelle or maybe even Setanta dead. So unthinkable that Sarai had lost her right hand to protect them, to be replaced with a magical prosthetic that moved, but had no feeling.

"You're up early," Marcelle murmured as she stirred. "Is the sun even down? How are you awake right now?"

"Just woke up early, I guess."

"Something on your mind?"

"Nothing new. I'm fine." She didn't look at her lover. They both knew it was a blatant lie, but it said enough. It said Sarai didn't want to talk about it and was the same song and dance they've been doing back and forth ever since Alma tortured Marcelle. Sarai was fine. Marcelle was fine. It was all just… fine.

"Did you just get in?" Sarai asked.

"Mm, yeah. Setanta kept me busy. I'm up though." The vampire rolled over, a pale breast freed from the smooth sheets. "Do you still want to come with me for training?" Marcelle asked.

"I dunno. Is there a point? I can't keep up with you."

"It's fun. Bear and Angela will be there. A few others, probably. Oh, we can teach you how to shoot, if that interests you."

Shooting a gun; that was something she never thought she would ever do. "Yeah, I guess. Not like I have any plans." Which had become more and more of a problem as of late. Sarai never thought she'd miss her old job chopping onions and bussing tables, but at least it kept her on a schedule. At least she knew what to do from day to day. The routine would have provided her much needed sanity.

Once they'd gotten out of bed and put themselves together, the witch in baggy but comfortable clothes with the vampire in tight leggings and sleeveless crop top possibly from the eighties, Sarai joined Marcelle in going down to the second deepest part of the mansion, a floor above the dungeons. It was a basement gym built for vampires to work out. There was a firing range and weaponry, boxing rings for hand-to-hand combat practice, and metal dummies. Interestingly, at the ceiling were a network of ropes, bars, and beams, on which a few vampires could be seen practicing agility and balance. There were no weights or cardio-related pieces of equipment in the gym, of course. Vampires didn't need them.

Marcelle looked at ease as they entered the location, more than Sarai had seen in a while. It was as if they'd entered her comfort zone, and the smile on her face as she greeted her coworkers proved as much.

"You brought a friend!" Bear, a large Mi'kmaq Native American man with long hair and tattoos on his arms, shouted as he flipped Angela onto her back and pinned her to a mat-covered floor. The Romanian vampire woman grunted but shook off the shock of the slam as she stood up and leaned against the rail, brushing loose blonde hair away from her face.

"Are you going to show us how it's done then?" Angela teased, letting a rare smile show on her lips. The more reserved of the two, it made Sarai relax to be teased by her.

"Oh yeah, definitely." She looked at one of the metal dummies with way too many dents. As if she could ever be capable of denting solid metal. "He looks wimpy, I bet I could take him." Everyone chuckled, and she tapped the metal to check that it was very solid. "You guys really busted this one up, huh?"

"Some of us have," Bear said, looking pointedly at Marcelle.

"They're meant to hold up against us, so we can practice strikes. But the closer your blood is to a pureblood maker, the stronger you are." Marcelle gripped its head and jerked it to the side, then back upright, the metal screeching as she did.

"Whoa."

"Show off," Angela sighed.

"Angela is jealous because she's not a first-generation vampire like me," Marcelle grinned.

"What generation are you?" Sarai asked.

"Fourth. It means that a pureblood of this family made a vampire, who made a vampire, who made a vampire, who made me."

"And I'm second, so my sire was turned directly by a Viking queen," Bear said.

"Which means my sire is better than your sire," Angela taunted, and flicked his ear. He yelped and swatted at her like a child.

"Pssh, say that to me in Norway."

"Go away to Norway and I'll consider it."

"Who was your sire?" Sarai chimed in.

"Didn't I tell you?" Bear said. "Norse guy, total jackass."

"No, not you," Sarai teased. "Angela, who turned you?"

"Me?" Angela looked surprised at the interest. "Oh, no one of particular importance. A lonely nomad. He was attractive enough and my family abhorred him. Probably should have listened to them since our wedding night ended in him killing and turning me without warning me at all of what he was, what I would be." She spat on the ground in disgust. "Not the virginal blood I expected on the sheets."

"Yikes."

"He was not an ideal groom," she agreed. "But he ended up killing himself a few years later when he realized that tricking a woman into being his undead bride wouldn't fill the void in his heart." She grinned. "I won by outlasting him."

"On that lovely note, I offered to teach Sarai how to shoot," Marcelle said.

"Shooting, huh?" Bear said.

"I don't know how I feel about guns," Sarai admitted. "They're... I dunno."

"Would you prefer a sword?" Angela asked. Sarai couldn't tell if she was joking or serious. "We have some light-weight ones that shouldn't be too much trouble for you."

"Is that... really?"

"Of course." Angela blinked; her eyebrows knitted in confusion. "Why would I joke? Our prince favors the spear but is well trained in sword combat. I wouldn't give you a greatsword, but perhaps a longsword or rapier—"

"I'm not sure I'm a sword person," Sarai said. "Always just used my hands. You know, magic." She wagged her fingertips in an over-the-top way, as if she were a cartoon magician.

"Maybe hand-to-hand?" Bear suggested. "You need to be in contact with someone to use your power, right? Puts you up close with bad guys, potentially. If you don't want to use a gun, then hand-to-hand combat is your best option."

"What, hand-to-hand combat with you guys?" Sarai laughed. "No, thank you. I like being alive. Breathing is one of my favorite hobbies."

"Bear has a point," Marcelle said. "It's not as if you'd be fighting us. It might be a good thing for you to know, just in case."

The truth stung. She had killed a man alongside Setanta, her hand to his throat and her power spreading through his body like a disease. If she hadn't been able to catch him by surprise, would she have been able to kill him, or would he have had the advantage due to her lack of combat knowledge? There was always a chance she would need to kill again. She hoped not... but then, she had thought herself safe from such situations at the Ellis Coven in the company of her vampire protectors.

"Yeah. Just in case."

"Don't worry, we'll go slow for you," Bear said. "Marcelle, come on up here. Let's show her a few things."

Marcelle hesitated. It was a short motion, barely a moment, but Sarai noticed it. The flicker of fear looked so out of character for the vampire. She hid it well and a smile spread across her face. "I could go for a fight, I suppose."

They launched into a lesson, teaching Sarai the basics of self-defense, pointing out the best weak spots for a witch like her to hit if faced with a mortal while demonstrating on Bear. How to ram an attacker's nose into their skull with the base of the palm, punch someone in the throat, what points of the body hurt the most when pinched or elbowed.

"We should teach you how to throw someone. You can try on Bear," Angela said.

Sarai looked the giant vampire up and down, then laughed. "Hi, have you seen me? I don't even crack five feet."

"It's not about height," Marcelle said. "Or strength, in some cases, though being stronger is a nice advantage. We have some seventh- and eighth-generation vampires around who could take down a pureblood with the right moves."

Angela snorted.

"Maybe a young pureblood," Marcelle corrected. "But you get my point. Honestly, your low center of gravity is a real advantage. Bear, come here. Just do a slow move, like you're trying to grab my shirt, so I can show her."

"Yes ma'am," he said, and hopped to obey, moving in aggressive slow motion.

"See how he's got me like this?" Marcelle said. "Now, pretending I'm not stronger than him for a moment, I can still get out of this."

"I would just grab his hand and use my power," Sarai said, looking at their position. "Can't hurt me if I control him."

"It's probably a good idea to be able to subdue someone instead of killing them," Angela murmured. Sarai blushed, embarrassed for some reason to be a natural killer. She shoved the feeling aside: these were vampires. They couldn't judge her for her first instinct being murderous defense. It wasn't her fault that her dark gift as a necromancer killed her victims to grant her control over them.

"Yeah, I guess so."

"All right, so he has me here. All you need to do is step as such." Marcelle stepped forward enough to get behind him with one foot. "Then like so." His knee buckled in response to her movement, sending him flat on his back with a loud thud. Marcelle pulled him back up and stepped aside. "Catch that?"

"I think so." She saw the moves but replicating them would be something else.

"Come on, give it a try," Bear said.

"On you? You're joking."

He gave her a stern look. "I never joke." The seriousness lasted less than a few seconds. "Okay, that was a joke. But I promise, I'm not really attacking you. I'll let you throw me."

She shrugged as if that was a perfectly normal thing to attempt and stepped up to him. Even with his friendly smile, Bear was imposing as he towered over her. Sarai was hyper-aware of her narrow shoulders, non-existent muscle, and short stature. Forget vampiric super strength; he would have been a monster to fight as a mere human.

"I'll go to grab your shirt now, okay?" he said as if speaking to a child. She was certain he could sense her discomfort; her heart was pounding as if she'd run a mile. "I'll stop there, and let you do the move."

Sarai nodded and let him put his hand out as if to attack her.

"Now bring your leg forward behind his," Marcelle instructed. "And push him, knock his leg out."

With the one simple move from Sarai, the goliath toppled onto his back. A grin spread across her face as the two women clapped for her. "I think I can get the hang of that."

"Not bad," Bear said as he got to his feet. "Let's practice a few more times."

Sarai found she enjoyed the fake sparring with the vampires, with them allowing her to throw them to the ground over and over, teaching her a few kicks and punches in addition to the tricks. Eventually they wore her out, and she was left the only one panting from exertion.

"I think I need a break," she said as she sat on the floor, wishing for a bottle of water.

"Take your time," Marcelle said. "Are you all right?"

"Just out of shape." She gave a half smile.

"You want to go for a real bout while she's resting?" Bear asked, jabbing Marcelle's shoulder. "You can fight the winner, Sarai." The witch rolled her eyes and waved a hand to shoo him.

Marcelle gave Bear a light shove. "All right, let's go."

"Fists or weapons?" he asked, stretching as if he needed to at all.

"Been in the mood to pummel someone. Fists are the way to go for that, aren't they?"

"Fists it is," Bear said with a grin. "Not going easy on you though, Commander."

"Wouldn't expect you too, Teddy."

Bear scowled at the nickname, but it got a laugh from Sarai, and even a smile from Angela, so Marcelle looked pleased with herself as she entered the roped-off section with mats on the floor set aside for sparring.

The pair stared at each other with intent, watching for some give Sarai couldn't detect. Then, Bear darted forward. Marcelle sidestepped, sticking out her foot and tripping him. He fell forward, then immediately sprang back up.

"I let you have that one."

"Come now, it's like you're not even trying," Marcelle said. "Show me you're worth keeping around."

They started to circle each other, then rushed to the center and collided like missiles. He had sheer mass over her, but she was far faster and more agile. He would punch and meet air, while she would jab at tender points then dart out of the way before he could retaliate.

They started moving faster, making contact more often, with speed Sarai couldn't quite track. Bones shattered under fists and healed in moments.

"Is this how you guys usually fight?" she asked Angela, who nodded.

"It's typical. We don't need to hold back as much when—"

There was a sickening, loud crack that echoed through the gym. Bear fell to the floor, his body limp and lifeless.

Chapter Three: Paralysis

"What the fuck is your problem?!" Angela shouted as she stomped forward.

Marcelle looked up from Bear's immobile body, as if in a daze, and Sarai didn't know what to think. She couldn't have seen what she thought she'd seen. Marcelle wouldn't kill a friend. Bear couldn't be dead.

Wait, no. He *couldn't* be. Vampires turned to dust when they were killed, and Bear was very solid.

"He's fine," Marcelle said. "He's only paralyzed. Put it back, he'll be fine."

Angela glared as she snapped Bear's head back in place, and a few moments later he got to his feet. He was healed, though visibly drained. Sarai slumped to the floor in relief.

"What the hell, Marcelle?" he said, though he didn't sound angry. More concerned.

"I... I just needed to blow off some steam."

"That was more than blowing off steam," Bear said. "You almost took my head off. You're not well."

"I'm fucking fantastic." Marcelle walked out of the ring, and Sarai reached for her, only to be ignored. It stung. The vampire glared at one of the metal dummies and swung at it. The force left a light imprint of her fist embedded in the metal. "Maybe you just need more practice. You should have seen that coming a mile away. You know that's my go-to."

"When you're against someone you're actually fighting, not sparring with a friend."

"Did you want me to go easy on you? I thought you were a warrior."

"You know what I meant."

"Marcelle?" Sarai asked.

"I'm fine."

The witch's eyes narrowed. The lie had outlived its welcome.

"No, you're not fine," Sarai snapped. "None of us are fine. I'm not fine. You're not fine. No one is fine, so let's not lie about it anymore."

Marcelle punched the dummy again and the sound rang through the gym like a bell tolling for a funeral.

"What, should I spill my bleeding heart all over the mat for everyone to see? Everyone, come see that your knight commander can't handle a little torture," Marcelle shouted. Everyone present had long stopped what they were doing to stare. "Dame Marcelle de Sauveterre can't handle a little flaying, come see!"

Sarai stepped forward and grabbed Marcelle's fist as it raised to strike the dummy again. It was dangerous, but she trusted Marcelle to hold back with her.

"It wasn't a little. You didn't look like a person. I couldn't recognize you."

Marcelle's lips curled in a snarl, and she pulled her hand away as she took several steps back. "You shouldn't have seen anything. You are *my* ward. You wear *my* ring. And you had to save *me*? From some fucking witch?" She scoffed and began spewing what sounded like venom in French, while Sarai's throat tightened with emotion. That "fucking witch" was her sister, after all. The relation felt like it gave Sarai ownership of the crimes.

Angela's expression softened and she responded in the same language. Marcelle shook her head, looking around the room.

"*Je suis désolé*," she whispered, then darted away, leaving Sarai alone with the vampires.

"What did she say?" Sarai asked.

"The crux of it is that she's unworthy and undeserving, that she's sorry," Angela said.

"She's unworthy? She saved me from my family and got tortured for it, but she's the one who's unworthy?" Sarai burst into incredulous laughter. At least they had moved beyond the "I'm fine" lies.

"Are you all right?" Bear said. "Would you want to stay with us for a little?"

She shook her head as she tried to stop laughing. She didn't need more people watching her humiliation. She found herself holding her own hand, the artificial one grafted onto her arm by the witches on Ellis Island the vampires had allied with. How could she have lost so much and yet felt like she'd done nothing?

"Want me to walk with you back to your rooms?" he asked.

Sarai shrugged. As she thought about it, she decided it would be best to have someone with her, just in case, and nodded. Bear put a cold yet comforting hand on her shoulder and she let him lead her out of the vampires' gym. It was like having a large, walking suit of armor or professional athlete as a personal bodyguard, and it did make Sarai feel safe. Especially since he really was so nice.

"She's not mad at you," Bear said. It was sweet, but she disagreed with him.

"I'm mad at me." She wiped her eyes a little, trying to be subtle about it but knowing she was failing. Was she crying, or was it from the inappropriate laughter? She wasn't sure.

Bear kept trying to reassure her and listening to him worked a little. By the time they got to the floor with the bedrooms, she'd calmed down a little and kept herself from any hysterical crying fits, which she felt was some sort of accomplishment.

"Are you okay?" she asked him. "She broke your neck, right?"

"Oh, yeah, don't worry about it," he said with a dismissive wave of his hand. "It doesn't even hurt. It just paralyzes us, which is a little weird to experience, and it's bad form to do it the way she did, but I can heal from it. Might pop down to the human quarters for a pick-me-up, though."

As they turned the corner, Sarai's heart jumped. Setanta stood there, closing the door to one of the rooms next to Marcelle's.

"Your Highness," Bear said, bowing his head. Even with his head bowed, he was taller than the prince, which was saying something since Setanta was tall in his own right. Of course, everyone seemed tall to Sarai's four-foot-ten-inch frame.

Setanta nodded in acknowledgement, then frowned, and looked up, his eyes landing on Sarai. "Is all well?"

Was it that obvious? "Y-yeah. Yes, Your Highness." Was she meant to be formal with him now? Bear had been, yet she remembered them being less formal before. And she'd had casual conversations with him in the past, though they had always been in private.

"Marcelle's having personal issues. Might want to

talk to her later," Bear said.

"Noted." He didn't look away from Sarai. "I actually have something for you, Sarai. It might cheer you up." He reopened the door to what she could only assume were his bedchambers, which made her gulp a little. "If you have a moment? Bear, you too, just a moment of your time. For an unrelated request."

She couldn't say no.

Chapter Four: The Grimoire

"Please, come in," Setanta beckoned.

Sarai followed Setanta through the doorway and into the room. With just one foot inside, it was obvious that this was his home. It was even more luxurious than Marcelle's rooms. She remembered when she first entered Marcelle's home, how she compared it to her old apartment, with its makeshift "furniture" and cracked walls. It couldn't hold a candle to Marcelle's room.

Likewise, Marcelle's didn't compare with Setanta's, but in a different way. The large living area and branching rooms were made for a king. Instead of a bright and baroque style, there was a gothic grace. Dark green curtains and colors adorned the walls, with carved rich oak in Celtic patterns accompanying them. The furniture (namely a table, desk, and some chairs) sat on a large green rug that looked like a medieval tapestry. Said furniture appeared to be made of solid black marble, like the floors, which she imagined would work best for a vampire. They needed everything to last a long time, after all. But was gold paint along intricate, carved designs in the stone necessary?

"What do you need?" Bear asked Setanta as he followed Sarai into the room.

"Sarai, why don't you sit down, we'll only be a moment," Setanta said and pulled out a chair at a table with a turn much too graceful for the simplest of gestures. Sarai nodded and did as she was told, allowing him to push the chair in under her before he led Bear toward the other side of the suite, to the bedroom.

"I haven't been asking Marcelle for her usual routine, if you understand my meaning, as to not put too much stress on her," Setanta said. "I've put it off for some time now, but much longer would be unwise. Would you mind terribly stepping in for her? If you'd rather not, I can ask Angela."

"Nah, I'm right here. It's no trouble. I was going to get a pick-me-up today anyway, so this is perfect timing. Help yourself."

Sarai's heart skipped a beat as she realized what the prince wanted with Bear. Setanta was after blood. Pureblood vampires fed not on the blood of humans, but on the vampires they created, as the power of human blood simply wasn't enough to sate their thirst. She'd never seen Setanta feed before, though she had seen him attack opposing witches once. Feeding was very different than a fight, as she knew from her own experience allowing Marcelle to bite her. Gripped with curiosity, she leaned forward to get a better look. The chair shifted under her.

Bear pushed his long, black hair to the side, then paused with a chuckle.

"Do you care?" Setanta mused.

"She can have a peep show if she wants." Bear turned and caught Sarai's eye, winking. She blushed.

"I wasn't—!"

"It's fine," Bear laughed. "Enjoy the show."

Smiling as his fangs grew and eyeing Bear's neck with which he was just a little above eye level with, Setanta said, "I'll make it quick."

Then he bit.

Bear gave a sharp inhale and clenched his fists as he closed his eyes, then relaxed into the bite, one arm wrapped around Setanta as the prince fed without so much as a drop spilt.

As he finished, Setanta rested a hand on Bear's forearm. "Thank you. I appreciate it very much."

"Feeling better?" the younger vampire asked, rubbing his healing neck.

"Much."

"Man. I don't know how Marcelle does that all the time. That is… that's taxing."

"I have some bags of hers, if you need a quick sip now. Would you like something specific?"

"Yeah, sounds good. Got any vegetarian?"

"Let me check."

Setanta went to a small mini fridge and opened it to reveal packs of blood.

"I have regular, regular, lactose intolerant, and, ah, yes. Vegetarian."

"Groovy." Bear smirked at Sarai. "Did you know that vegetarian is a Mi'kmaq word?"

"What? No, it's not," she scoffed.

"It is, I swear! It translates to 'bad hunter'."

Sarai snorted, while Setanta sighed and shook his head as he tossed Bear a packet of "vegetarian" blood.

"I'm positive I've read that one on a popsicle stick," she told him.

"Impossible," Bear replied. "Because *I* got it off a bottle cap."

He accepted a straw from Setanta and punctured the pack like it was a juice box. "I don't have anything against vegetarians though, really." He slurped his blood and smiled with a red gleam on his teeth. "They taste great."

The image of him smiling with blood would have frightened a younger Sarai. But somehow, it was just funny to her.

"Is this how it usually goes?" Sarai asked. "With purebloods, I mean."

"Usually, I rely on Marcelle," Setanta said. "Though I do ask others from time to time, should the need arise. All amicably, as you can see. New Ulster purebloods do not make demands of blood, we take only willingly here."

"I guess that's good then." Sarai pursed her lips. "You know, you could call yourself something other than purebloods. It's a little…"

"Eugenicist elitest?" Bear offered.

Setanta laughed but nodded. "You're not wrong. But it's a nice euphemism for a horrific Frankenstein's monster amalgamation of witch powers stitched together with the blood of a goddess or possibly a demon from another plane wandering the earth in thirst of blood for eternity. And much shorter."

"What about… I dunno, first ones?"

"Artemisia is hardly the first vampire, as young as she is. And I'm not either. There are even other bloodlines much older than ours. The Kemetic vampires in Egypt are a good example."

"Okay, uh, I'm spit balling here. Blood source?"

"We call the humans who serve us sources, so that's taken, I'm afraid."

Sarai sighed. "Well, it's a bit icky to call yourself pure. You should come up with something else."

"Perhaps the name will change in the future,"

Setanta said with a smile. "I don't think of myself as pure, if that matters at all. It's simply the name that's stuck for the past few centuries."

"This is all interesting but, if that's all, Highness?" Bear said. "I'd like to get going."

Setanta nodded. "That will be all, yes. Thank you, again."

Bear nodded his head with respect and gave Sarai a wave. "See you around, kid." He closed the door behind him.

And so, Sarai was alone with Setanta.

It felt weird being alone with the vampire prince in his home, trapped in his quarters. When she'd been alone with him at the Ellis Coven, it felt different. Witches were her territory, so to speak, while this was his. It was as exciting as it was scary, especially when he pulled out another chair and sat right next to her. She glanced up at him before focusing on the plain-looking notebook. Before she could wonder about it too long, he answered her unspoken question. "I have the translation of my grandmother's grimoire that I promised you in exchange for your assistance in contacting other witches. I thought we could look it over together, in case you have any questions."

"Oh." She stared down at the notebook in surprise. She wasn't sure what she had expected when he invited her into his room and sat her down but for some reason, it was a very unexpected revelation. "Um, sure. And thank you," she added.

Setanta flipped open the book to the table of contents. "Some of this is fairly standard. Though I'm sure whatever you've learned has changed over the years."

It was well organized for a grimoire. Most were a mess, written without neat categories; it made her wonder if the version in its original language was more chaotic, and Setanta had edited it for her.

"You probably have expanded knowledge. She only had access to herbs and plants from one region of the world. But past the beginning half with the basics of potions and spells and such, that's where she gets into uses for her power, incorporating it into her craft. One interesting potion to me was... this one here. The concept is fascinating at least. Decaying living plant matter and seeds to the edge of death and reviving them as it's drunk to revive a woman's fertility after menopause. Was very popular at the time. Not something you need, but it's a method to play with, using your abilities in potion making and in making talismans."

She scanned the directions. "That's genius. Your grandma's good."

"She was very good," he agreed. "Inventive as well as powerful. I'm sure this book contains all kinds of good ideas for you. Probably the most useful to you would be training yourself to be able to project your powers, so you don't need to touch people to affect them."

Healing from a distance would have its uses. Killing and turning people into zombies however... Perhaps it was all worth learning. She seemed to have more use for her violent half as of late.

"Granted," he continued. "She was turned into a vampire so she had a few more years to practice and teach herself these things, but she documented her journey, so you can take shortcuts just from reading her work rather than trying to figure it out all by yourself."

"A vampire?" she asked. "Can I meet her then,

or…"

"She isn't alive, or in existence, anymore," he said.

"Oh, sorry."

"No need to be sorry. She died centuries ago, I'm well past the loss."

Sarai flipped to the back of the book, landing on a page about reattaching severed limbs. There was nothing about regrowing them, unfortunately. She clenched her artificial fist, unable to feel the sensation. At least it was something that she had the use of the limb. "Damn… I mean, no offense, but I wouldn't have thought ancient witches could do something like this. It's advanced stuff even now."

"We weren't all incompetent hedgewitches, you know. Some of us could pass for civilized."

"I-I didn't mean…" She looked up to see amusement on his face and smiled with him. "You shouldn't mess with people, you know. You're too serious for that and I was going to take you seriously."

"Ah, but that's the perfect reason to mess with people."

"You're terrible."

He laughed. "Perhaps. Oh, I meant to discuss something else with you. The Ellis Coven sent a message from Hannah. They want to know when you would like to see her. Something about a haunting?"

"Not exactly a haunting," Sarai said. She couldn't view her mother's guardian spirit as a proper haunting, even if it did technically qualify as one. "My mother's ghost has been following me around. It's been mostly helpful. But, you know, something that someone with expertise should look into about why she hasn't moved on. Hannah offered to help."

"Is she here now?"

Sarai did a quick survey of the room and shook her head. "She pops up right before things go wrong to give me a warning. And she kept trying to sing me to sleep, but I got mad about that and chased her off for a bit. That was, well, before I knew she was my mom." Guilt twisted her gut. If only she'd known.

"A helpful sort of apparition then. I've heard of worse. It's been a long time since I've encountered a proper ghost before. Does she seem self-aware?"

"I'm not sure?" Sarai said. "She's like an alarm that goes off. I haven't had any real conversations with her. Though I could try harder."

"I'd be curious to learn as to how she perceives threats to warn you. If I were to startle you, or threaten you without true malice, I assume that wouldn't quite be enough."

"Probably not, but you can give it a try," Sarai laughed. "I don't think you count as a real threat anymore."

"A little roleplay never quite bites with the same risk as the real thing," Setanta mused.

Sarai raised an eyebrow. "I'll take your word for it."

He chuckled. "That aside, I wonder if perhaps you'd allow me to attempt some magical assistance, before Hannah gets here? If only to sate my own curiosity about this spirit wandering my home."

"What did you have in mind?"

"Nothing too strange. My own ability to cast spells is quite limited, but I do have in my repertoire a rather useful reflection spell. I can use it to experience magic either cast on you or to use magic you can use."

"Like my gifts?" Sarai asked in surprise. "Would

you be able to use my gifts, or other people's gifts? That's possible?"

"Yes, though I've no interest in that at the moment. Spirits are tethered by magic. As such, with the reflection spell, I would be able to glimpse the bond you have as if it were my own. Perhaps even commune with her or help you to do so."

Sarai's eyes widened. "That sounds like a great idea. I don't know much about ghosts. You've got to know more than I do, so yeah, any help would be amazing. All I know is that something has to be keeping them stuck. Unfinished business, a curse, an object their spirit's connected too. I think that's all the reasons, right?"

"Just about," Setanta said. "A few others, but those are the primary ones, yes."

"Then yes, let's do it," she said. "I… I'd like to know my mother's found some peace. I don't remember her, but I know she didn't have much peace in life. I'm about ninety-nine percent positive that my father kidnapped her to, you know, make her have me."

"A grim fate for any woman. For any person." There was a flicker of something sad in his eyes, of true empathy. "She deserves her peace, and I would consider it an honor to assist, though you will need someone with Hannah's skill set to do more than contact her." Setanta checked a pocket watch for the time, then snapped it shut. "Unfortunately, I can't stay much longer now. But come here tomorrow evening and I'll perform the spell for you."

"Yes. Thank you. I appreciate it a lot." She smiled and let him walk her to the door, grimoire gripped in her arms, then paused. "You… you're close with Marcelle, right?"

"Obviously."

"She snapped a bit just now. I went with her for some sparring. She broke Bear's neck and there was an argument with Angela."

"Bear can handle a broken neck," Setanta said. "But I see why there might be cause for concern."

"She's not dealing with what happened. Do vampires have, I dunno, psychologists?"

"Psychologists? An interesting notion. No, we don't as of now. Though the field of psychology is an interesting one, it's still relatively new to us. You'll be hard pressed to find a vampire willing to accept they need a doctor of any kind, let alone one for our minds."

"Well, you should tell her to go see one to help her deal with stuff. She doesn't talk to me about what happened. With my sister."

"I see." Setanta thought for a moment. "I'll speak to her. Perhaps make use of some psychology."

It felt like a weight off her shoulders. She felt that if Marcelle would listen to anyone, she would listen to Setanta. "Thanks."

He smiled at her. "Have a lovely evening, Sarai."

Chapter Five: Fight or Flight

Marcelle felt like shit. Somehow, the mansion felt stifling, and she craved a change of scenery. Angela's advice wasn't awful, and she thought about going into town alone for a bit, maybe buying herself something nice, but there didn't seem to be a point in that. She had plenty of nice things in her room, and they didn't make proper hair combs anymore. At least, the mall she went to most often didn't sell any. It crossed her mind to visit an antique shop, but that would just be depressing. Everything she liked was old and covered in dust.

Even if that hadn't been the case, shopping wouldn't have helped. Something inside felt hollow in a way that material possessions wouldn't fill.

"What are you doing up there?"

The child-like voice broke Marcelle's brooding, and she looked down to see the young pureblood princess Artemisia watching her. Immediately, she swung herself down from a tree branch and knelt on one knee.

"How can I be of service to you, Princess?" she said, bowing her head.

"Don't do that," Artemisia pouted.

Marcelle frowned and looked up. The little girl was spoiled beyond reason and always wanted vampires and humans fawning over her, kneeling before her. Her mother was to blame, as the woman had a superiority complex a mile wide.

"I want to talk to you," the princess said. Marcelle rose to her feet but bowed her head again respectfully.

"As you wish, Princess. What would you like to talk about?"

Artemisia crossed her arms over her chest and stomped over to a bench, where she sat with her feet just brushing the ground. "Now that we're friends with witches, are you going to kill all the Vasi with them?"

"That is the plan," Marcelle said, and sat down next to the princess. "I'll be going with some of the others to train with their witches, to work on fighting together."

"And if you kill them, all the contracts get destroyed, right?"

Marcelle looked over at her. It wasn't like Artemisia to be concerned about the welfare of others, let alone witches enslaved by the anti-occult fanatics known as the Vasi. Perhaps her limited time as their prisoner had changed her heart and made her a little less selfish, more empathetic.

"I don't think it works that way," she said. "My understanding is that a bond like in those contracts lasts until death."

"Until death?"

"Yes."

"Well, what if it happened to a vampire?"

"Most vampires aren't witches, so it wouldn't work in the first place. We're already dead."

"There's still a lot of live witches. What if you killed all the Vasi everywhere? The whole thing, all dead. Would all the witches they took be free then?" Artemisia pressed.

"Well, I imagine that with no one to give them orders, they'd be free to do as they pleased. I don't know a lot about this sort of magic," Marcelle admitted. "Are you worried about the witches?"

Artemisia didn't answer. Instead, she slumped over, curling up against Marcelle in a fetal position. Marcelle raised an eyebrow and contemplated placing a hand on the girl's shoulder or head to comfort her but decided against it.

"Yeah. I guess," the princess finally said with a shrug. "Don't tell Mama. She doesn't like witches." Marcelle felt power in the words and sighed.

"You don't need to compel me. I wouldn't have said a word." As if she ever wanted to speak with the stuck-up Queen Giovanna if she didn't have to.

Artemisia shrugged. "What about Sarai? Did she get compelled? I heard someone say that she's contracted." Marcelle could guess who that "someone" was. No doubt a certain antagonistic queen would enjoy spreading malicious rumors and sharing them with her precious princess.

"No, not contracted. We freed her before that could happen. She just has her old coven interested in finding her and they're not very nice."

Artemisia's body went rigid, then she sat up straight. "She's got Vasi *and* witches chasing her, but she's allowed here? Why didn't you kill her like the other Vasi witches?"

So much for empathy. "It's not like that. She's not a danger to us."

"Are the people who want her dead dangerous?"

"Yes, but I—"

"Then she's a danger, isn't she?! Until we kill all the Vasi—"

"She's not bound to the Vasi, Princess. I promise

that."

Artemisia pouted and stared down at the ground. "Do old compulsions disappear if someone dies? Like, if a witch is captured by the Vasi, and they compel her, but then all the Vasi are dead, does she have to listen still?"

"I'm not sure. It's not the same as our compulsions. At least, not from what I know," Marcelle said. She took a deep breath to force herself to relax. She wasn't in the mood for this at all but could not be rude to royalty. If only it were Setanta, she could get away with telling him to leave her alone when she wanted. Most of the time. "Why don't you talk to your brother about this? He knows a lot more about magic than I do."

Artemisia glared at her, and somehow the dead woman felt a chill. The princess was an unnerving sort of being, due to her youthful appearance while being thirty years old, but this was different. There was something wrong.

"Artemisia... Is everything all right with you and Setanta?"

"No. I can't talk to him."

"I know that he's a little distant, but he still cares about you."

"I can't talk to *him*."

Marcelle paused for a moment. There was such anger in the little girl's eyes... it was frightening. "My Princess, you know your brother loves you."

Artemisia shrieked in frustration, pushing Marcelle hard into the bench's armrest, causing the metal to bend.

"You're useless!" she screamed, her voice shrill like the smallest banshee. "You and everyone, you're useless! I tell you, you don't remember, and I hate you!"

"My Princess—"

"Shut up!"

Marcelle's mouth snapped shut, compelled into silence by the power of a pureblood's command.

"Just… just forget this. Forget everything I said and go run around the mountain or something."

Marcelle found herself sitting alone, a dent the shape of her side in the armrest of the bench she was in. Hadn't she been sitting in the tree just a moment ago?

Clearly she needed to go for a proper run, to get some fresh mountain air. Marcelle hopped to her feet and ran with vampiric speed from the property, up into the Appalachian mountains of North Carolina.

****

Setanta found Marcelle curled into a ball in the branches of a tree halfway up a nearby mountain. It was always easy for him to find her around the palace and its surroundings. While he shared a blood bond with any vampire of his bloodline, his connection to Marcelle was more intimate than only blood. He could pick up her rosewater scent whenever she was nearby and knew her favorite spots around the Appalachians that hid their home. Seeking her out was like following an animal instinct to find home.

"Come down from there," he said as he looked up at his love, perched like a gothic gargoyle.

"Is there something you want, Setanta?" she grumbled, not moving from her tree.

"Just to talk. I heard you and Bear got into a fight."

"No, we sparred. That's all."

"That's all?"

"Fine, there was a little bit of yelling. Angela and Sarai were there, go ask them."

"I did. Sarai suggested you see a psychologist."

"A psychologist?" Marcelle snapped. "She thinks I'm insane?"

"Not insane, just troubled."

"I'm fine."

"You are not fine."

"Maybe I've got the morbs. It's fine. I'm fine. I'm *fine.*"

He jumped up and landed in the tree next to hers, gripping the trunk like a cat. "First the safe word, then Bear's neck. I'm thinking Sarai might be onto something with the psychologist."

"I'm not crazy."

"No, you're hurt," he said. "If you were mortal and the wounds were in your skin rather than your mind, you would rush to a physic."

Marcelle audibly ground her teeth at him, then her lips curled to reveal her fangs as her eyes flashed an angry red. "I haven't needed a physic, apothecary, doctor, or surgeon since you killed me. I don't need one now. Or is it an order, *Your Highness?*"

"It might become one. Some of the humans see them for their troubles, and those doctors know of our existence. You could visit one of them."

"An order. If you order me to see some human doctor, I will... I'll eat the psychoanalyst."

"Psychologist. And no, I know you wouldn't do that. You'll just as soon milk a pigeon as needlessly hurt an innocent."

"I'm not so weak that I need help," she shouted. "I am not weak, I'm fine!" She leapt down from the tree and kicked the one that he clung to. There was a loud crack like thunder and the wood split. Setanta jumped to the ground just before it fell and crashed down the mountain side until propped up by other trees.

"Yes, clearly," he mocked. "You can tear down a tree and break a weaker vampire's neck. You must be the strongest vampire in New Ulster."

"Don't patronize me, Setanta," she growled. "Look, I'll apologize to Bear. I just needed a fight. I needed... I don't know."

"A good fight to get the bloodlust out of your system?" he asked and began to unbutton his shirt. "I'll give you the fight you want."

She eyed him cautiously, then nodded and stripped off her shirt before flinging it into the undergrowth, revealing a black sports bra. "No rules?"

"No rules." Setanta braced himself. "Go."

Marcelle didn't hesitate. She launched like a lioness, and Setanta met the force head on, feeling her push him back into another tree that almost shattered from the strength. He grunted. He was stronger than she was, but that didn't mean she couldn't hurt him. She was a skilled and well-trained fighter with centuries of experience under her belt, and one of the few non-pureblood vampires who could make him pause. But he had an advantage aside from his superior physical abilities: she was fighting angry.

He flung her in the other direction to slam her against a tree, then stood back as she picked herself up and shook leaves and bark from her skin. Setanta cocked his head to the side.

"Is that all you have?"

Marcelle bared her fangs and tried again. She attempted to fling herself around his neck with her legs, in a move meant to break his neck like she no doubt had done to Bear, but Setanta threw her off and into a large stone. A section of the rock cracked, but Marcelle was undeterred. With a high-pitched war cry worthy of Setanta's primitive ancestors, she pummeled into him, fists beating his sides. Ribs broke and bruised and healed in moments. The pain she managed to inflict was impressive. It made him feel invigorated, and his own fangs extended. With a snarl, he began to fight her back. They each landed and blocked blows, breaking their bodies on each other's fists again and again, clawing with their nails to draw streaks of blood that, like their bones, healed instantly.

Then, Marcelle found an opening and latched her teeth into his shoulder.

Setanta gave an animalistic cry somewhere between a shout and a growl as she moaned into the wound, feasting on his superior blood. It was an ultimate taboo, to bite a pureblood. Even when he fed others for pleasure or to turn them, he always made the cut himself. For him to say no rules was to allow it, but it was forbidden by their culture. No one fed on purebloods. No one dared. No one but his violent and beautiful Marcelle.

Deciding to end the fight, wings erupted from his back with a burst of bone-crunching agony, and he jumped into the air to the tops of the trees, then slammed her back down into the rock below. She let go of his flesh, staring at him in a daze as she lay on her back. Blood dripped down from him to her mouth.

"Better?" he asked, panting just a little.

She nodded, breathless as the dead, then hugged him as tears poured out, cold against his warmer skin. "I needed this," she whispered. "I shouldn't have bitten you. I'm sorry, that was crossing a line."

"So it was. Should I punish you?"

She sniffed a little, then laughed, burying her head against him. "I think you just broke every bone in my body. That's enough punishment for me, if it's all the same to you."

"You are forgiven," he said, and kissed her forehead with tender care, stroking his fingers through her disheveled hair. It felt like silk to his touch. It never ceased to amaze him that no matter how strong she was, how many centuries she spent fighting, her body was always so soft and giving.

Marcelle tilted her head up and pushed her blood-coated lips to his with need. His fangs ached in response, an indication of his desire to penetrate her in more than one way.

"Take me, Setanta," she begged, nails digging into the skin of his back and drawing blood yet again. "Please. Don't be gentle."

"Since you asked nicely," he murmured. Setanta used his wings to prop himself up over her while one hand undid his belt and the other pulled down her pants. She wore black lace underneath. It was a favorite style of hers, and he more than approved of the way it looked against her pale skin, but there wasn't time to appreciate her beauty or take things slow. The battle had been their foreplay, and the scent of her need was an elixir drawing him in. Harder than the stone landscape they had destroyed, he pushed the lace to the side and thrust inside her body, feeling her clench and reveling in the vibrations caused as she cried out.

Their union was primal. Setanta had had his way with many women and men over the centuries, but none felt like home the way Marcelle did. She was rainwater at sea, a hearth fire in winter, a soft bed after war. She was safety and passion and bliss. Comfort and consistency in a world always changing. The person who stayed with him the longest, with no indication of wanting to leave. She was his, forever. And eternity was theirs.

His speed picked up, to a pace no human could match or endure. Held up by his wings to allow his hands full access, one hand slid down to play with her clitoris as the other teased her breast. Marcelle shouted again and again, the warrior from before surrendered to pleasure, to him. Submitting to his will and body.

He held off his own pleasure until Marcelle had several orgasms, turning her into a whimpering and limp mess in his grip. When he knew she could take no more, he released inside her with a war cry, filling her with warmth. She moaned, and they lay together on the forest floor, where the only sounds were his breath and his slow heartbeat.

"Thank you," she whispered, her body still trembling around him as he softened. "I needed this. All of this."

He used his wings to push them up to a sitting position, arms tight around her, his member still inside her with her legs around his waist. Once leaning against a tree, he wrapped his wings around her like a blanket. He knew she loved the warmth as she snuggled against him.

"You know I'm here for you. If you need a kiss, a fuck, a beating, a fight. A taste of my blood. You can always come to me." He wiped a tear from her face. "Would you at least consider talking to a doctor once? For me, *mo anam cara.*"

Marcelle sighed. "Look, I don't know about the

psychological stuff. But if you really think it would help, I'll try it once. I don't think it can be better than this, though."

"That's all I ask. And we can always do more of this."

Marcelle smiled. It was the first genuine smile he had seen grace those now smeared painted red lips since she'd been tortured.

"I don't want to go back yet," she told him.

"What would you like then?"

"I… would like to go for a flight."

Setanta kissed her and unfurled his massive, powerful wings. "Then let us fly."

****

Sarai was on pins and needles waiting for Marcelle to come back. She had a midnight 'lunch' meal in the French bedroom, waiting for Marcelle there just in case she showed up, reading the grimoire when she could focus on it. She wished she had the mental fortitude to put her worries out of her mind and just indulge in the book but worry for her lover kept popping into her mind.

Would Marcelle be angry Sarai had tattled on her to Setanta? That she'd suggested a psychologist? She would find out soon enough, but not knowing when was a torment.

Suddenly, Marcelle was sitting at the foot of the bed. Sarai jumped a little; she hadn't even heard the vampire come in.

"I owe you an apology," Marcelle murmured. She reached out and rested a hand over Sarai's. "It wasn't fair of me to behave the way I did. You deserve better."

"It's okay," Sarai said as she put her book to the side and held Marcelle's hand. "How are you feeling?"

"Better. I went for a run to clear my head. Setanta found me, turned it into a flight."

Sarai raised both her eyebrows as she eyed Marcelle's appearance. A flight could explain the messy bed hair. But it didn't explain the missing shirt, blood, and dirt.

"All right, a fight, then a fuck, and then a flight. Then another fuck," Marcelle amended.

"You... fought Setanta?" Sarai asked incredulously. "That sounds like a great way to commit suicide."

"His suggestion, to let me blow off steam," Marcelle shrugged. "And fucking him is a much better suicide attempt. I feel like I need to put my organs back in their right places now."

Sarai snorted. "Sorry. Uh, yeah, looks like it. Is the blood from the fight or the sex?"

"I honestly couldn't tell you," Marcelle laughed. "I'll go wash up. Look, Sarai. Setanta told me what you suggested. About the doctor."

"The psychologist? It was just a suggestion. I want you to be okay."

"I'm fi—" Marcelle stopped herself mid word. "No, I suppose I'm not fine. I agreed to see one. For one session."

It was much better than nothing, though Sarai did not envy the poor psychologist who would now be tasked with helping a vampire through trauma. She smiled and leaned forward to surprise Marcelle with a kiss on the lips, but her lover pulled back. Sarai's heart raced with instant panic at the thought she had done something wrong.

"Sorry," Marcelle said quickly. "I'd kiss you, but some of this blood is Setanta's. I don't want to risk you having any since it could turn you. And… there's other fluids that you might not want to taste. We did a few things. A few times."

Sarai blushed. "Oh. Okay."

Marcelle squeezed their hands together, clear affection in her eyes. "I'll go wash. But I needed to tell you, thank you. And I'm sorry. I know you care."

"I do. Marcelle, I care about you a lot. I just want to see you happy again."

The vampire smiled. "I think I will be, Sarai. I will."

Chapter Six: Ghost Magic

The next evening when they woke up, Sarai and Marcelle went separate ways. The vampire went to meet with a psychologist in town that Setanta had arranged for her, while Sarai went to meet the prince in his chambers. She knocked, and he called from within for her to enter.

Inside, she found the furniture pushed to the side and a circle made from unlit candles on the floor. Setanta stood in the center, holding the largest weapon Sarai had ever seen. It was a spear of metal and possibly petrified bone that looked medieval, or perhaps older, with wicked barbs along the end. She could feel the ancient magic radiating from it.

"What is *that*?" she marveled as she closed the door behind her.

"My focus. A spear named Gáe Bulg."

"Sorry, gay what?"

He sighed. "Not gay. Gáe. It's the old Irish word for spear."

"Well, in English it means gay," she snickered. "I see why you don't bring it out in public. And I thought wands were conspicuous. You could see that thing from space."

Setanta smiled a little, shaking his head. "It has become more difficult to use as society changes."

"Compensating for something?" The joke slipped out before she could stop herself, and her eyes widened as she realized she had technically just asked him about the size of his privates.

Setanta blinked and stared at her a moment, as if shocked anyone would have the gall to say such a thing to him, then burst into laughter that echoed in the room.

"No, Sarai. I am most certainly not compensating for anything."

"I, I'm sorry, it just slipped. That was inappropriate of me," she said, though his laughter made her smile.

"So it was. Please, if you would enter my circle?"

Sarai stepped forward, her prosthetic fist clenching her own focus, a red fingerless glove. She'd never been more grateful that it was as inconspicuous an item as it was, in comparison to Setanta's spear. Traditional wands and staffs were considered bulky and archaic as a witch's tool necessary for channeling spells, but at least could be hidden in a jacket or passed off as a walking stick. Modern witches preferred subtle items: a piece of jewelry, item of clothing, and small objects were popular choices. Once crafted, the item was bound to the witch as the only form their focus could take. Setanta was stuck with something impossible to bring anywhere in modern life, and she imagined that even back in the days of his youth it hadn't been an easy thing to carry around, even if he was known and accepted as a witch rather than only seen as a vampire back then.

"How does this work? Do I need my focus?"

"No, I'll be casting the spell. You're not opposed to a little blood magic, are you? I know it's fallen out of favor in recent times."

"Uh, well, I guess it depends on the context and how it's used."

"I use my own blood to amplify the power of spells

since my ability to cast them is weak. That is all," he said. "No animal or human sacrifices. And none of your blood is required."

"Have you done that before?"

"Which part?" he asked and without warning impaled his hand on one of the barbs of his spear. She winced, feeling sick from the sight. Yet, he didn't seem to bleed. Instead of the blood dripping, the spear pulsed with magic, drinking it.

"The, uh, human sacrifice part."

"Would you like me to say no?"

"If it's true."

"No."

"No it's not true so you can't say so or no you didn't do it?"

Setanta smiled at her without answering and pulled his hand free of the spear. Almost instinctively, she grasped the hand and surged her healing gift into him.

"Thank you, though that was unnecessary."

"Oh, right." Of course; he was a vampire, he'd heal on his own. "How does this go?"

"All you need to do is stand there," he said and gripped the old, polished bone staff of the spear with both hands, closing his eyes. The candles around them flared with light, wicks catching fire. She hadn't even heard him mutter words of a spell. She knew that those who practiced long enough with skill and meditation could use spells silently but had never mastered the ability herself and met very few who had. For someone who spoke of how little power his spells had, he was an impressive witch. Having multiple millennia to practice helped, no doubt.

Setanta's magic was pulled invisibly from the spear,

like a thread from a spindle. It reached out and touched her forehead, winding into her body. It was as he said. His ability to cast spells was limited, she could sense that for herself now. Some people had weak gifts but a spellcasting ability equivalent to swinging a greatsword. Setanta's magic was more like a needle, but he knew exactly how to use that power to the greatest effect. Needles could paralyze if stuck in the right place.

"I feel her bond to you," Setanta said. The thread of power between them pulsed red with the power of his blood stored in the spear. "It's not all of her. She's caught between our world and where she's meant to be. If you'll allow me…"

The red power touched Sarai's core and she gasped. It was a similar sensation to experiencing Marcelle's blood in her system, in that it felt thrilling, but in a spiritual rather than physical way, and much more intense. She felt as if she'd touched an electric socket.

Liora, Sarai's mother, appeared between them, eyes closed and floating semi-transparent a foot above the ground. She looked almost as if she were asleep. The thread of red power was strung through her heart, connecting all three present in the candle circle.

"Liora Meir," Setanta said. "I am a friend of your daughter, Sarai. Can you hear us?"

The ghost did not give any indication of having heard anything. The vampire sighed, then impaled his hand once more on his spear. The thread of power burned brighter with blood from every thump of his slow heart.

Suddenly, Sarai's mind was overwhelmed, swamped with images and memories not her own.

She could see herself, singing in Hebrew to a baby in her arms. A baby that meant everything in the world

47

yet caused so much pain in her heart. She remembered running in the dead of night with the baby wrapped in a bundle against her chest. Breaking through magical barriers like beating her way through broken glass to escape with the child. Years in hiding, teaching the child to speak in Hebrew and English. Combing her golden-brown curls. Teaching her about magic.

Then, there was a man. No, multiple men, who attacked her and forced a silver collar around her neck. Sarai recognized the one in charge, Alaric Reinhart. Her father. No, not her father... but it *was* him. She begged and pleaded with him, only to be struck across the face. Sarai could feel the pain as if it happened to her. Alaric plucked a single strand of dark hair from her head and put it into a bottle of black liquid. The potion swirled, then turned clear as water. Sarai watched in horror as Alaric subdued the screaming, curly-haired little girl and forced the clear potion down her throat. Half of it spilled down her front, but the damage was done, and the girl fell unconscious, to be passed into the arms of a tall, blonde woman.

"For taking her from me, this is your punishment," he said as he knelt in front of Sarai. He touched a tear on her cheek. "Five years I've looked for you. Five years you robbed me of what belongs to *me*. I want you to know before I kill you, she won't remember you. Your face, your voice. Nothing. You will be nothing, Liora."

"Please, let me come with you," Sarai heard herself beg. "I'll do what you want. Anything you want. Just let me be with her. She needs me, she needs her *ima*."

"She'll have a mother," said Alaric. "She'll live with her sister and my wife. She doesn't need a second mother."

His fingernails grew into vicious claws and Sarai felt them at her throat. The pain stunned her, and she couldn't scream without swallowing mouthfuls of her own blood, drowning in it as she fell to the floor. She couldn't die. She couldn't allow it. Not when the girl needed her. She couldn't leave her.

"Sarai..." she whispered, and the world went dark. All she could see was the sweet, curly-haired girl, but magic shrouded her, kept the girl from looking back except in the occasional dream. The girl grew and grew, and time and again she watched dangers around the girl, beating against the blackness to try to warn her. The magic barrier between them thinned, and Sarai was looking at herself, as if she were gazing into a mirror. And finally, the girl who was now a woman could hear the warnings.

Sarai gasped, her vision returning to see Liora floating between her and Setanta, the red line of power connecting them all still. She stumbled back, tripping over the candles and extinguishing them as she fell.

"Oh my god," she whispered, trying to make sense of the memories she'd just seen. The power of Setanta's spell snapped and her vision was gone again. She found herself lost in a sea of memories. Voices and faces she couldn't recognize but seemed so important were all around her. Marcelle was there, then not. There were men and women, sometimes naked and on top of her or under her. Cold climates she'd never experienced bit her skin, castles and stone buildings loomed against gray skies. War. Blood. Pain. There was so much blood and pain.

The blood and pain became a vision. She was kneeling on a muddied ground surrounded by corpses, the stench of death a hell to her nostrils. There was a woman in her arms, lifeless and limp, with wild red hair, blue tattoos, and sightless red eyes. A deep wound was proof of a murderous stab in her chest, where a blade had pierced her heart. The blood stained her clothes and dripped into the earth in rivers that echoed the ringlets of her long hair.

Sarai was screaming, her voice deeper than she thought it should be. She knew she had to save the woman in her arms, but that she was too late, and the pain of her loss was unbearable.

Then she was back in Setanta's room, the pureblood's lukewarm hands on either side of her head as he looked into her eyes with worry.

"Sarai?" he whispered. "Sarai, say something."

"*Mo ingen*," she gasped, and sat up straight, nearly knocking her head against Setanta's and not knowing where the words came from.

"What did you say?" Setanta asked.

"I-I'm not sure," she said. "*Mo*… something?"

"*Mo ingen*," he said. "It means my daughter, in my native tongue. In ancient Irish."

"I saw my mom dying. I *was* my mom dying. My father, he made me forget it all with a potion," she said. She looked behind the vampire and was disappointed to see that Liora had disappeared. "Where is she?"

"She disappeared when you broke the circle," Setanta said.

"When I broke it, I saw more," she realized, and looked up at him. Those red eyes, the red hair, the blue tattoos. The woman dead in her arms in the vision looked like a female clone of Setanta. "I, I'm sorry. I didn't mean to see it."

"My memories," he said, with much calmer demeanor than she would have expected. "I felt it when the magic snapped. You were connected to my mind for a moment. I saw yours."

Sarai bit her lip. "Uh, what did you see?"

"I saw your father when you were a child. The way he treated you. I felt your fear." Setanta held her hand. "No one will ever beat you like that again. I promise."

Sarai felt almost embarrassed to have unwittingly shared such a painful moment with him. "I'm sorry."

"There is no need to apologize. I should have taken more care with the spell to avoid something like this." He placed his hand over her heart, near her breast, and closed his eyes. Her heart raced as he pulled a strand of his red magic from her soul and reclaimed it within himself. "What did you see?"

Sarai looked down at his strong hand against her. "A battlefield. Corpses. A woman with red eyes."

His expression softened. "*Mo ingen*, Boudicca."

"I'm so sorry."

"I lost her in… I believe what you consider the first century, almost two thousand years ago. It's not a fresh pain."

Sarai shook her head. "It felt so real. I was there, it felt… Nothing my father ever did to me hurt so much."

"Then I pray you never lose children, Sarai. There is no pain so profound, as I've been unfortunate enough to know."

It was hard to picture Setanta as a father. Not that she had any good role models to compare him to, but it seemed strange to imagine. She felt in her heart that he could be a good one.

"It's only you, your father, and your sister who live

here, right?" she asked. "You said children, are they all…?"

"I have no living children, grandchildren, or great-grandchildren anymore," Setanta said. "I once had twelve children. Four grandchildren. Two great-grandchildren. A few allowed themselves to age until death, the rest either killed themselves or were killed by others. Boudicca and her two daughters were my last descendants to pass. She'd moved from Ulster to Iceni, to marry a mortal witch she loved and to claim her own land. I had no more children after her passing."

"Twelve, wow." She shook her head with wide eyes. "Sorry, I don't mean to focus on that, just wouldn't want to be the woman pushing out twelve kids."

"The labors were distributed among multiple women."

"Well, that's a little more manageable. At the same time?" she asked with a raised eyebrow.

"Two were at the same time once," he admitted. "But mostly successive. Political arrangements with purebloods or witches who were strong enough to bear it. But enough about that. How do you feel?"

"My head hurts," she said, and he helped her to stand. Red overwhelmed her vision and she almost fell again.

"Some of my magic might still be in your head. Come this way, I'll remove it for you." Setanta led her to sit on a comfortable couch. He began running his hand over her without touching her, pulling fragmented strands of his power from her body. As he did, flashes of the memory and of his old life shot through Sarai's mind.

"Romans killed her," she whispered. "They

captured her first… her daughters… I see you, learning what they did."

She knew what he'd experienced. Learning by messenger while he was across the sea that his daughter had taken on the Roman Empire, including Roman vampires. She had been chained in silver and humiliated. Her daughters, Setanta's granddaughters, raped by soldiers. They were let go, expected to be subservient vassals, but fought back and rallied other Celtic tribes to fight as well. By the time Setanta had learned of everything happening, it was too late to help. His granddaughters had been recaptured and killed, his daughter dead in battle.

"I'm sorry for this," Setanta said. "We won't try a spell like this again."

"She was your favorite child, I can feel it in my heart," she said as images of the girl's childhood flashed through her mind. Setanta had such pride for her.

"I suppose we're not meant to have favorites," the vampire said. "But she was special. So much like me. I think this is the last of it." With a final tug of his fingertips, and the memory of holding a newborn child with bright red eyes and hair passing through Sarai's mind, she was free of the rogue magic.

"You're getting married again," Sarai said. "Marcelle mentioned it. That you need someone to give you children."

"It's a duty. There are too few New Ulster pureblood vampires. A dynasty needs heirs to succeed and a vampire kingdom needs purebloods to defend against rival bloodlines," Setanta said. "As the new king, I will do what I need to for my kingdom."

"You don't want to."

He sighed. "Sarai… if you could, please don't speak to others about my memories. Marcelle if you must, but none of the others. And do not mention my, ah, discomfort regarding my upcoming marriage to others. Such matters are private, as I'm sure you understand."

"Of course, yeah." Sarai had been given something special, if accidental, in being allowed to glimpse the mind and emotions of someone like him. It wasn't meant to be shared.

"At least, we've learned why your mother stays. I must say, I understand her reasoning."

Sarai's eyes widened. "You do? Why?"

"Her love for you." He smiled and caressed her hair in a manner her mother had done in her memories. "She's bound to you from the trauma of losing you."

Chapter Seven: Blue and Silver

Sarai was happy to hear from Marcelle when she returned that the psychologist appointment had gone well.

"None of that Freudian hogwash I was expecting," Marcelle explained. "No ridiculous diagnosis, no assumption that drinking blood should make me feel bad, no 'you wish you had a penis because you love women and you want to have sex with your father'. Much more intelligent than I expected."

"Will you go back?" Sarai asked.

Marcelle made a face. "She wants to see me again next week, but I haven't decided yet. She might be interesting to talk to, but I have a hard time thinking someone so young can know more than me about myself. We'll see. I'll grant you that perhaps psychology isn't useless."

"Glad to hear it. Even if I am so much younger."

Marcelle rolled her eyes. "Oh, and while I was in town, I picked something up for you." She darted away and returned with several parcels tied with black and gold ribbon in her arms, which were all promptly dumped on the bed.

Sarai's eyes widened. "Oh, I— You don't have to get me presents." She tried to remember the last time she got a gift and, aside from the amber jewelry Marcelle had bought her in New York, she vaguely remembered Alma once giving her half a chocolate bar.

"These are just a few things you'll need," Marcelle assured her. "And besides, a beautiful woman like you deserves to be showered in gifts. You might want to get used to it."

She leaned forward to place a cold peck on Sarai's cheek, causing the witch to blush, then sat back. "Go ahead, open them."

Smiling to herself, Sarai turned the smallest package over in her hands. This was a moment to savor, whatever was inside. She shook it a little and heard something rattle inside. Judging from the size, it had to be jewelry. A strange sense of nervousness and excitement gripped her, and she tore open the box. Her heart nearly stopped at what she saw.

"Marcelle, I can't accept this," she whispered. "It's too much."

A set of jewelry including a necklace, earrings, and a pair of bracelets like she'd never seen before greeted her with glittering gems. Deep blue sapphires adorned with what had to be diamonds and pearls were wrapped in delicate white gold filigree to create a work of art worth more than everything she'd ever owned in her life. The necklace looked the heaviest, like a thick collar that would cover at least half of the wearer's neck and dripped precious stones down the collarbone. The bracelets were similar in design, thick like cuffs to cover the wrist.

"Do you like it?"

"Like it?" Sarai said. "You can't expect me to wear this. What reason would I ever have to?"

"Well, there is a coronation approaching. I thought you might like appropriate accessories."

"Please tell me you're just lending this to me. What

if I lose it, or break it?"

"Then I'll enslave you for the rest of your life and make you work in the kitchens as a maid until you pay off the debt," Marcelle teased. "Relax, I lose and break jewelry all the time. Besides, this necklace is high enough up your neck to send a message to anyone getting ideas that you're not on the menu for the night. Same with the bracelets to cover your wrists. Consider it necessary armor."

"When you put it like that," Sarai murmured and traced the filigree with a fingertip. "Any chance this is glass and cubic zirconium?"

"Diamonds and pearls, I'm afraid. You'll have to make do."

"Absolute madness," Sarai said. She lifted out one of the bracelets, amazed at the weight of the white gold, and fastened it around her narrow wrist. It fit perfectly, as if it had been designed for her alone. "Did you steal Setanta's crown jewels for this?"

"Don't tattle on me. Go on, try out the rest," Marcelle urged.

Sarai picked up the heavy necklace and latched the back, while Marcelle held up a hand mirror she hadn't seen the vampire get.

The witch was at a loss for words. It looked so elegant. She brushed her fingertips over the largest stone, a sapphire that rested at the base of her throat. "Definitely the crown jewels from somewhere," she said. "The queen of England doesn't have a rock like this."

"Well, she did once," Marcelle laughed, and helped Sarai put on the second bracelet. The final piece were the earrings, and she couldn't stop looking in the mirror. After a little time watching with glee as her lover preened, Marcelle said, "You know, you still have two more gifts to open."

Sarai wasn't sure she could handle two more gifts if they even held a candle to the jewelry. She opened the medium sized box to find a pair of shoes. They were low heels, silver in color and surprisingly comfortable. The heel was just enough to give her a little height, but not so much as to make standing in them painful.

The final, largest box could only be one item.

It was her dress, exquisitely crafted by the vampire seamstress Sophie. It seemed so long ago the pair had gone to the shop to design a custom gown. Yet not long enough for something of such detail to be made by human hands, that was certain.

The back laced up like a proper ballgown, which it was with its full, pleated skirt. Said skirt was royal blue, with silver embroidery and beadwork that made the dress reminiscent of the night sky. The top was made with silver-colored material, with short sleeves of delicate silver colored scalemail. The most eye-catching feature was without a doubt the deep neckline. It went down to the waist. In retrospect, the request she'd made for the low neckline was a horrible idea. As someone who loved baggy shirts, she in no way had the confidence for it.

"This is art," Sarai said. "You need to put this on a mannequin or something. Put it somewhere no one can ruin it. Marcelle, I can't do this. I've never touched anything so nice; I just can't wear this."

"If I agree to go to another psychology meeting, will you agree to stop acting like you're not worthy of pretty things and accept that this is yours?" Marcelle asked.

"Maybe." A thought crossed her mind. "What are you going to wear?"

"Oh, you know, something sexy."

Sarai giggled a little. "That'll be fun to see. So, some fancy French thing for you, then?"

"Well, not the heavy authentic clothes with the petticoats and the corset and the pannier... Something modern that I can move in since I'll be on guard duty. But don't think about what I'm wearing, you've got all this to try on."

Sarai's fingers traced the laces in the back. "Should I wait? Until the actual ball?"

"You should try it on now. I know you want to. Besides, we need to see if it fits right."

She nodded. Some girlish part of her that had survived childhood with Cinderella fantasies desperately wanted to wear the dress.

"Okay. One step at a time." She slipped off her clothes without any self-consciousness in front of her lover and stepped into the dress as Marcelle held it up for her. The back needed someone else to secure it, so she had to wait while Marcelle laced it up. As she did, she could look down at the way the top hugged her curves, the way the iridescent skirt fell around her in a wide cascade. It made her breath shallow and fast with excitement.

"There, now come over here," Marcelle said, and led Sarai to stand in front of a mirror.

"Wow." The grin that spread across her face was uncontrollable. She pulled a hair tie down her curls to release her mane and shook her head to watch how it completed the look. Not a single detail was wrong. The reflection was regal as a queen's.

She spun around, and the skirt flared open like a blue and silver hibiscus. Sarai stopped her spinning and hugged Marcelle as tight as she could, looking at their embracing reflection.

"Oh, and let's not neglect the best part." Marcelle pulled Sarai close and put her hands down the witch's sides. "It has pockets."

Sarai's eyes widened and she shoved her own hands into the pockets. "Damn. You guys think of everything." She spun around again, this time her hands in the deep pockets, then stopped in front of her lover. "Thank you. Marcelle. I love... this." She caught herself before saying 'you', just in case.

"I love you too, Sarai," the vampire said softly. Their eyes locked in the mirror.

"You love me?" she asked. "It's not, I don't know, too soon to say?"

"Love doesn't need to be a taboo. I can love quickly. Or slowly. I think it would be cold of me not to fall in love with a woman who sacrificed her right hand for my life. And maybe the psychologist helped me realize a few things. About how I feel about you." Marcelle caressed Sarai's face with a cold hand, and the witch closed her eyes as she melted into the contact. Love was the warmth she needed. She hadn't realized how much she needed it until she heard the words and felt her chest tighten in response. "I don't know if it will last or if it's shallow or fleeting, but I know at this moment, I do love you. I want you to be happy, and to feel beautiful and loved. You deserve that."

"I'm happy," Sarai said and kissed her lover's red lips. "I think... I love you too. I'm so happy because I have you."

Chapter Eight: Fire and Firearms

Marcelle hated that Setanta made her take time off and was almost grateful when tragedy struck, forcing her back into the field. It was so much more interesting than lazing around trying to clear her head of intrusive thoughts, even if her time with her new psychologist did seem to be helping.

Thankfully, the tragedy did not directly affect her beloved vampire kingdom, but rather the witches: a large family living in upstate New York had been targeted by the Vasi. According to the information provided by the Ellis Coven, they were primarily plant witches, able to speed the growth of plants or bend them to their will. A few were elemental witches, able to manipulate earth and rocks or water, and some were even regular non-magical humans who had married into the family.

Under Setanta's orders, Marcelle, Bear, and Angela, along with others in the elite team meant to serve the royal family, were mobilized out to rural New York to meet the witches.

While not as attuned to magical protections as one who could cast them would be, Marcelle could feel the tatters of protective spells as they drove into the small farming community that had been the witches' home. Some were meant to keep out undead like her, but the spells had been so eviscerated by Vasi attackers and their enslaved witches that none of the protections would do more than make Marcelle's skin tingle.

The homes were small brick cottages, and old by the standards of buildings in America. She could tell they were meant to be an established family, one that assumed they were safe. They practiced magic in the open, as evident by a sponge washing a window all on its own with no hand to hold it. No witch would have spells like that in place if they thought they were in any danger of being seen by humans. Yet, as she stepped out of her vehicle, signs of battle were obvious. Scorch marks and lingering fires indicated the Vasi had used at least one enslaved witch pyromancer, a favorite of theirs. Parts of the earth and rock looked as though it had leapt up to try to provide cover. Overgrown plants drooped without a witch to command them and lay dying outside of their gardens. Bullet holes riddled every surface. One fact Marcelle could glean from her analysis of the battle was that the witches had been on the defensive, trying to hide, shelter, and take cover rather than return the attack.

The most depressing sight was a row of bodies that had been shot execution style, hands tied behind their backs. Their assumption of safety had been their undoing; complacency was never safe.

Captain Moretti, the Italian American woman who was head of the guards at the witch coven on Ellis Island, stood over the bodies, her usually heavy hair frizzy with static, as if she hadn't had the chance to slather it in hair gel, and so her power had wreaked havoc on it. She glanced up at the vampires and gave them a curt nod.

"Thanks for coming," she said. "I wasn't sure you guys would."

"We're allies now, are we not?" Marcelle said. "It would be a poor ally indeed who ignored an attack like this." She frowned at the bodies, a familiar scent catching her attention. "Those... are humans."

"The ones that married into the Fattore family," she said. "Vasi think they're traitors, to align with us. To love us."

Funny, Marcelle hadn't expected witches to be open to marrying humans. She looked around, trying to take stock of the situation. "This is a family, right?" she asked. "There are no children left here."

"They've been taken," the captain said. "Vasi took them, and some of the adult witches. They're building up their witch army to fight us." She rubbed her temples. "It's disgusting. Forcing us to fight our family and friends. My cousins. These are my cousins. I can't kill my cousins. And if they make the kids sign contracts?"

Then it was a race against time and every minute counted. Something about the whole situation set a fire in Marcelle's dead heart. Children, teens... they were rare to non-existent in her vampire world. They needed protection. *Her* protection.

"Do you know where they were taken?" Marcelle asked.

"Oh yeah. Our scryers figured that out just before you arrived," Captain Moretti said, then sighed.

"What is it?"

"We don't go on the offensive," the captain said. "We defend, we take care of survivors. We protect."

"It's a good thing you have us on your side now," Marcelle said. "We're very good at going on the offensive."

Moretti nodded. "Yeah. You know what, it's probably a good thing right now."

In an ideal world, Marcelle would have wanted more

experience working alongside the people she was about to go on a rescue mission with, but there was no chance of going in to fight these Vasi without taking the Ellis witches with them.

"We need to talk strategy on the way," Marcelle said. "We've never fought alongside witches before, and I'm sure you've never fought alongside vampires."

"Fought against vampires though," said a familiar voice. Marcelle inhaled, the scent of a campfire filling her nose; it was the smell of a certain vampire-hating pyromancer. Their first meeting had been memorable, when he attempted to kill her in a New York City alley, and she'd knocked him unconscious. She suspected he held a grudge.

"Lochlan, pleasure to see you again," she said, and turned around to flash him a fanged smile. He'd kept his appearance since the last time she'd seen him at the peace treaty signing, and sported purple hair, eyes, and fingernails. It was a far cry from the red hair and blue eyes he'd had when they'd first met. She doubted he would want to keep red hair after meeting Setanta. Those violet eyes narrowed with anger and smoke streamed from his hands.

"Why the fuck are they here?" he snapped to Moretti.

"They're here to help," she said. "It's in the treaty."

"We've fought and defeated Vasi before. Behave yourself like a good little boy and we might teach you something useful," Marcelle told him.

Lochlan opened his mouth to retort, but Moretti raised her hand to silence him.

"I don't want to hear it. Every second we waste here is a second longer my cousins are in Vasi hands. So, you're going to shut up about the vampires and get ready to barbeque some Vasi. Because we're going to go hunt them down."

The anger disappeared from Lochlan's face. "You got the approval from Dad?"

"From the council, yes. Unanimous decision that the risk is acceptable with vampire aid."

Lochlan pursed his lips pencil thin, then gave a curt nod. "They better stay out of my way."

"Do you want to ride in the car with us, or should I go with you?" Marcelle asked Moretti, ignoring the pyromancer. "To go over details."

"We used a portal door," Moretti said, and held up a bag with what had to be enchanted sticks to form a doorway poking out the top as she gave Marcelle an apologetic look. "It needs time to recharge though, and it only works between preset locations. So, we, uh, we don't have cars with us."

Marcelle frowned. That seemed like a poor decision. "What sort of weapons do you have?"

"Our gifts," Moretti said, as if it were obvious and Marcelle shouldn't ask. "Most of the people who sign up for the guard are elementals of some kind. Lightning, fire, ice. Most witch gifts aren't offensive and most spells and charms are protective or preventative."

Marcelle cursed under her breath. Not only did she have to go on a high-risk mission with people she'd never worked with before, but they were amateurs.

"So, no guns. I don't see any bullet proof vests. Do your spells repel bullets?"

"Our... Our spells can do things like fireproof our bodies," Moretti said.

It was something at least.

"Do any of you have any real fighting experience?"

"We practice with each other all the time."

Marcelle fought hard to resist the urge to roll her eyes. "Against outsiders, Captain. Have you ever killed a Vasi?"

"I've killed two Vasi," Lochlan said, sliding his bow off his shoulder. It sparked with fire magic. "And five vampires."

It was meant to jab at Marcelle, but at least someone had experience doing something other than twiddling their thumbs and patching up the wounded after attacks were over.

"Good," she said. "It sounds like you witches would be best at a distance. Targeted range attacks with your elemental abilities. My people excel at up-close and personal fighting. We're fast and we don't take prisoners. Think you can work around that, Captain?"

Moretti looked green but nodded. "We want our kids back. We might not have a lot of combat experience, but we're determined."

"Let's get going then. Time is wasting," Marcelle said. As they headed towards the cars, she grabbed Lochlan's forearm and stopped him.

"Get your undead hands off me—"

"We're not tenth generation weaklings picking on homeless scraps for blood in an alley," Marcelle cut him off. "My people are warriors. Knights of New Ulster. We're under orders not to harm allied witches unless we're provoked first. Provoke me, or 'accidentally' friendly fire my team, and I will show you what a trained vampire is capable of. Do we have an understanding?"

He tried to jerk his arm free, which she didn't allow the first time, then let go when he tried again so that he stumbled back a little.

"I'm going to protect witches," Lochlan said. "If you don't like it, stay the fuck at home, leech." He turned on his heel and moved to hop into the back of the van, then hesitated at the sight of the heavily armed vampires inside.

"Come on in, the water's great," Bear joked.

"If you want to come help us get those bastards, you're going to have to deal with these," Moretti said from inside, though she sat with noticeable space between her and the vampires.

Lochlan nodded and got in, squaring his narrow shoulders to try and fill up as much space as possible as he sat down between his captain and another witch.

During the ride, Marcelle got a breakdown of each witch's powers. The elementals were useful, but it seemed their two scryers would have to stay away from the action. One stayed in the front seat of the vehicle to guide the driver, and that would be the extent of their usefulness.

Lochlan, strangely enough, seemed to be one of the more useful witches, as he was the only pyromancer. That was assuming he didn't turn against the vampires and torch them all. Between him, Moretti, and a few other elementals who between them could control metal, ice, and water, it would make for a very interesting fight to be alongside them.

The scryers led the witches and vampires to a large building made of bricks. It was a new structure by Marcelle's standards, no more than a few decades old. Old enough for vines of ivy to have snaked up the sides, but not covered in the plants. It was a rather unassuming building, three floors and a cellar, but the moment they neared it, the cars all stalled.

"It's warded," Moretti said as she threw open the car door and stepped out. "They've got witches here that work for them." She lifted her hand and pressed it forward. The air thickened around it, impeding her movement.

"What can we do?" Marcelle asked.

"They're weak. I think we can break them." Moretti gestured for the other witches to join her. She rubbed a star sapphire embedded in a gold ring on her hand. It sparked with electricity and strummed, like the vibration of a string instrument plucked with precision and allowed to reverberate in the soul.

All the witches, even Lochlan as he adjusted his glasses, joined her, touching objects on their person that acted as their magical focuses. The magic they created, whispering spells to themselves, made the pressure in the air change. Marcelle's ears popped as if she were in a plane, and the other vampires all looked equally uncomfortable at the show of magic.

The warding spells shattered like glass, disappearing into nothing. Marcelle stepped forward and found that the magic protection keeping them out had been destroyed. She could move freely.

"They'll know we're here," Moretti said.

"Doesn't matter. We can take them," Lochlan retorted.

"Lochlan, stay back with me. Ranged attacks, remember," Moretti reminded him. He nodded, and the group advanced forward, Marcelle in the lead. With a few hand motions, she directed two small groups of her vampires each led by Angela and Bear respectively to go around the sides, to force the Vasi to fight on more than one front. The witches, unable to move as fast to keep up, stayed with Marcelle's group.

Lochlan burst open the door for them with a flung fireball to reveal the inside of the building. It was devoid of furniture or furnishings of any kind, but that didn't matter as much as the silver bars Marcelle noted on the windows, the shiny and slightly tarnished tint all the doorknobs had.

"Careful," she warned. "Silver doorknobs."

"I see them," Moretti acknowledged.

They began to funnel into the entrance, and fire lashed out from the end of the hall. Lochlan stepped forward and caught the blaze, grunting with the effort as if it had weight. Squinting against the light and intense heat that threatened to sear off her eyelashes, Marcelle saw three witches at the end of the hall, all with their hands out to control the blaze. It was impressive that Lochlan could take on three witches and counter their flames himself. He was one to keep an eye on.

As he wrestled with the flaming hell storm that threatened to press down on them all, several vampires knelt at his sides, steadying their weapons. Gunfire rang out though the hall, and the fire dissipated. The three witches were dead, their sweet blood coating the floors.

Lochlan panted a little, wiping lingering flames off his palms. "See," he said breathlessly. "I've got this. I'm the goddamn fire king."

Marcelle heard guns clicking from down the hall, and the vampires all grabbed witches and pulled them behind walls for cover moments before bullets filled the air. She couldn't smell the identity of their attackers, but guessed they were human from their use of munitions.

"Let go," growled Lochlan, attempting to push her

hand off his waist.

She ignored him, focusing on the problem at hand. They didn't have a clear shot. However, the floors were suddenly slick with water, and she looked over to see one of the witches, a short black man, with his hand on the tiles. Puddles collected from leaks he seemed to force in the pipes in the walls, flowing towards their attackers. He nodded at Moretti, who placed her hand into the water and closed her eyes, sending bolts of electricity down the hall. The gunfire stopped.

Marcelle was impressed. It was nice to have witches on their side for a change. She heard the beating of more footsteps and heartbeats and nodded to her fellow vampires. She and one other darted forward, making quick work of four more Vasi humans before they could aim their guns. Marcelle only broke necks, but her companion, an ex-pirate with one leg and an eyepatch named Crispin, ripped out their throats with his teeth and nails.

"All clear," Marcelle called.

All the witches seemed unnerved by Crispin but came out of hiding in cover.

"Are these any of your cousins?" she asked the witch captain.

Moretti didn't look at the dead Vasi witches. "We didn't have any pyros. Earth and plants, that kind of magic. Couple of weather witches."

"Could be good news." Marcelle closed her eyes, listening. There were too many heartbeats, too many living people around her. She couldn't discern where the other living beings in the building were but could hear fighting breaking out around where Bear's team had gone.

"Captives would probably be in the cellar," she said, going with an educated guess. "We should find our way there."

They encountered several more Vasi humans, making quick work of them between the vampires' ferocity and witches' gifts, but no further Vasi witches were found. From the sounds of fighting Marcelle could hear, they were preoccupied elsewhere.

The door to the cellar was old and wooden, with a tarnished silver handle Marcelle's black gloves protected her from. The rickety stairs led to a stone room where barred cells filled with people lined the wall. The moment she saw them, gunfire slammed her group, and she pushed her people back up the stairs. Crispin cursed next to her, grasping his side as blood soaked his clothes.

"Silver bullets," he warned her through his teeth and a British accent. "Damn, that hurts."

"I'll scorch 'em to a crisp," Lochlan said, starting to move forward, but Captain Moretti stopped him.

"You'll hit our witches at this range," she told him. She looked at Marcelle as suppressive fire rang out again. "Got any ideas?" she shouted over it.

Marcelle thought for a moment. Without the witches, she would have rushed in with vampires and torn the Vasi to shreds. But knowing there were children in the cages they needed to save made her feel that another course of action was needed. She looked over at the witch who'd used his control over water to help Moretti electrocute the other witches.

"Can you control blood?" she asked him.

His eyes widened at the thought, and he shrugged, making several hand gestures. Marcelle looked to the other witches for translation.

"He said he hasn't tried before," Captain Moretti said. "But it has water in it, so maybe."

"Can he hear me?"

"He can hear you; he just doesn't speak well."

Marcelle nodded. "I want you to focus on the water in their brains and mix it all up. Make it pop inside their skulls. Can you do that?"

He looked a little sick but signed again.

"He says he'll try," Moretti said, who also looked disturbed.

The man closed his eyes, and soon after the gunfire stopped, humans dropping to the floor. Marcelle peeked around the corner to see five Vasi humans dead, blood oozing out of their ears and noses.

"Very impressive," Marcelle noted.

The witch responsible gave a weak smile, then turned away and vomited. She and the other vampires quickly went down the stairs away from the stench and found the keys to the cells, letting the Fattore family free. There were tears, the usual emotional hugs. Captain Moretti rushed forward to greet them all, making sure none were harmed.

"My son," one middle-aged woman begged, grabbing Marcelle's arm. "Please, they took my son somewhere, I don't know where he is."

"We'll look for him," Marcelle promised. The woman let go of Marcelle's arm and stumbled away, her eyes wide.

"It's okay," Captain Moretti said. "It's okay, they're helping us. Tell us, what direction did they take your son?"

"Upstairs, somewhere. I heard... I heard screaming,

I—"

Marcelle closed her eyes, focusing on the sounds above them. The fighting was still going on, but her teams seemed to have made quick work of the Vasi they'd encountered. There were far fewer heartbeats above them. Or she just couldn't hear them over the sound of all the anxiety in the cellar.

"Witches, you stay here. We'll clean up the stragglers and look for the missing boy," Marcelle said. If there was a chance this woman's son had been forced into a contract… she would need to kill him. She didn't want the witches in her way for that.

"No way," Lochlan said. "I'm not being told to wait in the car like some fucking damsel. I'm coming with. You don't get to have all the fun."

"Killing people isn't fun," Captain Moretti muttered. "But I agree with him, you're not leaving all of us here." She glanced around. "Everyone, stay here until we come back. We won't be long. Lochlan, you come with us. We could use the firepower."

"Hell yeah. Let's bring the heat." He sparked flames in his palms and grinned as he followed the vampires back up the stairs.

There weren't many Vasi left. Bear and Angela's teams had cleared out most of the opposition, and Marcelle told them where to find the witches so they could provide further assistance.

"What about you?" Bear asked.

"There's a boy missing from the group. I'm going to find him," she replied. He nodded solemnly, then darted away.

A few busted down doors later, the boy was found. He was a young man, not much older than twenty or so, with a tear-streaked pale, freckled face, a hand with blood dripping from a cut, and a roll of parchment in front of him with a handprint in his blood. A Vasi woman next to him held a gun to his head, then turned to point it at the vampires.

Marcelle made quick work of her, snapping her arm in half as the gun fired into the ceiling, then punching her in the chest at just the right moment to make her heart stop. She fell to the floor, dead and broken.

The boy stood up and punched Marcelle with a fist so weak she barely noticed. The vampire raised an eyebrow.

"That is a very stupid move," she warned him.

"S-she said I have to," he blubbered as he punched again. "She said I have to, or they'll hurt my mom."

"Shit," Captain Moretti said as she looked at the signed contract. "Damnit, kid."

He punched at Marcelle again, and the vampire caught his fist. "I'll make it quick and painless," she promised Moretti.

"You— No!" the captain shouted. "Don't even think about it."

"You know there's no saving a contracted witch," Marcelle said. "He'll be forced to fight us until he drops of exhaustion, and then keep going at it. There's no hope for him."

"You… you want to kill him?" Lochlan said, raising his flaming hand. "He didn't do anything. I won't let you."

"You remember the last time we fought and how well that went for you?" Marcelle snarled at him. "I've been fighting Vasi longer than you've been alive. Let me do my job."

"What are your powers, kid?" Moretti asked.

"I, I can make light. Sunlight, kinda. It helps in the greenhouse," he said, as he tried to fight Marcelle's strength. Well, that explained why he wasn't using anything substantial to try to hurt them. She picked him up by both his wrists, holding him aloft in the air so that he flailed even more uselessly. "Please, there's gotta be a way to undo it, right?"

"Don't hurt him," Captain Moretti warned Marcelle, who rolled her eyes. This entire thing was dragging out the inevitable. Better to make it quick and not give the poor thing time to worry about his fate. Now he was suffering needlessly. "Let me look at the contract." The witch scanned the parchment, then sighed. "Anyone know Latin?"

Marcelle nodded and stepped forward, looking at the text. "He's bound until death to help the Vasi fight the occult, to kill witches and vampires, and obey any commands from a Vasi member. Straightforward enough."

"I can burn the contract," Lochlan offered. "No contract, no magic binding."

"We've tried destroying contracts before. The magic in them is still binding; the physical contract doesn't matter as much as the content agreed to," Marcelle said. Then a thought struck her. "You know... there is a loophole."

"Yeah?" the sunlight witch said eagerly as he tried to kick her. "What's the loophole?"

"It's until you die. If you weren't alive, it wouldn't be a problem."

"No, no, I don't want to die, please—" he stopped, staring in horror. "Oh."

"You're joking," Lochlan snapped. "Captain, you can't let that happen. That's even worse."

Moretti pursed her lips into a thin line as she thought, then looked at the boy. "What's your name, kid?"

"Peter Fattore. And I'm not a kid, I'm twenty-one."

"Older than you, Lochlan," the captain muttered.

"By one year!"

"Old enough to drink," Marcelle said. "If that's what he chooses. This is an excellent opportunity for us, Captain. To see if we can finally find a way around these infernal contracts. So, Peter, make your choice. If we leave you alive, you will spend the rest of your life trying to kill your family and friends, likely imprisoned and alone. Or you can choose to die and rise again as one of us." Normally, she wouldn't turn someone she didn't know. But, considering the circumstance, there was a chance it could be beneficial in building bridges for the alliance. Not to mention that Marcelle wanted to try the experiment to see if it worked in freeing him from the contract.

"I… I don't want to hurt my mom."

"She'll be hurt if every second of your existence you're fighting the irresistible urge to stab her in the heart," Marcelle said. "Do you want to be able to embrace her again? Decide."

Peter looked at the faces around her as he thrashed involuntarily, and then looked at Marcelle, at her red eyes and fangs.

"I want to hug my mom," he said, tears flowing anew. "Okay. Okay, do it."

"No," demanded Lochlan. "No, there has to be another way. Until death, right? Well, what if he were to technically die and then we resuscitate him? You know, CPR and shit. Captain, you can basically make your hands into paddles to jumpstart his heart with your gift, right?"

Marcelle raised an eyebrow at the witch captain. It was a smart suggestion, considering she'd been under the impression Lochlan had coal for brains. "Could it work?" she asked.

Captain Moretti thought for a moment. "I've never tried that, but it could work in theory. It… it isn't guaranteed. Peter, what would you like to try?"

"I'd rather wake up alive than a vampire," the boy replied. "I want that one."

Marcelle nodded. "I can kill him quickly for you. It'll feel a little like a heart attack. Then Moretti and Lochlan, you need to get his heart started once we're sure he's dead. Take too long and there will be brain damage."

"Right." Moretti took several deep breaths, rubbing her palms together as they sparked.

"Are you ready?" Marcelle asked Peter, who nodded fearfully.

"If I don't… if I don't make it, don't tell my mom I signed a contract, okay?" he pleaded. "Tell her Vasi killed me."

"I will," Lochlan promised. "But you're going to be fine. I'll see you on the other side, man."

Peter nodded again. Marcelle didn't wait for them to change their minds. She listened, struggling to focus on Peter's heartbeat over the other anxious mortals in the room, and struck at just the right moment. His eyes widened, but it was quick, and soon the witch had collapsed in death. Lochlan lunged and caught him, laying him on the floor.

"Okay, CPR. I got this," he said, focused on the problem before them. Marcelle stepped back. While she was an expert at murder, bringing people back without vampirism was well out of her realm of knowledge. Lochlan listened to Peter's still chest, ensuring that he was indeed dead, then began to beat the still torso with both hands together, using the full weight of his body to try and force the heart to function. He pinched Peter's nose, breathing into his mouth to put air in the motionless lungs.

Marcelle had seen CPR in a few movies, though never in real life. Being surrounded by vampires meant that making hearts beat was never a necessity. It was fascinating to watch and took longer than she expected.

"Captain, you got your hands warmed up?" Lochlan called, then blew more air into the dead witch's lungs.

"Yeah," Moretti said. "Get his shirt open so I don't fry his clothes."

Lochlan tried to rip the shirt, but it was a sturdy material. Marcelle darted forward and tore it for them, startling Lochlan.

"Okay, clear!" Moretti pushed Lochlan back and put both her hands on Peter's chest. Electricity snapped through from her palms, jolting the body slightly.

"More than that," Marcelle said, straining to try to hear if it had worked at all. There was no heartbeat. "Try more electricity."

Moretti tried again, this time causing the body to jump a little. Marcelle heard a heartbeat for a moment, but it didn't last.

"That was it," Marcelle shouted. "I heard his heart. Do that again, just a little more."

Moretti zapped him, her hair now standing on ends

from the electricity in the room. This time, it worked, and Peter's eyes opened as he gasped for air, his heart now pounding in his chest.

Marcelle stood back, amazed. She'd never seen someone come back from death and remain alive before. Lochlan whooped, jumping in the air.

"*Yes*," Lochlan shouted. "That's how we *do* it!"

"How do you feel, kid?" Moretti asked.

"Like an elephant was tap dancing on my chest," Peter groaned, wincing as he sat up. There were singe marks in his flesh from where the captain had shocked him.

"Do you have the uncontrollable urge to try to kill any of us?" Marcelle asked.

Peter looked around at the three of them and his face lit up. "No, I feel like me. Like I'm in control."

It worked. They had freed a witch from Vasi control, possibly for the first time in all of history. Marcelle smiled. This collaboration was going to turn the tables on the Vasi. Together, the Ellis Coven and the kingdom of New Ulster were going to be unstoppable.

Chapter Nine: Central Park

Since they were already out and away from the palace, Marcelle spoke with Setanta on the phone to arrange with him that they would stay out a little longer and accompany the witches to do further training.

It turned out that the Ellis Coven had a secondary pocket dimension set up in the middle of Central Park, where humans wouldn't be able to observe them letting their powers show to their fullest potential. After a short rest in the New York City haven, Marcelle led her team to the park. Captain Moretti met them just outside the Conservatory Garden and used her focus to bring them all into the human-free pocket dimension.

It looked the same as the mundane side, but devoid of the crowds and far quieter. In fact, the silence was unsettling and unnatural, the honking and screeching of New York City traffic absent. There weren't even any birds chirping or squirrels in the trees.

"I'm glad you could all make it," Captain Moretti said as she led them to the spot where her guards were waiting. "It's the talk of the coven; we freed a Vasi witch. I've been talking up your role in it. People are calling you a hero."

"A hero?" Marcelle mused. "I think I like that."

"You should. Freeing Vasi witches, it's a game changer. Everyone was skeptical about Setanta's speech at the treaty signing, but this? This is how you win witches over. No pretty words. Results, action. We keep this up, we learn to work together, and the Vasi don't stand a chance."

"Think fast, leech," called a familiar voice. Marcelle jumped out of the way of a fireball just in time, the earth where she'd just been standing scorched and smoldering. She frowned and looked to see Lochlan standing proudly on top of a large rock twice her height.

"Lochlan!" shouted Captain Moretti. "I swear—!"

"Oh, it's fine, Captain," Marcelle said, and darted up next to Lochlan, looking down into his suddenly wide and purple eyes. "The little pyro was just flirting with me."

He shoved her and took a step back, though the panic in his pretty eyes told her that she'd perhaps hit the nail on the head. "You wish."

"A greeting like that? I don't know, it seems to me that you want things hot between us."

"Not in this lifetime. Not ever."

"The lad doth protest too much," Marcelle teased.

He flung another fireball at her, but she sidestepped it, laughing at him as he stood there with smoke rising from his ears.

"Marcelle," Angela called. "Quit playing with the child. We're here to work."

"You can get me hot and bothered later," Marcelle said with a wink, then darted back to her vampire comrades. "So. We're here to teach you how to fight."

"I believe it would be more accurate to say that you are here for us to learn to fight together. We didn't do so bad at the Vasi as a team," Captain Moretti said.

"True. Though we need more time practicing with each other if we're to go into the field again."

They spent the next half hour discussing the witches who were there to learn and what each of their offensive capabilities were. Unfortunately, the silent water witch had quit the guard after killing Vasi made him too sick, but the others were still formidable.

They broke into smaller teams of powers well-suited to work together, with vampires attending each team with expert advice, as they learned to work alongside the powers without getting in the way.

Lochlan, being the only fire witch, wasn't suited to teamwork with anyone. Though, that was in no small part due to his attitude.

"So, what, Teach, no buddies and bloodsuckers for me?" he said. "That's fine. I hate group projects. Just point me at a monster and I'll flambé 'em."

"Since it seems everyone is paired up, I think you could use a lesson in humility. You can be my partner. We'll fight Moretti together. I want you to learn to fight with me, not against me. I think she was talking with Bear last I saw, let's find her."

If she could make Lochlan work well with others, someone with his power would be a huge advantage to have on their side.

Lochlan scoffed. "Whatever. I can take the captain. Which one's Bear?"

"That would be me." Bear darted over, putting a frazzled Moretti on her feet in front of them.

"Jeezus, that's going to take some getting used to," Moretti gasped. "Okay, what are we doing?"

"I think a sparring match is a good idea. You play the role of a Vasi witch. We get Mr. Hothead here to learn how to play nicely with others, and it'll be a good example for everyone to watch me and see how our best warriors work."

"I'm the best warrior," Lochlan said smugly.

"No, you're a little baby psycho with a temper who's being included because he's the only pyro here," Marcelle taunted. "Now let's get to it."

He scowled, muttering curses about leeches under his breath. The stage was soon set, and a ring was drawn in the ground for the four to use in their match. The other witches and vampires stayed outside as the two teams stepped in.

"No shots to the head or heart," Marcelle said, naming the shots that would instantly kill a vampire. "No permanently disfiguring attacks. The goal is restraint."

"And no biting," Moretti said.

"Agreed. Anything else?"

"I think that covers it?" The captain braced herself in preparation, electricity gathering in her hands.

Marcelle turned to Lochlan, who was cracking his knuckles and jumping from foot to foot as if there were hot embers in his shoes.

"You work best at range, right?" she said. "We work best as ambush fighters. If I pick you up and dart you over behind her—"

"Shut up," Lochlan said. "I don't need your help."

He shot fire at Captain Moretti, who was prepared to catch and disperse it with a net made of electricity. The fire disappeared, and Lochlan scowled.

"Right, let's do this together," Marcelle said and picked up Lochlan by his waist, jumping over the electricity that was shot in their path and flipping over onto the ground.

"Put me down!" Lochlan shouted and flames erupted on his arms, burning Marcelle. She yelped and dropped him as he turned on her, the fire like a cloak of death around him. She hissed, her fangs extended as her burns healed.

"Maybe this was a bad idea," Moretti said, and her electricity disappeared. Bear darted forward next to Marcelle, and Lochlan shouted in surprise, his heart rate spiking in a primal fear Marcelle could smell in the air. In response, he shot fire at the pair of them.

They both leapt out of the way and Marcelle lunged forward, grabbing Lochlan's throat and pinning him to the ground.

"Try that again, you little shit," she snarled through her fangs. "If you were one of my knights, you'd be in shackles for that."

"Get off him," Moretti snapped at Marcelle, who complied, baring her teeth once more at the witch boy.

Lochlan got to his feet, shaking. "We can't work with them. She was going to bite me; did you see that?"

"You tried to burn her and Bear first," Moretti said. "Sit this out, Lochlan. Maybe you shouldn't be in the guard if you can't keep your flames to yourself."

"That would be appreciated. Damn, I think he messed up some of my ink," Bear said through his teeth. Marcelle looked, aware of the smell of burnt flesh, to see that Bear was missing part of his shirt, his burned skin healing on his arm. Marcelle's eyes narrowed.

"Burn any of my subordinates again and you will regret it, Lochlan," Marcelle warned.

"Fucking leech," the witch spat.

"That's it. Lochlan, sit on the side and watch," Moretti said. "Marcelle, you and Bear team up against me to demonstrate to the rest of us how you work best."

Moretti's plan worked. The vampires and witches

were soon sparring and practicing together with relative harmony, Lochlan scowling on the side.

After the witches had gotten tired and decided to call an end to the practice, Marcelle was overall pleased with their work. There was true potential to do great things together. Except for one witch.

As the rest of the vampires and witches left, Marcelle stayed behind, murmuring to Bear that she would join them later as he left. He glanced at Lochlan and nodded, understanding her meaning.

Someone needed to teach the brat a lesson.

"I've had enough of your attitude," Marcelle announced as Lochlan got up from the ground. "I don't care what vampires have done to you in the past because I need you to focus on the future. So, we're going to have it out. You and me, right now. You win, I'll leave for good."

"Yeah? Perfect," Lochlan snapped. A fireball erupted in his hand, which he flung at the vampire. She dodged. He had raw power but lacked skill, something someone had to teach him before he got himself killed.

"And if I win?" she asked.

"You won't."

"If I win, your blood is my prize," she decided. Setanta would scold her if she bit a witch without permission, possibly have her punished with a night in silver since it was technically violating his treaty, but it would be worth it to show this mortal boy who was on top.

"It'll never happen." He threw another fireball, which she again dodged.

"It's a wonder you've managed to kill any vampires. Let me guess, you shot them from a distance before they knew someone was there?" Marcelle asked. She darted forward and grazed her smallest knife against his cheek, before darting back and holding up her prize. He stumbled back in shock, touching the blood as it dripped. His purple eyes narrowed with anger.

"You'll pay for that," he snarled.

"Will I?" She licked the blade. His blood was good, exquisite even. She had long forgotten what human foods tasted like and so could not compare it to anything like spicy peppers since she had never tasted any in life, but if she had to label his blood with a flavor, she would say it tasted the way Fourth of July sparklers looked.

"You bitch—"

"You taste fantastic," she said with a grin.

"I'll give you something to taste," he snapped, and fire burst along his arms, somehow controlled enough not to burn his clothes. It crossed her mind that as a witch, he likely fireproofed everything he wore with spells to avoid instant nudity whenever he used his gift. Before he could attack, Marcelle switched blades to her silver dagger with a hound's head on the hilt and rushed forward, pressing the edge against his throat. The flames died; his magic inhibited upon contact with silver.

There was no fear in his eyes, that she could respect. Only anger, determination, and… *oh how fascinating*, she thought to herself as she noted the flush in his cheeks and dilation of his pupils. So, she hadn't been wrong before.

"Do you hate me so because you want me?" she asked, the dagger firm against his skin. Lochlan's eyes widened, but he didn't reply. He just stood there, heart pounding. "Little schoolboy pulling on a girl's pigtails because he doesn't have adult words to say what he wants?"

"I... I don't know what you're talking about," he managed to stammer out.

"Oh, I think you do." Marcelle leaned in, inches from his lips, blade forcing his chin up to look into his eyes. "I can smell lust."

Lochlan glared at her. Then he pushed forward, the knife biting his neck as his fire-hot lips pressed against hers. There was a low aggressive noise in his throat, a rumble like a growl that made his mouth vibrate. He bit her lip, hard, and it took every ounce of self-control she had not to bite back. After all, her bite was much deeper.

Then, he shoved his tongue into her mouth, and they were kissing, almost fighting again with the need that he used to tear at her, his fingernails raking against her body. As if he realized what he was doing, Lochlan shoved at her to push her away, but Marcelle stood firm as a stone pillar.

"Fuck off," he said, looking helplessly into her eyes. "I'm built different. You wouldn't know what to do with me."

Marcelle laughed and grabbed the front of his long-sleeved shirt with her free hand, tearing the cloth from his fit body as if it were tissue paper so that it hung on him like an open sweater. She ran her fingers over twin surgical scars on Lochlan's chest, under his flat pectorals. He stared, rooted to the spot as she touched him.

"Because of this?" she asked. "Don't think it makes you special, pyro. You're not my first." She reached down between his legs and grabbed his crotch, pressing against that concentrated spot of pleasure to make him squirm and gasp. "I know exactly what to do with you."

She unzipped his fly and slid her hand under his

clothes, the throbbing point held firm between her thumb and finger, rubbing it just right to make him groan. It wasn't long compared to someone like Setanta, of course. Perhaps just more than the length of two finger joints. But it was longer than her comparatively flat equivalent and more than enough for a fun time, and to enjoy in her mouth. Most of Marcelle's previous experience with trans men had come from ages when transition had been social and performative rather than medical. The chance to tease the stiffness he offered courtesy of whatever hormonal or magical treatments he took and see what would happen intrigued her, and she felt like a kitten at play with a new toy.

The scent of sex was heavy in the air and sweet on her fingertips. Marcelle brought her fingers to her mouth and licked them slowly, her eyes locked with his as she made a show of using her tongue. His sex tasted hot, like his blood. She wanted more of both.

"The question is," she said, "Can you handle me?"

Her fangs dropped, and she let the dagger leave contact with his skin.

Lochlan hesitated. Then he curled his fingers into a fist and a rope made of fire sparked around Marcelle's wrists. He lifted his hand to guide the fire, forcing them to move above her head or be burnt. The rope had no weight or tightness, but the searing heat kept her still.

Lochlan took a step back, contemplation on his face. He walked around her, and she could feel his eyes on her curves. Then he grabbed her behind, digging his nails into the fabric of her pants. Heat flared and she yelped as she felt his hand scorch away part of the fabric, leaving his mark. He let go, and Marcelle smirked at him as he stood in front of her again, looking more determined.

The pain turned her on, and she was impressed by his confidence. Perhaps she didn't want to be on top.

"Bite me and I'll torch you," he warned.

"I won't bite until you beg me to, pyro," Marcelle said. "But I don't need my teeth to make you scream. Get your pants down and I'll show you what my tongue can do."

He hesitated, then nodded and unfastened his belt, pushing down his pants and boxer shorts. The heat of his fire ropes wrapped around her body pushed Marcelle to her knees.

"Fine. Show me."

Marcelle wasted no time in utilizing all her skill to make the witch hers. Using fingers and tongue, she found out that he was indeed a screamer. His knees buckled and he pushed her down to the ground using the fire ropes, sitting on top of her and clenching her face between his firm thighs.

"Fucking vampire," he gasped. "You goddamn vampire bitch. You're my bitch now."

Marcelle might have replied if she hadn't had her mouth full, but the hateful dirty talk was an interesting twist; a different level from what she was used to with Setanta, Sarai, or anyone else in recent memory, since the feelings were so raw. She was into it.

Soon he had turned around, giving her quite the lovely view of a rear end she could bounce a dime off and was pulling down her pants, rubbing her with the practice of someone who was skilled in bed. The warmth of his hands felt rough and glorious. They were hot, literally, just at the edge of comfort and pain. He spat down on her exposed body, and they kept attacking each other until both were writhing and shouting in bliss, drenched in the sweetness of sex.

When they were done, the flaming ropes disappeared, and Lochlan lay in the grass panting. Attracted to the warmth like a moth to flame, Marcelle rolled over and rested her head on his exposed navel.

The whole situation was amusing. That a witch with such hatred would lust for a vampire. Or, as he was fond of calling her, a leech. Perhaps he saved his most burning hatred for someone else?

"Why do you hate Setanta?" she asked him suddenly, wiping her wet mouth on her shirt.

"Because he's a vampire."

"No, specifically him. He told me about how you reacted to hearing his other name. CuChulainn."

Lochlan made a face. "Well, he's supposedly my…" He sighed. "This is stupid. So, I'm Irish on my dad's side. My parents told me my dad's a descendant of a great witch and Irish hero. CuChulainn, the hound of Ulster. When I was a kid, I wanted to be like him. I had a book with the Ulster cycle by my nightstand all through my teens. Had the whole thing memorized. He inspired me to be… me. When that vamp called himself Setanta, I thought it was a joke or he was some poser. Then at the coven, when he said he really was *the* CuChulainn of legend. I saw red. He was in front of me and real. And a vampire. And maybe my ancestor."

Marcelle laughed. "Ah, I see now. I can promise you that it's impossible for you to be his direct descendent. Cousin, maybe. He's from the Danaan and Fomorian Irish witch clans. Are you?"

"Danaan, yeah, that's me," Lochlan sighed. "One of the last. You know, I almost picked Setanta as my name. My youngest sister couldn't say the S though. Kept calling me 'aunta', like auntie? Decided to go with Lochlan instead. Really glad I did."

"Lochlan's a good name. I picked Marcelle after the Roman god of war. Mars."

He raised an eyebrow in surprise. "You picked a new name? Why?"

"Lots of vampires do. In most cases, we get to reinvent ourselves on our own terms when we get this new life. Start over as someone new, someone better. Someone authentic. I needed a fresh start, so I gave myself a new name. Marcelle de Sauveterre."

"I can see the appeal in that." He snorted. "So instead of a dead name, you've got an *un*dead name."

She laughed. "You could say that. My old name is thoroughly buried in the fields of France."

Lochlan shook his head, amused. "Say, isn't CuChulainn supposed to be dead? I remember the whole story: he tied himself to a standing stone by his own intestines to keep fighting his last battle, but his strength had been tricked away by a goddess, the Morrigan, so he died there."

"Oh, yes, that did happen," Marcelle confirmed. "He told me about it. Interesting story. He made a deal with her to subvert a prophecy about his death and when he killed his thousandth foe at the stone without using his powers, the Morrigan gave him back his abilities and his life. Not sure I would call her a goddess. She's a… confusing being. But that's something I don't know a lot about; I've only read the accounts of others about her. You should ask Setanta, he tells the tale much better than I do."

"I'm not suddenly okay with this, you know. I'm not asking him a thing. I still can't believe my ancestors *made* a leech."

Marcelle sighed. "All right, get it out of your system already. Let's hear it. Why do you hate vampires?"

"Just because you're a good lay doesn't mean we're friends," Lochlan said. "I don't need to tell you anything. This doesn't mean anything."

"You don't need to. I'm just curious. I told you the true story of CuChulainn. Fair's fair, story for story?"

"What, you want to hear my big, dramatic, tragic backstory?" he snapped. He pushed her off and sat up, staring at the quiet sky of their pocket dimension. After a moment of silence, he spoke. "Some vampires followed a five-year-old pyro kid home. Got tricked into inviting them in past protection spells and they strung the family up like livestock from the ceiling. Cut my parents' throats and they bled out into buckets. Left me for dead when they got bored of playing with me, but sure took their sweet ass time about it. Hours. All night. Kept teasing about whether or not they'd let me see the sunrise one more time."

He pulled off what remained of his long-sleeved shirt and revealed that he had far more scars than just the two surgical ones on his chest. Marcelle frowned. The scarring was most intense along his inner wrist, upper arms, and where his shoulder met his neck. It was clear evidence of having been subjected to bite after gruesome bite from vampire fangs. There were even dents where it looked as if his flesh had been gouged out by mouths, something no vampire feeding with any shred of decency would do. They had eaten him.

Marcelle remembered what he had said to Sarai when they'd first met, how he'd tried to warn her that vampires ate people. The hatred in his voice, the disbelief on his face when Setanta had lied to assure him they didn't. Lochlan knew firsthand it was true. Some vampires *did* eat people.

"This one was called Carrie," he said, pointing to the bites on his wrist. "She had long brown hair. Freckles all over her face. Red eyes. They all had red eyes. Fangs like animals. She laughed like a damn hyena every time she made me scream and made fun of me for crying, called me a stuck pig. This one was Bertrand." He pointed at the bites on his upper arms and along his shoulders. "Had some kind of British accent, blond hair. He cut my mom's throat and then gave me these while talking about how he liked the way I smelled. Like chili peppers. He said he missed the taste of food, so I would have to do. And Gareth took the big bites. He said he loved how pretty I was. Compared me to a rare steak that needed tenderizing."

Lochlan ground his teeth.

"And now that little girl they wanted for easy prey is all grown up, except he was never a little girl. He's a man and always was. A man who couldn't save his family. Who spends every night praying he could run into those leeches just one more time. Who grew into a magic gift only suitable for turning those monsters into a barbeque because he sees their faces every night and hears their voices taunting him for being too weak to fight back... Stuck pig... Weak... Pathetic... Helpless..."

He raised his hand up, reaching for the sky, and made his fingers into the shape of a gun to shoot off a bolt of fire like a flare.

"One day I'll run into them again. Then we'll see who screams."

They sat in silence, watching the flare sputter and die in the distance.

"I could heal your scars for you, if that's something you want," Marcelle offered quietly. "Smooth skin, get rid of their marks."

He shook his head. "No. No, they remind me where I've been. I live with a coven of witches; I could get all my scars removed if I wanted to. They're proof. I didn't even need to keep these," Lochlan said, gesturing at the twin scars on his chest. "I chose it. I need the proof of what I've been through. My scars are part of me."

"Setanta has a similar attitude about tattoos. Since we can't scar, he uses them to mark events like battles, war, marriage."

He smirked a little. "Didn't you just say the same thing three times?"

"Oh, you're so funny. Not just marriage though, he got one for me two hundred years ago. A little fleur de lis on his arm."

Lochlan's eyes widened. "Wait, what? What do you mean, for you?"

"I'm his mistress." She'd almost forgotten that he wouldn't know; it was such common knowledge among all vampires she hadn't even considered bringing it up.

"Fuck!" he shouted and got up, frantically zipping his pants. "What the fuck?! Wait, you're with Sarai too, aren't you? Oh fuck, fuck, fuck, I can't believe I forgot. Does she know? Does he know?! Is he going to be coming after me?"

Marcelle laughed. "Relax, it's not like that. We're not exclusive. I can do whatever I like, and so can he. Though..." She frowned. "I never had that talk with Sarai. Oh, she knows about Setanta and they get along fine. I just never talked about anyone else. Old habits: I'm so used to vampires who don't care. I'll have to talk to her when I get back."

"Yeah, you think?" He was still panicked but had calmed down. "One time thing, okay? We're not doing this again."

"If you say so. *La petite mort* is always relaxing after sparring, but I can take care of myself."

"A… little death? Is that French for vampires?"

"Slang for an orgasm. Because when I'm done with you, it feels like you've died and gone to heaven." She gave him a wink.

"You're not that good."

"Says the one who was screaming on the tip of my tongue not five minutes ago."

Lochlan blushed and buckled his pants. "Don't tell anyone about this, okay?"

"Don't try to burn me or my vampires to death again and I won't say a word. Except to Sarai."

He groaned. "Do you have to tell her it was me?"

"If I don't, someone will. They're all going to smell you on me." She looked down at the burn mark in the shape of his hand on the rear of her pants. "And you did leave a mark that'll be hard to hide."

Lochlan groaned again, louder, and flopped onto the grass. "You should have just killed me. That would be less painful."

"I'll make it up to you."

"By never speaking to me again?"

"By finding the vampires who killed your family."

Lochlan stared at her. "Are you… serious?"

"Dead serious. Vampires running around targeting free witches and children are breaking our laws. And, technically, since you're from the Tuatha de Danaan, they attacked a relative of the royal family, however distant. That carries a harsh penalty. This normally wouldn't be under my jurisdiction, but I know who to call about it."

"You don't say?"

"I do say. Would that be acceptable to you? Getting help from a leech?"

Lochlan laughed. "Lady, you get me those three and I will let you peg my ass in front of everyone in the coven."

Chapter Ten: A Rude Awakening

Sleep was easier for Sarai. The broken record in her head that tortured her had been shattered, at least for the moment. A pile of enchanted bay leaves under her pillow helped keep away any dreams, and everything started to feel better. She wasn't happy that Marcelle had been called away to New York, but at least she knew that they loved each other, and she had her friend Rosaline to hang out with.

She often followed Rosaline, one of the humans who worked at the palace donating her blood and doing chores, around as she worked. She even got the girl to teach her how to fold a fitted sheet. It was all menial work: laundry, dusting, and the like. But the company was nice, even if Rosaline did veer towards being a chatterbox at times. The normality was the beacon of sanity Sarai had desperately needed. Silly banter about some human boy Rosaline had a crush on and about her ongoing semi-reciprocated lust for Bear was fun.

Sarai's sleep schedule flipped to the vampires' preferred rhythm, which made things easier if she wanted to participate in anything going on in the palace. She started to build a witchcraft corner in Marcelle's room, using a small table to keep an assortment of items she procured from the kitchens. A pot and a plug-in burner as a cauldron plus a collection of herbs were her new prized possessions. She also kept a pair of candlesticks she'd requested from one of the vampire guards in the palace there to light on Friday nights in honor of Shabbat.

It felt good to have the freedom to practice both religion and witchcraft openly. She recalled how afraid she'd been of vampires when she first arrived, how one named Nicolas had played into all her fears and earned his death at her hands when he attacked her. No one else had ever caused her any problems. Perhaps they all knew what happened to Nicolas or were too afraid of Setanta's wrath to cause her any grief, but she couldn't be upset with the results either way. She felt right.

As sunset began to fall on a Shabbat eve, Sarai opened the balcony to let some fresh air in. It was a beautiful night. The clouds were just right across the Smoky Mountains that the setting sun made them glow purple. Life had never been better for her. She turned back to her witch corner and focused on her candles. It amazed her that she could have as many candles as she wanted, let them burn all the way down naturally. Back when she'd lived on her own, she had to conserve tealights and suffocate the light to be able to reuse them as many times as she could before needing new ones. Now she could do things right.

She lit the candles with a quick spell, then waved her hands over the candles three times and covered her eyes with her hands.

"*Baruch atah Adonai, Eloheinu Melech ha'olam. asher kidishanu be'mitzvotav ve'zivanu le'hadlik ner shel Shabbat*," she prayed in song. She didn't always do the prayer. At her old home, back when every penny counted, she would conserve her tealights by extinguishing them quickly, and therefore hadn't wasted time on prayer. But now that she had as many candles as she wanted at her disposal, she could let them burn and allow herself the time to say a proper prayer.

Strange. She usually felt Liora's presence next to her whenever she lit the candles, whether she said the prayer or not. But there was a distinct absence of the ghost in the room.

A light clinking noise chimed behind Sarai, like delicate metal against metal, and it caught her attention. Excited, she hoped it was Marcelle, back early from New York.

"Hello, witch."

She turned around in shock at the voice. The queen she barely knew at all stood in Marcelle's room, in an elegant white dress and large amounts of gold bracelets on her wrists, clearly having used the open balcony as a doorway. Vampires... no wonder Marcelle kept it closed.

"Uh," Sarai's voice trembled as she tried to pull herself together. "Hello?"

"Don't mind me," Queen Giovanna said, her voice sarcastic. "I thought, you've been living in my home for some time. I should see who this... witch sensation is. You've captured the prince's attention and time. Is that brutish whore calling herself a knight commander not enough for you?" She smirked, as if the insult were a joke, but Sarai cringed. Her eyes narrowed on Giovanna.

"Excuse me, um..." She cleared her throat a little to compose herself. "Is there something I can do for you?" She had an uncomfortable flashback to Nicholas, but the difference was that this was a pureblood, a queen. She knew that even Marcelle couldn't go against the queen. At least Sarai had her powers this time and kept her hands at the ready.

Giovanna's piercing red eyes drifted over to the table, and she approached, running manicured fingertips over the pot that served as her cauldron. Sarai couldn't help but tense at the sight of the queen touching her things. It was an unspoken rule among witches that strangers shouldn't touch a witch's materials without permission. The chance of tainting a spell or potion aside, it was just rude. And yet, Sarai knew she had no right to call her out on it. She was a queen, and Sarai was a guest, and not even a vampire.

"Did he get all this for you?" she asked. "I know Setanta gave you something much more precious too. He had my," she scoffed a little, "*beloved* husband help with the translations. And had to ask permission to give such a thing. He's not king yet, as much as he's been acting like one." There was obvious distaste in her voice, and she looked like she'd been sucking on a lemon as she mentioned the other purebloods. "It's strange having a stepson so much older than myself, you know. I was born in the Renaissance. They were trying to marry me to him first, but he refused." She looked up with those uncomfortable eyes. "So why is he spending time with you? What is it you do with him?" She raised an eyebrow, almost suggestively.

Sarai shook her head, trying not to think about the way her cheeks grew hot at the implication of that carefully plucked, raised eyebrow. "I think you've got the wrong idea. This is a misunderstanding."

"Do I misunderstand?" She smiled, but it was fake and threatening. "Come now, we're both women. We know what women want with men like him. A little enslaved witch like you suddenly finding herself in the lap of luxury and the arms of the next king of New Ulster? None of us are blind. Even a simple title like 'mistress' would get you power and stability for a lifetime. Is that what you want?"

"I'm not trying to do anything. Marcelle's got that title, and she's welcome to it. I'm not interested." She knew that mistress was a genuine position in the vampire court but couldn't help but think of the word mistress in a different context. She doubted Giovanna was accusing her of wanting to sexually dominate Setanta. As if anyone could dominate him in any way. "You've got this all wrong."

Giovanna studied Sarai. "If there's nothing happening, then why did he take so much time out of his schedule to spend it with you?" she demanded. Sarai opened her mouth to explain they only met up for magic-related reasons but didn't get the chance. "Has he said what he wants from you? This ridiculous alliance business is over and done with, you served your purpose. Why are you still here and not back with your own kind?"

Sarai glared at the queen. "Because I don't exactly fit in with 'my own kind'. Aren't you a witch, technically speaking? You fit in with them about as much as I do. You could always 'go back' to a witch coven."

Giovanna's eyes widened. "You impudent…" She stopped and smiled. Her hand touched Sarai, causing her to tense, then her body relaxed. Why had she been so upset? The queen was so pretty. She was a goddess.

"You're a horrible little girl, you know that?" the queen murmured.

"Yes, my queen," Sarai replied in a daze. "I'm sorry, my queen."

"You know you should be nicer to me, don't you?"

"Yes, my queen." Those red eyes were so stunning, Sarai wanted to drown in them.

"You'll do anything I tell you, won't you?"

"Anything for you, my queen."

The goddess before her smiled, and elation swelled in Sarai's chest: she'd made her queen happy!

"Let's take a walk on your balcony."

Sarai followed, gladly letting the goddess hold her hand as they went out into the open. She caught the scent of saffron from being so close to the queen, the perfume like an intoxicating wine to Sarai.

"Now, you can't really be this daft. You know you have no right to be with the crown prince, but you've got him at your beck and call. Yet you're so simple you're just sleeping around with some useless made vampire? Come now, tell me. He must want something more from you. He spends his time with the whore because of what she does for him in bed. What do you do for him?"

"Do for him?" Sarai tried to concentrate through the fog, but the queen was just so beautiful. She had to focus though, to answer the question to this goddess's expectations. She had to please her. "I... let him use me."

The queen's eyes narrowed. "How?"

"He needed someone to help him get into the Ellis Coven. He used me to start talks with the witches."

Giovanna made a noise of disgust. "You imbecile. How *else* does he use you?"

"I think... I think we're friends?"

A frown twitched on the queen's painted lips. "Everyone thinks you're just the sweetest little thing, and now I see why. The childish innocence act is nauseating." Giovanna gripped Sarai's chin and forced her to look away, out towards the forest. It was painful to do; she wanted to keep looking at the beautiful goddess. "Do you like the view?"

"Nothing is as beautiful as you, my queen."

"Climb up on the ledge. Keep holding my hand."

"Yes, my queen." Sarai leapt to obey and clambered up onto the balcony barrier, balanced precariously on the stone.

"Turn around and face the forest."

Sarai obeyed, though she wanted to keep looking at the flawless queen. To revel in her perfect face, her enchanting eyes.

"You've been through a lot, haven't you? The Reinhart Coven, the Vasi, all this pressure Setanta's put on you. Might be nice for you to just... make it all go away."

"Make it go away? Do you want me to go away?"

"Do I want the pretty witch who waltzed into my home to snuggle up with the crown prince about to dethrone me to go away?" Giovanna laughed. What an enchanting laugh she had. "I don't know, do I have a problem with him chatting up a mortal when *I* was originally put in his path?"

"I can go away. Anything to please you, my queen."

Giovanna grinned and let go of Sarai's hand. The blissful devotion evaporated, replaced by sheer panic. Disorientated, she slipped, screaming in terror. The queen caught her by her neck, dangling her over the edge as she now stood on the ledge.

"Do you feel that fear?" the queen hissed. "Remember how much you wanted to please me? You would do *anything* for me."

"Please—"

"Shut up," Giovanna snarled. "If you don't leave and go back to your little witch coven immediately after the coronation, then I will come back. I will force you to write your own suicide note. And I will make you jump headfirst off this balcony. Do you understand me, slut?"

Sarai's first instinct was to use her power, but that would do no good. If she did anything to compromise Giovanna's steel grip, she would plummet to certain death. She gripped the queen's hands in fear of her letting go, only moderately glad that the contact didn't cause the haze to return.

"If you ever grow up and figure out how to properly use what's between your legs, remember this. I can stomach losing the chance to put my daughter on the throne to an equal. To a proper princess of Kemet or Xian. To a pureblood. The thought of some mortal bitch like you swooping in at the last minute and stealing everything is enough to make me sick. Do you understand me?"

"I'm not trying to sleep with Setanta, just let me—"

"Let you go?" Giovanna grinned with sadism.

"No, no, no—"

"Then stay away from—"

"Giovanna."

The stern voice brought hope to Sarai's hammering heart and caused the vampire to snap her head towards the door. A fake smile plastered onto her face at the sight of a very angry looking Setanta in the doorway, even as she still held Sarai aloft in the air.

"Put her down. Gently," he growled.

The moment Sarai's feet touched the floor, she wanted to run to him, but just backed away from the queen, brushing down her clothes as she tried to calm down. She couldn't run to Setanta after Giovanna's accusations.

"No harm done. I was just playing with the pretty witch. Someone told me she could fly, and I wanted to see for myself. All in good fun," she teased, not bothering to even put effort into her blatant lie.

Setanta walked forward and put a hand on Sarai's shoulder, which helped her calm a little, but not much. "Is there something you wanted, Giovanna?"

"That's 'my Queen' to you," she snapped.

"Only for another few days," he replied. "Queen *Step*-mother doesn't quite have the same ring to it, does it?"

"Maybe just 'Mother' then?" she said in a sickly-sweet voice.

His eyes narrowed. "You should leave before someone throws *you* off the balcony. If I recall correctly, *you* don't have wings. I wonder what would happen to even a pureblood if they fell from a thousand feet in the air? Come up with me and I could arrange for you to find out."

"Your father would never forgive you," she said. "Would you like to be grounded for treason against the queen?"

"My father won't be king soon. Would you like to be grounded for attempted murder of an honored guest?"

Giovanna glared at him, then leapt with the grace of a cat off the edge of the balcony, disappearing into the gardens below.

Chapter Eleven: Waltz and Swing

"Fuck." Sarai leaned back against the wall and covered her face with her hands, taking a few deep breaths. "*Fuck*."

"Sarai…"

Sarai shook her head and slowly lowered her hands. "I'm fine. I've had people try to kill me before." Her hands started shaking as she looked at them. She tried to get them to stop, to no avail.

"I won't allow her to kill you," Setanta said, gently taking her hands in his. Sarai blushed. "You're safe."

"You shouldn't hold my hands. She thinks…"

"I know what she thinks," Setanta sighed, but let go of her hands and went to close the balcony doors. There was a slight creaking sound, and it made Sarai concerned to see that there were indents of his fingertips in the metal knob, despite how gentle his hands felt against hers. She could feel the anger and tension in him, even though he was across the room. Her logical side knew that he wasn't mad at her, but she couldn't help but feel threatened by a man's anger out of habit.

"Did she hurt you at all?" he asked.

"No." She cleared her throat. "Just accused me of… of trying to…" *Sleep with you.* "She told me that if I didn't leave after the coronation she'd make me write a suicide note and jump off the balcony."

"That vexing shrew," he muttered. "If I could send

her back to Rome, I would in a human heartbeat. I'll ensure guards she can't control are posted to the door."

"She controlled me. That was mind control, right? What was that?"

"Her gift," Setanta said. "You remember I have wings?"

Who could forget? She nodded.

"All the pureblood lines are a little different, blends of different powers and rituals, different spirits involved in the rites. I can grow wings and may or may not have inspired some myths about red-headed demons as a result. Some can levitate, turn invisible, control wolves. You recall Greek and Roman pantheons? That's Giovanna's bloodline. They were worshiped because her bloodline has the ability to cause devotion and obedience in mortals. Though, to be frank, they didn't need to. It used to be a lot easier to get humans to worship you as a god than it is now. There's even some left who still worship my father as a god."

"I did keep thinking she was a goddess," Sarai realized. "That's disturbing. Does Artemisia do that too?"

"No. There's a ritual when two pureblood lines marry, to give one line dominance. After that ritual, any children of that couple inherits the dominant traits. Without the ritual, it's luck what side a child falls on. Artemisia is of my father's bloodline in all that it entails."

She thought for a moment, intrigued. How did witches not know about any of this? They had a lot to learn about purebloods. "What's the coolest power you've seen?" she asked.

Setanta chuckled. "Egyptians are more immortal

than the rest of us. Cut off my head or pierce my heart and I'm finished. Cut off an Egyptian pureblood's head and you'll make her angry. You can cut them into a thousand pieces, and they'll still be alive and able to be put back together unless you destroy the heart and burn the pieces."

"Like... Osiris," Sarai realized. All the powers he'd mentioned had some tie to mythology, even vampire lore.

"Precisely. Osiris was the start of their line."

"I need to do more reading in your library," Sarai said.

"I'll have someone pick out the best history books for you."

"So..." She shifted a little. "Uh, did you hear me screaming or just dropping by at a convenient time?"

"A bit of both, to be honest," he said. "I wanted to bring something for Marcelle. But it was your mother who summoned me. Quite the surprise to be accosted by a ghost demanding I run to your side. I suspect after identifying myself to her as your friend, she trusts me to ensure your well-being."

Sarai's eyes widened in shock. Liora hadn't appeared before her to warn her because she had gone to Setanta for help. It made sense, though she felt a little jealous. She wanted to see her mother again.

"Is it a side effect of the spell going wrong?" she asked.

"I think not. It seems she's aware of my existence and ability to help if needed. In fact, this was quite useful. Much more so than any protective spells I'm capable of placing on you, except perhaps the enchantment keeping anyone from taking you beyond the palace grounds."

"I guess." She looked away and wished she had something to busy herself with so the jealousy didn't show. "You said you had something for Marcelle? More paperwork?" Sarai asked, amused by her own statement. She'd never have thought that being a vampire knight commander would involve paperwork, but she often saw Marcelle going over a decent amount of it.

"She gets enough of that, I think. This is just a present to complement her dress for the coronation," he said, pulling a small jewelry box out of his pocket.

It was a reminder that he and her lover were together, but the polyamorous arrangement was less and less taboo to her mind as she grew accustomed to it. "Can I see?"

Setanta opened the box to reveal a decorative hair comb with a golden Celtic hound design and a black pearl for its eye.

"That's beautiful," she said in awe. It gleamed in the light and looked heavier than any piece of jewelry she had ever seen, except perhaps the necklace she had been given. Who in any modern era wore so much gold? Though Marcelle did have a large collection of decorative hair combs, most of which looked just as if not more old-fashioned.

"She likes doing her hair up with these," Setanta said. "I thought a new one was in order for the special occasion."

"She's going to love this," Sarai smiled. "It's just her type."

"You know her style well then?"

"Well enough, I think. I know she'll like this. It's shiny. She likes shiny."

Setanta laughed. "She does. Maybe you could help me get her a set of earrings and a necklace to match?" he asked. "It can be from both of us."

It would be from him, financially. Like asking a child to go into a store and pick out a present for Mother's Day; the father would still be paying. Not that she had experience with that exact situation, but the sentiment was kind. "I'd like that," she replied.

"Speaking of fine things, has your dress arrived yet?"

Sarai broke into a wide grin. "Oh yeah." She bound to one of Marcelle's wardrobes and opened it. The large ballgown's blue and silver skirt spilled out. She blushed a little and looked down. "I'm sure it's not your thing… sorry."

"Don't apologize. It's exquisite," he said. "Have you put it on to check the fit?"

"First thing I did. I still can't believe you guys got me something like this. If I ever get married, I'll never be able to top this even with a wedding dress," she joked. "I shouldn't even be allowed to touch it. It should be in a museum."

"You remind me of Marcelle the first time she touched velvet and silk. She was, well, adorable. There were sumptuary laws at the time forbidding commoners from wearing certain fabrics, so it was a shock for her to have access to the finery of nobility."

Did he mean to imply Sarai was adorable, or was she reading too far into his statement?

"Yeah, that sounds like it would be."

"Have you tried dancing in the dress? I understand it can take some getting used to for women unaccustomed to the large skirts."

Sarai burst into laughter, then stopped when Setanta raised an eyebrow in silent question. "Wait, you're serious?"

"It is a ball," he said.

"I can't dance."

"Why don't you put the dress on? I'll teach you the basics."

"You are serious, aren't you? Look, I can't dance."

"Which is why I'm offering to teach you."

"Now?"

"After you put on the dress. Your bathrobes and night shift are lovely, but they're not for dancing."

For the first time aware of how little she was wearing in front of him, she grabbed new undergarments, using her body to block him from seeing it coming out of the drawer, then snatched up her dress and dragged the heavy thing into the privacy of Marcelle's bathroom.

Once she was there, she was faced with the prospect of putting the dress on without any help from Marcelle. There was no way she'd be able to get up into the dress from the bottom, so she stood in the middle and pulled it up around her body. Why had Marcelle made her climb through it like a tent? This method was easier. Though the waist did stick a little around her hips, making her shimmy it up until it got to the right place.

It looked spectacular. Unfortunately, she wasn't able to reach behind her to lace it. She needed Marcelle to do it for her, but the only person there was Setanta.

It took a couple of minutes for her to work up the courage to open the restroom door. "Uh…" She still wasn't sure whether she should call him a title, honorific, or his first name, so decided not to address him when she stuck her head out. "I can't get the back."

"I can help," he said, and so she walked out, holding the front up awkwardly over her breasts to make sure it didn't slip. It was so low cut. Her decision to expose so much cleavage felt foolish now in front of someone other than Marcelle. If he agreed with the sentiment or had any thoughts at all regarding how exposed she was, he kept them secret. Setanta stepped behind her and deftly pulled the laces just right, tying them. The thought popped into her mind that he'd had clear experience with similar lacings and wondered if it was less lacing up women than unlacing them.

"There." Setanta stepped back and looked at the dress. "Sophie's outdone herself. You look stunning, Sarai." He took her hand, and gave her a spin, causing the skirt to flare around her.

"I feel ridiculous," she admitted, a grin plastered on her face. "Sophie's your family's seamstress, right? I guess I should thank you. This is part of you bribing me for my help?"

"If you want it to be, but I prefer to think of it as a gift."

"Keep the bribes coming and I might be willing to talk to more witches for you."

He chuckled. "Noted." Setanta went to a collection of records Marcelle kept on a shelf, skimmed them, and pulled out one of classical music. He popped it onto a record player and waited for it to start playing before offering her his hand. "Shall we?"

Sarai gulped. "Is there a spell in your grimoire to enchant some dancing shoes?"

"I'm afraid not, though I'm sure one exists somewhere." He looked at her with mock concern. "Are you afraid of a little dancing?"

She scoffed at him and took his hand. "Who, me?" Of course, she was. And a part of that fear was a sudden hyper-awareness of how it felt to hold his hand. "You're really going to teach me how to dance?"

"It would be strange to learn the night of the party. And it would be rude of me to let you attend unprepared," he said. "Everyone who'll be there has attended this sort of event before, and I wouldn't want you to feel too out of place." He was as practical as ever.

Setanta pulled her in closer. It wasn't the first time he'd touched her; being near while holding hands wasn't remotely as intimate as curling against his naked chest as he flew through the air. Yet, it felt more intimate as his red gaze captivated hers.

"Put your hand on my shoulder here." He guided her hand in place, then put his hand just above her waist, supporting her arm on his shoulder with his arm. "And we hold hands as such."

This is just a tutorial, she told herself. *That's all.* Still, she felt the urge to hold her breath, as if she were about to dive underwater.

Setanta raised an eyebrow a little. "Don't forget to breathe," he said.

"I'm breathing," she retorted.

"Of course you are."

She blushed. "Just show me how to dance."

"We'll do a simple waltz," he said. "One, two, three. Your partner will lead, so you only have to follow. There's much less chance of stumbling that way." He smiled and led her through the first simple step. She looked down at his feet and tried to follow them, wishing she could see her own feet. He should have let her practice without the gown.

"You're doing fine," he said to coax her. "Hold your head up tall, and don't hide your eyes. We can't see your beautiful eyes if you have your chin glued to your chest. All you need to remember is to start on your right foot. The memory trick is that women are always right." He stepped with his left to mirror her as he led.

It seemed impossible to dance without looking down, yet once she was looking up it was impossible to look away from him.

"Pretend you're a princess."

It made her snort. "Now you're a comedian?"

"Well, you're wearing a dress like one," he said. "And if my sister can be a princess, then anyone can. You look radiant, Princess Sarai." He gave her a twirl and pulled her back towards him, hand finding her waist with the practice and ease of someone who'd been dancing for centuries. Her hand caught his shoulder with much more comfort than before.

Radiant. He was probably just being nice, but she basked in the complement anyway. "Thanks." She blushed. "You're sweet."

"Sweet?" he mused as they danced. "You know, I don't think anyone has ever called me that, outside the context of exchanging blood... no, not even then." His eyes were so stunning.

"I-I aim to surprise."

"You succeed."

Setanta spun her out again, then held up her hand, bowed to her before letting go, and turning off the music.

"I wonder, would you indulge me in a small favor?"

Her mind snapped to the sexual favors Queen Giovanna had insinuated they traded. Some part of her wondered what that would be like with him, given the chance.

"It depends what the favor is."

He smiled. "I hope you won't judge me too much for this. But I found I rather enjoyed the dancing in a recent period of history very much. I used to take Marcelle to clubs just to dance."

As he put on a second record, the sharp contrast was obvious; an instrumental, upbeat band started to play swing music. He couldn't keep the smile off his face, his eyes glinting with genuine enjoyment of the moment as he did a spin and offered her a hand once again.

Sarai's eyes widened and she couldn't control the laughter that leapt from her body.

"Sorry! Just, never would have guessed you would be into swing."

"You should have seen my disco phase," he said before pulling her in again. "I may have worn bell bottoms." He placed his hand just a little lower. "Of course, the truly wild stuff was back in my youth; drums, nudity, bonfires. Sometimes drugs. Not much has changed in that way, though it was usually the priests who did the drugs."

"Drugged priests and bell bottoms. Now that would be an interesting mix."

"Very nineteen-sixties," he agreed.

Setanta showed her the first few basic steps to let her get the beat and the moves that the rest of the dance would revolve around. It was fun, and less anxiety-inducing than the first dance. Sarai found herself enjoying the movement, but also fantasizing about what Setanta looked like in ancient Ireland, in nothing but his blue tattoos and with drums thundering around a bonfire.

As she picked up on the steps, their dancing became faster. He manipulated her body with ease, even eliciting yelps by flipping her around like a toy. Amazingly, her skirt never caught or got in the way, just flared like a flower in bloom.

When the song ended, they were both smiling ear-to-ear, and Sarai was panting from the exercise.

"I appreciate this," he said as he held her. "I don't get to dance quite like that very often anymore."

"No problem. It was fun. Really fun." She held onto him, wishing the dance hadn't ended. She couldn't take her eyes off him and his gorgeous face. "I don't think I've ever seen you smile like this. It's a good look for you, you know."

"Don't tell anyone. I have a reputation to uphold; it'll be our secret."

They were so close… her heart was pounding so hard; she knew he had to be able to hear it. Had to be aware of how she was feeling. And he was still there, complimenting her, holding her. He was even leaning down just enough. He had to know, just like Marcelle always knew.

Some crazed instinct gripped her. Sarai stood up on her tiptoes, closed her eyes, and pressed her lips against Setanta's.

The moment after she did it, she froze. Afraid to pull away, and afraid to stay, her body left her paralyzed. His lips didn't move against hers, and they were rougher to the touch than Marcelle's. Slowly, she pulled away and opened her eyes.

Setanta stared at her, an eyebrow raised.

Heat flushed her from head to toe in embarrassment,

then drained out as a cold dread settled in.

"Interesting," Setanta said, his expression not changing.

"I, I'm sorry, I thought…"

He sighed and let go of her. "I appreciate the dance, Miss Sarai. Perhaps you should change into more casual clothes?"

"Y-yes, I… yes." Once again, she found herself stumbling at the thought that she couldn't manage the lacing at the back of her dress herself. She had to figure it out though, she couldn't ask for his help now. She pulled away and started to go towards the bathroom, head down as she tried to keep herself from crying.

"Wait."

Sarai froze in her tracks, and felt him behind her, his expert hands undoing the laces. Was it her imagination, or was he going slower than he had gone when lacing it up? She could only stand there, staring straight ahead as Setanta took his time helping her undress. She imagined what he saw from his point of view, what her naked back must look like. Was he teasing her, enjoying the view? Her hands moved to hold on to the front of the dress as if it would fall to the ground the second the laces were done. When he finished, she still stood there frozen for a long moment until she snapped herself out of it.

"Thank you," she whispered.

She felt the floor shift under her as he leaned forward, his voice close to her ear and causing goosebumps to ravage her neck and arms. "I will see you again at the ball, Sarai."

His fingertips lingered against her skin, and then they were gone. She heard the door open and close, and when Sarai turned around, she was alone in Marcelle's room once more.

Chapter Twelve: New Arrivals

When Marcelle returned, Sarai was panicked about the prospect of telling her what had happened. Sure, it was fine for Marcelle to do what she wanted with Setanta. That was an understanding Sarai had the moment she first kissed the vampire woman. But she'd never considered going after him for herself until their dance. What if Marcelle saw it as encroachment? What if she was angry?

"I need to talk to you about something that happened," were the first words out of Marcelle's mouth and immediately Sarai knew that the pureblood prince must have told her.

"I'm sorry," Sarai blurted out. "I don't know what happened. One minute we were dancing, and I thought he knew what I was feeling like you knew, so I kissed him and—"

"Who did you kiss?"

"You... you wanted to talk about something else?"

"Yes, but now I need to know who you kissed," Marcelle said with a grin. At least she didn't look angry.

"I, I kissed Setanta."

Marcelle's eyes widened. "Well then, that's much bigger news than I had. *You* kissed Setanta? On the lips? On purpose?"

"On the lips. On purpose."

"My goodness. All I did was sleep with that pyro

witch Lochlan and promise to try to hunt down the vampires that killed his family, but this is much bigger news."

"Me kissing Setanta is bigger news than... I'm sorry, wait, Lochlan?" She laughed. "Oh man. Last time I saw him, he called me a traitor for being with you. I can't wait to see him again; I'm going to rub his face in this."

"Been there, done that. He's pretty good, so I would recommend it."

Sarai snorted. "No way. Hot-headed idiots aren't my type." She smiled sheepishly. "I guess, with you doing that, you're not mad about Setanta?"

"Oh, you dear little witch, of course not. I had honestly forgotten I should discuss it with you beforehand. I thought you might be mad at *me*."

"No. Well, I'm absolutely judging your taste in men. But not mad at all. Go for it. Hunting down the killer vampires for him then? That's gotta be interesting."

"It's boring, to be honest. He gave me some possible names and descriptions, but there's well over ten thousand vampires in New York City alone. I'll have someone go through some old records, ask around, see if a trio named Carrie, Bertrand, and Gareth passed through around fifteen years ago. Chances are they might be dead by now, with how brazen their attack on Lochlan's family was. Vampires who act out like that get caught or killed by their prey."

"Hope they're dead," Sarai muttered.

"If not, they will be soon. But enough of that. What did Setanta say?"

"Don't make me relive it," Sarai groaned. "He said, 'interesting'. Interesting is never good. That's what you say when you don't have anything nice to say but you're trying to be polite."

Marcelle just laughed and kissed Sarai sweetly. "You poor girl," she teased. "Don't worry so much."

For better or worse, Sarai had plenty to preoccupy her mind as far as worries went. Specifically, the start of the ball and the arrival of the witches, Hannah, Danior, and Captain Moretti, from the coven to the palace. Too nervous to worry about her appearance, Sarai let Marcelle pick out a simple and professional-looking green dress for her, her favorite color. It gave her a little bit of confidence to look good, but it wasn't enough.

"Relax," Marcelle said, giving her lover a gentle kiss. "You don't have to say anything, we're just showing you off to prove I didn't eat you yet."

"Well, you kinda did with…"

"I've told you before, pussy doesn't count," Marcelle said with a wicked grin, and it brought a smile to Sarai's face.

"So just Hannah and Danior tonight? Not that other guy… Tobias, right?" Sarai asked.

"Smart of them to keep a leader at home, just in case of a trap. If I were in their shoes, I would have just sent Danior with his truth powers, but I suppose the rest were curious. Also smart to bring the captain for her firepower, though it'll be extra work to keep an eye on her." Marcelle sighed. "These events are always intense with our natural ability to stir drama, but this is going to be something else. I have ten vampires dedicated to watching them from the shadows to make sure none of our people try anything."

"Maybe don't tell the witches that." Sarai paused. "Wait, do you have them stalking me too?"

Marcelle just smiled and gave her a kiss. "Come on

now, we don't want to be late."

They went together down to the main entrance hall, and the royal family was already there at the foot of the grand staircase, including Setanta and the queen. Giovanna's jet-black hair was done up elaborately, and she wore a casual but stunning white dress that hugged her curves and gave her a statuesque appearance. Her hand was protectively on her daughter's shoulder, the gold bracelets on her wrist jingling with every slight move the little girl made.

Artemisia had a look of immense boredom on her childlike face as she fidgeted but perked up a little when she saw Marcelle and Sarai coming down the stairs.

"That's the witch they found with me?" she asked her mother. Before the queen could respond, the girl had darted away and appeared in front of the new pair. "Mother and Father said I'm not allowed to drink from you, but I wasn't going to. Since the Vasi want both of us, I think we should be friends." She extended her hand to shake.

Sarai didn't know what to say. She knew that Artemisia was in fact a thirty-year-old woman, yet her body and mannerisms were so child-like. Being friends with her could entail something as simple as playing dolls, or it could be some sort of political maneuver made with the same sort of conniving mind as her older brother. Still, she couldn't say no to the princess.

"I'd like that," she said. "It's nice to meet you. Properly."

"You healed well. You would, though, being a healing witch," Artemisia said.

"Artemisia," Giovanna snapped, and spat out a sentence in what sounded like Latin. Sarai wasn't sure what the foreign words meant, though she did catch the word "maleficarum" which she knew often referred to witches in a derogatory way in old texts. The little girl rolled her eyes in response before disappearing and reappearing at her mother's side.

Sarai's heart beat faster as they walked to join the royal family. Last she saw Giovanna, the woman threatened her life. And last she'd seen Setanta, she had made a fool of herself kissing him. But there they all stood as if nothing had happened.

Politics, she thought to herself. She bowed her head just enough to show respect, though she didn't want to give any to Giovanna. As she lifted her head, she looked at Setanta, and her heart fell. He wasn't looking at her, but rather at the door. If only he would look at her, maybe give her a smile. Perhaps he was angry at her for stepping out of line.

"Sarai, is it?" said the other rather tall man present. He had a kind voice, and kind eyes when Sarai met them. He looked older, with gray streaking through his red hair and beard, and wrinkles surrounding his red eyes. There were blue tattoos at his wrists and neck, and even one on his scalp under his hair, similar in style to Setanta's body tattoos.

"Sarai, this is our king, Lugh," Marcelle said, making the formal introduction.

She took a deep breath, and gave him a smile, once more bowing her head to him. "It's nice to meet you, sir."

"Likewise. I've heard about you from my son. All good things. Your assistance in his new pet project has been very appreciated."

"Thank you, sir, Your Highness. It's no trouble."

Danior might have seen that as a lie, but thankfully he wasn't there. As if summoned by the thought, the front door opened, and the witches were escorted in by Bear, Angela, and a male vampire with an eye-patch whose name Sarai didn't know. Danior's cane clunked against the ground as the middle-aged, tan, bald man entered the palace, accompanied by an older Lakota woman, Hannah, with long gray hair and a black pantsuit.

Their eyes were wide as they took in the luxurious palace's interior, and Setanta stepped forward to greet them.

"Danior Teli, Hannah Little Hawk, Miriam Moretti; welcome," he said. "I hope the journey was an easy one?"

"Of course. It is a privilege to be here," Danior said.

"Please. Allow me to make introductions," Setanta said. "This is my family. My father, King Lugh; my stepmother, Queen Consort Giovanna; and my half-sister, Princess Artemisia. You already know our Knight Commander Marcelle. And Sarai, of course."

"It is a pleasure to make your acquaintance," Lugh said, stepping forward. "I'm very excited to see an opening of the relationship between our peoples once again." Evidently, he told the truth, Sarai thought to herself. Or at least if it was a well-intentioned lie, Danior didn't give away what he knew. She did note that the king said "I" rather than "We", as it was clear Giovanna had no interest in relationships with witches.

"A pleasure for us as well. Forgive me, I'm not quite sure if there's proper etiquette we should follow in meeting royalty. This is a new experience for us," Danior said.

"There's no etiquette necessary here," Lugh said

with the kind smile of an amused old man. "Consider this an informal meeting. Your escorts will prepare you with proper formalities for the main event."

"Our escorts?" Hannah asked, glancing back at the made vampires.

"They will ensure your safety. While our own people who live here know to behave, we are expecting a large number of guests, including foreign vampires. I must ask that you not wander, at least not without proper security, or we may not be able to ensure your safety."

"We appreciate your concern," Danior said. "Do you anticipate any trouble?"

"It is always best to be prepared for trouble regardless of whether it is anticipated or not," Lugh said.

"A respectable position to take," Danior said. And also not a straight answer, so no lie would be noticed by the truth-detecting witch's gift, something Sarai was sure he would note as well.

"Indeed. I shall leave you in the capable hands of my son for now. Please, enjoy our hospitality. If there is anything you need, do not hesitate to speak to any of our knights."

Giovanna almost snatched the king by his arm to drag him away, looking down her nose at the witches as if she had been forced into the presence of cockroaches.

"Bye, Sarai," Artemisia called, before they disappeared. She raised a hand to wave, but the girl was gone before Sarai's hand was halfway up. At least the stuck-up queen was gone too.

Still, Setanta hadn't looked at her or addressed her at all the entire time. She wanted to blurt out, "What did you think about our kiss?!" But of course, she couldn't do that.

"Sarai," Hannah said with a warm smile. "I hope you're well?"

"I can't complain."

Danior raised an eyebrow, and she quickly amended her statement.

"I mean, I'm sure I could complain if I wanted to. But I don't want to right now." She smiled. Needing to speak only careful truths would keep her on her toes. It satisfied Danior at least, who turned to Setanta.

"We were hoping to learn more about how you live firsthand while we're here. I must admit curiosity about, well, more delicate topics," the witch said.

"I expected nothing less," Setanta said. "Angela, would you mind taking their things up?" The vampiress scowled at being reduced to the work of staff, but obediently nodded and darted away. Sarai wondered why Setanta hadn't asked one of the humans who worked at the palace to do the job and suspected that Angela was off to inspect the luggage, perhaps alongside the absent spymaster, Lilly.

"Thank you!" Hannah called after Angela but got no response.

"We have rooms for you, if you'd prefer to see them first," Setanta said. "I know you wanted to see how we treat humans in our care, but there's the rest of the mansion as well, if you'd like a tour. Mundane things like the gardens, some old artifacts and paintings, whatever strikes your fancy."

"Whatever you would like to show us," Hannah said. "Though I must insist on time with Sarai at some point, so I can help with the spirit."

"There will be time, you have my word," Setanta said.

"I would like the chance to talk to the humans who live with you first," Danior said. "Just to put us more at ease."

"Of course," Setanta said. "Before we venture further." He held out his hand and offered all the witches gold arm bands that looked like miniature versions of the golden torque necklace he wore with wolf heads on the ends. Not only that, but they looked like large versions of a gold ring Marcelle always wore to indicate her relationship with him.

Danior picked one up and looked it over, tapping it with his cane. "What are these?"

"There are no spells on them," Setanta said.

"Then, the purpose?" Hannah asked as she took one and passed the other to Captain Moretti behind them.

"They let any vampires here know that you're under my protection when worn on your left hand. Few to none would risk a fight with me," he said with a smile.

"I can protect my leaders," Moretti said.

"Can you?" Bear said, suddenly right behind her.

She jumped with a shout, her hair rising with electricity sparking in the strands.

Hannah shook her head. "We *all* appreciate the gesture, Setanta. And accept your gift." She looked up at Bear and gave him a disapproving tsk-tsk noise with her tongue. "Here I thought, the older you are the more mature you should be? Or are you as old as you look?"

He laughed and gave her a broad grin. "My apologies. Only making a point, Ma'am."

"Your point is made," Setanta said, and the knight bowed his head and stepped back. "If you would like to speak to our humans, allow me to be your guide. This way."

Setanta gestured for them to follow him up the stairs. Bear took up the rear alongside Marcelle and her lover. Sarai found herself following Marcelle and Bear's gaze around the halls and spotting what they were doing: warning off other vampires coming to glimpse the witches. A stern look from either of the guards would cause the fleeting shadows in doorways to disappear. And it seemed that the three witches were none the wiser, which was for the best.

"You should know that the humans you are to meet will be present at the ball and I'd rather that not be a shock to you, that you not worry about their safety."

"Really?" Hannah asked. "I hadn't thought other mortals would be attending. That does put me at ease."

"Attending might not be the right word for it," Setanta said. "When you have events, it's proper to provide guests with refreshments, yes? The concept is similar. They will be serving drinks to our guests."

"That's more like what I expected to hear," Danior muttered with disapproval.

"It's just out in the open then, is it?" Hannah asked. "I have to admit, I imagined it would be behind closed doors."

"It's not so bad," Sarai piped up. "I mean, we do worse to animals. At least they don't kill people for their blood."

"I suppose that is a relief," Danior said. "I hope the wine glasses are kept separate, so we don't take a sip of the wrong red liquid."

Setanta chuckled. "Mostly we wouldn't use wine glasses, though some might. Something more direct is preferred. We crave warmth, after all."

Then why didn't he kiss her back? Were her lips not

warm enough? No, that was ridiculous.

Sarai looked down at her feet. Marcelle thought she was warm enough. But then, Setanta wasn't as cold as Marcelle was. It was as Giovanna said: she wasn't good enough for the vampire crown prince. And that was why he didn't return the kiss, why he wouldn't look at her or speak to her.

It was fine, Sarai told herself. She didn't need to be with him, she'd just been so wrapped up in the moment, in the dancing. If she hadn't been surrounded by vampires and their permissive and open culture, she never would have kissed anyone while involved with Marcelle in the first place. She did adore Marcelle, and clutched her hand as they walked, leaning in affectionately. It felt so right. It *was* right.

Still… It would have been nice to see Setanta smile at her.

Chapter Thirteen: The Human Quarters

Led by Setanta, the small group came to a stop at one of the doors in a part of the palace Sarai recognized. She'd been there a few times to hang out with the humans, mainly with Rosaline. There was a bit of a ruckus on the other side of the doors, and when Setanta knocked for the first time, no one seemed to hear. He sighed and knocked again, louder.

"Shut up a sec, I think someone's at the door." There was the sound of bare feet against the tile floor, and the door opened a crack. It was one of the humans Sarai remembered from her trip to the mall with Marcelle, a girl not older than her early twenties. She had a goofy look on her face that slipped off to be replaced by pure shock.

"Oh! Oh, shi—, um. Sorry, Your Highness. Uh, Sir. We're a bit of a mess right now?" she said. "We didn't think any of, well, we don't usually get you royals."

"It's all right. I didn't want you to have a warning. I brought guests interested in seeing how you live. May we come in?"

The girl nodded, opening the door. There were empty beer bottles on the floor by the couch, and several different types of gaming equipment. Video games by the TV, as well as a pool table, foosball, and several arcade games. Despite the fancy equipment, it looked like a trashed college dorm room, much worse than Sarai remembered ever seeing it. The humans must have had a party and not yet had the chance to clean up. A dozen or so were milling about. Several of the girls painting each other's nails scrambled to stand up out of respect as the company entered the room.

"We thought we wouldn't be meeting anyone until later on," said the girl as she sheepishly tried to throw some things in the trash. "I would have cleaned up better after last night if—"

Setanta raised a hand to silence her, and she immediately went mute.

"It's quite fine. I wanted to introduce our newest guests to you. These are the witches from our latest alliance, Danior Teli, Hannah Little Hawk, and the captain of their guard, Miriam Moretti."

The witches were staring, taking it all in. It was impossible to tell what they thought, hiding their opinions behind semi-pleasant but sharply observant expressions.

"It's our pleasure to meet you," Hannah said. She stepped forward and grasped the girl's hands in hers. "Oh, but you're so young."

The girl glanced over at Setanta. "I mean, I guess compared to them." She laughed awkwardly.

"SARAI!" shouted a thrilled voice from the doorway to the rest of the humans' quarters. Rosaline ran right past the vampires and witches to give her friend a hug, then stopped, her eyes widening as she saw Setanta standing there with his piercing red eyes and took a step back. "S-sorry, Your Highness!" she gasped. "I didn't see, well, I mean, I didn't expect, um…"

"Please, I'm not here to make you uncomfortable," Setanta said.

"Does he make you uncomfortable?" Danior asked.

"What?" She looked around at the expectant faces of the witches.

"I assume I make her uncomfortable because royals like myself rarely visit our human sources," Setanta said.

"No, no," Rosaline laughed in a nervous, cheery tone. "It's all good. But, yeah, unexpected. We're not used to guests in our space. Nine times out of ten, this is a no vampires zone."

"We don't mean to intrude. We're simply curious about this arrangement you have with these vampires," Danior said.

"These are the witches from the Ellis Coven," Sarai told her. "Everyone, this is Rosaline. She's a friend of mine here."

"Ohh, gotcha. Are you as weirded out as Sarai was by all this?" Rosaline joked.

"That would be a word for it," Captain Moretti said.

"Would you mind talking to us for a bit? Assuming no one objects," Danior said.

"No, no, all good! If I'd known I was gonna do an interview, I'd have done something with my hair," she laughed, and ushered them to follow.

"If you don't mind me asking," Hannah said, "How old are you?"

"Twenty-seven," Rosaline said. Sarai was surprised. Rosaline had a very young face, and she'd assumed the human was closer to her age or younger.

"Ah. And some of the others?"

Rosaline shrugged. "It varies. They don't let anyone who's not a legal adult here though, if that's what you're asking. We're all legal to sign up for the army."

The witches hid whether or not they approved.

"Anyone want something to drink? Tea or coffee? Or…" Rosaline glanced at Setanta and the other vampires. "*You* guys gotta sign up on the schedule if you want a drink."

"Tea sounds lovely, thank you," Hannah said. "Could you tell us more about this schedule?"

"Oh, yeah," Rosaline said, and led them to the kitchen where she, to Hannah's displeased gaze, began to microwave water for tea. "We have a signup sheet with who's available when to give them blood. We dictate when we want to do it, how often. If we don't like someone, we can veto them. We all have our regulars though." She winked at Bear.

"You're her… regular?" Hannah asked the large vampire.

"That's right," he confirmed. "Unless I need something in an emergency situation, we meet every few days. Of course, who knows what might happen with someone pretty as you here. Maybe I'll skip a feeding with her."

Rosaline's smile faltered, and Sarai bit her lip. Bear had to know that wasn't fair, to flirt with the older witch in front of a girl he slept with who was so clearly infatuated with him. As if he realized what he'd done, he cleared his throat.

"Only joking, of course," he added. He looked from Rosaline to the stern expression on Setanta's face. "No intentions of making our guests uncomfortable. Honest."

"I hope so," Hannah said, a little flustered. "We're not here to be your… what was the word you use?"

"Sources," Rosaline said flatly. "We're called sources. 'Cause we're their source of blood. Green tea?"

133

"Please."

Rosaline dunked a packet of green tea in the hot water and slid it to the elder witch, then got more hot water for Danior and Setanta. "You want one?" she asked Sarai.

"I'm good. Thanks though."

"So, Rosaline, what's your story?" Danior asked, watching with some surprise as Setanta sipped his tea. "How did you come to a life such as this?"

"Well, I was a runaway. They like us when we're kinda desperate, you know? Got into some stuff I shouldn't have. I was a mess. Like, really a mess. Caught some things from sharing needles and I wasn't going to be okay, you know? And being an addict… it's not an easy existence. Then one particularly cold night I thought I was gonna freeze under a bridge, this gorgeous woman buys me a nice meal and tells me that she can fix me up and give me a job." Rosaline laughed. "I thought she was trying to pimp me out, but I was desperate so, you know, whatever. But it was so much better. They gave me a legit job here. We do housework, get paid. Give a little blood now and then. It's a great set up. And now, look at me. They healed me up with their blood, so I got no diseases. No drugs cause we gotta be clean to stay. It's practically a public service they're performing."

Hannah nodded deep in thought. "That's better than what I imagined. And you don't mind them, well, biting you?"

"Barely hurts at all. Bear looks tough, but he's got gentle teeth," Rosaline said, smiling at him. "He's my favorite drug now."

"I suppose, we'll be seeing a lot of that tonight,"

Danior said, looking at Setanta for confirmation.

"It will happen, yes. I hope you won't be too alarmed when it does. We do our best to ensure the safety and health of our sources. To do otherwise would benefit no one in the end."

Danior nodded. "It is your home. It would be rude to object."

"Hey, Rosaline," called someone from the back where the bedrooms were. "Where the hell did you go, you still have to help me paint my—" A girl froze in the doorway, stunned as everyone had been to see Setanta and the witches.

"Perhaps we should leave you now," Setanta said. "I appreciate you taking the time to talk with us, Rosaline."

"Oh, yeah, no problem." Rosaline smiled, and curtsied. "Thanks, Your Highness." She gave Sarai a quick hug. "I'll be around tonight, but don't worry about me. You have a good time, okay?"

"I'll try." Sarai smiled. She could only hope that a good time would be possible and that no rogue vampires tried to kill the visiting witches.

Chapter Fourteen: The Button

After the human's quarters, Setanta left the group with Bear leading the tour and Sarai assuming the worst-case scenario that Setanta would never speak to her again. Bear showed them various rooms and sections, mentioning which were off limits: specifically, the wing that the vampires lived in, which was where Sarai stayed with Marcelle.

Once the group was finished with the tour of the nicer places of the mansion, they were led up to the guest rooms, the same wing Sarai had been kept in when she'd arrived.

"Here we are," he announced as he stopped in front of a door. The door was opened to display the layout to their guests. The accommodations were similar to those Sarai was familiar with. A simple but large bed, a nice restroom, and a spacious living area where the luggage had been placed. On the desk were large stacks of books and maps.

"The next two doors down are yours too, so you each get your own space. We figured you would like some time to settle in before the event," Bear said.

"That would be wonderful," Danior said. "What are all these books?"

"Information," Marcelle said. "Not to give you too much work, and I know the prince already had some basics sent to you at the coven, but we thought you might like to review more about who will be in attendance tonight, how our society is run. That sort of thing."

"Oh, that is helpful," Hannah said and began going over the materials. "Not all of us managed to grow old with the steadfast memory of twenty-five-year-olds. This is very appreciated."

"Would you like one of us to stay and help you review things?" Bear said and flashed her a charismatic smile, which Hannah returned with a blush.

"That would be kind of you. Though, I wanted to ask, when would I be able to have time with you, Sarai? Concerning your mother."

"Oh." Sarai thought for a moment. "Um, I'm not sure what the schedule is like."

"Tonight is the main event, but you'll have plenty of opportunity over the rest of the week," Marcelle said. "I'll make sure you have time to handle it."

"That would be good," Hannah said. "To be honest, I think I'll have an easier time focusing on that sort of magic once we get tonight over with. It's hard to focus on my astral gift when I have so much else to worry about that's grounded in this plane."

"You have a few hours to get settled. The coronation is at midnight, but people will be gathering to socialize once the sun sets. I suggest by then you be ready," Marcelle told them. "Is there anything you might need?"

"No, you've been wonderfully accommodating. I hope you don't expect this level of luxury should you ever stay at the coven," Danior said, glancing around the room. "One thing though, I wanted to speak to Sarai? If you could give us a moment."

Marcelle exchanged a look with Sarai, who gave her a nod. It was fine.

"I'll be waiting outside," Marcelle said, and left the witches alone.

"I know I can't persuade you to come to the coven," Danior said, fishing in his pocket for something. "But I am concerned about your safety here."

"I can handle myself," Sarai said. "And I trust them to keep me safe."

"I know, but still. I wanted to give you a little extra something." He held out his hand to reveal a button.

"What does it do?" Sarai asked as she picked it up and looked it over. It looked like a plain, black button but as she held it in her real hand, she could feel the magic enchantment on it.

"It's spelled so that when a lie is told to you, it will feel warm. For example: I am a talking duck disguised as a person."

The button warmed on her palm, and she nodded appreciatively.

"A talking duck, huh?" she said.

"A character in one of my daughters' books," he said with a smile. "But the demonstration worked?"

She nodded and held it in her prosthetic hand, the one with her focus. "*Lirot ha'emet,*" she said. See the truth. She could feel that it was exactly what Danior said it was, and nothing more. It was good to know it didn't have a secret listening enchantment.

"Thank you. I appreciate it," she said. "Really." Being able to discern truth from lies when she was about to go into a week-long festival full of vampires playing politics could only serve her well. She thought she might need to ask Marcelle for a needle and thread to attach it to her glove, but then remembered that her amazing ball gown had pockets. Perfect; now she had something to put in them.

"Stay safe," he said sternly. "And if you need anything... I know your experience with other witches hasn't been the best, but we're here if you need us."

She nodded. "I know. I just," she sighed. "I feel right here. Yeah, they're vampires, but with Marcelle." She shrugged and gave an awkward smile. "She loves me."

Danior sighed. "At least I know you think that's the truth."

"It is the truth," she assured him. "We click. I trust her. And I guess I trust Setanta."

The truth witch raised an eyebrow and she sighed.

"Okay, mostly. I trust him not to hurt me. And I trust him when he says he wants to protect me. He's... I dunno. Always full of surprises. But not in a bad way."

Danior nodded. "I suppose that'll have to do for now then. Just be careful."

Sarai promised, and left, meeting back up with Marcelle.

"A magic button, hm?"

"You were listening," Sarai accused.

"It's not my fault guest quarters have thin doors," she teased. "Sounds like a useful tool. Hold onto that."

"Oh, I plan on it. After all, what's the point of having a dress with pockets if I don't stuff them full of magic trinkets?"

The two laughed and made their way back to Marcelle's quarters. There was time to kill, so Sarai spent it with Marcelle. They took a bath together, taking advantage of the intimacy to kiss and cuddle in the tub that comfortably fit them both. The hot water helped Sarai relax, and Marcelle's dexterous fingers found their way to just the right spots, helping her find release. In particular, she found it very fun that Marcelle didn't need to breathe, and spent ten minutes submerged in the water, her tongue swirling against Sarai's sex.

When Marcelle finally reemerged, her black hair slick against her pale skin, Sarai sighed in bliss. "That is the best trick ever."

"You have so much more to experience," Marcelle said, and kissed her lover. Her lips tasted like sex, but Sarai felt sufficiently satisfied that she wasn't in the mood for more. Though, it felt rude to only accept pleasure and not to give it.

"Do you want a turn? I can't do that though; I do need to breathe."

"I think I'll wait for now," Marcelle said. "But thank you for the offer. Though… I think I will take something from you." She smirked. "Safe words are red to stop, yellow to slow down. Snapping your fingers if you find you can't speak. Repeat?"

"Red to stop, yellow to slow down, snapping my fingers if I can't talk."

"Good girl."

The sensual purr in the words brought heat to Sarai's cheeks. She was about to ask what the vampire had in mind, when Marcelle resubmerged under the water and sharp twin pains stabbed into her inner thigh. She gasped, clenching her fists. It was such a tender and sensitive location to have a bite. They were shallow bites, avoiding any major arteries or veins, but enough to hurt. Once Marcelle pulled her fangs free, the water turned pink, and the wound healed, but the vampire wasn't done. She bit her again, and again, making Sarai cry from the pain, but determined to endure it. When she wasn't sure she could take another bite, Marcelle emerged, her face clean thanks to the water, grinning. Sarai stared at her, breathless.

"Have a good snack?" she managed to ask.

"Delightful snack." They kissed. "Come, now that we're all clean, let's try to do something with your hair."

After using magic to dry her damp curls, Sarai sat still as Marcelle tried to help them do something other than be wild. Eventually she gave up and let them be, to Sarai's relief considering Marcelle appeared not to have much experience with curly hair, though the vampire seemed disappointed about it. To make up for it, Sarai allowed Marcelle to do her makeup. A thin line of silver-colored eyeliner on top of a line of black liner was an interesting touch Sarai wasn't sure she liked, but it did match the dress.

Once she was finally in the outfit, shoes, and jewelry, Sarai felt powerful. Perhaps there was something to be understood about Marcelle's constant obsession with nice clothes. There was a unique strength that feeling good in what she wore gave Sarai. Though the idea of walking around with such a low-cut dress was still daunting.

The dress hadn't lost any of its glamor, of course. Just standing in front of the mirror felt like something out of a fairytale, with the silver and blue fitting her to perfection. She was regal. Just one thing was amiss; her red fingerless glove stood out like a sore thumb on her magical prosthetic hand. Holding up her hand, she whispered, "*Kachol*," and the glove turned blue to match the dress. Much better.

As she looked behind her at Marcelle, who wore a sleek, beaded, black dress with a modern flair, she was completely distracted away from her own appearance. If the way Sarai's curves were accentuated was sensual with the deep neckline, then what Marcelle wore was obscene. It had a low, open back and a deep cut front. For good measure, there was even a long slit in the side to leave the dress open enough to reveal alabaster legs. It was almost funny that she wore long, black opera gloves when the rest of her was so exposed. Marcelle's hair was done up in a bun, held in place by the gold hair comb Setanta had given her and several long pins, showing off her elegant neck. She looked like death's femme fatale sister.

"You look like a goddess," Marcelle said with adoration, coming to stand behind Sarai and wrap her arms around her. "Like starlight."

Sarai curled a lock of hair around her finger. "It's amazing," she admitted, looking back at the mirror. "And wow. You. I literally don't have words. You look like sex."

"What, this old thing?" Marcelle asked as she kissed Sarai's neck, sending a needful shudder through her body. Perhaps the intimate bath hadn't been enough. "Just kidding. I did have it specially made for tonight."

That wasn't a surprise; Marcelle did have a materialistic penchant for custom, expensive, and shiny things.

"We should get going, before the witches get nervous and send someone up to rescue you from my devious clutches," the vampire said.

"What if I don't want to be rescued?"

Marcelle gave a mischievous grin and nipped Sarai's earlobe as the witch whimpered. "Later tonight, I promise," the vampire murmured.

Sarai turned around and kissed her. "Not now? Just

one more quickie? I should return the favor you did for me earlier."

Marcelle sighed and pulled back, keeping them at arm's length. "I'd love to, but I should go over with you what to expect tonight."

"Dancing, right?" Sarai glanced away as she thought about dancing with Setanta, the way he held her, the way his lips felt... She blushed and tried to think of something else. It crossed her mind that other than fancy dresses and dancing, she knew nothing of what was going to happen.

"Yes, though that's after the main events. It's a little old-fashioned. I'll be your escort to the throne room and for the night, so stick by me."

"I need an escort? Is that like a chaperone?" Sarai asked, half in jest and half serious.

"Basically. Mortals don't go to vampire events unescorted unless they're sources," Marcelle explained. "Once we get to the throne room, we'll be announced. We walk to the dais and greet the royal family. Just give a little curtsy."

"Uh, and how does one curtsy?"

"Doesn't matter with that big dress on. Just bend your knees a little and nod your head," Marcelle said. "Just enough to show respect, but not subservience. Like this." She demonstrated.

Sarai gave it a try and looked up to see her lover's approving nod. "Okay, got it. And after that?"

"Then there's the coronation. It's a blood ritual, but no magic. And you obviously aren't participating, but I will be, and anyone else who serves the kingdom."

"A blood ritual?" Of course there was a blood ritual. They were vampires. "I can't wait to see those Ellis witches react to *that*."

"We did give them a bit of a heads up," Marcelle said, looking a little smug. "But I may have been vague on details just so the rest of us can enjoy their expressions."

"How much of a heads up are we talking?"

"I believe we told them that some of our traditions may be unnerving and that we have rituals we adhere to that may be unusual to them, but that they won't be asked to participate."

"That's it?" Sarai burst into laughter. "That's going to be a shock. You're trying to stir the pot, aren't you?"

"You can't blame me, vampires love drama," Marcelle smirked. "Those witches are the entertainment of the evening. After all that, we get to relax. There will be dancing, some shows around the palace. Human food will be available for the purebloods and witches, as well as for the humans. I do hope you'll save a dance on your card for me?"

"I haven't done a lot of dancing," Sarai said. She bit her lip. Having Setanta lead her around the room in private had to be different from dancing in public at a genuine ball. "What kind of dancing?"

"Ballroom, various types. Waltz is standard, of course. There'll probably be all sorts of other kinds throughout the night. Everyone likes different styles. Waltz is easy enough to do a simple version; I can lead you."

"Yeah, I know that one."

"You know?"

Sarai blushed. "Setanta showed me." She looked down, pretending to stare at the floor, but did catch a smile on her lover's face.

With the sun well set beyond the horizon of the Smoky Mountains, Marcelle offered Sarai her arm and the pair left the safety of their bedroom to brave the menagerie of bloodsuckers that was the Midnight Festival and Setanta's coronation.

Chapter Fifteen: Shield, Sword, and Hearth

Sarai followed Marcelle out of the room and as they approached the main entrance, she could hear a low murmuring like a cloud of conversation growing the closer they got, as did her anxiety. But even as she felt her own nerves fraying, she held onto some confidence. Marcelle was there, holding her hand.

The main entrance hall was the busiest it had ever been, with multiple cliques of vampires in clusters as they socialized. Many, if not all, were bound to be old and powerful beings. Sarai was only twenty-four years old; not even legally able to rent a car in America. Not that she knew how to drive one since she'd never gotten the chance, but it would have been nice to feel a little more confidence in her age.

The vampires weren't just old and powerful though; they were also beautiful. Their outfits indicated presences from all around the world, in every time period imaginable. Dark reds and blacks seemed to be a popular color, but a good percentage wore brighter colors, such as the Egyptian woman with heavy jewelry and headdress, wearing an intricately pleated tight dress made of white linen so fine it was almost transparent.

Another bright dress worn by a pale woman with long, strawberry blonde hair was also white, but jeweled and reminiscent of czarist Russia. An Asian woman in a cloud blue robe-like dress drifted like a glimmering specter between conversations. A tan man with a heavily embroidered tuxedo chatted with a red-eyed black woman wearing a purple ball gown that was decadent. Everyone looked flawless.

"Are you ready?" Marcelle asked.

Sarai wasn't at all ready, but there was no sense in holding off the inevitable. She took a deep breath and nodded.

"I know this doesn't help but try to calm down just a little. Everyone can hear that heart of yours going off. You'll just get yourself more attention."

"You're right. That doesn't help at all." Sarai closed her eyes, trying to avoid thinking about what she was doing. She could do it. Remembering her reflection in the mirror gave her a sense of steadiness. If she didn't belong there, at least she was wearing a dress that fit in. It was like camouflage, a strange armor for a strange situation, and her makeup was war paint. For the first time, the dress didn't feel like it was too much. It was necessary and gave her a seat at the table, metaphorically speaking. Showing up in anything less would have made her look like the inferior no doubt many vampires already thought she was.

Sarai opened her eyes and clenched her teeth. "I got this."

With her arm on top of Marcelle's, the two descended the stairs to the entrance hall. Every eye turned in their direction. Specifically, in Sarai's direction. The silence that stilled the din unsettled her, but she kept her head up. She belonged next to Marcelle, and anyone who said otherwise was no different than the homophobic human woman who once scorned them for holding hands on their date in the streets of New York

City. Keeping that in mind, comparing their witch/vampire union to their orientation, helped. So, she acted the way some part of her had wanted to act towards that woman. Proud and unabashed.

"Is there something I can help you with?" Sarai asked loudly as the vampires all stared. A few frowned, but most looked amused. The hush broke, and they returned to each other, with only the occasional glance back at her.

"Not bad," Marcelle murmured in approval.

"Indeed," said a voice. In the time it took to blink, a decorated Egyptian woman adorned in heavy gold like Sarai had never seen in her life had appeared before them, her wide, kohl-lined, red eyes betraying her pureblood status. "Calm your heart, little one, I do not seek after your veins."

Sarai gulped but kept a brave face. There was no point in denying what was a fact. "I'll see what I can do."

"A pleasure to see you, Your Highness," Marcelle said, nodding her head with respect. Sarai noticed it was very different and much less than the kneeling respect the knight paid to her own regents. "Might I introduce Queen Arsinoe of Kemet? She rules the vampires in what you know as Egypt."

So, they were jumping into the deep end: a foreign queen. What did one do when meeting a foreign queen? They didn't shake hands, that much she was certain of. Instead, Sarai copied Marcelle's head nod, doing her hardest not to stare at what had to be the most distracting outfit ever to exist.

"It's a pleasure to meet you, Your Highness."

"Please, please," the queen said, waving her hand.

"So formal, dispense with it. I heard the rumor there were to be witches, but I had not realized they would be attending. It is my pleasure to meet you. What do you call yourself?"

"Uh, my name is Sarai…" She hesitated, not wanting to align herself with her father's surname, but afraid to lie.

"She's Sarai Meir," Marcelle interrupted. It made Sarai smile.

"Yeah. Meir. Sarai Meir," she said proudly.

"Delightful to see you here, Sarai Meir. And I mean my words, truly." Her smile did seem genuine, as far as Sarai could tell. She clenched her fist in her pocket to feel the button Danior gave her in the palm of her hand. It hadn't changed temperature at all. "I will not keep you from the ball. Please, go on ahead. I'm sure our hosts are eager for you to make your grand appearance."

She disappeared back to her group of Egyptian vampires, and Marcelle steered Sarai towards a grand pair of tall double doors.

"Meir?" she asked Marcelle.

"You told me you prefer your mother's name once, don't you?"

"Yeah, but I always figured technically I have to go by my dad's. Don't I?"

"Not if you don't want to. Choose your own name," Marcelle said. "Besides, I put you down under your mother's surname. I thought you would have enough to worry about without the stress of representing your father."

Warmth filled Sarai's heart. Sarai Meir… it sounded much better than Sarai Reinhart and didn't make her cringe. It was best to accept it as her name.

"Thank you."

"Think nothing of it." Her lover glanced back at the Egyptian queen. "That was very interesting though."

"Why?" Sarai asked.

"She just gave you her approval in front of other vampires. It's a good thing, I promise. Her country isn't the largest or most powerful militaristically, but it is one of the biggest diplomatic players. Just keep that chin up and that brash attitude, and you'll be fantastic." Marcelle gave her a gentle peck on the cheek, and they entered the main ballroom.

Whenever she'd passed by the room before, the grand doors had been closed. Never could she have imagined the beautiful room behind them without seeing it for herself. The illumination came primarily from dim candlelight, perfect for creatures with sensitive eyesight, and for creating an anachronistically romantic yet mysterious atmosphere. There were elaborate chandeliers above, easily the size of cars, and tall windows with exquisite old curtains pulled open that spilled moonlight over marble floors. There was a portion of the room off to the side where a small orchestra was set up, playing light classical music on string and wind instruments. It was dazzling.

People gathered around the edges of the room, just as glamorous looking as the room itself in their silks, velvets, and jewels, leaving a path down the center. At the end of the walkway were all four of the New Ulster purebloods: the crowning glories of the night.

King Lugh and his wife stood together on a dais, with Setanta on Lugh's right side and Artemisia looking bored on Giovanna's left. The men both wore dark fur cloaks over their shoulders, long dark tunics with knotwork embroidery along the edges in gold thread, embossed leather belts around their waists, and similar golden torque necklaces. While Lugh wore a green tunic with black and gold embroidery, Setanta's was black with gold and hints of green embroidery. Lugh's red and white hair was open and he was crowned with a plain, possibly iron circlet. Setanta wore his hair simply as he always did, pulled back by his usual black ribbon.

Queen Giovanna wore a smaller circlet, similar to her husband's but gold, and a draped white gown reminiscent of ancient Rome or Greece, accessorized with heavy gold on her wrists, ears, and neck. Her hair was done up elaborately, with half of it in ringlets down her back and half woven into elaborate patterns on her head. Artemisia was the simplest, wearing a modern green velvet gown to her knees, bright white tights, and shiny black shoes. Her black hair was open, and she looked like a collectable doll of some sort, the expensive kind that was meant to sit on a shelf and stare at children with haunted glass eyes.

There was a single throne behind them, unfilled for the moment. It was made of solid black marble, with white snaking through it like veins and Celtic knotwork carved around it for decoration with gold paint to accentuate it, and some sort of animal fur draped over the seat and back. All in all, regal did not begin to describe the family.

"Announcing the Knight Commander of the Realm, mistress of Crown Prince Setanta CuChulainn mac Lugh, the Dame Marcelle de Sauveterre, escorting her ward and honored guest of the New Ulster royal family…" The announcer hesitated for a moment, but it felt like an eternity. "The witch, Sarai Meir."

The sound of conversation lowered to near nothing as every set of eyes, pureblood red and natural human-colored of made vampires alike, turned to stare. Did he have to say she was a witch? Yes, of course he did. That was the point of all it all, to have witches alongside vampires in public. At least Marcelle had given them her mother's surname, sparing her the burden of being a Reinhart. She was just a witch. A witch surrounded by vampires.

Somehow, the situation didn't make her feel small as she feared it would. She felt powerful in commanding attention around her. It was a thrill, just as sure as skydiving and bungee-jumping had to be. Sarai *Meir* was a confident witch.

The women's heels clacked against the marble underfoot, and low murmurs surrounded them. Sarai squeezed Marcelle's hand, right up until they reached the dais. When they stopped, so did the whispers. It was quiet enough to hear a pin drop, or Sarai's rapid heart beating. She tried not to look at Giovanna, and kept her eyes on Setanta, who to her great relief made eye contact with her and gave her a reassuring nod. It relaxed her; the first comforting gesture from him since their awkward kiss.

Marcelle let go of Sarai, giving her a moment of panic, then knelt. Remembering what she'd been told, Sarai tried to curtsy. Just as Marcelle had said, no one could tell that all she did was bend her knees under the dress rather than attempting any fancy proper curtsy. Hopefully, it would be respectful enough for the royals.

Lugh held out his hand as he looked at Marcelle.

"Commander, rise."

She did, and took his hand, bowing as she kissed his

ring before standing up.

"Miss Meir, it is a pleasure to welcome you as the first mortal witch to any event like this in many years," Lugh said. There was relief in hearing his words, and she bowed her head.

"Thank you for having me," she told him. "I'm honored."

"The honor is ours. Please, enjoy your evening," he said with a kind smile.

"I will, thank you."

Marcelle led her away from the royals to an empty space on the sidelines, allowing Sarai to breathe more steadily.

"Did I do it right?" she asked.

"To perfection," Marcelle promised.

Soon, there was yet another announcement that stunned the gathered vampires, taking the attention off Sarai for a few moments.

"Announcing the witch, Councilman Danior Teli of the Ellis Island Coven, escorted by Knight of the Realm, Dame Angela Lupu, the witch Councilwoman Hannah Little Hawk of the Ellis Island Coven, escorted by Knight of the Realm, Sir Bear, and the witch Guard Captain Miriam Moretti of the Ellis Island Coven, escorted by Knight of the Realm, Sir Crispin Wright."

"Does the 'realm' thing mean anything important?" Sarai wondered aloud as she watched them, thinking to herself how no one but vampires called it the "Ellis Island Coven". It was just the Ellis Coven.

"Well, there's knights for different parts of our territory. Like, that fellow over there is a knight commander too, like me, but he's the knight commander of Maine. Being commander of the realm means I have more responsibility, and the others ultimately all report up to me. Knights of the realm are more elite. We serve the kingdom as a whole instead of one state or city and directly are involved with the protection of the royal family," Marcelle answered, keeping her voice a little low to not disrupt others.

Hannah had kept a simple black pantsuit look with her signature white-lace gloves, though her belt was beaded and decorative, and she'd added a wide-brim black hat with a colorful scarf around it to her look. Sarai tried to remember if she'd ever seen the elderly woman in anything other than a pantsuit. Under the suit was a frilly lace button-up dress shirt that, despite looking very formal, didn't quite fit the level everyone else in the room was at. Her expression seemed unaware of this, and she walked with confidence on her escort's arm. Bear almost seemed to match, dressed in all black with bright geometric floral patterns, accessorized with the standard black gloves of a New Ulster knight. It looked almost modern, which was funny considering Sarai knew that he was over one-thousand years old. She wasn't sure what she expected from him: something older or maybe even flaunting the formalities with one of his favorite band T-shirts. Or perhaps one of those joke casual T-shirts with a tuxedo design printed on it.

Danior dressed as if he were going to a wedding, or perhaps participating in one, in a dark green tuxedo, his cane tapping along with his heels. He looked confident, proud, and after a moment Sarai realized why. His outfit had been magicked, and slowly changed color from dark green to navy blue, beginning to cycle through a dark hued rainbow. It captured everyone's eyes, as a boasting of his powers was meant to.

Beside him, Angela wore a basic black dress and black uniform gloves, with her hair done up in a tight bun as usual. Different from Bear, she wore a rapier strapped to her waist. Sarai glanced back at Bear, then at Marcelle, to see if she could spot any obvious weapons on them. Bear had a dagger with a hound's head on the hilt on his hip, but Marcelle didn't appear to be armed. Sarai didn't believe the facade for a second. There was no chance Marcelle would go into any potentially dangerous situation where she was on guard duty without a weapon of some kind on her.

The last to come in behind the witch leaders was an uncomfortable Captain Moretti next to a vampire Sarai didn't recognize by name but had seen around the palace. He was rather distinct with an eye-patch, scruffy five o'clock shadow that never grew, and a prosthetic leg. Moretti with her heavily gelled hair looked like she had a deer in her headlights and was uncomfortable in a frilly looking pink prom dress, while the vampire with her looked like he'd walked through the costume departments for both a regency era romance movie and a piracy epic while grabbing whatever happened to be near him off the racks and throwing it on. He looked amused, and she looked horrified. Sarai suppressed a snicker.

The vampires paid their respects by kneeling before the royal family, as Marcelle had, and kissing the king's ring. Hannah and Danior nodded instead of bowing or curtsying, while Moretti looked mortified and awkwardly followed suit a few moments after her leaders when she realized it was expected.

"It is an honor to have you at the New Ulster court. As guests of my son, and as visiting leaders of your coven, you are due every respect, and it is a great pleasure to welcome you," Lugh said. He looked at the witches before him, but it was obvious who he was really speaking to as the volume of his words rose just a little when saying they were due respect.

The murmuring began again from the crowd, with the words "witches", "outsiders", "insanity", and "delicious" floating around liberally.

"We're honored to be here representing the Ellis Coven," said Danior.

"Please, enjoy your night," Lugh said, and the escorting vampires led them towards Sarai and Marcelle.

"Not too strange yet?" Marcelle said, smiling cordially to the witches. "We're a little formal, I know, but it's fun to have an occasion to dress up."

"If you say so," grumbled Moretti. "Is there somewhere we can sit?"

"You're not in high heels, are you?" Sarai asked, trying to glance under the layers of pink tulle and taffeta. A whole evening in proper high heels sounded awful.

"What, like if I get into trouble here I should worry about how fast I can run?" she said. "I didn't have anything else that worked with this dress, so now I'm stuck in stilettos."

"About that dress…" Marcelle said, while Moretti rolled her eyes.

"I didn't have anything I thought would be appropriate, all right? It's my sister's prom dress; it's not mine. Not my style."

"Clearly. You could have asked for help. If I'd known it was an emergency, I would have offered you my wardrobe," Marcelle said. Sarai snorted as she tried to stop herself from laughing. Bear didn't bother hiding his laugh, while the other witches seemed unsure if they were supposed to join in.

"Just point me towards the bar so I can drown myself," Moretti sighed. "Please tell me there's going to be alcohol?"

"Don't worry, you won't have to endure that outfit sober," Bear said. "They always have alcohol for the humans. How else are vampire guests supposed to get drunk?"

"The humans?" Hannah asked, looking around. "Are they here already?"

"They're the ones in the identical uniforms," Bear said, nodding upwards to gesture with his chin in the direction of a group of humans standing off towards the back, chatting with a few vampires. They were distinct in their clothes, with plain black pants or skirts and tops that all had a crest embroidered on the left side of the shirts. Their necks and arms were all accessible, free of sleeves, collars, necklaces, or bracelets.

Hannah inhaled sharply as one of the vampires lifted a human's wrist to his mouth and bit.

"They are here of their own free will," Angela reminded their guests.

"Yes… we understand," Danior said as he grimaced. "We don't have to approve."

"Announcing her majesty Queen Arsinoe the Sixth of Kemet, her highness Princess Meritaten the Third of Kemet, General Radmases—" The voice proclaiming identities was lost as Sarai saw the beautiful Egyptians glide into the room, five in total, with two pureblood women at the front. They were stunning and carried themselves like the royalty they were in their elaborately pleated, nearly sheer gowns. They greeted their fellow royals gracefully, the king standing and taking the foreign queen's hand, both greeting each other with a nod.

"Might I introduce my granddaughter to you, Prince?" she asked, looking at Setanta. He stepped down towards the second pureblood and took her hand, kissing it.

"It is an honor to meet you, Princess."

Marcelle tensed next to her, and Sarai looked up. "Are you okay?"

"Fine." But her eyes were laser-focused on the new princess. She looked sad almost, but Sarai couldn't understand why. There had to be politics behind the scenes, she reasoned, but it was best not to talk about those in earshot of every other vampire present, let alone the witches.

"They're quite… lovely women," Danior said after clearing his throat.

Marcelle turned her attention back to him. "Calm your blushing, Mr. Teli," she teased.

"Yes, yes. Of course." His outfit shifted to a deep red color.

As the last of the vampires made their way into the room, Sarai was transfixed by the beautiful outfits. Setanta greeted another country's princess named Xian MeiXiang the same as he had the Egyptian princess, and a thought struck her. These countries were presenting their princesses to the next king. To a king without a queen, who had already told her privately that he was meant to marry a pureblood soon. The reason became clear: they wanted to be potential brides.

No wonder it made Marcelle sad, when she couldn't marry the man she loved herself. Sarai slipped her hand into Marcelle's and gave her a gentle squeeze, which was returned.

When the procession completed, a silence fell on the room, cued by Lugh raising his hand up for attention. Queen Giovanna took her daughter by her shoulders and led her off to the side, to stand with an expression befitting an angry statue frozen in place at the front of the gathered crowd. Setanta also moved, capturing Sarai's attention as he stepped down from the dais to stand before his father, waiting.

"Good evening," the vampire king began. He had a gentle voice, but it carried through the room with ease. "My heart is gladdened to see that so many could attend this night. I have led this coven for many years now, first from its creation, and second after my late daughter Aoibhinn's passing. I established this kingdom of New Ulster in the New World with a vision in mind, and to see it grow to be so successful has been one of the most fulfilling experiences in my life. But tonight, my reign comes to an end. This world... it has changed, and I am tired. I leave the kingdom and its subjects in the capable hands of the man who helped me build New Ulster. My only living son."

Setanta knelt on one knee, his head bowed, as Lugh removed the iron circlet from his own head, holding it in both hands.

"You honor me, *Atháir*," Setanta said.

"And you honor me. You followed me from the Old World to the New, built a kingdom for our people. Do you swear to uphold the laws and customs of New Ulster with justice and honor?"

"I do swear."

"Do you swear to be a shield to the innocent, a sword

to your enemies, and a hearth to your allies?"

"As shield, sword, and hearth, I do swear."

"From this night forward, I decree that you will be known as King Setanta of New Ulster."

Sarai held her breath as the crown was placed on Setanta's head, enraptured by the moment as the former prince rose and climbed the dais as his father stepped down, both literally and figuratively. Then, Lugh knelt before his son.

"Long live the king."

Chapter Sixteen: Blood of the Kingdom

"Long live the king."

Sarai repeated the words, unable to look away as Setanta ascended. Marcelle whispered them breathlessly next to her, with reverence and love in her voice, as the rest of the vampires present gave loud shouts of approval and celebration. And somehow, Sarai felt a similar excitement.

"Long live the king!"

Lugh stood and gestured to his daughter, who darted away a moment, then bounced over holding a table that looked too large for her to carry with two large stone goblets balanced on its surface. She placed it at the foot of the dais and bowed as she and her father backed away.

It didn't surprise Sarai as much as it should have to see Setanta draw a dagger from his belt under his cloak. She glanced at the other witches. While she didn't know what was about to happen exactly, she had the warning from Marcelle and they did not. They looked concerned, at the very least.

It proved to be not without cause: Setanta slit his wrist without the slightest flinch and kept the dagger against his skin to keep the wound open by force so that it wouldn't heal. He held it over one of the goblets with a stoic expression as the red liquid flowed, filling it. How much could he safely lose?

"I swear to rule fairly and justly as your king, until I

am no longer able. By my blood, I bind myself to the kingdom. By my blood, may it be sealed."

His wrist healed and, after placing the dagger on the table and looking a little paler than usual, he stepped back to sit on his new throne. A king's throne.

"I'll be back in a moment, little witch." Marcelle kissed Sarai's cheek as she looked at her in confusion, and watched the vampire walk to the front, standing in front of the table.

Marcelle picked up the dagger and slit her wrist, making Sarai flinch just a little. The wound was held over the second goblet.

"I, Knight Commander Marcelle de Sauveterre, submit myself to your rule until my existence ends or you release me. I am your shield, your sword, and your hearth. By the blood in my veins and the blood you offer, I bind myself in oath."

Then, Marcelle picked up the first goblet, filled and heavy with the pureblood's offering. She put it to her lips and drank a mouthful before setting it down. How did Setanta's blood feel, Sarai wondered. How would a pureblood's vein differ from a made vampire's? He'd once told her that it would kill her. To a vampire, it must be the ultimate high.

"Long live the king!" Marcelle shouted as she knelt before her sire, then returned to the group. Her eyes were blood red; she looked like she'd drained an energy drink or maybe five cups of coffee at once with the alert exhilaration in her eyes. It made Sarai smile.

Bear went next, and there was something enjoyable about the stunned expression on Hannah's face as he spilled his blood and swore his service to King Setanta. Next went Angela, several other knights of the realm, and (as she was informed by Marcelle) the vampire nobles who ruled states or large cities. Two-thirds of the vampires present swore themselves to Setanta's rule, bled before him, and drank his blood before the new king. The ritual was so primal, yet refined. Sarai was in awe, and some part of her wanted to know what it would be like to participate, to stand before him and look into his red eyes. To swear her life to him, offer her blood, and drink his. To be a part of their society and culture, to kneel before him next to Marcelle. It was almost... the only word to come to mind was erotic.

He walked slowly towards the table. The goblet he'd bled into had been drained dry, and the one the others had contributed to was overflowing.

"I accept the oaths of the kingdom. By our blood, I am your king."

Setanta's fangs extended as he spoke, and he grasped the goblet in both hands. He lifted it to his mouth, drinking deeply from it until it was empty. Not a single drop spilled, and there was only a red gleam on his teeth as he raised the goblet over his head with one hand in triumph and grinned. The kingdom and its subjects were his.

Again, a chorus of "Long live the king," sounded through the room, this time accompanied by clapping and cheers. A group of tall, blond vampires cheered the loudest, stamping their feet and distracting Sarai for the first time since Setanta had stood.

Marcelle rolled her eyes, which had returned to blue. "Nords," she said. "So obnoxious."

Setanta put the goblet down, walked to the top of the dais, and raised his hand to silence the room as he sat in his throne.

"As your king, I intend to bring vampires to a better future. I will see the end of the Vasi menace. But they have become stronger, as many of my nobles and knights can attest to, and more threatening with the advances of modern technology. Left unchecked, they could bring about our end."

There was a murmur of agreement through the crowd.

"To defeat them, we need alliances," Setanta continued. "I hope that tonight will strengthen the friendships already in existence and create new ones. To that end, I have reached out to the largest witch coven within my territory." He gestured to the witches and all eyes turned on them. Sarai wished she'd worn camouflage. "I know many of you have wondered about their presence. I want to bring back the times when witches were our allies. I know some of you, like me, remember family who were witches. Friends. It can be that way again. I hope that when it comes time to gather the council, you will be open to working together with my new allies." It was similar to the speech Sarai remembered him giving the witches in the Ellis coven, but different. More forceful. His "hope" with witches was meant as a request. With vampires, it sounded like a demand.

"He's fucking with us," snapped one of the vampires under his breath; a large, tanned black-haired man who'd just dedicated himself in the ceremony. His voice was half to himself, but everyone heard and looked at him. The vampire's eyes turned red with anger as he looked between Sarai, Hannah, Danior, and Moretti.

"You have something to say?" Setanta asked.

He stepped forward. "Your Highness, we thought

you lured them here for entertainment. Spill their blood at your feet, tear their hearts out. That's what should be done with witches. If you want to return to the old ways, those are the practices you should reinstate."

Sarai swallowed hard and gripped her lover's hand for security. She knew some of the vampires would think that way and, looking at the man and the rest of the audience, she wondered how many. Was Marcelle able to keep her safe from them all?

"Your objection is noted and dismissed. They are to be treated with the same respect as any other member of the New Ulster kingdom or visiting vampires," Setanta said. "They are my honored guests."

The vampire glared at the witches, shaking with anger. His fangs extended and he launched forward.

Sarai didn't have time to yelp or even follow what happened next with her inadequate mortal eyes, but suddenly Marcelle's hair was down and a slew of silver needles were sticking out of the vampire's chest, their sheaths and the golden hair comb clattering to the marble floor.

Moretti stepped forward doing an impersonation of the Greek god Zeus with electricity sizzling in her hand but didn't have a chance to act as the attacker shouted in pain, thrown to the ground with expert technique by Angela who drew her sword and had it pressed against the malcontent vampire's chest over his heart. It pierced the fine Edwardian clothes, hissing where the silver blade touched his skin.

Attention turned towards the vampire king; the room was quiet as a crypt. With a look from him to his knight, Angela sheathed her sword and grabbed the rogue by his collar, throwing him to the steps of the dais at Setanta's feet.

"I said, they are to be treated with the same respect as any other member of my kingdom," Setanta said, his tone and gaze cold as he took a step down toward the vampire. "That means unprovoked assaults are to be punished in the same manner as if you had attacked a member of my household."

The attacker's eyes drained of red and returned to green as they widened in fear, his threatening demeanor reduced to quivering terror. He crumbled into a crouched position, prostrated before the throne.

"Y-your Majesty, please... I meant no disrespect to you, I only thought of your honor. Have mercy!"

Setanta met Angela's gaze. "Ground him."

Angela yanked the man to his feet and dragged him toward the doors as he shrieked, begging for clemency, and passed him off to two vampire guards wearing black gloves. Marcelle sighed, picked up her fallen hair ornaments, and put her arms around Sarai as Angela returned to stand protectively by Danior's side.

"You're safe, don't worry," Marcelle murmured. It did feel comforting, but Sarai's heart was still racing. "What's a vampire event without drama?"

"*Anyone else who dares to defy me meets the same fate*," Setanta shouted to the shocked crowd in a voice that vibrated in Sarai's bones. He strode back to his throne and sat down. No one would go against him now, Sarai was certain. The ferocity she saw in him was even more overwhelming and powerful than when he'd threatened Giovanna on her behalf. She was rooted, his power oppressive in the room to the point that she almost forgot to breathe. Then, he spoke again, his voice calm as if nothing had happened. "I believe this is a celebration, yes? Please, let the festivities commence."

The band took their cue and light classical music filled the room. A loud ruckus erupted among the vampires talking about the new turn of events.

"Well, that was an exciting start to the new reign. You have our apologies for that man's lack of decorum," Marcelle said to her company as she redid her hair. "There shouldn't be any more trouble now."

Hannah pulled herself away from Bear, whom she had clutched in her fear, and straightened her suit top. "Yes, well… It isn't a surprise that we're not welcome by some. Miri, dear, your hands are sparking."

Captain Moretti, rather, Miri wiped her hands on her dress as if the tulle could clean off the electricity. The heavy gel in her hair failed its duty as static caused several stray strands to stand on end.

"Sorry," she said, glancing around at the many vampires staring. "Just a little jumpy."

"Try to be less jumpy." Lilly, the spymaster dressed in a sleek forest-green dress that had a corseted waistline far too waspish for a human and large puffy sleeves down to her elbow, stepped forward from the shadows behind them. Moretti jumped. "It makes you less of a target."

"A-And how does showing that I have strong powers make me more of a target?"

The spymaster smiled. "It means you taste better than these other two."

Moretti's olive complexion paled, and snickering could be heard from eavesdropping vampires in the vicinity.

"Captain, this is our spymaster, Lilly Thorn," Crispin, the witch's escort, said. "Lilly, this is Captain

Miriam Moretti."

Lilly bowed her head, showing that her hair had gold entwined in her usual swirled braids. "Delightful to make your acquaintance. Do you prefer to be called Captain?"

"Miri is fine," the witch said.

"Spymaster?" Danior asked. "Did I hear that correctly?"

"You did," Lilly confirmed.

"So, you work together then?" Moretti asked. "You and Marcelle. Do you work for Marcelle?"

"No," Lilly said. "We're in charge of different departments, so to speak, but in control of our own teams. Though we do coordinate many aspects of our work."

"Then, perhaps you could answer a point of confusion, just for those of us uninitiated?" Hannah asked, stepping forward. "I was curious about something here."

"Of course."

"What does it mean, grounded? It sounds…"

"Like we seal our people in stone coffins, chained in silver so that they're too weak to break out while they wither into a husk as bloodlust and isolation corrodes their sanity?" Lilly smiled. "Yes, that's correct."

Hannah blinked. "I hadn't thought… it's quite a brutal thing to do to your own people."

"We don't really have jails, and imprisonment as humans practice it would be petty to us considering our lifespan," Lilly explained. "Grounding makes an impression."

Hannah pursed her lips. "I imagine it does."

"We're not here to judge their society. As long as we're not subject to it," Danior said to his companion.

"Only vampires are subject to vampire law," Marcelle reassured them.

"If you say so. But it doesn't kill them? Being denied blood?" Hannah asked.

"No. Fortunately or unfortunately, starvation won't kill a vampire. We end up losing ourselves to bloodlust, and if we're starved long enough we do wither into husks," Lilly explained. "Blood revives us. It's not a common punishment; the king must be making an example to make a point. He'll probably be let out in a year."

It was unnerving, to think of Setanta sentencing someone to such a punishment. He and Marcelle were both so contradictory. Both were kind to Sarai yet could be downright medieval.

Lilly cleared her throat and gestured for the group to look towards the king with a nod of her head. "It seems you're being summoned."

Setanta nodded when Sarai met his gaze. "Do you mean, us?" she asked, squeezing Marcelle's hand again for reassurance.

"Well, not all of us."

"Just you and me, little witch," Marcelle told her. "Come."

Together, the pair approached the throne. Marcelle knelt in submission, and Sarai instinctively began to kneel as well, but stopped herself, and repeated her curtsy from before.

"Rise, please," he said, and his mistress stood. "I'm meant to open the dance floor tonight. Might you do me the honor, Marcelle?"

She grinned in response. "I would love to, sire. But I'd rather not leave my beautiful date behind."

"Well then... Quite the predicament." Setanta stood, unfastened his fur cloak, and draped it over his throne. Then he descended the dais and bowed his head like a gentleman as he offered Sarai his hand. Time froze. "I'd like you to join us. Sarai, may I have this dance?"

Chapter Seventeen: The Dance Floor

Sarai was taken aback and gazed up in fear. Sure, all she could think about was how amazing Setanta looked, and her mind was trapped reliving her awkward kiss over and over. But the previous dance had been just to teach her how, hadn't it? Had he intended to dance with her at the ball? She trembled, but how could she say no; everyone was watching.

"I would like that very much. Your Highness. Sir." Her hand tingled as she took his.

Just look at him. Don't think about everyone else, she thought to herself as her heart raced and she was led out to the middle of the floor.

Marcelle darted behind the pair at Sarai's back as she joined them, her hands teasing against her skin with electric caresses. Every hair on her body was standing on end, knowing that everyone had their eyes on her.

Setanta nodded toward the band, his lips moving but his voice too quiet for Sarai to make out what he had said.

A cold, soft hand caressed her cheek, and Sarai melted against it.

"Don't worry," Marcelle said in her ear. "We won't bite." She whirled the witch around, their lips inches apart, and Sarai felt her body flushed with heat at the sight of Marcelle's blue eyes turning red with lust.

The first few cords of string instrumentals played

and introduced a tango. Marcelle's body undulated in response. Setanta grabbed his lover's hand and pulled her towards him, then spun her out towards Sarai. They began a duet in those first bars of music, Marcelle's leg sweeping out sensually from the slit in her dress. Setanta's movements were more powerful, demanding, and full of purpose as he manipulated her body to press against him. He commanded, she responded. Her fangs slipped from her mouth, and he smirked just enough to reveal his own.

It looked like foreplay and Sarai wanted to participate in the celebration of sex and power. Setanta maneuvered Marcelle closer towards her. They made eye contact before Marcelle let go of her sire and circled Sarai, a hand trailing across Sarai's collarbone, just above her breasts.

Sarai felt her heart nearly stop as she was tilted back, then spun around to face Marcelle.

"Ready to dance?" the woman said.

Sarai didn't have time to respond that she didn't know how to do more than the waltz Setanta had taught her before she felt herself pressed against Marcelle's body.

"I can't—"

"Shh, don't worry. We'll lead."

Sarai followed Marcelle through a few steps that seemed basic compared to what she'd just seen. Far from thinking about her own awkwardness, she was distracted by Marcelle's expertise. Her lover's body was sensuality incarnate. Her touch, moves, and intense eyes sent flames through Sarai in the best way possible. Then, Marcelle wrapped a leg around her waist and leaned forward so heavily that the pair tipped backwards. Sarai gasped, anticipating the crash to the floor, but it didn't come.

When she opened the eyes she'd instinctively closed, she found herself looking up at the powerful man above her. Setanta had stepped in to support them, dipping them low over his knee, his body in a deep lunge. One hand supported Sarai's back, the other wrapped around Marcelle's waist. At that moment, all three were entwined with each other and the only thought in Sarai's mind was *yes*.

The king pulled them both to their feet, the two vampires pressed against Sarai: the man at her back, Marcelle facing them both. They began to dance again, guiding Sarai. It was the most unbelievable experience she had ever been a part of. Every so often, Setanta would spin one of the women. Every time she turned, Sarai's skirt flared with silver and blue, catching the light in a way that equaled the splendor of the chandeliers above them.

Just as she thought it couldn't be any more overwhelming, Setanta pulled away from them both, leaving Sarai standing alone in the center of the floor as he led Marcelle to the side, her legs exposed due to her pose and the way the slit in her dress opened. It had to be the end of the song, but it wasn't.

Setanta turned, and his red eyes locked on Sarai's, his focus shifted onto her. He had to know, she thought as her heart pounded at his approach. He had to know the effect he had on her. Was this his response to her kiss?

Coherent thought disappeared as he took her into his arms, and she began to dance with him one on one. It was so different from the waltz and even from the swing. They were so close; she couldn't breathe from the intensity. His body was strength in fluid form as he manipulated her.

Setanta lunged forward into her again so that he pulled her into another low dip; their faces were close for a moment, and his mouth turned into a crooked smile, the very tips of his fangs visible. Sarai's entire body seized with need.

"Are you enjoying yourself?" he murmured. "I am."

Sarai bit her lip, unable to find the air to respond, but there was no need. He knew. The gleam in his red eyes told her he knew. And... she could feel something hard pressing against her upper thigh. Her eyes widened in shock at the thought of what it might be, but before she could think of anything else, he pulled her back up with a secure arm around her waist, and lifted her clean off her feet, spinning her around so that her skirt unfurled like an elaborate fan. He twirled her again, then spun her into Marcelle's waiting grasp, who repeated his move with a more feminine flair.

Then the three were together again. Hands ran down her sides. She wasn't sure whose were where, and it didn't matter as long as they didn't stop.

In an instant of pure passion, they were entangled once more, both vampires above her and looking down into her eyes, red eyes and fangs revealed for the pair of them. They were the most erotic beings she'd ever seen in her life, like two beautiful beasts ready to pounce, and she embraced the role as their willing prey. The music ended and the room exploded with applause, but she wanted to stay where she was forever.

"You should think carefully about tonight," Setanta said, using the applause as cover so that their words wouldn't be overheard. "About what you want, Sarai. I am not as gentle nor as kind as Marcelle. I will hurt you."

She almost melted, her eyes drawn to his fangs when he spoke. "Is that a promise?" Sarai whispered, and Marcelle snickered.

Setanta smirked. "A warning, a threat, a promise. Take it as you will."

He pulled her back to her feet, and kissed Marcelle's hand first, then locked eyes with Sarai as he did the same to hers. Her face burned.

"That was lovely," he said with a smile. "Perhaps we can try it again sometime?"

"I'd very much like that. And, of course, we know Sarai loved it," Marcelle teased, grinning at her date.

With the dance over, Sarai could finally think clearly enough to realize that every vampire present in the room could probably smell her arousal. Unable to stop herself, she looked to the audience, to all the eyes on her. They had all watched her lose herself to the king and knight commander. She trembled a little and refocused on the two vampires she cared the most about.

"That was amazing."

"He usually is," Marcelle said.

Setanta bowed his head just a little, appearing very proper. "I'm glad I could entertain you." How had he changed from erotic force of nature to regal and almost aloof so easily?

He led them back to the sidelines. "Now that we've caused a stir, I should tend to other matters. But thank you both for the levity. I hope to see more of you later." Sarai inhaled sharply at the last sentence. He'd looked specifically at her. See more of her? More of her presence… or more of *her*? The promise to hurt her had to be more than the promise of a bite, but she didn't dare guess, even as he kissed her hand once more. "Please, enjoy the party." He turned and left to join a small circle of other red-eyed vampires. Included were the Egyptian and Chinese princesses who seemed less than pleased, but Sarai couldn't find it in her to care.

"Are you going to be all right?" Marcelle teased.

Sarai closed her eyes and took a deep breath. "Maybe. He is…" Her silence said it all.

"Intense?" Marcelle volunteered.

It was the perfect word. Setanta was intense.

Chapter Eighteen: The Queen's Brother

"Well," murmured Hannah as Sarai returned with Marcelle to greet the group. "That was an interesting display. Are dances here always so vigorous?"

Sarai blushed, but the taboo of the situation and the disapproval was like fuel. Every inch of her skin from her toes to her fingertips tingled with adrenaline. She hungered for more.

"We like to make statements," Marcelle grinned, and slid her arms around Sarai's waist from behind, pulling her in for a kiss on the neck.

The three witches tensed, and Moretti took a half step forward.

"Something the matter?" Marcelle asked.

None of the three witches said a word.

Sarai giggled.

"Aren't you and your king, ah, involved?" Danior said. "I believe I heard the phrase 'mistress'?"

"One of my favorite titles," Marcelle said.

"What sort of statement was that dance meant to make?" asked Hannah.

"I would have thought it obvious." Marcelle gestured to the vampires around them. "Do you think any one of them will lay a finger on her after his display? That a guest or lord would pressure her into a feeding, threaten her, or in any way disrespect her? Not a chance in hell. She's the star now, the king's chosen, and that grants protection."

"I suppose I can see the," Danior pursed his lips a little, "wisdom in that."

Hannah stared down at Sarai as if she had been the one leading the dance. "Still, it didn't need to be so—"

"Sexual?" Marcelle asked. Everyone stared at her bluntness, and Sarai bit the inside of her cheeks to stop herself from laughing. "Yes, but on the other hand, it didn't have to be chaste. You are here to learn about vampire culture, aren't you?"

"Culture. That's a word for it," Danior said, and turned to Sarai. "Are you comfortable with all of this? Vampire 'culture'?"

No amount of biting her cheek could keep her from smiling, and she had to stop herself short of drawing blood.

"Oh, yeah." Her voice cracked, and she cleared her throat a little. "It's…" What could she say to this older witch? That she loved sleeping with Marcelle who was also sleeping with Setanta who hinted he may be interested in sleeping with her? "Look, it's my choice. I decided to stay here for a reason. I like it. I told you earlier why. I just want you to believe me." They couldn't do anything about it other than look at her like they'd sucked on lemons. At least Danior knew she was being honest.

"You don't need to be jealous," Marcelle toyed with them. "Now that the dance floor is open, it won't be long before people start enjoying themselves. I'm sure we could arrange a gentle waltz if it suited you. We'll even provide you with partners. Bear?"

"I'd be happy to take the lady for a spin around the floor," he grinned, and bowed to Hannah, whose brown eyes widened.

"I think I'm a little too old to be dancing around," she laughed.

"You do realize you're one of the youngest people here, right?" he said. As if on cue, the music shifted to a waltz and couples began to migrate to the floor. He offered Hannah his hand. "Don't worry, I'll go easy on you. *Wayáchi yachíŋ he?*"

Hannah's eyes widened in surprise. "What did you just... You speak Lakota?"

He winked at her, still bowed with his hand extended. "Don't leave me hanging, Hannah."

The witch looked to Danior for rescue, but he seemed just as uncertain.

"I suppose, when in Rome?" Hannah said and gave Bear her hand. He kissed it, causing her to blush. "Be gentle, these old bones have wear and tear on them."

"I would never dream of hurting you," Bear said as he led her away. Sarai did notice the wording and wondered if it was on purpose. Danior would sense it as the complete truth for the simple fact that vampires couldn't dream.

"Would you like a dance as well, Mr. Teli?" Marcelle offered.

Danior looked at Marcelle, at her dress, and shook his head. "No offense meant, but my wife didn't want me to come in the first place. I don't think I could dance around with, ah, well, a woman such as yourself and face her when I got home."

"Angela could put on a turtleneck sweater and give you a twirl," Marcelle joked.

Angela rolled her eyes.

"Ha. Thank you, but I'll have to decline. My knees

aren't what they once were so I don't think I could keep up," Danior said.

"Just as well, I don't dance," Angela murmured.

"Would you dance if I asked nicely?"

Sarai blinked, and a new vampire with an Italian accent had joined them, standing behind Angela and putting a hand on her shoulder. He was impeccably dressed, in a very modern deep purple suit that looked like it had been tailored perfectly to him. He had curly dark hair, the bright red eyes of a pureblood, and the same olive complexion as Giovanna. In fact, he had a few similarities to her, as far as the shape of his oval face and straight nose like something from a statue of Greek antiquity.

"Still not interested, Valens," Angela sighed, shrugging off his hand.

"Baby, come on. I've got something fun for tonight," the vampire Valens said and pulled back his suit just enough to reveal a flask. But what could a vampire need in a flask? There were plenty of humans and vampires around if he was thirsty, a bar somewhere for alcohol if he wanted a 'real' drink.

Angela's eyes narrowed, and she shoved him. "I could have you sent back to Rome for having that on you. Never again, do you hear me? Never."

"Is that what I think it is?" Marcelle snapped.

"It's wine, obviously," he said with a smile. "Certainly not an illegal mind-altering drug to make drinking from weak little humans halfway enjoyable. I had to bring my own wine. Ours is better than anything you can get in America. Besides, what are you going to do, take my flask?" His smile turned into a smirk that dared them to try.

Angela's fangs extended, and she grabbed his arm and twisted it behind him. Sarai winced when she heard the crack of his bone snapping in her grip, but the pureblood just laughed. Angela took the flask with her other hand and popped it open, smelling it.

"I told you, just wine." He had the widest shit-eating grin anyone had ever worn. Angela let go of his arm, and he set the wrist she'd broken, letting it heal before he took his flask back.

"We'll have your room searched. If you're thinking of dosing anyone with ambrosia…" Marcelle started.

"Oh, I would never," Valens said with mock concern. He turned his gaze on Sarai, and she took a step back. "You're, what, a new mistress for the king?"

"She's with us," Captain Moretti said. It felt a little comforting to have the lightning witch as back-up.

"Obviously she's not or she would have walked in with you," Valens said. "Real shame. The only witches around are two old fucks, you, and Sparky here. And his newest majesty might as well have been a hound pissing on you to mark his territory with that display." He sighed, as if with regret. "Dangling treats like you out here and not letting us have any is just rude."

His blunt words took Sarai by surprise. Was that how the vampires watching had seen the dance? As Setanta marking her as his, what, property? Prey? She didn't mind the dance as a protective act or flirtation, but the way Valens phrased it made her burn with embarrassment from her cheeks to the tips of her ears. Or maybe it was shame.

Danior opened his mouth to respond, but Angela was faster.

"Miss Meir, Mr. Teli, Ms. Little Hawk, and Captain

Moretti are honored guests, and you will remember to speak to them with decorum befitting your station, and theirs," Angela said, stepping between them. "You wouldn't speak to Princess Artemisia in such a crass manner? Then you shouldn't speak to our guests that way."

Valens rolled his eyes. "Oh, my dear mother, I shalln't ever forget."

"Perhaps you should enjoy the rest of the party?" Marcelle suggested.

"Perhaps. I just had to come see the little girl in person. My sister won't shut up about her."

"Giovanna's your sister," Sarai realized. He smiled at her.

"Yes, interloper, the former queen is my big sister. And I'm sure she's having a fit about all the attention you're going to get tonight."

Sarai might have blushed again if the thought didn't fill her with dread. Setanta had made it clear that something was definitely on the table, for her and Marcelle. Which was exactly what Giovanna had threatened her about.

Valens's smile widened. "Does she frighten you that much, young one?"

Well, Giovanna had almost thrown her off a balcony… But with Moretti on one side, Angela in front of her, Marcelle on the other side, and the new king's protection, she felt more confident.

She smiled back at him, which threw him off. "I'm sure I'll be fine."

"She is my ward, in case it slipped your mind," Marcelle added.

"And you can keep her safe with all these foreign

purebloods around?" he asked.

Marcelle looked him up and down, and smirked. "You think I can't take one of you purebloods down? I spar with his majesty regularly. Mind your step, Prince."

He laughed, shaking his head. "As amusing as that notion is, I should be off to console my sister. Ladies. Gentlemen." He nodded his head as if tipping an imaginary hat and was gone when Sarai blinked.

"Fascinating individual," Danior said with an even tone.

"I think you mean pompous ass. And yes, I hope he can hear me," Angela said loudly. She paused, and Sarai noticed Marcelle's lips making minute movements; speaking, but too low for her to hear. Angela gave a small nod. "Danior, there's a piano lounge, if you're not interested in dancing. You'll find more scintillating conversation than what we just experienced, more refined company. I know a few friendly faces you should meet. The Duke of New York would be a good friend to have. And we have a representative from the New Orleans vampires who would like to meet you. I can escort you."

"I would like to get to know more of the individuals here," Danior admitted.

"I should stay by your side," Moretti said. "That is, if you'll be all right, Sarai?"

Sarai nodded. "Never better."

The rest of the night went very well in comparison to Valens's veiled threats. To Sarai's great surprise, the Egyptian queen made a point of inviting her and Marcelle to join in conversation, drawing Sarai out of her shell.

The light banter with foreign purebloods and

domestic nobility was like a game. Every time Sarai was blunt and forward, the responses she received were positive and encouraging. She felt a little like a court jester on display, or maybe some sort of pseudo-socialite. Either way, it gave her confidence.

Several vampires respectfully asked her for a turn on the dance floor when waltzes continued from the orchestra and, after a nod from Marcelle granting approval to a few, Sarai accepted.

It was *fun*. To be spun around the dance floor by several vampire men and women, all of whom were interested in giving her attention or learning more about her. Her dress was a topic that came up multiple times, with a Duchess of Maryland complimenting the fashion and begging to know the name of the seamstress before whisking her around the dance floor, followed by a visiting pureblood with elaborate braided blonde hair and a Nordic accent complimenting her grace in such a heavy dress and insisting on a turn.

While the dances with Marcelle and Setanta had been heavy in erotic energy, the dances with other vampires felt like a platonic activity. They never slid their hands too low or touched her in any way that wasn't appropriate and proper. She never would have dreamed she could feel so right being social, yet there she was. She was the literal life of the party.

"You should save your energy," Marcelle said, catching Sarai as she spun away from the dance floor and her partner, a duke of either New Hampshire or New Jersey.

"I'm having so much fun," Sarai said, breathing heavily.

"Yes, but you're exhausted," Marcelle said. "And

there are other activities I'd like you to participate in tonight, before the sun rises."

Sarai blushed. "I guess I could use a rest. Let's get something to drink? For me, not you."

They left the throne room and its beautiful, swirling dancers to travel towards a side room for food and drink. On their way there, Rosaline caught up with them.

"Sarai, wow. Just, wow," the human girl said, dabbing at a red, wet spot on her neck with a napkin. "Your dress. I can't handle all of this."

"I know, I can barely believe it myself," Sarai said with a grin. "I'm parched. If you're done being a drink, want to come get a drink with us? Well, with me. Marcelle's just going to watch."

Rosaline laughed and followed the pair into a quieter room with less activity, where there was a buffet in the middle lined with exquisite food and drink for mortals along with a few tables around the room for sitting at while eating. At first they thought it was empty, then they stopped, staring at a strange couple in the corner of the room.

"You can't tease an old woman like this," said a familiar witch's voice.

"I'm not teasing you. Hannah, listen to me. I'm interested."

And then, Bear and Hannah were kissing with passion befitting a pair of teenagers, Hannah's trembling hands gripping his strong arms as if she were afraid to let go.

Rosaline froze. "Oh," she said, alerting the pair to their presence. Sarai was too shocked to say anything.

Bear and Hannah looked up, and Hannah looked as if she wanted to sink into the floor.

"She's not too old for you then?" Rosaline said, bitterness in her voice.

Bear scowled. "Rosaline, I'm a thousand years old."

"Yeah, but she's the one who looks like it."

Hannah looked horrified. "She's right," the woman said, pulling away. "This, this never happened. I'm too old for this."

"No, you're not," Bear reassured her. "Rosaline, if you want someone in your bed tonight, go talk to Crispin."

"But I thought *we* had a thing."

"We slept together a few times. Casually. That's it. And maybe it was a mistake," he said. Rosaline looked as if she might cry. "We're not together."

"This isn't something I want a part of," Hannah murmured. "I'm too old." She started to walk away, and Sarai felt a pang of pity for the witch, as well as for her friend whose heart was no doubt breaking. But Rosaline had to know vampires' view of casual fun. After all, the human girl was the one who initially encouraged Sarai to have meaningless fun with whatever vampire guard caught her eye. Perhaps it was easy in theory, or before Rosaline's true feelings were involved. But presented with the truth in front of her, it was too painful for the girl. Sarai didn't know what to do and felt helpless as she watched the scene unfold.

Bear grasped Hannah's hand, keeping her from leaving. "Hannah, look at me," he pleaded.

Hannah sighed, then looked up at him, steel in her eyes as she yanked her hand free, and he allowed it. "I am not a child to be playing games like this. I am here representing my people on a mission of diplomacy, and I will not be manipulated by some Two-Face feigning interest in someone he would never truly want. Go with your girlfriend. Her body won't break as easily as mine."

"No, it's fine," Rosaline snapped. "I'll go find Crispin. He's bigger than you anyway."

Bear scoffed as Rosaline left, and Sarai felt torn between staying and going after her friend. She looked up at Marcelle for some sort of guidance, but all she saw on her lover's face was amusement.

"No, he isn't," Bear muttered under his breath before turning his attention back to Hannah. "I'm not a Two-Face. I'm not— Well, I guess maybe, but no. No, I'm not. Is that what you think of me? Just a monster? I'm not a cannibal."

"Maybe. You certainly seem to have two faces to show. One sweet, the other... this."

"Then let me have a chance to speak with you so I can prove I only have one face. Let me take you for a walk away from the people here. Peace and quiet, just the two of us. I want to know you better. If you can give me the opportunity."

"To talk," she said skeptically. "With your sweet words. I have a hard time believing that your king didn't put you up to this. First Sarai, now me?" Sarai noticed the witch slip her hand into her pants pocket, making a fist. Intuitively, Sarai put her own hand in her own pocket, gripping the button Danior had given her. It made sense Hannah would have one too.

"Setanta cannot control me," Bear said. "I follow him by choice, because I admire him, but I do nothing for him I do not wish to do. I am my own man. And I don't play games with women the way others might. Never for politics."

Sarai felt no change in temperature to the button.

Bear spoke the truth.

"If all you want is to talk, then we will only talk," he promised. "I haven't met someone like you, someone I can be honest with about who I am in every way, in a long time. Someone who sees more than a vampire when they look at me. Hannah, when you live as long as I have, you start to see the same eyes in new faces. I know I've seen your eyes before. And I know that you need this connection to the past, to what I can offer your mind, as much as I do. I'm not looking for just a bed warmer. *Waštéčhilake*."

Sarai wasn't sure what it was he said, but the steel in the elder witch's eyes turned to confusion, then melted.

"To talk only," Hannah emphasized, but put her hand back in his. "Keep your poetry to yourself."

"To talk only," he agreed, and led the witch past a dumbstruck Sarai towards the palace gardens.

"Well then," Marcelle murmured. "I can't say I'm surprised. But that was fun."

"Should I go after Rosaline?" Sarai asked, looking around to see where the girl had gone. A loud fake laughter echoed through the halls as she spotted Rosaline almost throwing herself onto the one-eyed vampire escorting Captain Moretti.

"I think she'll be all right," Marcelle said. "Still thirsty?"

Sarai remembered her dry throat and nodded, getting a glass and pouring herself a cup of water. "What did he say to her?"

Marcelle shrugged. "No idea. I don't speak Lakota. I think that's what that was, anyway. He speaks so many languages I lose track sometimes. Lakota's not even close to his first language. He puts Lilly to shame with how many tongues he knows, and she's made a point of learning every language she can for her work. I think even he forgets how many languages he speaks."

"How could he forget how many languages he speaks?"

"Some older vampires have memory troubles. Not all do; Setanta's memory is impeccable. But Bear once told me he can't remember his children's faces or his parents' names, like it's some foggy dream for him." She shrugged. "I'm just glad I've been spared that. Being a different bloodline might be a factor. I'm sure he'll remember tonight for a long time though."

"I guess they're kind of cute together. I mean, how perfect is it she's got someone flirting with her in Lakota?"

"I suppose. It'll be funny to see how long it takes him to realize she can't understand him."

Sarai frowned. "Can't she? How can you tell?"

"There was too much confusion in her expression. My guess is the language got beaten out of her in a boarding school, given her age. But that's her history to reveal or keep to herself with Bear. He'll figure it out eventually if he keeps trying to chat her up in Lakota."

"That's sad, if you're right." She felt fortunate to have held onto her own mother tongue of Hebrew, given her father's family's hatred of it. Sarai sighed and sat down. As she did, she realized her feet ached from all the dancing she'd done. She didn't want to get up for a while. "I think that's enough excitement for a while," she announced. "And there's supposed to be a week of this? It'll be a miracle we all survive the drama."

"What about your invitation?" Marcelle said, sitting

down next to her with a suggestive smile. "Not too tired already, I hope."

"What invitation?"

"To Setanta's bed, of course."

Sarai choked on her water. "Was that an invitation then?"

"Oh yes, little witch," Marcelle laughed. "You have a choice. We retire to my bed… or we can go to his."

Sarai wiped her nose from the water that had shot out of it, feeling very unsexy as she did, and nodded. It was amazing how the thought of being in Setanta's bed had her ready to stand again. As everything was with Setanta, his invitation wasn't a question to her. She could only accept.

Chapter Nineteen: Master

It was Sarai's third time coming to Setanta's bed chambers, but that didn't make it easier for her to relax at all. Marcelle let them in with a key from her bedroom, so they could wait for the new king.

"Are you still up to this?" Marcelle asked.

Sarai paced around the room by the black marble fireplace but nodded. "I thought he didn't like me, when he didn't kiss me back," she said.

Marcelle lounged on a couch. "Little witch, I can promise after that tango, he likes you very much."

"You do this a lot? Seduce 'little witches' to bring to him on a platter?" Sarai joked and sat down next to Marcelle. Then she got up and continued to pace, kicking off her shoes for a little extra comfort.

"Not witches specifically, but we've shared mortals before. You'll survive."

"I'll survive," Sarai repeated. "Cool. That's not terrifying at all."

The door clicked at the front, and Sarai froze in place. Setanta entered, as regal as ever and not a hair out of place. Sarai's heart skipped a beat. She could chat with him, dance with him, and even joke with him. But now that she was there in his room, and they both knew the night was to end in sex, she felt woefully unprepared.

"Sarai," he said. The way her name sounded in his voice made her knees weak. "You were beautiful tonight.

I'm glad to see you both here."

"Marcelle said you invited me," she said. She didn't remember the exact words ever leaving his lips, though it had been implied. "I... I'm not intruding?"

"Not at all. I was curious to see if you would accept or not. I admit, I suspected the night might end this way," Setanta said as he removed his cloak and draped it on the back of his couch as he sat down, gesturing for her to sit with him. "Tell me, Sarai. What interests you?"

She bit her lip as she sat at the edge of the cushion, glancing between him and Marcelle. "Um, sex?"

The vampires chuckled.

"You're going to need to be more specific than that," Setanta said. "Do you not have much experience with men?"

"I have experience. Not a lot. I think I like both? I'm not a lesbian. Like, half lesbian?"

"Bisexual then, or pansexual," he offered.

Sarai had never had the language for herself, but it sounded right. "Yeah, one of those. I never really thought of those words as mine before. Which one am I?" She directed the question at Marcelle.

"That's up to you. My understanding is bisexuals are attracted to gendered traits, while pansexuals find that limiting and are attracted to people regardless of gendered traits."

Sarai glanced at both vampires, at Marcelle's hourglass curves and Setanta's triangular torso. She was definitely attracted to gendered traits.

"Bisexual then," she said.

"Great minds think alike," Marcelle teased.

"My mind isn't great in this context?" Setanta asked.

"Evidently not, since you're now outnumbered by

bisexuals, Mr. Pansexual," Marcelle said.

Sarai's eyes widened. "Oh. I just assumed you only liked women." A ridiculous assumption, she realized, since she recalled glimpses of naked men when she'd been connected to his memories.

"Men, women, people. My only requirement is they be interested adults capable of handling what I do to them." Setanta trailed a finger along the length of Sarai's neck. Her heart skipped a beat. "Now that we've established you do indeed like us both, why don't you tell me what kind of sex you like?"

"I'm not sure. The other men never asked me what I like." Sarai looked down at her lap, playing with the fabric of her dress. "What do you like?"

"No, don't deflect like that," he said with a firmness that made her feel guilty. "You're not here tonight to cater to my pleasure. You're here for your own pleasure. Or pain, if it intrigues you."

Sarai blushed as she looked up at him. "Did Marcelle tell you about that? I do like when we've gotten a little rough sometimes. When she, well, makes me bleed."

He smiled. "No. But, generally speaking, anyone involved with a vampire has at least mild masochistic tendencies. We bite, after all."

"Don't be so shy, my little witch," Marcelle chided as she slid into the narrow space left between Sarai and the armrest. She leaned against her vampire lover, gripped her hand, and gave it a squeeze.

"Yeah. I… I like pain. Well, not pain. I'm not sure how to explain it." It was so hard to look into Setanta's red eyes and speak bluntly. "I like feeling vulnerable. And waiting to feel it. Waiting, it's exciting. Intimate."

Just the thought had her squirming in her seat, her body reacting as she remembered how it felt to be pinned down, quivering in anticipation of Marcelle's fangs. "Like when she bites me, and the way her hand feels when—" Her own free hand drifted up to rest against her neck. Setanta's gaze made her shiver, and Sarai knew in that moment she craved the sensation of his hand against her throat. He reached up, his hand hovering just inches away from her skin.

"May I?"

Sarai nodded and lowered her hand, breathing heavy with anticipation. He rested his hand against her firmly, but not rough, his fingers pressed against her pulsing veins. It was almost gentle, but she felt in that moment he had complete control over her. Then, he let her go.

"Do you want me to bite you tonight?" Setanta asked. To feel his lips against her neck, his fangs in her veins... she nodded perhaps too eagerly. "What are your safe words with Marcelle?"

"Red to stop, yellow to slow down, and snapping my fingers if I can't talk," Sarai replied.

"Is there anything you know you don't want to experience?"

She shrugged. "I don't know yet. If I don't like something, I'll let you know."

Setanta held out his hand to her. Sarai hesitated, her heart pounding, then reached out to take his hand. Instead of accepting hers, he gripped her wrist and pulled her closer. The power in his movement made her whimper. She looked back at Marcelle for reassurance, and felt Setanta's lukewarm finger touch her chin, indicating for her to turn back, but not forcing her.

"Look at me."

She looked, and he was closer. Their lips met, his arm wrapping around her waist to pull their bodies together. The kiss was different from when she had tried to kiss him, when he hadn't returned it. Now, his mouth felt demanding, like he might consume her. His lips parted in an invitation, and she accepted, letting her tongue flick against him. As she did, she felt his teeth elongate into sharp fangs. Setanta pulled back, leaving less than an inch between them, and a set of Marcelle's cold fingers danced across Sarai's back and tugged at her laces, loosening them. Then her top was yanked down, her breasts spilling forth.

Setanta's hand slid up Sarai's body to cup her soft flesh. It felt rough, and his hand was so much larger and more forceful than her own or Marcelle's. "Before we really start," he said, and looked past her to smile at Marcelle. "I'd like to show you something… fun."

He pulled Sarai to lean against him, as if they were a normal couple cuddling in front of a television. "Marcelle?" The vampire woman smiled and stood in front of them. "Strip."

"Oh, so that's the game we're playing, is it?" Marcelle asked as she unzipped the side of her dress and slipped it off. Sarai wasn't sure if the vampire had slipped underwear down at the same time, or if she'd just not worn any the entire night.

"Am I missing something?" Sarai asked.

"Shh," Setanta said to her as Marcelle pulled off her gloves and removed several small hidden sheaths to stand before them naked. "Just watch. Marcelle?"

"Yes, Master?"

"Embrace bliss."

Marcelle's eyes widened and she dropped to her

knees, shouting with sudden pleasure. The look in her eyes was one of shock and enjoyment, and something else Sarai had never seen in the powerful vampire woman. Submission.

"How did you do that?" Sarai whispered.

"I can control all made vampires of my bloodline," he said with a smirk. "So, I have her under orders to orgasm whenever I say the right code phrase, and she has no choice but to obey. It's a fun game, even if it is cheating."

"Definitely cheating," Marcelle gasped, looking up at the pair from her position kneeling on the floor.

"I don't hear any complaints from you," Setanta replied. He slid away from Sarai and circled around Marcelle, his hand at her neck. He stopped behind her and gripped her by the throat, pulling her to her feet. He whispered something in her ear, and Marcelle laughed, nodding as much as his grip permitted. It was a strange, yet erotic image, to see Marcelle's body bare while Setanta remained fully clothed as he held her. They both fixed Sarai with a red-eyed gaze, and her heart skipped a beat.

"You're right, she is over dressed," Marcelle said. "We should do something about that."

They approached her, and Marcelle pulled Sarai up to stand with her between them. Setanta pulled her close to his body, so that she was facing Marcelle.

"We're going to take off your clothes now," Setanta told her. "Are you ready?"

Sarai nodded and watched, mesmerized as Marcelle pulled down the rest of the elaborate ball gown, leaving her only in underwear and her jewelry as she was led back to sit between them, the gown draped over a chair.

Setanta's hands brushed aside her wild curls and unlatched her necklace, while Marcelle slipped off the bracelets at Sarai's wrists. Her slender fingers caressed Sarai's inner wrist as she opened her mouth so the witch could watch fangs extend. Light breathing at the nape of her neck had her hair standing on edge as Setanta's rough hand grasped her hair and pulled her head to the side to expose her vulnerable neck.

"I warned you," Setanta murmured in her ear. "I am not as gentle as Marcelle. I will hurt you."

"Then do it," Sarai breathed. "Hurt me. Or I'm going to think you're all talk and no bite."

Both the vampires gave a dark chuckle.

"Oh, my sweet Sarai… I bite." Setanta rested the tips of his fangs against her throat. She trembled in anticipation, watching Marcelle kiss her wrist, then cried out as he pierced her veins.

Setanta hadn't understated his power at all. His bite was much harsher than Marcelle's. The sheer force of the puncture made her feel weak, even lightheaded as he swallowed mouthful after mouthful of her blood. He didn't need to suck at the wound at all; the way he'd bitten her meant the blood came to him freely. All he needed to do was take what he wanted.

"You make such enjoyable noises when you're in pain," Marcelle teased. Sarai couldn't have replied if she wanted to, and simply relented when the beautiful woman pressed their lips together. Sarai whimpered; her lips belonging to Marcelle and her blood claimed by Setanta. She was trapped between Marcelle's raw sex appeal and Setanta's primal power, their erotic prisoner.

Then, Marcelle pulled away and sunk her teeth into the free side of the witch's neck, causing another cry of pain.

Sarai held onto Marcelle tight, inhaling that sweet rosewater scent. It was perfect. She could feel a now familiar light tingling from the vampires' saliva, and that little bit of numbing helped her cope with the intensity. As did the distraction of Setanta's hard grasp of her breast. And something else hard as well... despite the fact he was still wearing all his clothes, she could feel he was erect and pressing against her from behind. It frightened her, in a good way.

Both vampires pulled free of their bites at the same time, and Sarai would have fallen if Setanta hadn't held her up. Marcelle cut her fingertip on her fang, then pressed it to the witch's neck as it healed, allowing their blood to mingle to help with recovery.

"She does taste good," Setanta murmured. "Bittersweet, like a rich, dark hot chocolate."

"Isn't she delicious?" Marcelle said, and kissed Setanta. Sarai stood there between them as they shared her blood on their tongues, watching in disbelief that she was allowed to be so close to something so intense. They parted.

"How do you feel?" Setanta asked Sarai.

"I'm a little dizzy," Sarai whispered.

"Let's get you to the bed." He lifted her up in his arms and brought her to his bed in the other room. It was a large bed, much too large for one person, or even for two or three, made of solid oak and... were those shackles hanging from the corners of the four posters?

"I'm supposed to relax here?" she asked, eyeing the chains.

"You're supposed to recover. You can relax when I'm done with you." He placed her gently on the bed and saw her looking at the unusual bed adornments. "Do you want to try those tonight?"

She blushed. "Maybe."

"I can put Marcelle in them for you as well, if that's something you'd like to see. There is a thin line of silver in them, to tame her. I can switch them out for a leather pair if you'd like to try a more comfortable option. And there's always rope."

Silver, leather, ropes… it all sounded so intense. Marcelle had warned her Setanta was intense. *She wasn't kidding*, Sarai thought to herself.

"Maybe not silver. Leather though… You guys get pretty kinky then?" she asked as she got up to her knees on the bed, to get a closer look at the shackles and tentatively ran a finger against the inside. Just as he said, there was a thin line of silver.

"We invented kink," Marcelle bragged.

Setanta laughed. "There might be some truth to that."

"So then. Why are you still wearing clothes?" Sarai asked, her cheeks burning as she looked at the man. He grinned at her, a light red gleam of her blood still on his teeth. She noticed, despite the wet feeling on her neck, he hadn't spilt a drop from his lips. He was far too experienced to be messy.

"A good question." He looked at Marcelle. "Why am I still wearing clothes?" The vampire woman smiled at him and he beckoned her closer. She obeyed and helped him out of his shirt, first by unbuckling the long belt around his waist, then unbuttoning his sleeve cuffs as he held them out to her, and finally lifting it up over his head to reveal his extensive blue knotwork tattoos and muscular body. As Marcelle laid the shirt and belt off to the side, he snapped his fingers at her, as if she were a servant, smirking. "You're not done yet. Get on your knees."

Marcelle knelt in front of him. "Sarai, do you want to watch, or would you like to help?"

Sarai bit her lip. "I think I'll watch for now."

Marcelle nodded and first removed Setanta's boots and socks, then finally unbuttoned his pants, pulling them down to his ankles so that all he wore were his signature golden torque necklace and the iron circlet that marked him as the vampire king. Sarai gulped a little, wide-eyed at the sight of his proud member, which it turned out was the only part of his body other than his head and hands not covered in blue tattoos. He was larger than her previous partners, and uncut, and she was immediately worried about how it was going to fit.

Marcelle, in answer to the unasked concern from Sarai and with the skill of a practiced prostitute, made the erection disappear down her throat. Setanta gave a sigh of pleasure and watched as his mistress gagged herself on his length.

"Isn't it lovely that she doesn't need to breathe?" he said, grabbing her hair and forcing the last inch into her. Marcelle made a wet, muffled, choking noise, but Setanta held her in place. "She can stay down for as long as I want her to. The perfect little toy." He grinned at Sarai. "Though sometimes a warm mouth is just as enjoyable a sensation." Her heart raced in a panic at the thought that she was far out of her league. There was no way she could do what Marcelle was demonstrating. No way to keep up with them. They had to know that. "How do you find her mouth?"

"I, I love it," she whispered, reminded of just earlier

that evening when Marcelle had made her orgasm in the bath.

"Would you like her now?"

Sarai took a deep breath, then nodded. Setanta pulled Marcelle off and roughly lifted her to her feet by her hair.

"The witch wants your mouth," he told her. "Give her what she wants."

"Yes, Master."

"Didn't you once tell me she wasn't your slave?" Sarai asked, raising an eyebrow.

Setanta laughed and yanked Marcelle's head back by her hair, forcing a gasp from her. "Marcelle, are you my slave?"

"Only when I want to be, Master." Marcelle winked at Sarai, making her blush.

"Good girl." He gave her a kiss on the side of her head, to which the vampire woman purred in response, then he pulled her forward to kneel on the bed. "Lay back, Sarai. And spread your legs."

Taking deep breaths, Sarai started to do as he'd instructed, then stopped, and looked up at the naked couple, mischief on her mind.

She grinned. "Make me."

Both Marcelle's and Setanta's red eyes burned with lust.

"I like this one," Setanta said, darting forward and pinning her to the bed. Her heart skipped a beat. "You want me to make you?"

"If you think you can," she said with false bravado. Her time with Marcelle had given her far too much confidence. All she could think was that this was a horrible idea, yet there she was digging herself a deeper grave.

"If I think I can," he repeated. "What a challenge. Let us hope I can *rise* to the occasion. *Marcelle*." He didn't look up as he spoke to the vampire, the R in her name rolled in a French accent Sarai had never heard from him before. "*Obtenez les menottes en cuir.*"

Marcelle disappeared from the room.

"What did you just tell her?" Sarai asked, then whimpered as he kissed her. She forgot about her concern over what he said, losing herself to the demands of his mouth.

Cold hands grasped her wrists and Sarai looked up to see Marcelle buckling a soft, leather cuff in place.

"Not too tight?" Marcelle asked. "Not too loose?"

Setanta pulled back from the kiss. "Answer her."

"It feels okay," Sarai said, looking at the cuff on her wrist. It latched together like a small belt, and there was a D-shaped metal ring on it. Most interesting to her were the Celtic knotwork imprints in the black leather. It almost looked classy and marked the equipment as belonging to Setanta. If she was captive in it, did that mean she belonged to him as well? The thought was more exciting than it should have been.

Her other wrist was captured in a second cuff, then the two vampires manipulated her to lay back on the bed in a move so synchronized that they must have practiced it on others, each holding one arm spread as close to the edges as Sarai could reach. Something snapped in place, and Sarai tugged on the restraints with both arms. Chains clinked, exciting her, but did not give.

"All right," she said. "All right, this is interesting."

"What was it you wanted me to do again?" Setanta said, trailing a hand along her naked torso, around her breast to her navel. "When I told you to spread your legs?"

Sarai smirked. "Make me."

"I'm sorry?"

"Don't you have supernatural hearing? You heard me. I said, make me."

"Oh, I heard you." Setanta gripped her breast, his fingers caressing all its sensitive flesh to cause her to moan.

Then his hand was at her throat. He didn't press down on her esophagus; he instead applied a gentle but firm pressure on either side of it to restrict the blood flow. She could breathe, but her head grew dizzier by the moment as she stared up into his eyes. Their expression was something new she hadn't seen in him before: full of lust, yet with a flash of intense cruelty. The vulnerability of being at his mercy as he choked her and had her completely under his control made her slick with need for anything he wanted to do to her.

He leaned forward, watching her intently as she began to feel just a twinge of concern, his lips so close she could feel his breath. "I was giving you the chance to back down."

"Never," she gasped. It was the biggest lie she'd ever uttered. He grinned and immediately released her.

Setanta was then at the foot of the bed, gripping her ankles and pulling them apart to spread her legs. She tried to fight his strength, which he clearly found amusing from the look on his face. When he let go of one to start to latch a leather cuff to her right foot, she twisted, trying to pull and push with her left, getting a thrill out of straining against his impossible grip. He tucked her left leg under his arm and fastened the cuff in place, chaining her right leg to the right bed post, then doing the same to the left. When he was done, he looked pleased with himself as he appreciated her spread-eagle form.

"That is a perfect view," Marcelle said.

"Then perhaps you should get a closer look." Setanta had her by the back of the neck faster than Sarai could blink and pushed her down between the witch's legs.

Sarai moaned as Marcelle's familiar tongue flicked against her. The view was spectacular from her end as well: with Marcelle bent over, her rear end raised in the air, and Setanta standing behind her. Then there was a loud noise of impact and scream vibrated against Sarai's sex. It felt so good, but she strained to see what the cause was, curious. Setanta stood there, a black leather flogger in each of his hands, spinning dangerously and with skill that came from regular practice.

"Did you like that?" he asked. Marcelle gave a muffled response of approval, and he hit her again, causing another cry from the vampire that made Sarai tremble with need. "Not you. Don't speak with your mouth full. Sarai, do you like the way her screams feel?"

Sarai nodded.

"Shall I hit her again?"

She wasn't sure she wanted to be the one to make that decision but couldn't speak when Marcelle thrust fingers inside her and curled them just right, causing her to groan in bliss.

"I'll take that as a yes."

The floggers hit against Marcelle's raised and vulnerable behind to a regular beat, every fifth or so landing hard enough to make Marcelle grunt or cry out in response, the vibrations of her voice lovely against Sarai's sex. Soon, Marcelle's expert attentions had the witch screaming and thrashing against the restraints as she orgasmed once, twice, then three times in a row. Tears swelled in her eyes when Marcelle finally stopped, and Setanta put aside the floggers.

Then, it was Marcelle who screamed in pleasure. The vampire woman was on top of Sarai, pinned in place, rocking back and forth from a harsh force behind her. It took Sarai a few moments to realize from the motion and the sounds that Setanta was inside of Marcelle, having sex with her, while Sarai lay under them both. While it was a beautiful act to witness and had the bonus of giving the witch a moment to breathe after her pleasures, Sarai was overwhelmed with need as she looked deep into Marcelle's red eyes. They were wide, her mouth open and ruby lips trembling as she whimpered with each inhumanely fast thrust. Sarai had never seen anything so beautiful as the mindless desire in her lover's expression.

"Embrace bliss, Marcelle," Setanta ordered, and Marcelle began shouting in pleasure, her nails digging into Sarai's soft skin, drawing blood in crescent shapes that healed moments later. When Marcelle was done, Setanta laid her next to Sarai, allowing her to rest. Sarai wanted to hug her lover, cover her in kisses to taste herself on those red lips, but the chains kept her in place. Setanta looked down at the two women, then smiled.

"Sarai, how do you feel?"

She wanted more. She knew he had more for her, and she wanted it. "Horny as hell," she told him.

"Mm, that's my little witch. *Ma petite sorcière*," Marcelle purred, her body curled against Sarai's curves.

"Would you like a turn with him?"

Sarai looked down between her spread legs at Setanta, at his naked warrior's body.

"I'm pretty sure you're going to kill me with that," she whispered. "Yes."

Setanta moved slowly over her, kissing her body as she lay exposed to him. He nipped, not drawing blood, just causing the slightest of sharp pains against sensitive spots at her waist, under her breasts, and her nipples. In his clenched fist, he revealed a thin necklace with a gold charm on it and fastened it around Sarai's neck.

"What is that?" she asked.

"An enchantment. To ensure you don't become pregnant," he said. "Now, where were we?" There was mischief in his crimson eyes as he made her wait. Suddenly, the intrusion of his finger caused her to arch off the bed. His fingers were much thicker than Marcelle's, and her orgasms left her feeling so much more sensitive to his touch. And, it seemed, he was just as skilled as Marcelle. He used his free hand to press down on her lower abdomen, just above her mound, causing the most interesting pleasurable sensation as she moaned. "Ah, yes, just there."

To her surprise, his mouth was the next experience. She wasn't sure why she'd thought he wouldn't go down on her but was glad she was wrong. Marcelle's cool, delicate mouth was one exciting feeling, and his warmer, demanding mouth was another. They were both exquisite in their own ways. He slid one hand under her to rest at the small of her back and lift her up a little off the bed, granting him easy access to everything he desired. Sarai pulled against her restraints, groaning at how good his skilled tongue and harsh fingers felt.

"Doesn't he feel good?" Marcelle whispered in Sarai's ear.

Sarai just nodded, her body shaking as she neared yet another orgasm, clenching tight around his fingers.

"How many fingers is she taking?" Marcelle asked.

"Two," Setanta said from between her legs. "I think she might be ready for a third."

Sarai shouted as he pressed into her with an added finger, rubbing the button of sweet pleasure with his thumb, and she gripped the bedsheets under her.

As he rocked her on his hand, Sarai's eyes rolled back, and her body tensed in anticipation of the building climax. Then, he stopped, and she sobbed in frustration.

"No, not yet," he said. "Not yet. I've let you be greedy with Marcelle, but not with me. You're going to ask permission."

"You fucking sadist," she accused, squirming as she longed for that delicious pleasure to return.

He laughed; the sound was dark like a villain whose evil plot had come to fruition. "Yes, exactly, Sarai. I am a sadist."

As she looked down, she felt something much larger than a finger teasing her.

"Are you ready?"

Sarai nodded. Setanta grinned maliciously, his fangs exposed, and eyes filled with sadistic enjoyment.

"Good girl."

He pushed forward, slowly. Sarai's eyes widened, locked on his as he watched her expression. The scream felt caught in her throat. It was almost too much, just past the point of pleasure, though she imagined it was much easier to take than if he hadn't used his fingers first to warm her up. The stretched, full feeling made her crave more.

Satisfied with her expression, he bared his teeth and struck. Sarai lay there unable to protest as he swallowed mouthfuls of her blood and drove into her body again and again with powerful thrusts as he fed. Words evaporated and Sarai gave a half-choked sob of need.

The chains clinked at her wrists, and she found that Marcelle had unlatched them, but left the cuffs on. Setanta released her from his mouth and pulled her half up to a sitting position as he thrust into her, hard, so deep that it caused her to shout. Marcelle slid behind the girl to hold her up, murmuring something Sarai couldn't understand in French in her ear as she kissed and nibbled her neck.

Setanta kissed Marcelle over Sarai's shoulder, sharing the witch's blood on his lips, then became more brutal. His pace increased, making her scream again and again. She thought for a moment of the safe words they'd discussed in the beginning. But then, it seemed ridiculous that she could take his vicious bite, but not sex. She wanted to endure, wanted to let him take his pleasure with her body. It was different from Marcelle, where they would take turns granting each other orgasms. With Marcelle, sex was about giving. With Setanta, he was about taking. Sarai wasn't sure anymore where the border between pleasure and pain was and she didn't care. Her body tensed around him, and she tried to speak, but couldn't make words.

She was so close, yet couldn't seem to get over the edge, as if Setanta had control over her. She just needed a little more attention to that one sweet spot, and she could make it.

"Can you speak?" Setanta asked, not letting up.

Sarai shook her head. "Are you trying to ask for permission?" She nodded desperately.

Setanta gripped Sarai's chin in his hand and forced her to look him in the eye as he touched her just right to give her what she wanted.

"Embrace bliss, little witch."

Sarai screamed as did Marcelle behind her, set off by the words. Pain, pleasure: it didn't matter. It was pure mind-blanking bliss.

She collapsed back against Marcelle's cool body, but Setanta wasn't done. With a primal war cry that made Sarai tremble in arousal and fear, his speed increased again to something beyond human she knew she couldn't endure for long, then she felt him burst inside of her. Teeth were in her neck, and she wasn't sure who they belonged to. There was too much power around her, in her, stealing from her, and she was exhausted by it.

Setanta stilled inside her, his arms around both the women to support them, and Sarai realized it was Marcelle who had bitten her. She closed her eyes, surrendering completely, gasping as the vampire woman pulled her fangs free.

"You did so well," Marcelle told her, kissing the wound as it healed. "You are so beautiful, *ma petite sorcière*."

"I think I died," Sarai whispered.

Setanta laughed a little and pulled himself free. A wave of his seed and her orgasmic nectar spilled onto the bed. "You are very fun, little one. *Mo cailín álainn*." He leaned over her to give her a slow, sweet kiss that tasted of sex and blood, then released her to unfasten her ankles. The couple shifted so that Sarai was cuddled between them in the massive bed.

"What does that mean?" she asked.

"My beautiful girl," he said, pushing back a curl from her face behind her ear. "Rest now, you've earned it. Would you like anything; a drink, some food?"

She did feel a little hungry and her throat was dry, but she didn't have the energy to eat and she didn't want either partner to leave her side. She didn't even want to get up to go to the restroom. Sarai just wanted to be lazy and lay in bed forever.

"I like this," she sighed. "I'm good here."

To the sound of Setanta's slow breathing and trapped between their bodies, her eyes closed. They lay in perfection, in quiet. Sarai couldn't resist the soft bed and comfort any longer and was soon fast asleep.

Chapter Twenty: Two Rings

Waking the next night just before sunset was the best thing in the world. Sarai didn't know whose hands were where initially but realized soon it was Setanta pressed against her on her left and Marcelle on her right. Both were naked.

"Good evening," murmured Setanta in her ear.

"Morning?" she asked.

"Evening," he corrected.

"Did you sleep well?" Marcelle asked. "You fainted on us."

"Well, you did wear me out. And drained my blood."

Setanta kissed the back of her neck, sending aroused chills down her spine. "So we did."

Sarai shivered with desire, but unfortunately, nature called. "I kinda have to go to the bathroom," she said sheepishly.

"Go," Marcelle said. "We'll be here when you get back."

Sarai scampered away and did her business, taking a moment to appreciate just how nice Setanta's large bathroom was. She had to try out the bathtub sometime. It easily would fit all three of them.

When she came back, the couple were curled together, discussing something in French.

"What're you guys talking about?" Sarai asked as

she crawled back into the bed and brazenly landed between them.

Marcelle sighed and shook her head. "It's nothing."

Well, that was a lie. Sarai frowned and looked up. Marcelle looked upset.

"Did I do something wrong?" she asked.

"No, no. It's nothing like that," the vampire said as she shook her head. "It's... forget it."

"But—"

"I'm picking a bride today," Setanta said. "It's not Marcelle's favorite topic."

"I don't have a problem with another woman," Marcelle said with a sigh. "I just don't like you having no choice."

Sarai frowned. "You're the king, aren't you? How do you have no choice?"

"There are very few of my line left. As a king, to secure my position, I need heirs to the throne. Only a pureblood woman can do that for me."

"Or a wit..." Sarai caught herself before she said it. Or a witch like her. Both her lovers looked up at her in surprise, and she decided to finish her sentence. "A witch. Like me. Right?"

"In theory. Wasn't the idea of keeping you from your father to avoid you having to birth a pureblood?" Setanta mused.

"Or about me being allowed to make my own decisions."

Setanta paused and leaned forward, his expression unreadable. "Are you trying to suggest something?"

Sarai blushed and toyed nervously with the anti-pregnancy charm he had put around her neck. "I was just stating a fact. You could marry a witch. If all you need is someone who can have children with you. And, you know, you've got a whole new witch alliance to promote."

"And I suppose I could do that by marrying a mortal witch to cement that bond?" Setanta asked.

"I mean, in theory." She stared down at her feet, feeling vulnerable and self-conscious of her nudity. She crossed her arms over her chest and leaned forward a little so that the blanket would hide her body better. "I'm not suggesting, you know. Forget I said anything."

"She has a point," Marcelle murmured. "You don't need a stronger alliance with countries on a different continent. The ones on this continent haven't offered any of their daughters. This alliance with the witches is the most important one right now. Proving that they're not a passing fancy by marrying one would make a statement that would reverberate throughout our world. And there are other witch covens we will need to prove our good will towards. What better way to do that than to have a witch for a wife on your arm?"

It was so silent; Sarai was sure she could hear her own heart beating.

"Are you saying that we should get married?" she asked, a tremble in her voice.

"No, no," Marcelle said. "Not you. I'm not trying to push you into an arranged marriage after everything with your family, I promise. But maybe we should talk to Danior and the rest about an arranged match?"

"The Ellis Coven wouldn't push any of their people into an arranged marriage, let alone with a vampire. Most modern people don't do arranged marriages anymore. The witches see things as final with the treaty being signed. A marriage would mean the most to other vampires," Sarai said. The way Marcelle put it, the idea made sense. A witch would make a great statement as his wife, to other witch covens and to other vampires as well. It was the kind of commitment he needed to show them, and he needed a woman who could survive carrying pureblood children. A healing witch, even one designed by her family to have vampire children. Someone like Sarai. "You should pick me. If you want a witch."

"I don't think you know what you're asking," Setanta said, though his expression was intrigued rather than uninterested. Still, he had a point: Sarai wasn't quite sure what she was asking for. What was she thinking? Be the wife of a vampire? He was attractive, there was no doubt of that. She wanted him, in a primal way. But marriage? That was something else entirely. It was insane. Besides, she had much stronger feelings towards Marcelle.

And children... She'd always been terrified of the idea of having children, but she was terrified less of children and more of the idea that her father would take them from her. Or maybe kill her after she had them and her use was at an end. If she were with Setanta, then she could have children and feel safe about it.

"I'm not sure I know either," Sarai admitted. "You need to have kids, right? That's the main goal? I could just surrogate for you, if you wanted. It doesn't have to be super official or fancy. You've let me stay here, which saved my life in a lot of ways."

"So, you want to be my concubine to pay me for your life?"

Sarai made a face. "Well, I don't know if I'd call it *that*."

Setanta sighed, and exchanged glances with

Marcelle, who was watching the situation unfold with wide eyes. "Would you mind letting us talk in private for a little, Marcelle?"

"Of course," she replied. She got up and pulled on a silk robe. "I'll just be in my chambers."

A moment later, she had disappeared, and Sarai was alone with Setanta. She felt hyper aware of her breath, her heartbeat. Both had increased in rate, and no doubt the vampire could tell with his hearing.

"I won't be with anyone who is giving me their body as payment," Setanta said flatly. "When Marcelle was young, she felt sex was transactional. That she owed me her body in return for the blood I gave her to turn her. I don't pay to fuck, even if the payment isn't monetary. I refused to lay with her until she came to me because she wanted the experience for herself rather than for my benefit."

"I get what you mean," Sarai said. "You know that's not why I came to your bedroom, I hope. I wanted to experience you."

"And you want to have children?"

She thought for a moment. "Growing up, I didn't want my dad's family to take the kids when I had them, so I thought I never would. But it wasn't because I didn't want to. I was afraid of what would happen to them. This is the first time I've been, well, allowed to think about having kids in an environment where I wouldn't be expecting abuse. At least, I'm assuming you're not going to beat your kids and lock them in a dungeon if they aren't subservient to you."

"No, of course not. We did practice corporal punishment for misbehavior the last time I had children, but that was over two thousand years ago. I don't strike children; it just teaches them to lie better, be more deceitful. And the only reason anyone is imprisoned in a dungeon is for breaking laws. Not for refusing to clean their room."

That was good to hear.

"You realize that I do not love you, Sarai."

She took in a sharp breath. Of course he didn't. She didn't love him. She hardly knew him, even if she did know he was very good in bed.

"Yeah, I know."

"Does that bother you, the thought of having a child with a man who does not love you? I know that means more in this time period than it once did."

Why did they have to have this conversation while they were both naked? She felt so vulnerable, and yet he looked so comfortable and confident. "I don't love you either," she said. "But I think maybe I could one day?" She hoped that wasn't too much to say to him.

"I can't promise that I will. But I won't keep you from other relationships that might fulfill you in that way. Such as with Marcelle, or anyone else who might come along. My only stipulation would be that you not have unprotected sex with someone capable of impregnating you. It would be a bad look for me if you were to carry another man's child, politically speaking."

"That sounds fair." Sarai found herself laughing.

"Something amuses you?"

"It feels like we're negotiating a contract. It's funny, I suppose."

Setanta smiled a little. "Marriage is a contract, in my experience. There is one more thing to discuss. Your position here."

"I can just be a surrogate," Sarai said. "I'm not

looking for anything else."

"But I'm not looking for a concubine or surrogate, Sarai," Setanta said with a sigh as he leaned forward. "I am looking for a queen."

Queen. The word sent a shiver down Sarai's spine. How had she overlooked such an important detail? "Oh, I'm not trying to be a queen," she blurted. "That's way too much. I'm not monarch material."

"The technical title would be Queen Consort. You would have no ruling power, as I would be the regent and only a pureblood can rule. But you would have respect."

It still sounded daunting. "What would being 'Queen Consort' entail?" she asked. "Is it a figurehead position?"

"Essentially. And a social position, representing New Ulster at events not unlike last night. You would be subject to our laws and be considered a citizen of my kingdom. You'll also be required to publicly swear fealty to me. Do you think you can do that?"

She already felt more at home in the vampire kingdom than anywhere else. Nowhere else welcomed her, kept her safe, or made her feel like being a mother was something she would be safe to do. "Yes," she said softly. "I can do that." Sarai's eyes flickered down to his body, lingering on his tattoos. "I can't say this is how I ever would have pictured this."

"Pictured what?"

"Getting engaged."

"Not romantic enough for you?" he mused.

"Well, I used to think it just wouldn't happen." She could feel the heat rising in her cheeks. "I should get a ring or something, right?"

He chuckled. "If you want a ring, I can get you a

ring. Though in vampire culture, wearing someone's ring means that you're their ward and under their protection. Would you like one like Marcelle's?" He tapped the gold torque around his neck. "Wearing the hound symbol would mark you as connected to me. To New Ulster."

"What about Marcelle's ring?" she asked, looking down at her hand. She'd grown quite fond of the bulky fleur-de-lis jewelry.

"It would return to her right hand. On the right hand we wear our personal symbols. On the left, we wear the symbols of our protector, if we have one." He raised his right hand to reveal a miniature copy of his torque necklace, complete with hound heads at the ends. He slipped it off and took her left hand, removing Marcelle's ring from Sarai's finger and putting it aside on top of a nightstand.

As he slid his ring in place on her hand, it felt a little large. Due to the style, he was able to pinch it to fit just right.

"Am I your ward or your fiancée?" Sarai asked.

"You could be both." He held her hand and kissed the ring. "But, before we agree to this arrangement, I want you to accompany me today. You impressed me last night at the dance and impressed many of my guests. I'd like to see you interacting with them in a less formal, more intimate setting. I'm having tea with the other purebloods representing North American countries tonight. They'll view you as entertainment but consider them an introduction to royal circles. If you decide after this that it isn't a life for you, I will respect that and marry the Egyptian girl."

"When you say entertainment, what do you mean?" she asked with suspicion.

"You're young. You're a witch. You're a novelty. Don't worry, the entertainment value is purely in your personality."

As long as she wasn't expected to entertain them with anything else.

"All right," she said. "Let's give this a try."

Chapter Twenty-One: Teatime with Vampires

Tea. It sounded so proper and yet strange, to be invited to "take tea" as Sarai's trial run interacting with pureblood vampires. She wasn't sure what to expect but allowed Marcelle to pick her outfit for the day, after a quick conversation reassured Sarai that the idea of becoming Setanta's witch bride was brilliant, if unexpected, and Sarai had Marcelle's blessing. A navy pencil skirt and a short-sleeved blouse that had a high collar was the choice, which made her look like a businesswoman. Or maybe a joke.

Sarai did make a point of putting on the heavy elaborate bracelets from the night before. They looked a little too much for her new clothes, but they made her feel more secure to have an obvious bite point covered. Not that she believed Setanta would allow anyone to do anything to her, but it felt good.

Tea was to be served on the terrace she'd once had lunch with Setanta on, which was nice to return to a familiar room. However, the furniture had been changed. Instead of an intimate setting for two, there was a coffee table surrounded by comfortable couches and chairs for lounging. Setanta led Sarai in on his arm, and the vampires there took a moment to take in the strange sight.

"Setanta, is this why you kept us waiting?" teased a red-eyed Asian woman wearing a beautiful, semi-transparent, red kimono with blossoms embroidered along it over a simple white robe.

He smiled. "It is. Everyone, thank you for joining me. I'd like to introduce my companion, Sarai Meir."

Sarai knew they could all hear her heart pounding and tried not to dwell on it. This was to see if she could mingle with pureblood royalty and find a place with them, not to panic about who they were and how powerful they all had to be. And she was certain she had danced with the blonde woman present the night before at some point. "It's a pleasure to meet you all," she said, and nodded her head to show respect. Setanta had brought her, so she had to act like she belonged.

"The pleasure is ours," said a very dark black man with red eyes and dreadlocks down to his waist. His clothes were custom and exquisite, though much more casual than the outfits from the ball of the previous night, with a vibrant purple cloth cut almost like a modern dress. She wasn't quite sure if it was feminine or masculine but loved it and was sure he wore it better than she ever could. In fact, thinking back to the ball, she remembered seeing him and realized she had mistaken him for a woman in a purple ballgown, so she had no doubt he could wear anything he wanted better than her.

He stood and approached, taking her left hand in his to kiss her new ring, his eyes lingering on the hounds embedded in the gold. Setanta stepped forward with just enough speed that it might have been aggressive, and the man dropped Sarai's hand. She wasn't sure if he was being protective or possessive and decided not to question it in case it was the former.

"Sarai, this is Prince Celestin. He is here representing his grandfather, King Legba, from the capital of American Guineé in New Orleans, and is a member of the Loa bloodline."

"A proper New Orleans vampire?" Sarai noted, giving him a little smile. "Hollywood didn't do you justice."

He laughed and nodded in approval. "No, it did not. Please, sit with us, Sarai Meir."

There were four other vampires present, two of whom had the bright red eyes of purebloods, and the others who appeared to be undead vampires.

Sarai let the prince lead her to a chair and sat down, self-conscious of how her ankles crossed and legs were positioned to keep the pencil skirt from riding up too far. It had been a terrible idea on Marcelle's part. Sarai should have worn pants.

"This is Shogun Hattori Ryoko and her handmaid, of the Yokai bloodline in Japan," Setanta said, gesturing to the pureblood in the red kimono and the made vampire woman in a pale pink kimono next to her. "She controls Alaska and the western territories in Canada on behalf of the Edo Empire."

"Good to meet you," Sarai said.

"And you as well, Miss Sarai Meir." The woman seemed amused and curious. At least she didn't seem aggressive.

"And this is Jarl Yrsa Lagethasdottir," Setanta continued. "Representing our friends to the north, the United Nordic Clans. Of the Eagle clan and Aesir bloodline, specifically, one of the five pureblood Norse clans."

A blonde woman with animalistic and runic tattoos along her arms, upper chest, and head flashed a smile at Sarai.

"Yes, we met yesterday. She granted me the honor of a dance," Yrsa said.

Setanta continued to the last vampire in their circle, a Hispanic made vampire with kind brown eyes wearing a modern button-down shirt. She began to wonder if there was going to be a quiz on all the names and resolved to do more reading about other vampire countries.

"This is our newest addition to our North American alliance other than myself as a new king. Senator Felipe Garcia."

"Senator?" Sarai asked in surprise. "I didn't know vampires had senators."

"I represent the only existing vampire democracy in the world, located on America's western coast," he said politely. "The Vampire's Republic of California. The VRC, if you please."

"And he still won't tell us what his bloodline is," Yrsa said with a sigh. "We keep guessing, but he's as tight lipped as a virgin."

Felipe shook his head. "I was sent because I'm not of any of your bloodlines. Revealing my bloodline would compromise my safety. I'm sure you understand."

"I do. Though I must admit some curiosity," Setanta said as he sat down.

"Rest assured, the ones who can control me are not here," Felipe said. "Which is why I was sent."

"Aztecs," Celestin said. "He's Hispanic, it must be one of those Aztec bloodlines."

"As before, I will neither confirm nor deny any bloodline you may guess."

"Don't be ridiculous," Yrsa said. "Aztecs never let their thralls leave. Mayan perhaps?"

"He could be a dead bloodline," Ryoko suggested. "Not the Gauls, surely?"

Felipe sighed and shook his head. "I'm sure there are more interesting things to discuss than my blood. For example, I must offer my congratulations, King Setanta. Your coronation was a beautiful spectacle." He raised an eyebrow. "I particularly liked the attempt on the witches' lives. A lively performance by all."

Setanta smirked. "I suppose to us seasoned politicians it was obvious, was it not?"

Sarai's brow furrowed, then her eyes widened as realization dawned on her. "It was a set up," she realized. "For drama. Was anyone in any real danger?"

"There's always real danger in a room full of vampires," Celestin said with a wink.

Setanta shook his head. "The attack was genuine. With witches who can sense truth from lies, one must be careful. I had a knight speak with that individual before the coronation to plant a few thoughts, fan the flames a little, and, well, an over-eager bloodlust and hatred of change did the rest for me."

"Seems a little harsh to ground him for it," Sarai noted.

"Perhaps." Setanta moved forward in his seat to reach for the tea pot and cups. "But he did intend to kill the witches. I think the punishment is justified."

"Oh, please, allow my dear Yuki-chan," Ryoko said. "We brought our own set so she could serve us. She's a witch too, you see. Consider it my gift in honor of your coronation, CuChulainn."

Sarai's eyes widened on the silent handmaid. "You're a witch?"

"She doesn't speak much English, dear. But yes, she

is. A craft witch, she makes all sorts of beautiful weapons at the forge. I couldn't ask for a better companion and smith. And her blood is divine."

Yuki lifted a tray with a Japanese tea set from the floor, but there was one item on the tray that didn't seem like it belonged. A dagger, one that looked like a smaller version of a katana and had a fancy tassel at the bottom of its wrapped hilt. The vampire picked up the instrument and to Sarai's horror, slit her wrist over a large porcelain bowl. Sarai inhaled sharply and looked away. It wasn't worse than the blood ritual at the coronation, but it was much closer and therefore more unnerving.

"Squeamish about blood?" Celestin teased.

"It doesn't suit my palate."

"Mm, not even a little sip? She's not a pureblood, it would be very enjoyable for you and free of any danger," Ryoko offered.

"I keep kosher."

There was silence for a moment, then the vampire guests burst into laughter, Ryoko covering her smile with a hand. "Oh dear, oh dear. Well, then, no blood for the Jewish girl."

"Goodness. You know how to pick them, Setanta. A Jewish girl like her at our profane little tea ceremony?" Yrsa asked, wiping a tear from her eye.

"There are some Jewish vampires in my kingdom," Setanta said, though he was clearly amused himself. "I should introduce you sometime, Sarai. One of Lilly's spies is a fine fighter from the Polish resistance in World War Two. Crafty sort, expert with explosives. You could talk about kosher laws in regard to vampires sometime."

"That would be nice. But I'm still not gonna drink blood in a teacup anytime soon," she said, glancing at the

Evelyn Silver

filling bowl. Yuki's wound healed, and she set to work making a small fire to heat the blood. There was an added barrier between the direct fire and the bowl, likely to prevent it from heating too much and causing clots, if Sarai had to guess.

"We have real tea," Setanta reassured her. He reached for the English style tea set and poured a cup, handing it to her.

"Thanks," she said, and inhaled. It smelled like a black tea. She saw a small bowl with a spoon in it and used it to take a spoonful of sugar.

"Senator, would you like me to call for a human source?" Setanta asked.

"I'm quite curious about this witch's blood," he said, looking at the blood in the bowl. "It smells delectable."

"It is," Ryoko assured him. "Quite the treat for an undead like yourself."

"For any of us," Yrsa said. "A vampire witch... A rare delicacy."

Yuki poured the blood from her bowl into a teapot and closed the lid, then poured it into a small collection of handless cups that she served one by one.

"Speaking of witches..." Ryoko glanced at Sarai, then addressed Setanta. "I'm impressed with your little collection. You have powerful allies."

"Powerful allies are always a good thing to have," Setanta said, gesturing around him.

"That fellow, Danior. I could chat with him for hours," Ryoko said. "Celestin and I met him in the piano lounge, and we had quite the discussion. Sly of you to set a truth-compelling witch among us, Setanta. Sly indeed."

"He is a fascinating individual," Setanta said. "I

226

expect to benefit greatly from our association."

Yrsa looked at Sarai. "Might I ask what you do?"

Sarai looked at Setanta, who gave her a nod as if to tell her to proceed, but this was all about games. She shouldn't give something for nothing.

"If you tell me what all of you can do first, I might share what I can do," she said.

Ryoko nodded with approval. "Very good, Sarai, very good. Well then, I assume you mean other than the usual strength, speed, and physical gifts of vampirism?" She stood and lifted her arms. Her skin, clothes, and hair faded, turning a transparent white and fluttering as if in an unfelt breeze. She looked like a ghost, and floated through the table, doing a flip in the air before landing back in her chair and becoming solid again.

Everyone gave her a polite clap, so Sarai restrained herself from clapping too enthusiastically despite how impressive it was.

"Might I demonstrate next?" Celestin asked, reaching for Sarai's hand. Setanta caught him in a gloved grip before he could make contact.

"The Loa bloodline is said to be able to read your future and absorb knowledge of languages you speak with a touch," Setanta said, and smiled with ice in his eyes at the prince. "A demonstration will not be necessary."

"You kissed my hand," Sarai accused.

"I did," the vampire prince chuckled.

"See anything interesting?"

"Nothing clear. I didn't have the time to sort things out before your valiant protector stepped in. But I appreciate learning Hebrew from you."

"*Bevakasha*," she told him as a test. It meant please,

but also worked as a way of saying you're welcome.

"*Ein be'ad ma*," he replied perfectly. No problem. She could see that being the most practical of the vampires' gifts, on a day-to-day basis.

"Well, just to get it over with, I can control ravens," Yrsa said. "It was useful until the telegraph was invented."

The older vampires laughed.

"If your curiosity is sated, would you tell us what is your gift, Miss Meir?" Ryoko asked.

"I'm a necromancer," she said, feeling proud that she had a power that vampires feared. "And a healer."

That got everyone's attention. She knew from her talks with Setanta that they all knew what it meant. That she was capable of creating new purebloods, with the right ritual. And necromancy always made vampires uncomfortable, regardless of any other implications her abilities had.

"You are quite powerful then," Celestin said, taking his cup from Yuki, but not tasting it.

It was funny to her, the respect her powers granted her in front of these powerful vampires. Sarai smiled at them, then sipped her tea. Setanta looked pleased with himself as he accepted his cup from Yuki.

"Setanta, you keep fascinating company as of late," Yrsa said. "If you ever tire of his machinations, child, the Nordic court would be glad to welcome a woman of your talents."

"Or the Edo courts, should you feel the desire to travel," Ryoko said. "And you wouldn't be the only witch. Though perhaps the only mortal one."

That surprised Sarai. Other vampire courts were interested in her? And even had a few witches already among their ranks, even if they were vampires. It almost sounded like a job offer.

"Now, now," Setanta said. He locked his fingers in Sarai's free hand and brought her knuckles to his lips for a quick kiss. "I'd like to remind everyone I don't permit poaching in my territory."

Ryoko smiled and winked at Sarai. "I suppose I can't offer you the same... perks... as he can." She glanced up and down the pair, knowingly, and Sarai realized they hadn't showered since having sex. Everyone knew. Her cheeks burned. Had he done that on purpose? Paraded her as his sexual conquest in front of the other purebloods?

Of course he did, she thought. Everything he did was on purpose. She wasn't sure what she thought of that and decided she had to own it.

"I do like the perks," she said. "Though I appreciate the offer. I wish we could have met last night to discuss it more, but I'm afraid I was a little tied up."

Celestin snorted into his blood in a poor attempt at suppressing a laugh and Setanta smiled with approval.

"She's a delight, Setanta, a delight," Yrsa said with a grin, and took a sip of the blood. "Mm, as is this. Warm vampire witch's blood... I don't think I've ever tasted anything so flavorful."

"It is quite good," Setanta said, drinking from his own cup. "Thank you, Ryoko. And you, Yuki. *Arigato gozaimasu*." The vampire woman bowed before sitting down next to her leader.

"You speak Japanese now?" Celestin asked.

"No, only a few words. My Cantonese is much better."

Ryoko rolled her eyes. "Yes, but Japanese sounds so

much better. Although maybe not on your rough tongue."

"Did you learn Cantonese for that Xian princess?" Yrsa asked.

"I picked up a little when I traveled Asia some centuries ago," he said. "Though it did come in handy when I spoke to her yesterday."

"Is she your choice then?" Celestin asked. "We're all very curious as to who your new queen will be."

"You'll learn soon enough," he assured them.

Sarai looked at him, trying to read his tone, his expression, something. Some hint as to how she was doing. She found she rather liked this horror-themed teatime. The back and forth with these purebloods was fun, a game. That was what he was after, when he said she would be entertainment. To see how she played the game.

She caught his eye and smiled confidently, nodding. She wished she had some silent way of telling her that this excited her. That being part of vampire society was thrilling, and that she wanted to spend more time playing the game. That she wanted to accept and be his queen.

He looked at her, and their exchanged looks seemed to do the trick. "If you're sure then?" Setanta asked.

"I am," she said. "I like this."

He smiled. "Then, I have an announcement." Setanta put down his cup and Sarai followed suit, letting him take her hand and bring her to stand. "I would like to introduce to you my future queen consort, Sarai Meir."

"Is this serious?" Ryoko asked.

"Absolutely," Setanta said.

Yrsa clapped, laughing. "Oh, well done,

CuChulainn. Well done. I cannot wait to see the look on MeiXiang's face. And Giovanna; now that will be a beautiful defeat. Will you have her sent back to Rome?"

"Perhaps," he said. "She is rather attached to her daughter, and I don't intend for Artemisia to leave. If Giovanna wishes to stay, I won't forbid it as long as she behaves."

"When will you be announcing it officially?" Celestin asked.

"I think tomorrow at sunrise may be the best option," Setanta said. "Try not to spread too many rumors, if it's all the same with you? Consider it privileged information."

"Then, I consider it an honor," Ryoko said with a nod of her head. "Welcome to our ranks. To the new queen." She raised her cup in salute. "To your health and prosperity, young Queen Consort to be, Sarai Meir." They all raised their cups.

Sarai smiled. "Thank you. I appreciate that."

When the meeting had concluded and Setanta and Sarai were alone on the terrace, he drew her close and kissed her on the forehead.

"You were excellent. I was impressed," he said.

"It's all about games with you purebloods, isn't it?" she asked. "I wouldn't have guessed that was a setup, with the vampire who attacked us at the coronation. You plan everything, don't you?"

"Not everything. But most things."

"Did you plan on me being your queen? Was it all some web you spun?"

"I can honestly say no. You surprised me, which is a hard thing to do. Perhaps that is why I accepted your offer."

"If you did plan it, would you tell me?"

Setanta smiled. "Would you believe me if I said yes?"

She thought for a moment. "Probably not," Sarai admitted. He'd once told her that the key to living forever was strength, cunning, and a dash of hedonism. He hadn't been kidding about the cunning. Or strength and hedonism, but it was the cunning she found herself most concerned about.

"Then, let me pose to you a question: does it matter what I might have planned as long as you're not doing anything you don't want to do?" Setanta asked.

"I guess not." She sighed. "If I'm going to be your queen, I don't want to be a pawn, Setanta. We're on the same page there?"

He nodded. "I understand. I can promise I will do my best to protect you rather than use you. My family is my priority. Anyone who becomes my wife is my family."

"I'll hold you to that."

"I would expect nothing less."

Setanta kissed her farewell and left Sarai with Marcelle, having further duties to tend to than having tea parties, the witch assumed. Sarai felt good about the whole encounter, and excitedly clung to Marcelle, eager for what the night would hold for them. After all, it was a festival, and she was in a good mood.

Marcelle, ever one for entertainment, led the witch to a music room where several vampires were chatting as someone played a grand piano in the back. Everyone took note as Marcelle and Sarai entered, and Sarai expected to be introduced to more vampires. However, she received a surprise when Marcelle sat her down on a chair in front of the pianist and kissed her cheek.

"I wanted to give you a surprise," she said, smiling like a cat with a canary.

"What is it?"

"A little something for you." She turned to the pianist. "*Ma chanson, s'il vous plait?*"

The vampire at the keys nodded and stopped his song. The rest of the vampires gathered close.

"This song is dedicated to you, *ma petite sorcière*, Sarai," Marcelle said as the witch blushed.

And then, Marcelle began to sing. Her words were French, so Sarai couldn't understand anything beyond the deep emotion in them. And the voice… Marcelle had the beautiful voice of a cabaret singer, longing and sensual. Intimate, yet powerful.

After a few verses, Marcelle pulled Sarai to her feet and spun her around, holding her close from behind and singing with passion that made every cell in the witch's body burn for more.

With Marcelle's lovely voice in her ear, her hands at Sarai's waist and throat, clinging to her with need, the witch was speechless. She was lost somewhere between love and lust, the song's melody giving her the same sensation she felt when Setanta had danced with her, and she wanted to stay as Marcelle twirled her back into her chair for the last verse, ending the song with a final, beautifully belted note as she tapped against her chest then her head in repetition, almost mimicking a heartbeat.

When Marcelle finished, she bowed, to a round of applause from all the vampires. Sarai stood and threw herself at her lover, pressing their lips together for a passionate kiss.

"I have no idea what any of that means," Sarai said. "But I loved it."

"I sang to the sound of your heart beating. I sang of how your heart drives me mad," Marcelle said, and dipped her, giving another kiss to another round of applause. "You and your blood make me remember life and love in such a warm and intoxicating way. Sometimes, when you have such love for a woman, all you can do is sing it."

Sarai smiled. "Well, just don't expect me to sing for you. My voice isn't that good. Would you accept something else?"

"Whatever you wish, *ma petite sorcière.*"

"Then… just a declaration. *Ani le'dodi ve'dodi li.*"

"What does it mean?" Marcelle asked.

"It means, I am my beloved's and my beloved is mine."

"My beloved," Marcelle repeated. "Yes, I like that a lot. You are my beloved. And I am yours."

Chapter Twenty-Two: The Trial

The first night of the Midnight Festival was a celebration of the new reign, and the second was for casual socializing. The third would be for official business. Court was held properly for the first time, and Marcelle was glad to help make it a memorable opening.

Finding the trio who killed Lochlan's family was easier than Marcelle had thought it would be. A seventh-generation colonial-era woman named Catrina who sometimes went by the nickname Carrie and her husband, an eighth-generation vampire named Bertrand, had lived in New York City for the past forty years, registered as upstanding vampire citizens. There had been a third living with them, a man named Garrett, not Gareth, who had disappeared some ten years prior and was suspected to have ended himself, as many vampires did when they were tired of eternity.

Considering the severity of the crimes they were accused of, the timing of the discovery, and the impression Setanta wanted to leave regarding the beginning of his reign, the couple were quickly captured and brought to the palace for a full trial before the throne.

Convincing Danior to invite his vampire-hating son to the palace to be a witness was difficult, but after a long discussion behind closed doors with Setanta, the adoptive father agreed.

Lochlan was there by nightfall, stiff and almost

twitching every time he saw a vampire. Which, it turned out, was often, as many wanted to see the new witch.

"Are you going to be okay, Lochlan?" Danior asked as Marcelle led them as well as Sarai and Hannah to the throne room.

"I'm fine, Dad. Stop worrying. I'm not going to blow the place up." He glanced at Marcelle as he pushed recently dyed dark blue hair out of his matching dark blue eyes. "Don't think I didn't consider it though. I could if I wanted to."

She rolled her eyes at the bravado. The second he tried anything, there would be silver needles in his body from multiple vampire knights watching him from the shadows.

"Please do keep in mind that this is a delicate situation, and we have a large gathering of important foreign and domestic leaders visiting at present," Marcelle said. "Have some decorum, for your own safety. You don't need to bow, but it would be a good idea if you could stomach it. After approaching and when leaving is appropriate."

"Bow?" Lochlan scoffed. "What, to Setanta?"

"He *is* a king here," Danior reminded him. "And we're in their world right now. Just nod your head a little."

Lochlan made a face. "Only 'cause you said so, Dad. Not 'cause I respect him or anything. I respect you. That's it."

"I appreciate that very much. Lochlan, I… want to say, before we go in. I talked to Setanta about what will happen. I don't approve of this; I want you to know. I didn't want you to be subjected to any of this. But you're an adult now. And I know what those monsters did to you, that you need closure. I just hope," Danior paused and embraced Lochlan. "I know we see things differently and we've fought about the vigilantism you practice but remember everything I've tried to teach you. I know you'll do what you think is right, my son. I hope we agree on what the right thing is."

Lochlan hugged his father back but didn't reply. When they parted, Marcelle opened the doors to reveal the throne room, lit in the flickering light of candles in chandeliers above them.

Vampires lined the sides and Setanta sat on his throne, looking regal as ever. His focus, a massive spear, in one hand and an iron circlet on his head. Marcelle knew the significance of the iron, as opposed to bejeweled gold other monarchs wore for crowns. The iron had come from the shackles of an ancient lover of Setanta's who had once been enslaved. It served as a reminder that all royalty of New Ulster was meant to serve their people, not the other way around.

"Your Highness," Marcelle said as they stopped at the foot of the stone dais and bowed. "I present to you the sole witness to the crimes on trial today, Lochlan Kelly. A member of the Tuatha de Danaan."

Lochlan stepped forward, to hushed voices whispering, "*Tuatha de Danaan*," through the room. It was a rare bloodline, having once been hunted to near extinction by fearful humans in the Dark Ages, and everyone knew what it meant: this witch was technically a relative of the royal pureblood family. He looked pale, sick almost, but determined. His lips formed a thin line, but he nodded his head just enough to count as some sort of acknowledgement to King Setanta.

"Lochlan Kelly. I appreciate you answering my

summons."

"I didn't come because you summoned me," Lochlan said. "I'm here for justice."

"Of course. My understanding is you accuse Catrina and Bertrand Watson of killing your parents and attacking you when you were five years old," Setanta said. "In our world, when a crime such as this is brought before the king, you can consider me judge and jury. What would you like to say on this matter?"

"Just that. They killed my parents. Slaughtered them like cattle and tortured me for a whole night. If you want proof, here it is." He stripped off his jacket to reveal a sleeveless shirt underneath, his numerous old scars along his toned arms. He bared them out to the court, fists clenched. "Five years old and they did this to me."

Setanta didn't show any emotion on his face in response, though Marcelle could hear murmurings of the court. His scars were vicious enough to make even older vampires pause. That he had survived was nothing short of a miracle.

"And, when this happened, was it a sudden attack? As if they smelled a witch and lost control?"

"Sudden?" Lochlan laughed without mirth. "They planned the whole thing. The one they called Carrie gave me a lollipop the day before. I remember because my dad, my… my other dad. Bio dad. He took it out of my hands and threw it in the trash then rushed me home. I saw the lady again and she asked if she and her friends could come into my house to give me a new one." He fought back tears. "I got my parents killed for a fucking piece of candy. But the leeches were in control the whole time, I can promise you that."

Setanta nodded. "I see. Is there anything else you

would like to say?"

"They're guilty. They did it. And if you let them get away with it, I don't know what I'll do."

It sounded like a threat, but Marcelle was just glad it wasn't an explicit threat. Perhaps the pyro had some sense after all.

"Very well. Angela? The prisoners, if you would."

The blonde vampire woman left the room, then returned pushing a pair of disheveled vampires in silver chains into the room. A woman with brown hair and freckles, a short man with blond hair. They were brought before the throne and dropped to their knees of their own accord, prostrating themselves fearfully before their sovereign.

"*Sit up. Show your faces,*" Setanta ordered, magic compulsion in his words. The pair immediately obeyed. "Mr. Kelly, are these two of the vampires who attacked you?"

Lochlan was shaking in anger at the sight of the vampires, smoke rising from his skin. Yet, he looked almost afraid. Like he was a little kid again, faced with the monsters that hid under the bed and in the closet, waiting to devour him.

"That's them," he said, and his voice cracked with fear. He took a step towards them. Danior put a hand on his shoulder, holding him back. "Where's the other guy? There were three of them."

"Tell me," Setanta said to the vampires with a compulsion. "You were living with a vampire named Garrett Hayes. What happened to him?"

Catrina tried to fight the compulsion but couldn't. "I killed him," she blurted out. "We got into a fight, about him getting more witch blood than us. I stabbed him in the heart." She moved to cover her mouth with her chained hands, tears welling in her eyes as the silver shifted and burned against her skin.

"What, what was that?" Lochlan asked Marcelle quietly. "What happened?"

"Setanta can control any vampire of his bloodline. He ordered her to speak the truth, so she did," she explained in a low voice.

"You are accused of attacking a witch child and killing two uncontracted witches with the blood of Danaan," Setanta continued. "Relatives of mine."

"You can't mean... what are you talking about?" Bertrand said, angrier than his fearful wife. His accent wasn't quite the British accent Marcelle expected. It was more Cockney, but she could understand where a five-year-old might have made the mistake. "We'd never attack the blood of the crown. We've only done what vampires do."

"Unfortunately for you, targeting children for torture and death isn't something vampires are permitted to do in *my* kingdom. And, though you might not have known it at the time, it does appear that you targeted my cousins," Setanta said. "Tell me the truth, now. Did you attack this man's family fifteen years ago?"

They both stared at Lochlan, then at each other.

"I... I don't know, Your Highness," Catrina said. She couldn't be compelled into speaking the truth if she didn't know what the truth was. "He doesn't look familiar."

The heat around Lochlan built, like a hearth poked with a stick. Marcelle took a step back.

"Squeal, little pig, squeal," he said slowly. "I like it when they squeal like little pigs." He glared at Catrina.

"That's what you told me. And you. Blondie. You told me you liked that I smelled like spicy peppers. Chili peppers, you said."

Catrina's eyes narrowed with recognition. She laughed, a high-pitched noise very much like a hyena, just as Lochlan had described to Marcelle.

"This is a joke," she laughed. "The witch girl grew up into this? A joke!"

"Then you recognize him as the child you attacked?" Setanta asked. "Tell me the truth."

"It wasn't an attack, just feeding," Catrina snapped. "I recognize her, sure. Him. Whatever. It's the kid from fifteen years ago, yes. We were hunting in the street that was our territory and found some witches. Witches always taste better than humans. Not everyone has a full household staff of humans to snack on at their leisure. Some of us have to work for it. Not everyone can enjoy the flavors of real food like you purebloods can. You know the same as I do how good it feels to take that last drop while they're begging for their lives. Or their wife's life. Or husband. Or child. We were bored and it was a game. Just a game! We're entitled to a treat once in a while."

"I'll accept that as a confession," Setanta said. "For feeding in a manner not permitted by targeting a child and killing two uncontracted witches unprovoked, I pronounce you guilty."

Catrina started to stand to protest, but Angela hit her hard on the shoulders, forcing her back down to her knees.

"Mr. Kelly: their lives are yours. You may choose to take them using the method of your choice, or you may choose to delegate one of my people to stand as the executioner. If you wish to show mercy, I will sentence them to a single lifetime of seventy-five years entombed in a silvered coffin as payment for the mortal life you lead suffering from what they took from you. The choice is yours."

Lochlan looked stunned. Marcelle could only imagine what he was thinking. And she knew what she herself was thinking; of the options, Marcelle wasn't sure which was crueler. A week grounded in a coffin was harsh. A year was maddening. After seventy-five years, they would be broken beyond sanity. Most sentenced to such extreme punishment killed themselves when released. Setanta was making quite the statement with his sentence, and the tale of the trial would spread throughout the vampire world for that alone. Anyone considering whether or not to attack mortals illegally would, at the very least, hesitate.

"I want to kill them," Lochlan said, his voice confident with resolve.

"Lochlan," Danior said, disappointment in his voice. "You don't need to do that. You don't need to follow their rules. Let them take care of their own. Wash your hands of them. It's your chance to find peace. Maybe even learn to forgive and move on."

"No. They don't deserve forgiveness. I'll move on when I get justice. These bastards are mine. They killed my parents. Look at me, Dad. Take a good look at what they did to me. Every bite they inflicted I've been wearing on my skin my whole life, so I know what they did and why they deserve to die. I will never forget it. I've been dreaming of this for fifteen years." Lochlan pushed past his father, flames growing along his scarred arms.

"L-let's not be too hasty," Catrina stammered. Lochlan stared, disbelieving the moment was there before him. But his eyebrows knitted together as his expression darkened, mind decided. Heat washed the room in a wave of power, a prelude to the fire to come.

"Squeal, pigs," he spat at the guilty vampires, who looked up at him with terror.

Lochlan's flames shot out in a stream from his arms. The vampires were engulfed, shrieking and twisting as if they could fight their way out of the fire, fight off the death that they had been sentenced to. Lochlan stopped, panting, the charred vampires screaming and twitching as their blackened skin smoldered. It hadn't been enough to sufficiently damage their hearts or heads to kill them, leaving them in agony.

But Lochlan wasn't finished. With a cry of pure rage, he shot out the flames again. They blazed so hot they burned blue as his hair, and the shrieking vampires soon were silenced, their ashes turning to dust in the continuous blast. When Lochlan finally stopped the fire, he was shaking, staring at the spot where two scorch marks were left on the marble floor. Air above it warped with waves of heat in the afterglow of the attack, evidence of his raw power far beyond the average pyromancer. The power of the blood of Danaan, the same blood that ran in Setanta's veins.

The room was silent but for the beating of mortal hearts and the labored breathing of the fire witch. Marcelle recognized something in his expression. A familiar numb satisfaction. She remembered killing her father, the relief she'd felt in ridding the world of his abuse. In taking revenge for the cruelty he'd inflicted on others in his life. Whatever Danior, a disturbed looking

Sarai, and the other witches thought of vampire justice, Marcelle was happy for Lochlan. And she hoped he could move on to a more fulfilling life.

Lochlan looked up, sparks still hopping off his skin like they would off a campfire, the air thick with the smell of smoke and burnt flesh. He locked eyes with Setanta.

"I guess I could have worse cousins." He bowed, a little mockingly, a lopsided grin on his face. "Thanks." Setanta nodded in acknowledgement. The witch then stood upright, turned on his heel, and left the room, every vampire present giving him as much space as they could.

There was a smirk in Setanta's eyes, and an aura of fear and respect from the vampires in the room. Aside from satisfying the need for vengeance, Marcelle knew there was one more positive aspect to the display Lochlan had put on in executing the vampires for them. Knowingly or not, he had just demonstrated to numerous vampire world leaders that Setanta had immense power in his new allies not only at his beck and call, but now in his debt. Despite the pureblood family being a small one with few living members in comparison to others around the world, Setanta would be taken very seriously. All according to plan.

Chapter Twenty-Three: Petition to the King

Sarai was headed up to Marcelle's room to change into clothes that didn't smell like a fire pit and toasted vampire when she bumped into Artemisia in the halls, to her great discomfort.

"Hello," the girl said, blinking her large red eyes. Sarai nodded towards her and tried to walk past, but Artemisia wanted to have a conversation. So, Sarai stopped.

"Hey. Uh, do you need something?"

"Yes. You're friends with the fire witch from the trial?"

"I wouldn't say friends, but I know him."

"He's shooting my mom's apples in the garden. You should tell him to stop before she finds him and he gets hurt."

Sarai gulped. Two people she knew should absolutely not meet were ex-Queen Giovanna and Lochlan. "Thanks for the heads up. I'll go get him." She rushed off to the garden where a few apple trees stood. She'd eaten from them before and if she'd known they were Giovanna's, she'd have never come near them.

Lochlan was right where Artemisia said he would be, throwing apples as hard as he could into the air and shooting them with his bow and flaming arrows. She wasn't sure when he'd gotten the weaponry, but he certainly knew how to make good use of it.

"Dude, you need to leave the apples alone," she said, glancing around as if she were afraid Giovanna would jump out from the bushes.

He ignored her, picked a new apple off the tree, and chucked it into the air before blasting it out of the sky with a flaming arrow.

"I'm not joking around. They belong to the ex-queen and she's a total bitch with some freaky mind-control thing going on."

Mind control would make anyone pause. Lochlan nodded and allowed her to lead him to a bench to sit down, where he held out his hand and shrunk his bow down to pocket size to put it away in his cargo pants. That explained how he'd gotten in with it.

"They took me off the team," he said unprompted.

"What team?"

"The Vasi murder team. Dad and the captain, they said I'm too into this and need to take time to cool down. 'Cause of what I did back there. Just when things are getting interesting and we're going after Vasi for a change instead of sitting around to get picked off."

"Well, they probably took you off because you just called it the Vasi murder team."

He shot her a glare. "What, you think we should let them all go free to keep killing and enslaving us?"

"No, no. Not what I meant," she said. Sarai sighed. She couldn't fault him. She'd once been given her own Vasi prisoner to kill by Setanta and Marcelle, an alleged doctor who had terrified her and butchered other witches before her. Even if she hadn't gone through with it, she wasn't sad the man was dead. She knew what the Vasi did and why they deserved to be hunted. There was no reasoning with a group of people whose goal was to wipe her kind off the face of the world. They were at war, whether other witches wanted to admit it or not. Lochlan had a soldier's heart. He wouldn't accept being sidelined during a war.

"They need me," Lochlan insisted. "You know as well as I do how few and far between real gifts like ours are. The stuff that can go on the offensive. I mean, my dad's ability to make people tell the truth is great for a leader, but he's a pin cushion in a fight. All my adopted siblings have gifts that are just as useless. One sees in the dark. The twins can breathe underwater. My older brother can sense metal. Not even move or manipulate, just sense it. Great if you're a fifth century peasant trying to find a vein of copper to mine, but useless now. You get the idea. What I can do can make a difference. There's not a lot of free pyros left, you know. We've been targets for centuries 'cause we're so damn flashy."

"Yeah, I get it. There's not a lot of necromancers out there. I'm not even a full-blown one." Strong witches were an endangered group, she realized. No wonder her father was so obsessed with enhancing and preserving power. "They could use someone who can do more than sense that they're about to get shot," Sarai admitted.

"Exactly!" He slumped against the bench. "I got to finally torch the bastards who killed my parents, and I get my own ass fired for it."

She half laughed at the pun, then furrowed her brow in thought. "You know," she said. "If you got fired from one group, maybe get hired by another?"

"What, join a different coven? No one else is actively fighting back against Vasi."

"Vampires are."

Lochlan opened his mouth to protest, then closed it.

Then opened it again, and closed it again, doing an impression of a fish out of water. He leaned forward in thought, then shook his head. "I don't know, Sarai. That's not my thing."

"That's not what I heard." She gave him a knowing look and he blushed.

"Shut up. It was one time. It's never happening again."

"Yeah, but last time I saw you, you called me a traitor for it. I had to."

He looked at her sheepishly. "Maybe I shouldn't have said that. Sorry."

Sarai smirked, feeling vindicated.

"But just because I..." He stopped before admitting he'd had sex with Marcelle. "Just because that happened doesn't mean I want to be buddies with vampires, you know. Fine, maybe they're not all as bad as I thought. And I never would have guessed they had actual rules to follow like decent people. I'm kinda a fan of Setanta's idea of justice. But come on."

Sarai shrugged. "They're going to be working with the Ellis Coven anyway, right? You wouldn't even be changing who you're working with, just maybe putting on a different uniform."

"I guess. It's not the worst idea in the world. And I'd still get to take the fight to the Vasi. That's what I want," Lochlan said. "You think they'd let me?"

"As long as you don't try to blow them up."

He snorted. "Yeah, fair. Just... joining them. I had some issues with Moretti when I joined the guard when I was eighteen. She asked what I was going to do to make others respect me." He rolled his eyes. "I'm a goddamn pyromancer, and she wanted to know what I would do to make people respect me? Bitch, I make *fire*." He shot off a few bolts of fire from his fingertips into the ground in front of them.

"What, was it because you were a kid?"

"Ha, that's cute. It's because I'm trans and had just started wearing a binder at the time," he said. "Think I'd have that issue here? Marcelle didn't seem to mind. Said I wasn't, you know, her first."

Sarai shook her head. That didn't surprise her at all, coming from Marcelle, though she was a little surprised at the reveal from Lochlan and had the distinct notion she was the only one in the vampire palace who didn't know without being explicitly told. That aside, she doubted there was any sexual experience the vampire woman didn't have.

"I don't think anyone cares. I just met this prince from another vampire kingdom who wore a ballgown to the coronation. They let vampire girls get married to each other here, even though that's illegal for humans. The way Marcelle explained it to me, they can all kinda sense what other people are feeling by reading our reactions. So, if you were miserable all the time trying to be someone you're not, that would upset them more."

"No kidding?" Lochlan looked almost impressed. "I would have thought they'd be way more old-fashioned."

"They can be, just not about that. Like, put electricity in every room, it's not that hard. The only issue here for us is not being undead. Come on, let's go find Marcelle, we can ask her about it."

Marcelle was found socializing with some foreign vampires Sarai didn't recognize in the main entrance hall, and Sarai felt a little bad to pull her away, but the woman looked relieved to have to say goodbye.

"Sarai, just who I hoped to see," Marcelle said and gave her a kiss. "I was wondering where you'd gone off to."

"We need to ask you about something," Sarai said, not waiting at all. "Lochlan wants to be part of your team. Fighting Vasi."

Marcelle looked as if she'd been given an early birthday present. "*You* want to be part of *my* team?"

"My dad and the captain kicked me off ours," he explained.

"I see. Well, if you were a vampire, I could give you a fast-tracked promotion—"

"Fuck no," he interjected. "Alive or not at all. I think my firepower is worth it."

"Be that as it is, I'd need special permission," she said. She looked behind her, at a line of vampires waiting to go into the throne room. "Why don't you get in line and make a petition?"

"A petition?"

"To Setanta. The trial was just to kick things off with a bang, the real purpose of today is for the new king to hold court and hear petitions from citizens. But you can get in if you want, make a request to be on my team. Try to be respectful about it, or he will deny you. He's king and has a reputation to maintain, especially with everyone watching."

"Right. Right, all right." He looked sick at the thought. "Gotta bow again, huh? I really hate that."

"That would be a good idea. Maybe kiss his ring."

"No way in hell," hissed Lochlan. Sarai couldn't tell if it was a joke or not, or if Marcelle was playing with him. It was a bit weird to think of bowing to the man she'd slept with the night before, but Sarai decided she could manage that to help the self-conscious fire witch. And it crossed her mind that it would give her points towards her value at Setanta's side to be the one responsible for bringing Lochlan into the vampires' fold. A twinge of guilt struck her. Maybe she had more cunning than she gave herself credit for.

"I'll go with you," Sarai offered. "Won't be as bad if you've got another witch with you, right?"

He didn't look any less sickened but nodded. "My dad is gonna be so pissed."

They stood in line, and it felt like an hour at least before they were at the front and let into the throne room before the court. Sarai bowed her head, and saw Lochlan do the same out of the corner of her eye.

Setanta leaned forward a little on his throne. "I must say, this is a surprise. I assumed our business was concluded for the night. What more have you to say to me, Mr. Kelly?"

"I got fired. Off my team, at the Ellis Coven. They don't want me to be in the guard anymore. They think I'm too..." The witch hesitated.

"Bloodthirsty?" Setanta supplied, amused. Lochlan made a face.

"Yeah. I guess. So, I want to join Marcelle's team. I want to fight Vasi. She said I needed to ask you."

Vampires around the court whispered in response to the request, and Setanta held up a hand to silence them.

"I am intrigued by your proposition," Setanta said. "You realize we have a rather strict hierarchy you would need to respect. And we haven't yet allowed anyone who isn't a citizen of our kingdom and sworn to my service to become a knight of the realm. Certainly, no mortals."

"I don't need this to get crazy. Just want like, an

exchange program or something. I want to barbeque Vasi and I can keep up with you leech-er, vamps. I've got the power for it. If you let me hit back at Vasi, I'll fight for you."

Setanta looked past the witches. "Marcelle, what are your thoughts?"

"I think I can work with him," the vampire said. Sarai jumped a little. She hadn't realized Marcelle was standing right behind them the whole time. "He could be useful, if he agrees to take orders."

"How is he in a fight?"

Marcelle smiled. "I've witnessed him battle firsthand and sparred against him. Not only is he powerful, but he can even be used non-lethally to subdue others. There's this neat little trick he does with ropes made of fire I was lucky enough to experience personally." Setanta raised an eyebrow and Lochlan blushed. It was hard for Sarai to imagine someone other than Setanta doing anything like that, but she knew it had to be a sex thing given Marcelle's tone. "In short, he's powerful and versatile. He meets the requirements well enough, considering his disadvantages as a mortal and his temperament. I will vouch for his abilities as a warrior."

Setanta nodded. "Mr. Kelly, I will permit you to join Marcelle's team of knights temporarily under the condition that you swear an oath akin to military service for the duration of your time on Marcelle's team. Breaking your oath will result in banishment from vampire society. If you target or harm innocent citizens of mine, you will be subject to our laws. I do warn you; our punishments are harsh, draconian even, compared to current human standards. Disobeying orders can mean time imprisoned in a dungeon or worse, depending on the situation. Additionally, in exchange for this service, I will not order any investigation into the alleged vampire hunts you conducted in the past and will grant amnesty regarding those possible crimes against my people."

Sarai glanced at Lochlan. She'd almost forgotten that it was possible he'd targeted vampires who hadn't deserved it in the past, considering how he assumed Marcelle had hurt her when they first met. The look on his face said he knew Setanta had a point. Community service seemed like a light sentence from the king who had just that night sentenced two of his own people to fiery death. All that aside, the rest sounded perfect for the hotheaded pyromancer. He was a fighter, and Marcelle would be able to direct that passion into something positive.

"I think that's fair, all considered?" Setanta said.

Lochlan wiped smoking palms on his pants legs, shifting nervously. "An oath of service. You want me to be your soldier."

"It is you who requested to be a soldier by petitioning to join Marcelle's team. We are not a handful of guards protecting a small island, Mr. Kelly. This is not an after-school club to join on a whim. We are warriors in service of a kingdom. The Vasi are waging war on us, and we will meet them. You will see battle; of that I have no doubt. If you cannot respect our ways, you may leave."

Lochlan nodded. "Okay. I guess that's fair, yeah. I had to swear to protect people to get on the guard with the Ellis Coven, so it makes sense. What am I swearing, exactly? I like to read contracts before signing, you know."

Setanta thought for a moment, then replied, "Will you swear to obey orders from your commander and from me, to never fight a vampire unless in self-defense or for non-lethal training purposes, and to use your abilities to work towards the goals set for you by Commander de Sauveterre in defense of New Ulster?"

Lochlan nodded. "Yeah. As long as those goals involve torching up some Vasi, I'm good with that. I... swear by your terms."

Setanta looked at Angela. "Would you be willing to impart your blade? Another can be forged for you."

"I prefer the rapier anyway," she said and unfastened a sheathed dagger from her waist. It looked similar to one that Sarai had seen Marcelle wear, with a hound's head on the hilt. Angela stepped forward and handed it to Lochlan.

"What is this?" he asked, unsheathing the dagger to inspect it. He seemed pleased, and Sarai thought with some amusement that it was a significant upgrade to the switchblade he had once pulled on Marcelle.

"A silver dagger. Treat it with care and wear it at your belt. It is a symbol that marks you as a member of Marcelle's team." Setanta stood, spear in hand. "Kneel."

Lochlan hesitated, his expression tight with displeasure. "Oh, come on."

Setanta raised an eyebrow. "Kneel, Lochlan Kelly. That *is* an order."

The fire witch looked around him, at all the expectant and waiting people. Sarai could see the wheels turning in his head, debating if it was worth it or not. If he should renege on his oath already. After a pregnant pause, he got to one knee, not breaking eye contact with the pureblood king, a silent warning not to push him into anything too humiliating.

Setanta held out his spear, like a sword, and tapped Lochlan on his shoulders as he spoke. As the witch listened, his expression softened to one of near awe. "For the duration of your service, I will grant you temporary knighthood under the tutelage of Knight Commander Marcelle de Sauveterre. I charge you to defend against the Vasi. You are to be my shield for the innocents they target with your valor, your gift, and your life if need be; to be my sword in the hearts of those who would threaten the peace of New Ulster; and to be my hearth to our allies and for those who need our protection. Lochlan Kelly, do you swear to be my shield, sword, and hearth as a temporary knight in service of New Ulster and of its king?"

Lochlan took a deep breath and let it out. "Yes. I swear."

"Then arise, Sir Lochlan Kelly, the first mortal knight of New Ulster."

As Lochlan stood, applause filled the room. He looked uncertain, but a little pleased with the positive attention, and with the recognition of his abilities.

"Thank you," he said. It sounded genuine.

"Congratulations," Sarai said, patting him on the shoulder. He looked down at the dagger in his hands, then up at Setanta again.

"I really do appreciate this chance. Thank you." He took a deep breath, then bowed, much more respectfully than he had before. "I won't let you down."

As they left together, Lochlan pulling out his silver dagger and touching the edge experimentally, Marcelle took Sarai's arm and leaned over to murmur in her ear.

"I can assume this was your idea?" the vampire asked.

Sarai nodded, proud of herself while also guilty. Was it a good thing that she'd put the idea into Lochlan's head when he so hated vampires? If he snapped on them or caused problems, it was indirectly her fault. She didn't like that feeling.

"Very nice. I'm impressed," Marcelle said. "We'll make one of us out of you yet."

One of them, worthy of being their queen. Sarai was both unnerved and proud of herself. Perhaps she would make for a good queen of New Ulster? The future was shaping up to be very interesting indeed.

Chapter Twenty-Four: Doda

After the excitement with Lochlan, Sarai had assumed the most interesting part of her night had been concluded. Hannah pulled her aside to prove that thought wrong. She expected a lecture about Lochlan, but there was something more pressing that the witch wanted to discuss.

"I have someone who wanted to meet you, now that word about who you are has circulated more widely around the coven," Hannah said. "You know that our coven takes in, well, a wide variety of witches, many of whom feel they need to escape from bad situations or who feel they don't belong where they came from. It took a bit of time to put the pieces together, since you're known as the Reinhart girl, but the woman who made your prosthetic hand wanted to meet you."

They stopped in front of one of the drawing rooms, but Sarai couldn't see past Hannah as she held her hands. "I know that you have a difficult time with your family, but I hope the idea of family isn't something that is painful to you?"

"I mean, my mother's dead ghost is following me around," Sarai joked.

"We'll try to work on that after this, if you'd like," Hannah said.

"Sounds good to me."

"But family. Is it a difficult topic?"

"As long as it's not my dad's side of the family, I guess," she said. "I like the idea of a family. I just don't have any real experience with it."

Hannah smiled and led her into the room. Two women, perhaps in their late thirties, stood up from the couch, both their eyes wide and excited. One woman was a short, Middle Eastern woman with curly, black hair peeking out slightly from under a colorful, paisley *mitpahat* headscarf, light brown skin, and brown eyes, who wore a loose shirt with elbow-length sleeves and a floor-length skirt. The other was much taller and also looked Middle Eastern, with darker brown skin and nearly black eyes, but wore a colorful, embroidered, dark red hijab so none of her hair was visible, along with a long-sleeve shirt under a short-sleeved shirt and comfortable looking mom-jeans.

"Sarai?" the first woman asked with a thick Hebrew accent. "Oh, you must be. Look at her, she has to be."

"I'm Sarai, yes. Who are you?"

The woman glanced at Hannah.

"I haven't told her yet. I thought I would leave that to you two," Hannah said.

"Right, of course, thank you." The woman approached and took Sarai's hands in hers, caressing them as if they knew each other. Something about her face looked so... familiar. So comfortable. The nervous smile on her lips made Sarai feel happy. "Sarai, I'm your *Doda* Mazal. You know what *doda* means, *ken*? Yes?"

"My... my aunt?" Sarai's eyes widened. "My aunt, Mazal?" That was why she looked so familiar. Mazal and Liora looked like sisters. They *were* sisters.

"Yes!" Mazal threw her arms around her, holding her close. "You look just like her, just like Liora."

"I could say the same to you," Sarai said.

"Let me look at you," Mazal said as she pulled back. "Oh, how beautiful you are. When I heard, I could not believe. Didn't I say? I said, a Meir witch, who is a Reinhart? It cannot be, could not be. But then look at you! Oh, your *ima* would be so happy to see you, such a grown-up girl, such a beautiful and brave girl. Only Liora's girl would be so brave as to be here with vampires, that is the truth." She wiped a tear from her eye.

"I didn't know my mother had any siblings."

"We have more. Two brothers, Ezra and Chaim. Ezra lives with the coven, but Chaim stayed in the Negev, where all the good Meirs who haven't disgraced the family stay." Mazal laughed. "Speaking of which, please, please, come, come. I want you to meet…" She looked up nervously. "The rumor is you and one of the vampire women, you are in a relationship?"

"Uh, yeah. Marcelle. We've been on a few dates."

The two women giggled. "Your grandmother would be so angry. Well then, this is Zeinab. She is also your *doda*."

Also her aunt? Then, that meant… "Oh! So, you two are a couple?"

Zeinab smiled. "You can see why we might not have been welcome with our families," she said. Unlike Mazal, she had an English accent.

"Just a few reasons," Sarai joked. An interfaith lesbian couple contending with traditional Jewish and Muslim families would not go over well, she imagined.

Hannah left the three, and they sat down together. Sarai learned more about her family than she ever expected to know. She knew that her mother was a

Sephardic Jew, but that had such a wide potential for geographic origins. It turned out that her grandmother had come from Morocco while her grandfather had come from Iraq, settling in the Negev with a witch coven that was much more orthodox than Sarai had suspected. Hidden from the mundane world, they could be open about practicing magic and it was there in the Negev Coven where Sarai's grandparents met and fell in love. It was reaffirming and validating to learn about her family's history. About *her* history. To learn that she came from two long and proud lines of Jewish witches who had survived so much hardship.

She learned about how her mother had wanted to go to America to learn more about the world and go to college one day, which Sarai's grandparents had disapproved of. Then one day, Liora stopped all contact, never to be heard from again. Sarai was able to fill in the sad details about what had happened, how the Reinhart coven had imprisoned her, about the circumstances that lead to Sarai's birth. How Liora died trying to protect her.

Mazal wept to know for sure her older sister had died, but stated she was proud of her.

"Oh, I have something for you. Something Liora would want you to have," Mazal said, blowing her nose, then dabbing tears and stuffing her tissue into her pocket. "It, well, we talked about this a lot. We have a little girl, see, and we thought maybe we would give it to her one day."

"I have a cousin?" Sarai asked.

"Yes, her name is Yaffa Ali-Meir. She's only a little girl, so I didn't bring her here because of all the vampires, but you should meet her one day. Our little girl. Well, mine, biologically. Technically she might be considered a clone? I could have done the spell with Zeinab's DNA incorporated, but that wasn't an option for us. Still, we might have another little girl in the future."

"Oh, wow, that's some intense magic," Sarai said, impressed by her aunt's skill. "Not a little boy?"

"No, the spell can only work with what we have," Mazal said. "There's not a Y chromosome in sight in my genome, so we can only have girls."

"There's spells like that?" Sarai asked.

"It took some time to develop. Having healing magic was a good baseline, but it was all spellcraft and potions skills. Zeinab was so helpful."

"You're too sweet, *habibti albi*. Your healing powers were what helped it work. I just didn't get in your way; I'm no witch."

That was surprising. "You're not?" Sarai asked. "Sorry, I just assumed."

"No, I could never participate in magic. That's why Yaffa is an adopted daughter to me, and I couldn't be involved in that spell," Zeinab said. "But loving a witch…" A gentle smile appeared on her face. "Love is love, as they say. You can't fight true love."

"I'm just trying to wrap my mind around that. So, if you drink a potion and have healing powers and do this spell, you can have a baby without a dad? Or with two women? That's amazing."

"My understanding is that it's a little more complicated than that, but yes," Zeinab said. "I keep my distance from Mazal's magic business."

"I suppose I could have a boy if we were willing to pick a man to donate, mix his DNA in with mine?" Mazal mused.

Zeinab scoffed. "Who needs men when I have you? Besides, I'd rather Yaffa's sibling be a full sibling, not half. Three parents are too many to put on a birth certificate."

"Oh, but we're off topic," Mazal said. "We need to give you your gift."

Zeinab picked up a large package and held it out to Sarai. "Your grandma gave this to Mazal, before she left the coven and disgraced the Meir name by loving a Muslim woman, and we've been keeping it all these years. It should have been Liora's, since she was the older sister. With you alive, we felt it would be best given to you."

Sarai lifted the lid, and her heart skipped a beat. Inside was a dress. It wasn't as stunning and elaborate as the dress she'd been given by the vampires, but it held a sort of mystical power with its bold, golden, spiral embroidery on a rich, black velvet. Just looking at it, she could feel that it was old. Maybe even magical in some subtly cosmic way. It wasn't unheard of for protective spells and good luck magic to be woven into elaborate clothes passed through families. Also in the package, among the many pieces that made up the dress such as the wrap skirt, bodice, short jacket, and separate flowing sleeves, was what looked like a tall crown covered in small pearls and a few colorful stones. "What is this?" she whispered.

"A berberisca dress with all the bells and whistles," Mazal said. "It belonged to my *ima*. Your *safta*. She brought it with her from Morocco, where it was gifted to her by her father. It's for brides, for a ceremony the night before a wedding, and for important ceremonies. Used to be a wedding dress too, but not so much now."

A dress that belonged to her grandmother, a gift from her great-grandfather, all the way from Morocco. A family heirloom, given to her from family members who didn't hate her or want to use her. Who just wanted to be family. Tears swelled in Sarai's eyes, and she leaned forward, hugging the couple tight.

"Thank you. You have no idea... I've never had anything of my mom's. Of my family's. This means so much to me."

"*Titchadshi*. Wear it in good health," Mazal said. "For your *ima*."

"It might be more timely than you'd think," Sarai said with a nervous laugh as she touched the gold embroidery, then glanced up at the religious headscarves from two different cultures on both the women. They had to be religious enough for such tradition to matter to them, which meant there was a chance they wouldn't be open to the idea of a marriage with a vampire. Or two.

"What do you mean?" Zeinab asked.

"I... might be getting married."

Both the women stared.

"To the vampire woman?" Mazal asked.

Sarai's gut twisted with nervousness. How was saying she was going to marry the vampire king so much more awkward than admitting to a relationship with Marcelle? "So, vampires do things a little weird. I'm still with Marcelle, but she's also kinda the new king's mistress. And, um, Setanta, the king..."

"That bastard," Hannah exclaimed from the doorway. All three turned to look at her, not having noticed when she'd returned. "You can't be serious. Are you engaged to Setanta? Whatever for?"

"Well, the idea was mentioned that he needed a marriage for alliance purposes. To make a statement to other vampires who won't accept witches easily. What's a bigger statement than marrying one? And I'm one of the few who could have a kid with him safely, so…"

"This is ridiculous," Hannah snapped. "No, I will be having words with that man. I don't care what kind of king he thinks he is, but this is unacceptable."

"It's my choice," Sarai said as she stood, clutching her grandmother's dress.

"You haven't thought about the gravity of something like that, I guarantee," Hannah said. "Is this about having a place to stay? You know you can have a place with us."

"If you need a home, we would be happy to have you," Zeinab added. "I know you've had some trouble with your other family before, but we aren't like that."

"No, I know. I mean, you guys are great. And I'd love to come over for dinner sometime to meet my cousin and get to know you both better. But I do want to do this, and it's not about just trying to have a nice place to live."

"Though the place is nice," Zeinab murmured, glancing around at their opulent surroundings.

"What is it then?" Hannah demanded.

How did she explain it all to a witch? It had made so much sense when she spoke to Setanta and Marcelle. "It's sort of an arranged situation. But it was my idea. It helps other witches by making us important to other vampires."

"Sarai, are you trying to sacrifice yourself to a vampire for the sake of other witches?" Mazal said. "Please, don't think you need to do that. No one would expect that of you."

"Yes. No. I mean, I'm not sacrificing myself. And I do love Marcelle. She means more to me than anyone else ever has. I lost my hand protecting her, for fuck's sake." The look on Mazal and Zeinab's faces in response to the profanity made her apologetic. "Sorry. But, well, Marcelle loves Setanta. And Setanta has been kind to me, even if he is a little overwhelming. He's making the announcement soon."

"We'll see about that," Hannah snapped. "I could understand if it was Marcelle. I've seen the way you two look at each other. Even with her, it's far too soon. But Setanta? And think of the age gap! He's clearly taking advantage of you."

"So was Bear taking advantage of you last night?" Sarai retorted. "I think there's an age gap there of about a thousand years or so."

Hannah's eyes widened and her wrinkled face blushed as she took a step back. "I... No, it doesn't matter. It's not the same situation. I'm not marrying Bear."

Sarai shrugged. "Your choice. And this is mine. Come on, think about it for a minute. Generally speaking, vampires don't respect witches. They look at us and see pretty party favors or comedians. If they saw one of us as," she took a deep breath then continued, "as their queen, then it would force them to give us more respect. Vampires are old-fashioned. This is a way that they would see the alliance as valid and worth honoring."

Hannah pursed her lips. "I'm going to talk to Setanta," she finally said, and stormed off.

"Our niece Sarai, queen of the vampires," Zeinab said. "I can't say that was news we expected to hear."

"Liora would be laughing at how much it would make *ima* mad," Mazal said. "You have no idea how much like her you are. Sarai, queen of the vampires. *Sarai, malka ha'alukim.* It does sound interesting. And, well, I'm not one to judge a match between two individuals whose people have a history not liking each other."

Zeinab shook her head. "I think it's a bit different, but yes, we would be hypocrites to decry an unconventional relationship others might frown upon. It sounds as if you have a very unconventional situation on your hands. With this Marcelle and also this Setanta. My concern is you're marrying Setanta, but you're in love with Marcelle?"

"Marcelle's my girlfriend, but Setanta..." Sarai's voice trailed off. A brilliant idea struck her. "Your spell. The one you used for your daughter. Could you make it work for three people?"

The couple exchanged glances. "I'm not sure I should get that involved," Mazal said. "And these are vampires. I don't know if it would even work."

"Please, could I just have the spell?" Sarai begged. "I love Marcelle. If I'm going to have kids, if there's a way for them to have Marcelle as their mother too, that would be amazing. You have to let me have the option. At least to see if it would work and ask if they would go for it."

Zeinab sighed. "You did give the spell to Greg and Oliver, to use with their surrogate. And Amy and Liz. And the Victorias. It's not like you've been keeping it to yourself."

Mazal knitted her brow. "All right. But don't use it immediately. Think about this more, make sure it's what you want. Children are very permanent. When is the wedding?"

"Well." Sarai gave a nervous laugh. "Soon. Tonight is to announce the engagement, then there's some formalities and stuff for tomorrow. And probably by the end of the week, before all the vampires go back to their countries and stuff. Though I'd honestly prefer a smaller crowd."

"That is pretty immediate," Zeinab said with visible discomfort. "Are you sure you love Marcelle enough for this? And you trust Setanta?"

"I gave up my right hand for Marcelle. And kinda also for Setanta. They're the only people I've ever felt right with."

Mazal thought, toying with a gold star of David charm around her neck, then sighed. "I'll get you the spell. I'll need a pearl."

That was no problem. Marcelle had tons of jewelry, so snagging a pearl would be easy.

Sarai grinned. It would be amazing to present the option to Marcelle. "And could you both come to the wedding? It would mean so much to me to have you there. I don't know how vampire weddings go, but I'd rather you two walk me down the aisle if there is one. If you're okay with that?"

"Walk my sister's only daughter down the aisle at her wedding?" Mazal asked. She kissed Sarai on the forehead. "My dear, it would be an honor."

Chapter Twenty-Five: The Offer

Marcelle wasn't surprised when Sarai asked to speak with her and Setanta privately. After all, the marriage they had discussed was no small thing. There was queen consort potential in the girl. She had the strength to meet vampires stronger than her head-on, and that was a prerequisite. But whether Sarai would want to be involved in their world on such a permanent basis or if she would walk back the decision, Marcelle didn't know. Still, she hoped.

"I have something," Sarai said, excitement in her eyes. "For both of you. Well, for you, Marcelle."

"For me?" Marcelle asked.

"You want to be Setanta's queen, right?"

Marcelle sighed at the sore point. "If you're worried I would be jealous, not of you. Not at all. I know that I'm dead, Sarai. I can't carry children. I know my place, and I'm happy with it."

"You can't have kids, but I can. But would you want kids? If you could?"

Marcelle shrugged. "It doesn't matter, I can't have children." It was starting to be annoying. "If you're asking if I would want to be involved in helping you, then yes. I do... I do find them precious. I don't think I was a very good mother, but I adored my little girl."

"But what if I said you could have children? With Setanta?"

Marcelle's mouth went dry. She looked at Setanta, and he looked just as confused as her.

"I don't think we follow your train of thought," Setanta said. "Undead cannot have children. There's no solution to that. The men can't create new sperm, and women can't ovulate or change according to the needs of a pregnancy. Only the living can become parents."

Sarai grinned. "Well, I just met my lesbian aunts from the Ellis Coven. And they have a daughter. Apparently, all you need to become a parent with modern magical advancements is DNA." She revealed a small mason jar that held some sort of dark tea and a single pearl at the bottom. "So, if you each contribute to this, we'll have a baby. A baby that's from all three of us."

Marcelle felt numb at the offer. Never in her wildest dreams had she imagined such a thing could ever be possible. "I, I need a moment." She sat down. Her hands were shaking, so she gripped the edge of the chair, denting the wood.

Setanta took the jar from Sarai, examining it. "This is… new. They made this themselves?"

The witch nodded. "Well, one of them did. The other isn't a witch."

"She must be a very talented spellcaster indeed. This is complex."

"I could be a mother again." But Marcelle had failed so horrifically with her first born, placing the girl in the care of family who then sold her to a life of prostitution, which led to her death. Did a mother who had lost her daughter in such a terrible way deserve a second chance? What if something happened to the new child, and it was her fault? "I'm not good enough."

Setanta knelt and took her hands in his, caressing the

backs of her hands with his thumbs. "Because of Henriette?"

"What if I fail again?" she whispered. Even as she said the words, she felt ridiculous, speaking to him. She had a single daughter who died. Setanta had lost far more. "How do you do it? How do you take that risk?"

"I didn't, for two thousand years," he admitted. "From Connla to Boudicca... Not since Boudicca. You know that. And now. Now I must. It's my duty to keep the bloodline strong, to protect the made vampires of my blood by ensuring they have a good leader and protector should something happen to me. But it's not your duty and I would never ask it of you."

Marcelle looked down at their hands together. They'd had so many adventures together, so many experiences. The idea of this new adventure was terrifying. And yet, somewhere in her unbeating heart, she craved it.

"When you first turned me and I told you about my daughter, you promised to help me raise her," Marcelle whispered. "Give her a good home. Comfort. An advantageous marriage. That she'd never go hungry, never know sickness. I wanted to raise Henriette with you. I had such beautiful fantasies in my head for that one night of blissful ignorance."

"I did promise. I can give you those fantasies." He held out a hand to Sarai, who stepped forward and took it, kneeling next to him on the floor. "We can give you that fantasy."

"Sarai..." Marcelle slid off the chair and embraced the little witch, holding her tenderly. "You would do this for me? For us?"

"I love you," Sarai said, pulling back to look into

Marcelle's eyes. "I know I'm younger than you both. And I know this is fast, but I know I've never felt right anywhere other than in your arms. I want my life to be here."

Marcelle wiped tears from her eyes and nodded. There was no question in her mind. She loved her little witch. She loved how forward she was, how strong she was. She would make a perfect vampire queen.

"And, and Setanta, you always get married for political reasons, right?" Sarai said, looking at the pureblood.

"Yes."

"Have you ever married someone you love?"

"Once, a very long time ago, to a woman named Emer. I've since learned that love is for *affaires de coeur*. Affairs of the heart. Anything else is a luxury."

"Well, then, you should marry Marcelle. She'd be a better vampire queen anyway, since she's actually a vampire. If you have to marry the mother of your child, then marry Marcelle instead of me. Fuck politics, do this for yourselves."

Setanta smiled softly, and kissed Sarai's cheek. "You don't know how much this gift means to me, Sarai. But I don't see why I must limit myself to only one mother of my children. I think I should marry you both." He kissed her lips, then kissed Marcelle's lips.

Marry Setanta, Marcelle thought. *Finally*. No longer the mistress, the highest relationship status she could claim as a made vampire, but his *wife*.

"Now, Sarai. What is involved in this spell?" Setanta asked.

She opened the jar and a smell like old licorice assaulted Marcelle's nose. She almost gagged, grateful

271

she wasn't the one who needed to drink the potion.

"I need a drop of blood from Marcelle," Sarai said.

"Done." The vampire woman scratched a fingertip on her fang and let the red liquid drip into the potion.

Setanta frowned. "You know I can't let you drink my blood."

"Thankfully, I don't need to drink it. So, this is kosher, sorta. But…" Sarai blushed. "It's not your *blood* I need you to give for the spell." Her eyes flickered down between his legs, then back up.

"Ah." He grinned. "Well, I could use a little assistance then. If you two would join me?"

Chapter Twenty-Six: Queen Consorts

Sarai was nervous about the announcement. Becoming Setanta's fiancée in front of the vampire world was daunting. She felt more confident after the approval of Setanta's tea party gathering, but they were the easy ones. She was more afraid of the reaction from purebloods like Giovanna, or the Chinese and Egyptian vampires who were losing out on a chance to marry Setanta. There was also one more person whose response she was nervous about, after Marcelle explained their significance: a druid vampire. She wasn't sure if the vampire was male or female, only that their name was Muach. They wore lose robes that obscured any secondary sex traits, and their head was shaved, with blue tattoos similar to Setanta's and Lugh's covering it and their arms.

As Marcelle explained it, the druid was the head of a caste of priest-like people who passed on the ancient religion Setanta had been born into. They were responsible for approving matches. While her vampire fiancé assured her that his choice would be respected, it was still nerve wracking. What if he was wrong? And there was the detail that she wasn't sure if she should participate if it meant honoring another religion. It crossed her mind for the first time that she was in an interfaith relationship. It helped to have her aunts there as role models, and she was able to ask them how they managed that aspect of their relationship, since Zeinab clearly was a practicing Muslim and Mazal wore a gold Star of David necklace.

"We respect each other and had two wedding ceremonies, one for each faith, with open-minded officiants. And we each teach Yaffa our faiths, and we will let her choose for herself when she's ready," Zeinab answered.

It was a good answer, Sarai reasoned. And a philosophy she would need to adopt if she wanted to go forward with the engagement. A quick talk with Marcelle and Setanta reassured her that she wouldn't be expected to convert to any sort of Druidic religion for Setanta's sake, and he had no qualms about their children being exposed to multiple faiths. It solidified Sarai's decision. She was as ready as she would ever be.

She chose to feel bridal and wore a simple, white, circle-skirt dress with a lace hem that had languished in Marcelle's closet since the fifties, while Marcelle wore a sheath-like, knee-length black one with gold embroidery along the front depicting a Celtic hound. It was minutes before sunrise, and the sky had started to lighten with a thin line of purple growing along the misty mountains of Appalachia.

Every vampire guest, as well as the witches present, gathered outside just beyond the gardens where a circle of standing stones was located. On them had etched writing like in the grimoire Setanta had translated for her, alongside spirals that she had seen in some of his tattoos, and on the druid.

It seemed like a spiritual place, and Sarai was a little nervous that the event was meant to be her wedding. After all, she wanted to wear her new berberisca dress for the event. But Marcelle assured her it was a formal approval and that a handfasting ceremony and celebration would be at the end of the festival.

The vampires gathered around the circle in attendance, and Setanta waited for them in the center, next to the bald druid. He wore a black tunic with a line of gold Celtic embroidery along the hem, his gold torque necklace, and iron crown. Missing was his ponytail, with his red hair open and flowing.

"We are here to judge the worthiness of the bride of CuChulainn, now King Setanta mac Lugh of New Ulster," said the druid, Muach. "Who is your bride?"

There was anticipation in the air like electricity. The Chinese pureblood and Egyptian pureblood vampire women exchanged quick glances, and the handful in attendance who already knew looked at Sarai, waiting.

"I have chosen two women," Setanta announced. The hope on both the eligible pureblood vampires' faces was almost cruel as Setanta extended his hand out to Sarai and Marcelle.

Her heart racing, Sarai took a deep breath and walked forward hand in hand with Marcelle to the center of the circle.

"It is acceptable for you to marry two women," the druid said, but their brow furrowed in disapproval as they looked at Marcelle. "The witch is acceptable. The corpse is not."

Marcelle bristled at the words, but Setanta cut in.

"We have devised a method that will ensure she and Sarai are both shared mothers of my children, by blood. It would be irresponsible to forbid the union of all three of us, as we all will be in equal parts the children's parents."

Sarai squeezed Marcelle's hand to reassure her as Setanta produced the enchanted brew her aunts had given to them, now completed with Marcelle's blood and Setanta's seed. The druid took the potion in their hands and looked it over. Muttering words in ancient Irish, Sarai realized this druid was a witch. The potion glowed a light green, and the druid nodded.

"I see. Then I stand corrected, my king. If your children bear the blood of both these women, I will allow their acceptance as your wives. Let us confirm this new magic."

Sarai breathed a sigh of relief, her heart leaping for joy. The druid turned to her, unscrewed the lid, and held up the potion. Her eyes widened. "Oh. Now?"

She had hoped to wait until after they were married.

"There is no other way to confirm the efficiency of this potion," Muach said. "Such a thing has never been attempted with the undead before."

Sarai accepted the potion and regretfully inhaled. It smelled awful. But it would work. It had to work. She glanced at Setanta.

"It, um, I'm not supposed to drink it. The pearl…"

She'd told him how to do the ritual, but now felt embarrassed. Setanta nodded, looking at the druid.

"Some privacy would be acceptable, for her sake?" Setanta said. It wasn't a request, and the druid nodded.

"You can decline," Marcelle interjected. "Sarai, if this is too much, you can decline, so we can do this in private some other time."

"If I cannot confirm the effects, I cannot accept the vampire," the druid said.

Sarai wouldn't let Marcelle lose her chance. How bad could it be? "No, I'm here. I'm committed. Let's do this."

Muach removed a layer of their robes, revealing only more robes, and they and Marcelle held it up so that between the cloth and the standing stone at the center, none could see Sarai. She glanced up nervously into Setanta's eyes.

"I was hoping for someplace I could relax a little for this," she joked.

"I appreciate your bravery. Let's just be grateful no one insists on bedding ceremonies anymore," he said with a sigh, and backed her up against the standing stone. He took the pearl between his fingers and lifted her dress up. His hand found her sex and she bit her lip, desperately not trying to make noises every vampire would hear. He rubbed against her clitoris a little, and she was instantly wet in his hands. Surely it wasn't the public nature of the act that had her aroused? Or perhaps it was. At least, the lubrication was helpful to reduce pain from the intrusion as his finger pressed inside her and she gripped his arms for support as it moved deep. She remembered the spell instructions and was nervous as he pressed against her cervix. Mazal had warned her to do it lying down, someplace she could recover afterwards. That she was still working on a magical way to include pain relief in the spell, since she'd used a separate cream that took longer to craft than the potion to cause numbness when she'd done the spell for herself. Sarai had hoped to wait for Mazal to be able to get that cream to her.

It seemed that wasn't an option anymore. But how bad could it be?

"Take a deep breath," he warned, and she nodded, obeying. Pain shot through her as the pearl was forced into her womb, and she felt a cramping like the worst period pain she'd ever experienced in her life, forcing a cry from her as she held onto Setanta, her nails digging into his tattooed arms. He pulled his hand free and held her gently for a few moments as she took deep breaths, doing her very best to hold back tears. All she wanted to do was double over on the ground and sob. She couldn't let herself cry in front of the vampire guests.

If a tiny pearl being pushed passed her cervix hurt so much, how was she ever expected to push out a baby? She'd thought her healing gift would perhaps spare her the pain, but that had been proven false. She resolved to accept any and all pain relief options presented to her when the time came.

With her dress pulled back down, Setanta pulled down the cloth covering and revealed Sarai to the gathering. She put on a brave face to hide the cramping pain as best she could and her healing gift kicked in, making it more bearable.

The druid stepped forward and traced a spiral with their finger in the air in front of Sarai. They focused, then nodded.

"I will accept both your choices, my king," Muach said.

Sarai smiled weakly at Marcelle, who looked ready to cry tears of joy. Setanta held out his free hand to the vampire woman, who stepped forward.

"I would like to present to you, your future queen consorts of New Ulster, Marcelle de Sauveterre and Sarai Meir."

The loudest applause came from Mazal and Zeinab, and from Celestin, Yrsa, Ryoko, and Felipe, who had already known.

Danior, Hannah, and Moretti clapped, but didn't look as though they approved. Lochlan just stood quietly, as if he weren't sure what to make of the situation.

To Sarai's surprise, the Egyptian queen stepped forward from the crowd. Sarai caught her breath, nervous as to what she might have to say. The woman had been kind and inviting, but that was before knowing that Sarai had stolen away an opportunity from her family.

"It's no great secret that Setanta and I have been negotiating terms for a possible betrothal to my granddaughter, Princess Meritaten," she announced. "And no great secret we as a society have had difficulties interacting with witches. As such, I would like to be the first to offer my sincere blessings to the three of you." She raised her hand as if in a toast, but without the drink. "May your reign be eternal as the stars, your legacy as vast as the sands of the desert."

Sarai was touched. While she didn't consider herself well-versed in her own religion, she had the distinct impression that the blessing was a reference to her Judaism, something about descendants as numerous as the stars and grains of sand and appreciated that detail.

Setanta bowed his head to her, and Queen Arsinoe returned the gesture. It felt good. Right. They had approval from at least some of the vampires. She glanced towards her future father-in-law and sister-in-law, and the former queen, Giovanna, next to them. The ice in her stare could have killed.

Sarai steeled herself, then smiled, gripping Setanta's hand tight. Giovanna glared, then gave a forced smile in return and darted away into the palace. That was fine, Sarai thought. They didn't need her negativity or threats. Avoiding her was going to be for the best. And after making a quick round for congratulations, with the sun rising into the morning sky, Sarai was happy just to follow her fiancés up to Setanta's room to rest.

****

Giovanna had never been so humiliated in her life. Over and over, she imagined how easily she could break the witch Sarai's body and into how many pieces. How fun it would be to rip out her heart to stuff down the throne-stealing slut's throat. But that would break decorum. So, she would have to be rid of Sarai some other way.

It was easy enough to leave the palace without any guards. Everyone assumed she was sulking in her room. But, instead, she'd used a hand mirror and a spell to get in contact with someone who could do something to help.

A public place in the middle of the day was the best meeting spot, so Giovanna picked one of her favorite restaurants. It was as close to an upper-class establishment as could be found locally. Their caviar was a touch too salty, but it would do for a snack. She, of course, was recognized by the staff, who took her to her favorite table overlooking a nearby stream. It didn't compare to Rome, but the view was beautiful in its own quaint way.

"I'm expecting a guest. They may not be dressed appropriately but send them to my table regardless. The meeting should be short and unpleasant, so I would appreciate a mimosa," she instructed the waiter and slipped him a hundred-dollar bill, lingering her fingers against his so that for a moment, he was overwhelmed with the need to worship her. While she could have them all at her beck and call with her power, she preferred to spend her husband's money. At least he could do something good for her. Since the kingdom now belonged to her blasted stepson, it felt even better to splash around their carefully accrued fortune.

She took off her large, designer sunglasses and blinked to adjust to the uncomfortable sunlight. She preferred dusk and night hours, but it was better for her to sneak out during the day. Less vampires would notice. To ensure her presence remained undetected among humans, she had used an eye dropper with a special potion to change her red, pureblood eyes to deep brown. Of course, any vampire who saw her would know who she was, regardless of her eyes.

She heard some commotion at the front, and a blonde, tattooed woman in a black crop top, jeans, and poor-quality prosthetic hand shoved a waitress who tried to tell her there was a dress code. That had to be her.

She nodded to the waiter she'd paid off, and he smoothed over the situation, leading the girl to Giovanna's table.

She looked the queen up and down with a pair of heterochromatic green and brown eyes.

"Well," Giovanna said. "Take a seat, child."

The witch scowled but did as she was told.

"You're the big shot vampire?" she said. "I'm Alma Reinhart. My dad said you had something for us."

"So direct," Giovanna sighed. "No niceties, no hello?"

Alma glared. "I don't do niceties with vampires." She slammed her prosthetic on the table, causing Giovanna's mimosa to slosh and spill a few drops over the edge. The ex-queen frowned. "Last time I had one in front of me, I lost my hand."

"Then you'd better be a good girl and do as I tell you, or you'll lose the other," Giovanna said.

Alma rolled her eyes. "Get to the point."

"You want Sarai, isn't that right? I want her gone."

Alma leaned forward. "You have my attention. What do you have in mind?"

"It's simple. Sarai is protected within the palace by a reverse invitation, if you will. She needs an invitation from a pureblood vampire to be able to leave. And you, of course, can't enter without an invitation."

"All right. So, how do we get me in and her out?"

"I happen to be a pureblood vampire," Giovanna grinned. "We don't get you in, first of all. I will never invite another witch into my palace. But I can invite her to leave in a way that will release her from the protection and lure her from the grounds. Do you think you would be able to handle it from there?"

Alma picked up Giovanna's mimosa and downed it like a shot. The former queen's nose wrinkled in disgust.

"Yeah. I can handle it. Just tell me when and where."

Chapter Twenty-Seven: A Letter and a Pin

When she awoke the next evening, ready for what the night would bring, Sarai was saddened to discover that she would have some time to herself alone. Setanta had to organize some friendly tournament between purebloods, who took such gatherings as opportunities to test their strength against each other, and Marcelle was called away to handle a security issue when it was discovered one of the visiting vampire purebloods had been discovered with a banned substance called ambrosia. Without even questioning, Sarai knew it was the Roman vampire, Valens. Giovanna's brother. It seemed suspicious, but she wasn't surprised Giovanna's brother was the vampire equivalent of a drug addict.

Sarai was told ambrosia acted like vampire catnip and would often lead to vampires becoming violent against humans, hence the ban, so she understood why Marcelle had to tend to the matter. At least it meant that she could have breakfast (or lunch? Who could tell when the day started at sunset) with Rosaline, whom she hadn't seen since she had stormed off, spurned by Bear. Feeling like a bad friend for not checking up on Rosaline sooner, but that she was justified in it considering all the wild developments in her life, she made sure to send word to the human woman as to her new location in Setanta's room.

"I'm still in shock," Rosaline said, shaking her head

as she set out the food for them both. Normally, when the sources who worked at the palace brought meals for Sarai, they didn't bring their own to eat with her, but Sarai had requested it so she could have company and catch up. "I can't believe you actually slept with him. And you're going to be the new queen? I just... wow."

"Trust me, I'm still in shock too," Sarai said, chewing on six pomegranate seeds. "Him and Marcelle... I'm amazed I'm still alive."

"What was it like?" Rosaline shook the chains on his bed, raising an eyebrow. "Did those get used?"

"Not those," Sarai admitted, her cheeks burning. "Some other ones. Leather cuffs. I think I'm kinky?"

"Well, this is the place for it. I've seen some of their collections while cleaning. Honestly, it's a little much for me. Like, a little spanking is cool, but knives? And they have *real* whips? But as long as you're having fun." She winked.

Real whips and knives seemed a little much for Sarai as well, but then... she already let them both make her bleed with their fangs. And the leather floggers spinning in Setanta's expert hands looked interesting to try.

"By the way, I had a great time too," Rosaline said. "Not getting made *queen* anytime soon, but damn did I feel like I was." She laughed.

"Yeah, uh, I wondered how that went," Sarai said, trying to be delicate with her words so that she didn't just blurt out her curiosity about the situation with Bear.

Rosaline sighed. "Well, I did have a nice night with Crispin once he passed guard duty to someone else. I thought..." She shook her head. "Bear's good. Just..."

"What?"

"Can I be honest with you?" she asked, a hint of

some nervousness in her eyes.

"Yeah, of course."

"I'm scared of dying."

That wasn't what Sarai expected to hear at all. "Well, okay, that makes sense. Lots of people are scared of dying," she said, trying to put the pieces together. "Wait, did someone threaten you?"

"No, no. Nothing like that. There's a rule. New Ulster vampires aren't allowed to turn anyone who has a history of serious addiction. Apparently, as a vampire, blood can be like an addictive substance to some and those of us who've... struggled... we lose control easier. They made it a rule at some point in the eighties that you're not allowed to turn someone with a serious addiction history, if you know about it. And if you do, anyone they kill is your responsibility and you get in trouble for it. So. No one is allowed to turn me into a vampire. And I want to be one, Sarai, I want to be one so bad. I've seen some shit. Seen people I know die. I don't want that to be me one day. I don't wanna die."

Sarai didn't know what to say to that. "Um, well, if it helps, there is some kinda afterlife. We don't disappear. I know that for a fact. Witchy stuff." Though if ghosts disappeared after they moved on, she had no idea.

"That's fine, but I like this. Me. I like being me, in this body. Interacting with the real world. And I'm not getting any younger. I've got gray hair starting to come in and I'm not even thirty." She sighed. "I know I've had my problems in the past, but their rule is stupid. I'm clean now. Squeaky clean. They're just discriminating so that they don't have sources begging all the time to be turned. They can be all, 'nope, sorry, I'd love to, but it's company policy.' It's ridiculous."

Sarai wasn't sure what to say to that. She was no expert on addiction or its effects on people, certainly no expert when it came to how it affected vampires. But she did remember the first time she'd seen Rosaline do a feeding for Bear. The girl treated the few drops of vampire blood she got in return to heal like her new drug, if the look on her face had been anything to judge from. But, there was no sense in upsetting her by saying it. "Uh, yeah."

"Bear isn't a New Ulster bloodline," Rosaline continued. "He's from one of the Nordic clans. I mean, sure, he swore the oath to the kingdom and Setanta and all that, but he's not bound by any compulsions. I thought if I could get him to care about me enough, maybe he'd be willing to run away to someplace else with me. Turn me in a kingdom without that rule."

Ohhh.

Sarai nodded in understanding, and Rosaline sniffed a little, wiping her eyes to hide tears. "I know, it's a stupid plan."

Well, the stupid part was the desire to be a vampire if the risk in losing control and killing people would be much worse for her, in Sarai's opinion.

"It's not stupid. Just, well, I don't think he'd do that," Sarai said. "He's a big goof, but I don't think he'd risk something like that. And I don't know if I can see him as the oath-breaking sort."

"Yeah. I… I'll figure it all out some day, I guess," she sighed. "Or I won't. I don't know. I should apologize to him. I do still like him. I don't want him to think I'm a mistake."

"You should probably apologize to Hannah, too,"

Sarai pointed out, and Rosaline made a face.

"Ug, maybe. Whatever. She knows she's old."

"Everyone but us is old here. And you're the one going gray." She smiled a little to indicate it was a joke.

"Touché." Rosaline rolled her eyes. "Oh, speaking of thousand-year-old vampires, I found this on the food tray when I went to pick it up. I think it's from your boyfriend?" Rosaline wiggled her eyebrows as she handed over a parchment letter sealed with black wax and an address to her written in red ink. *Setanta*. It was similar to the letter he had once given her to invite her to the Midnight Festival, though the penmanship was a little sloppier than she remembered.

Sarai quickly opened the letter to read it.

Dear Sarai,

I would like to celebrate our engagement properly. At midnight, I invite you to please follow the main garden path to the third left turn and take that path to the clearing by the creek. I look forward to seeing you.

Sincerely,

King Setanta mac Lugh

Sarai smiled to herself. He must have changed plans to finish with his tournament early, just to celebrate with her.

"What does it say?" Rosaline pressed.

"Oh, um." It felt so weird to talk about Setanta aloud as her fiancé. "I'll tell you later, okay?"

"Come on, you can't leave me hanging."

Sarai shook her head.

"Is it a sex thing?"

Not really, but she had a feeling it could become a sex thing. Sarai nodded and Rosaline giggled.

"Say no more. But I want the deets when you're up

to it."

Sarai nodded. She finished her food and, glancing at the clock, tried to figure out what to wear. Something sexy, just in case. Back in Marcelle's rooms, Sarai found the one pair of black underwear she owned. It wasn't lace like her vampire lover's many sexy pairs, but it was the sexiest thing she'd been comfortable buying since it had come in a pack with several other colors. Then she found a pair of shorts and borrowed one of Marcelle's tight tube tops. Checking her wild hair in the mirror, she went off to the gardens to meet her fiancé under the romantic light of a full moon.

A few vampires out for walks eyed her, but she didn't stop to see if any wanted to talk. Still, one darted to her side to follow her. It was Angela, the blonde-haired Romanian woman.

"Hey," Sarai said.

"Where are you off to?" Angela said, forever the professional guard. "I expected you to be with Marcelle."

"Marcelle's dealing with the ambrosia situation. I got an invitation from Setanta." She blushed, and Angela nodded.

"Congratulations on your engagement, by the way, I don't think I said yet. What is the invitation for?"

Sarai shrugged. "I don't know all the details; I'm just going with the flow right now. He said to meet him at a clearing by a creek."

"He did? That's an unusual choice." Angela frowned. "I'll escort you there. The night is dark. You shouldn't be alone."

Sarai felt a little awkward about having an escort but decided not to argue. There were a lot of vampires at the palace for the festival, and she didn't want to run into someone like Valens alone.

As they stepped into the clearing by the creek, Sarai felt something weird, tingling like magic at the back of her neck. Perhaps it was a magical place? Setanta was a witch, after all.

"When did he say he would meet you?" Angela said, glancing at a slim but expensive looking gold watch on her wrist.

"Midnight is what the letter said."

"A letter? Let me see."

Sarai unfolded the letter, which she'd brought in case she needed help remembering which path to turn on and gave it to the vampire. As she did, Marcelle darted into the clearing.

"What is she doing here?" she said urgently to Angela. "She can't be outside the palace grounds."

Angela frowned. "This is outside the grounds?" She looked back along the path. "Doesn't it end after the creek?"

"Technically, not at this spot," Marcelle said, then took Sarai's hands. "How did you get here? You shouldn't be able to walk past the barrier."

"I-I got a letter from Setanta, to meet him here," she stammered. "Angela has it. Weren't you dealing with Valens?"

"Something was off. He was acting too cocky and mentioned you being all alone without my protection. It was like he was daring me to leave him. Setanta's sparring with Queen Arsinoe right now. Angela, what does it say?"

Angela opened it and frowned as she read, then held it to her nose and inhaled.

"Setanta didn't send this." The wind shifted, and the

two vampires looked up, like bloodhounds who smelled something alarming.

Then, there was a popping noise. Angela's eyes widened and she froze, her face one of shock. Before Sarai could ask what was wrong, a gray, cracking texture covered the vampire's skin, radiating out from a dark spot in the center of her head. With the next brush of a breeze, she disappeared into dust. The letter dropped to the ground; the hands that had held it were gone.

Sarai stumbled back in terror. "Angela?"

Angela couldn't be dead. She couldn't be. She had been standing right there a moment ago. Marcelle crouched as if ready to spring into a fight, her fangs bared.

"Show yourselves!" Marcelle shouted, drawing a gun from the small of her back.

There was another popping noise and pain shot through Sarai's shoulder. She screamed and grabbed it, feeling warm blood soaking her hands. Then, hands grabbed her. Blinded by the pain, she felt for a moment that she had fainted as the ground under her spun and she had the distinct sensation she had been squeezed through a straw. But when she found her feet on the ground again, she was in the back of a car, looking up at her sister, Alma Reinhart. She had been teleported.

"What—"

She didn't have time to process what had happened. Alma stuck a syringe into the side of Sarai's neck and pushed down on the plunger, sending her into dark nothingness.

****

When Sarai awoke, she felt sick to her stomach. The pain had gone from her shoulder, but she felt wrong somehow.

She sat up and something felt heavy on her neck. Silver, locked in place.

"Welcome to the world of the living."

Sarai's blood ran cold. It couldn't be. She'd stopped having nightmares about him. He was gone from her life. She couldn't be hearing his voice.

She turned around to see her father, Alaric Reinhart, standing by a lit fireplace and nursing a glass of whiskey. He was a tall man, to Sarai, and wore his usual tailored suit. He liked tailored suits, liked the respect people gave to him when he wore them. He kept his blond hair dyed to avoid going gray with age and slicked back with too much gel. Next to him, handcuffed to a chair, gagged, and wearing silver that burned her neck black, was Marcelle.

"Dad," she whispered as she stood up, then immediately bent over and vomited, nauseated by both anxiety and whatever drugs her sister had injected her with.

The man made a disgusted face. "On my Persian rug. Really?"

Sarai sputtered a little and wiped her mouth on the back of her hand. Her stomach felt better at least, but she still was in danger.

He sighed and walked away, found a towel from the bathroom, and then threw it at Sarai's feet. "Clean it."

As if she had forgotten every scrap of independence she'd fought for over the past six years of freedom, she knelt to the floor with the towel and obeyed, her hands shaking.

She looked up, locking eyes with Marcelle. There was sorrow there, guilt even. Sarai wanted to rush to her, to pull the collar off. To run away together. But with both of them in silver, it was impossible.

"You know, I couldn't believe it when Alma told me. Vampires. And a vampire girlfriend," Alaric said. "I thought I raised you better than that."

Sarai didn't say anything, just looked down and focused on trying to clean vomit with the towel.

"She's a pretty thing, I'll give you credit for that."

Marcelle gave a muffled grunt and Sarai looked up to see Alaric yanking back the vampire's head by her hair.

"Don't hurt her!" Sarai shouted.

"That depends entirely on you, Sarai." Alaric stood in front of Marcelle, took a sip of his whiskey, then kicked. Marcelle's chair was pushed back onto two legs, and Alaric held her there with his foot, precariously poised over the fireplace. "Are you going to behave, Sarai?"

"Yes, please, just don't hurt her!"

Alaric smiled and set Marcelle's chair back on all fours.

"I have something special planned for you, Sarai. And as long as you cooperate, I won't turn her to dust."

Sarai felt numb. She knew what he had planned for her. The ritual Setanta warned her of, to create a new pureblood line. Human sacrifice and... a sex ritual with some stranger assigned to her. Rape. And if she didn't relent to his plans, Marcelle would pay the price.

I just have to stall, Sarai thought to herself. Buy time, and Setanta would come for them. She had to believe it. Setanta would come for them. They just had to survive until then.

"All right," she whispered.

"Excellent." He murmured something in German and a series of marks on the floor glowed white around Marcelle's chair, ensuring that even if she were to somehow free herself, she was trapped within the circle. "Then I have someone to introduce you to. Your fiancé."

For a moment, Sarai wanted to ask how he knew about Setanta, but terror gripped her as she realized he meant someone else. The mystery arranged match she had run from when she had been eighteen years old. Some man she'd never met that her father wanted her to create a new pureblood vampire line with using a hellish ritual of blood and death.

Sarai didn't reply, but slowly got up, abandoning the vomit-soaked towel on the floor.

Stall for time, she thought. "I, I need to finish this." She got back to her knees and scrubbed the rug, though all she managed to do was rub the vomit into the fibers.

"Leave it." Alaric's voice was sharp, harsh, and made her freeze. He slammed open the door of the room. He didn't need to speak to make Sarai get up and follow him out, taking one lingering look back at Marcelle.

"You'll be okay," she whispered. "I promise."

With that, she was led through the halls. It was an old plantation mansion, the sort with dark history. She grew up wandering its halls whenever she was allowed in the main house, avoiding her father and stepmother. Seeing it again years later felt… foreign.

Alaric led her to her old bedroom, a room with locks that could only be opened from the outside. At present, they were open. Inside, a man with platinum blond hair stood waiting at the window. He had a sharp, hawkish face, a neatly trimmed mustache, and forest green eyes. He might have been attractive if Sarai didn't know what his purpose was.

"Sarai, I'd like to introduce Victor Hess."

Victor Hess frowned as he looked Sarai up and down. "You didn't tell me she was so brown." Sarai bristled with instant hatred for him.

"Her mother was Moroccan or something, regrettably. It's hard to find healers of that caliber, so I took what I could find. Jews do have a habit of having the best healers and lightning powers. It is what it is. Her hair has some lightness to it, thanks to me at least." Alaric twisted his hand in Sarai's curls and pushed her forward. She stumbled a little and looked up at the new man. He walked around her, looking her up and down like a piece of meat.

"I guess she'll do. Sarai, is it? We should get to know each other."

"I'll leave you to it then. Nothing too rash. Save it for the ritual," Alaric said, and left the room.

Sarai's chest clenched in fear. She remembered the last time a predatory man had her alone. Nicolas, the vampire she had killed for trying to assault her. And once again, her powers were locked by the silver she had been made to wear.

"You're all right, I suppose," he said as he reached out to caress her cheek.

"Not too brown?" she snapped and stepped back out of his reach.

He chuckled. "Well, I was expecting someone like your sister. She's not bad. Shame she doesn't have your powers."

"Yeah, she thinks so too."

"We don't have to make this unpleasant, you know. I can be nice."

"So, if I say I don't want to do anything with you ever, that'll be fine with you?" she asked.

"We have a duty to fulfill. You're a Reinhart, you should understand that. The strength of the coven is our priority."

"*Your* priority. I'm a Meir witch."

He made a face. Victor stepped forward with a sudden speed that frightened her and gripped her chin, forcing her to look up at him. She realized in that moment, what his power was. If she embodied the healing and necromancy necessary to create a pureblood vampire, then Victor had to have the physical prowess of one. "That fire in your eyes… You're a Reinhart."

He pressed his lips to hers and fury burned in her heart. She bit down on his lip, hard, drawing blood. Victor gave a muffled scream and pulled himself free, slapping her across the face with a force that made her ears ring as she was slammed across the room and into the wall. She tasted blood in her mouth and wasn't quite sure whose it was.

"Definitely a Reinhart," he muttered, wiping the blood from his mouth. "If you want to do it like that, fine. Have it your way. I'm stronger than you. This will happen. But I can wait. You think about how you want things to go. You can be my wife, or you can live your life in silver. The choice is yours." He left the room and slammed the door, locking it behind him.

Sarai sighed in relief as she struggled to her feet. He hadn't hurt her too bad. She'd anticipated far worse, but supposed she still had time until she was forced to endure that. In the meantime, she had to plan.

Marcelle was captive. As long as Alaric had Marcelle, Sarai couldn't risk being too openly rebellious.

Still, she had to figure out a way to signal to Setanta. To do something. She had no magic, but she did have something magical. If silver didn't touch it…

Sarai pulled off her enchanted prosthetic hand. It was controlled by her mind, and apparently having a source of magic separate from her own power kept it functioning. Perhaps it could still work when not connected to her physically. She tried to reach out with magic, and of course could use none of her own. But…

"Can you still move?" She focused, trying to imagine her fingers wiggling. To her delight, the fingers moved. She almost whooped for joy but bit her lip to keep silent. She couldn't have someone come back and stop her.

She focused on wiggling her fingers and practiced making the hand crawl around the floor. It wasn't enough to break Marcelle out, and she didn't know where the key to her silver was. No doubt her father had the key, and he was too careful to leave it anywhere she would be able to get. But the window was open, though she couldn't make it out herself with the bars in place over it. She could make her hand crawl out of the plantation, beyond their territory. If anyone were to scry for her, that would be the best chance. To have a piece of her outside the protective bounds of the Reinhart plantation.

She looked out into the Virginian night sky. It was funny how beautiful a place with such bloody history and purpose could be. She picked up the hand and thought for a moment, then added the hound head ring Setanta had given her to the hand and took off her focus glove to put inside-out on her remaining hand. Then she threw it with all the force she could manage into the darkness. It landed somewhere in the lawn, and she focused, making it flop up onto its fingertips and scuttle forward. She could see a thin line of movement as it moved towards the forest tree line in the distance. She had hope.

****

Marcelle was furious and terrified. She anticipated torture, again, and mentally steeled herself. She remembered sitting on her psychologist's couch, telling the psychologist about how angry she felt that she'd been helpless, that anyone had been allowed to hurt her without permission. Angry that she'd been in a position she had needed help from the one she was meant to protect. Once again, she was trapped. And her ward was the one trying to keep her safe. It was maddening.

The door opened and Alaric Reinhart returned, adjusting his shirt cuff. She could appreciate the fine craftsmanship that had gone into his outfit. It looked Italian, and the cut was custom. Setanta wore suits better though.

"What am I going to do with you," he murmured and sat down on the couch, staring at her, swirling the ice in his drink. "If Alma hadn't insisted you were the key to controlling Sarai and if we didn't need to take the silver off her for the ritual to work, I'd never allow a vampire in the house. Fucking corpse."

He got up and pulled her gag out. So, it was time to talk. Time to interrogate him.

"Who the hell are you anyway?" he asked.

"Marcelle de Sauveterre," she said. "I'd say I'm pleased to make your acquaintance, but we both know that's a lie."

"Clearly. And what is your relationship with my daughter that she's willing to give you her blood and fight for you?"

"I'm her girlfriend." She smiled. It wasn't information he didn't already have, though it did anger him. She could see the way his eyes narrowed that he wasn't a fan. Given his coven's roots, he was likely homophobic. "I've heard a lot about you, Alaric. About how you went out of your way to capture a healing witch to be Sarai's mother. About your interest in vampires. I must say, I'm impressed at your planning. I thought all copies of the ritual you're planning were destroyed."

"It was difficult, but we found what we needed," he said. "You work with purebloods, don't you? Like the one that almost killed my Alma."

"Mm, yes, I do. One must have something to do to keep entertained through the centuries."

"They control you, don't they? Make you their little puppet. How does that work? Like a mind control witch gift?"

Marcelle shrugged. "I wouldn't know, I've never been mind-controlled by a witch before. But yes, it's common enough knowledge. The purebloods of my bloodline can control me."

"Even the young ones?"

She sighed. "This isn't going to work well for you," Marcelle told him seriously. "Purebloods don't like it when their territory or power is challenged by other purebloods. You should reconsider. It's not too late."

Alaric laughed. "You're a funny one, aren't you?" He shook his head and took another long drink. "You know, I don't really need you. Sarai saw you once. She knows I have you. I could just," he got up and ran a hand along her collarbone. "End you now. She'd never know until it was too late."

"Sarai drank my blood," Marcelle said, her mind

spinning to keep herself alive. "Do you know what that does?"

"Some healing properties. And it could turn her if she drank enough. But since she's still breathing, I don't think so."

"It means we're connected. Magically," Marcelle lied. "She can sense me. Can tell when I'm near, if I'm hurt. If you kill me, she'll know."

Alaric frowned. He had no way of knowing it was a bluff, considering how little most witches knew about vampires. Though, he might know. He had learned enough on his own to create a new line. But he also might not want to take the chance.

He lowered his hand and stormed out of the room, slamming his glass on a table on his way out, and closing the door with such force that the light fixtures rattled.

Marcelle allowed herself to relax. It appeared the lie had worked. At least, she thought she was safe. What felt like an hour or so later, he came back, several other witches with him.

"Back so soon?" she asked in surprise. "Is the party for me?"

"Shut up," he snapped, then dispelled the magical circle around her chair. Two of the men with him got to work uncuffing her from the chair and forced her with them.

"Where are we going?" she demanded.

"You'll see."

She was marched outside, passed several large trees, and was able to look back at the home. It was large, beautiful. It had colonial architecture from the Civil War era, and she remembered when such styling had been quite popular. Of course, given that they were in the south, it likely hadn't been used for any good purpose. Especially given the large fields around them, and the less well-kept buildings off to the side that looked like they had once housed slaves.

The Reinharts took Marcelle to an old graveyard, and she froze. There was a fresh grave dug, six feet deep, and an open coffin on the ground beside it.

"No," she whispered. Not in silver. Not in the ground. She had never been grounded before, but at least when it was done as punishment by vampire law, there was a set end period to the imprisonment. Here, on this witches' plantation, no vampire would know she was there. The territory was no doubt heavily warded, so Setanta wouldn't be able to scry her. She would be buried, conscious, trapped. Forever.

"As long as you're alive and unharmed, Sarai will comply with our demands. But that doesn't mean I want a vampire in my house. So, since you're a corpse, you'll be kept where you should be kept. In a grave."

"You fucking bastard!" she screeched. As the men holding her tried to move her towards the coffin, she twisted hard and broke free of their grasp. Just because she didn't have her strength didn't mean she couldn't fight. She was weakened, and she couldn't heal, but she had her skills and centuries of experience. She sidestepped one and tripped him over her knee, then spun and tackled a second, latching her fangs to his throat and ripping it out. The blood felt good, invigorating. As she turned to fight her next foe, a hand touched her back and magical pain shot through her like a hail of bullets. She screamed and fell forward, looking up weakly to see Alaric Reinhart glaring down at her.

"Bury the bitch."

She was dragged, kicking, twisting, and screaming, by four men and forced into the coffin. Her legs and hands were cuffed, and the lid closed over her. It was quiet, and she found herself gasping for air, as if she needed to breathe. A reflex, some long dead instinct lingering in her mind from when she'd been alive. There was banging on the edges of the lid, and she knew she had been nailed inside.

"I'll kill you for this," she raged, kicking up as hard as she could. "I swear, I will eat your heart!"

The coffin moved and was lowered until she felt it hit the bottom of her prison. She shut her eyes, taking deep breaths. She had to figure out a way out. There had to be a way out. But she couldn't think with the sound of dirt being shoveled on top of her. Slowly, the sound became muffled until there was nothing but darkness and silence.

Setanta had once been grounded, she recalled. It had happened as a punishment handed down from his sister, who had been queen of New Ulster prior to her death fighting in World War Two. The punishment had happened during the Revolutionary War. He had become enraged at the actions of some American soldiers who had killed a group of Iroquois, and so he slaughtered the soldiers, going against orders from his sister. She'd ordered him grounded until the end of the war.

He'd told Marcelle about it. That of all the things he'd experienced, the mind-numbing silence and loneliness was the only thing he would ever compare to a true hell. It had taken him years to recover. He'd clung to her in bed, afraid of the silence and loneliness. Anything that made Setanta afraid would terrify any sane person.

And now, it was her turn. As a mortal, she had been Catholic and had always imagined hell to be a place of fire and heat, full of the screams of the damned. It seemed hell was quiet, dark, and cold. The only damned scream to be heard was her own.

No... she couldn't lose her mind screaming. She had to get out. Her little witch was at risk, and this time Marcelle *would* save her. Marcelle was no damsel in distress; she was the knight commander of the realm. She took several meditative breaths and focused.

The biggest problems were her handcuffed wrists and silver collar. If she could fix one or the other, she had a chance.

While she could usually escape from ropes, handcuffs were a little more difficult. Still, it wasn't impossible. It would just hurt. But before breaking her thumbs, she decided it was a better idea to see if she had any other options available to her.

Marcelle took stock of what she had. Her clothes: pants with no pockets, a shirt, undergarments. Her hair had been pinned up in a bun and now lay in a braid, since they had removed anything from her person that might be used as a weapon, hair pins included. She ran her hands along the braid, hoping. There was always one that got missed, when she took it out herself. Perhaps... *yes*. Close to her scalp at the nape of her neck was a single, small pin. That was all she needed.

Chapter Twenty-Eight: The Warning

King Setanta was thrilled to get a chance to fight Queen Arsinoe. While he was not one who actively sought out those he knew to be stronger than himself for battles to the death, as he enjoyed living very much, a non-lethal test against an equal was always welcome for the excitement. The other purebloods at the festival all had similar philosophies and relished the opportunity to fight each other. Friendly fights were a given. They took place in the basement where his knights trained and would often attract an audience. A handful of knights were present, as were Captain Moretti and Setanta's newest recruited knight, Lochlan. They lined one end of the ring, while visiting purebloods were on the other end, taking bets and debating who would fight the winner. To his surprise, he saw Giovanna in the corner. She would never fight, Setanta knew that. The woman was a coward in the face of true power. He'd hoped to see Marcelle and had left a letter for Sarai to invite her to watch the tournament yet, saw neither. While part of him wished to wait for them, he knew the visiting purebloods wanted to get on with the show.

"Come now, good king," Arsinoe taunted, swinging twin khopesh blades. She wore only a loincloth, which might have distracted someone else, but he was too focused on the monstrous need for violence that so often lay subdued and dormant in his soul. "Have the centuries since you visited my court made you fat and slow?"

He grinned and twirled his spear, magic crackling in the air around them both. He made a quick slice across one of his many tattoos, as he'd discarded his shirt before the bout, and used the spilt blood to activate protective enchantments in the blue, woad-based ink in his skin.

"Not at all, my dear queen. Merely trying to decide how long I shall hold onto your head when I cut it from your body. Shall I mount it on my mantle for an hour or a day before I give it back to you?"

Bloodlust burned in her eyes and her fangs extended. "And when you lose to my blades, what shall be my reward? Perhaps I'll cut off that pretty ponytail as my trophy."

"You would have to win first, dear queen."

They grinned, then launched forward. They blocked each other, moving with the deft speed and power only purebloods were capable of. If their weaponry hadn't been magical, the items would have shattered from the force. His spear pushed past a khopesh to nick her skin, but she spun out of the way before he could do more than let his spear taste her, absorbing the few drops of power from it.

Then, as he was about to attack, a transparent Sephardic woman appeared before him. He stopped, stepping back with a frown.

"Please," Liora begged in a voice that sounded an ocean away. "My daughter."

Setanta barely had a moment to block Arsinoe as she spun with a banshee shriek at him, nearly cutting his throat. Such a wound wouldn't be fatal, as long as he was able to put it back together and didn't lose his head. He hoped she remembered that only Egyptian vampires were capable of putting their heads back on after a decapitation. He glanced around. No one else seemed aware of the ghost. It was just him who could see her.

"Stop," he barked, and Arsinoe hesitated, looking at him with a frown.

"What is it?" she asked, but he shook her head.

"I concede. Fight the next in line," he said, bowing his head and turning his attention to the ghost.

"Oh, CuChulainn, really?" she said with a disappointed sigh. He ignored her and bowed out, following the ghost as she led him up out of the basement and to the gardens, spear in hand.

"What is it?" he said quietly to the ghost.

"They have her," was all Liora said, a frantic fear in her eyes.

As he passed through the gardens, Bear, who sat in a treetop with Hannah in his lap as he ran his fingers through her hair, took notice.

"Your Highness," he called, then seemed to realize the sternness on Setanta's face. "What is it?"

"It's Sarai's mother," Hannah whispered, her eyes following the ghost's movement, flickering with the magic of her astral gift. "She's distressed. Please, set me down? I may be able to help."

"I believe Sarai is in harm's way. It may be dangerous," Setanta said, then looked at Bear. An extra hand could be useful if vampire guests had gotten out of hand, especially if they were purebloods. If his own citizens had harmed Sarai, he would kill them. But if they were foreign vampires, imprisonment would be necessary so he could discuss matters with whatever country they came from.

"Do you want me to get Hannah somewhere safe?"

Bear asked.

"I might be able to help," the witch protested. "What's wrong?"

"I don't know yet." Setanta followed the ghost down a path towards a small creek. There was no sign of Sarai, or anyone. But there was a smell of gunpowder and dust. His blood ran cold.

Setanta grasped some of the dust from the ground and inhaled. It was almost a relief that it wasn't Marcelle. He knew what her dust smelled like only because whenever she would become frustrated with too many knots in her hair she would cut it off to allow it to regrow free of the knots. The cut hair always turned to dust. This dust...

"Angela," he realized. A moment of sorrow hit him. Angela had been a fine warrior, and he knew she was a close friend of Bear's.

Bear darted to his side, inhaling, his eyes narrowed in fury. "Who would dare?" he said in a low voice. The bitter-sweet scent of Sarai's blood hit them as the wind blew, and Setanta noticed it on the leaves and a few spots on the ground.

"Sarai's. Not too much, she should be alive."

"Marcelle was here," Bear said, pointing to a dropped hair comb. It was gold, the gift Setanta had left. "What's this?" Bear picked up a letter from near the stream. "Your Highness, it has your seal."

Setanta snatched the letter, anger clouding his mind as the familiar scent reached him. It was perfumed oil with the distinct scent of saffron. His letter to Sarai had been switched out with lies.

"I wrote no such letter. This was Giovanna."

Hannah closed her eyes, and Setanta felt magic

weigh down on the clearing like a change in air pressure.

"Witches took your Marcelle and Sarai," she said. "I can see magic on the astral plane. Teleportation magic. I can't say where they went; it's warded. Strong, old wards. Like a coven or Vasi stronghold."

Hannah was a useful witch to have around after all, Setanta thought to himself. Even if she would be useless in a fight.

"Giovanna will know," he said.

"Where is she?" Bear asked.

"She was in the basement with us, watching the bouts. No doubt to shield herself from suspicion." Setanta glanced at Hannah. "Would you like Bear to take you somewhere safe? There may be violence."

"I'm fine," she said. "Take me with you."

Bear scooped her up in his arms, and the three raced back to the basement, where Queen Arsinoe had decided to face off against Prince Celestin.

The fight froze when Setanta reappeared. He spotted Giovanna in the corner of the room, who looked like a frightened rabbit. Without hesitating, he drew back his arm and shot his spear into her abdomen, pinning her to the wall behind her.

She shrieked in pain as the magic polearm drank her blood, reducing her strength. Her eyes were wide. Setanta knew she wasn't used to pain, and the agony of such an attack was vicious even for a pureblood to handle.

"Where are they?" he snarled through his fangs, darting forward and gripping her hair to force her to look at him.

"I've been here the whole time, everyone's seen me here. I don't know what—"

"My knight is dead, my mistress is missing, and my witch is abducted. Only a pureblood who lives in the palace could have invited Sarai beyond our barrier and I caught your scent on the false letter. I will ask you one more time, Giovanna. Where are they?"

She spat up at him and slid a hand against his wrist. He could feel her attempting to use her mind control power against him as his golden torque necklace warmed, the protective magic saving him.

In response, he gripped the spear by the pole and twisted it. She screamed in pain. Torture wasn't an effective interrogation technique, and it was long out of favor in New Ulster as well as in many vampire courts for that purpose. Hurting Giovanna wasn't about getting information: it was punishment and satisfaction for his inhuman bloodlust.

"Tell me where they are and if they return here in one piece, I'll consider letting you keep your life," Setanta growled.

"The Reinhart coven," she sobbed. "In Virginia. I told that witch Alma how to get to her. Told her to take Sarai far away. She said Virginia."

Setanta yanked the spear free. Not a drop of her blood had been wasted, absorbed into the spear to store away the power for future spells. Giovanna dropped to the floor, gasping and heaving as her massive wound began to heal.

"I want her imprisoned," Setanta instructed, and two of his knights were immediately by his side, pulling Giovanna to her feet and sticking her arm with a silver needle that caused her to whimper. "Keep her locked in silver until I return."

He turned to face the other purebloods, who were

shocked into a stunned silence. In retrospect, he should have sent them out of the room before assaulting Giovanna. But what was done was done. At least they would have good stories to tell.

"A momentary disruption to our festivities," he told them calmly. "I would like to request that you all adjourn upstairs for the evening. Enjoy the entertainment. I have business to tend to with my knights."

The purebloods left, and Setanta's knights of the realm stood at sharp attention, with the three present witches off to the side in stunned silence.

"Giovanna's jealousy invited enemies into our palace and they have abducted your future queens," Setanta announced. "We will journey to Virginia and lay waste to the Reinhart coven for this offense. We will raze their coven to the ground so none will dare threaten our queens again. Gather your weapons and make ready to leave."

Dismissed, the knights left to obey. All but one very new knight.

Setanta looked at Lochlan, at the dagger on his belt. "You swore an oath to me. Will you fight other witches, even if they are not Vasi?"

"Reinharts?" Lochlan glanced at Moretti.

"Don't look at me. You don't take orders from me anymore, remember? That was your call." She seemed upset with that and pointed at Setanta. "You wanted the proactive murderers? That's them right there."

Lochlan nodded and turned to Setanta. "Yeah. Yeah, okay. Yeah. Reinharts are the Nazi bastards, right? Let's fry some fucking neo-Nazis." Then he frowned. "They took Marcelle?"

"Marcelle and Sarai."

Moretti's brow furrowed in thought. "I get why they took Sarai, that's who they wanted this whole time, but why would they take Marcelle?"

"I'd imagine, to ensure Sarai's cooperation. Last time we met, Alma was made aware of how much Marcelle means to Sarai." Setanta's eyes narrowed. It was a race against time. He knew enough about the ritual he suspected the Reinharts desired to be aware that Sarai could not be kept captive in silver for it. So, they needed to threaten someone else, someone like Marcelle, to force her. After all, one could not be possessed by a demon if they wore silver. And the ritual... it was monstrous when the participants consented. When someone didn't consent... He knew personally the hell of being forced to couple with someone and have a child against his will. Over two thousand five hundred years later, he remembered vividly the silver burning into his wrists while that infernal witch Aife climbed on top of him and told him to relax and enjoy himself, all because she wanted a powerful child. He could not let that happen to Sarai. And no doubt once they had no need to keep Sarai out of silver, they would kill Marcelle. Life without Marcelle was unthinkable.

"I am going to Virginia to destroy the Reinhart coven," Setanta told Moretti. "Your assistance as our allies would be appreciated but is not required. If you are staying, please remain with knight escorts for your own safety."

"I'm going to come with you," Moretti said. "Marcelle helped us save a Vasi witch and a bunch of my cousins. I owe her one."

"And, apparently, I'm your soldier now," Lochlan said with a half mocking salute.

"I need to go with them," Bear told Hannah. "You'll be well cared for with Crispin as your guard."

Hannah nodded. "Be safe," she whispered. She closed her eyes and toyed with her focus, the feather tied into her hair, whispering a protection spell softly. Bear took her hand and kissed it.

"Thank you. I appreciate that." Bear turned to Setanta and gave a nod. "I'm ready."

As Setanta waited for the strike team to assemble, Hannah offered to attempt to scry for them. What she found was unusual; Sarai's disembodied hand scuttling across the ground by its fingertips at the edge of an old Virginia plantation covered in protective spells. The hand had just managed to slip past the edge into grounds where they could scry for it.

Clever that Sarai would think to help them by using such an unusual means at her disposal. With Sarai's hand, they could pinpoint the Reinhart coven on a map.

It didn't take long to assemble the strike team, and all the knights were on edge. For Setanta to be in the lead, and one of their own dead with another missing, it was more than a routine raid.

Hannah and Danior assisted in their own way, going from vampire to vampire to impart protection spells much sturdier than anything Setanta was capable of. Lilly watched them with some interest, making note of the wording the spells used, and helped the vampires arm themselves.

Then, with the spear Gáe Bulg in his grasp, Setanta and his army were ready for a fight.

Chapter Twenty-Nine: The Cellar

"It's time."

The voice was Alaric's in the doorway to Sarai's room. She cringed, wishing she could fight him, but she was too afraid of the consequences.

"Where's Marcelle?" Sarai demanded.

"Unharmed. And she'll remain unharmed as long as you cooperate."

Sarai glared at him, and he frowned.

"Where is your right hand?"

She raised up the stump, ready with a lie she practiced several times. "It brushed against the silver collar. It was a magical prosthetic, so it disintegrated."

That answer seemed to satisfy him.

"Are you going to come with me, or do I need to drag you out?" he said.

Sarai didn't reply. She walked forward, her remaining hand trembling. Maybe if she walked very slowly, Setanta or Marcelle would burst in at just the right moment and save her. That slim hope was all she had.

She followed her father down the stairs and into the basement. There were others there, other Reinhart witches in white robes. She recognized her stepmother Regina among them, Victor Hess, and several cousins. All monsters in their own right.

The people she didn't recognize were the thirteen

naked men and women shivering in silver chains. They were placed in a circle around an indent in the stone floor that looked like a large basin, bound on their knees with no way to escape and gags in their mouths to muffle their fearful protests. *Sacrifices*, she realized in horror. The ritual required human sacrifices. But what could she do to save them? The Reinharts would restrain her if she tried anything. She shut her eyes, as if that would erase the memory of their terrified faces.

"Are you going to behave?" Victor asked her as he approached.

"She will," promised Alaric. "She knows what will happen to her vampire pet if she doesn't." He produced a key from his pocket and, to Sarai's surprise, unlocked her silver. "Use your gifts against anyone here and you will regret it. You're outnumbered."

He was right. She looked around the room. There was a teleporter, Victor with his strength and speed, her father with his ability to cause pain and death with a touch, and that wasn't even taking into account the other witches there, all powerful. Sarai had no chance. She could kill Victor and destroy all their plans in that way, but then Marcelle would suffer. She couldn't let them hurt Marcelle.

Victor took her hands and led her to the center of the indent in the floor.

"Let us begin," said Alaric.

As Sarai looked around her at the unwilling sacrifices, the thought crossed her mind that regardless of the cost to Marcelle, she needed to stop the ritual for their sake. Not to do so was immoral. But she also wasn't sure if Marcelle would view the lives of thirteen strangers as more important than her own. Sarai wanted to think that was the choice the vampire would make, being a guard who was willing to throw herself into danger to protect others. Yes, Marcelle wouldn't want this on her behalf. Sarai had to kill Victor.

Before she had the chance to focus on her dark gift, Reinhart witches stepped up behind the sacrifices and, in a single synchronized movement, cut their throats.

Sarai clapped a hand over her mouth to keep from screaming in horror. The red spurt from their bodies and gushed out in rivers, draining into the basin Sarai stood in. She curled her toes inwards, as if that would keep her from coming in contact with it as the blood pooled around her feet. It was hot and smelled of copper. She wanted to be sick.

Alaric opened an ancient book and began to read. If Sarai had to guess, it was some form of an ancient Germanic tongue, but she didn't know what he said. As he read, the world around Sarai began to shimmer.

Then, she and Victor were standing somewhere else. The sky was open above them, and the stars were wrong. Brighter, and red. The landscape was desolate and cracked except for the pool of blood under them.

Something grabbed her leg and she screamed. Even Victor looked shocked as he stumbled back and pulled her with him as he gripped her hand tight. They were not alone.

Out of the pool of blood rose what Sarai could only describe as a monster. It was larger than any human being, and its skin looked like black latex as blood dripped down. It had no hair to speak of, nor any nose, lips, or ears, and its eyes glowed a burning red far more terrifying than Marcelle or Setanta's eyes. It opened its mouth and instead of revealing fangs, it revealed rows of teeth like large needles, stark white against its jet-black body. It lowered its maw to the ground and a long, black tongue licked at the blood.

"*What an opportunity*," said a voice in their minds. Sarai covered her ears with her hand and stump, as if she could block out the telepathy, staring in horror at the creature. The voice was like nothing she had ever imagined. It was as if she were hearing every voice she had ever heard in her life and every language to ever exist all at once. The weight of the sound threatened to burst her skull. She glanced at Victor and saw that he was just as terrified as her.

The creature stepped closer, and Sarai was too afraid to fight. It ran its claws over her, not touching her body, but inches away. Then it pushed its long fingers like spears into Sarai's chest like a ghost passing through a wall, and she was too overwhelmed to scream. It didn't hurt, not physically. Yet, it was so much worse than anything Victor could threaten her with, anything she had expected. She felt the creature's skin growing over her flesh where it touched her, trying to consume her from the inside out.

She couldn't scream. Couldn't move. It was going to use her like a puppet. She glanced at Victor and saw it was doing the same to him with its other hand, spreading its consciousness and gleaming obsidian skin across them both.

Its consciousness was painful. Experiencing it was like trying to inhale acid, like trying to wear fire. And it was much more than something so mundane as fire. It was much more advanced than simple elements, but so primal and raw as well. She could see her world, the tears in the fabric of the universe, the other creatures who drank magic and blood like water. Impossibly long-lived creatures who saw mortals like her as ants. Who would see even Setanta and his two-thousand-five-hundred-year lifespan as an ant. And... they were right. She was an insect, a mindless drone or toy compared to their magical presence. Tears streamed down her face, against the latex-like skin that threatened to consume her soul, but she couldn't feel them.

Then, it reached her abdomen and there was a gentle warmth there. Sarai could sense it, the pearl from the spell she'd done with Setanta and Marcelle. It glowed inside her, as if protecting her. The creature stopped. The darkness receded, and the claws were pulled from her chest.

"*Useless,*" it growled in her head. The desolate landscape disappeared, and they were standing in an empty basin, the blood from around their feet and from the sacrifice victims completely gone.

"What the hell just happened?!" demanded Alaric. Sarai didn't reply, only sank to her knees, too weak from the encounter to move. What *had* just happened? What had it been? What hell and insanity had her mind touched the edge of, and how was she supposed to make sense of it?

Victor looked just as shell-shocked and stumbled away, making a beeline for the corner of the room, and pushing past the other witches so he could sit there with his knees curled to his chest.

"Where did the blood go?" Alaric asked. "Did it work? Is that it?"

"Water," Victor rasped, and someone brought him a bottle of water. He took a shaking sip, then downed the entire bottle. Sarai wanted to ask for some as well, realizing as she watched that her throat was dry as if she had been screaming for hours. Had she been screaming for hours? Or had it been moments?

"Well?" said Alaric. "Is that it?"

"It didn't want us. Her. It didn't want her," he said, still shaking. "You didn't warn me what that thing was. It was in my head and I..." He looked as if he might cry.

Alaric rounded on Sarai. Before her encounter with the creature, he might have been intimidating. After... she felt she could face down an army of angry pureblood vampires and not even flinch. None of it mattered compared to that *thing* in her head.

"What did you do?" he demanded.

Sarai just stared. What had she done? Nothing she was aware of. Yet... Perhaps she had. Her hand moved involuntarily to her lower abdomen as she remembered the warmth, the feeling of the pearl inside her. No, it wasn't a pearl... The existential horror disappeared as new knowledge grounded her. That pearl mattered more than anything else. It made her feel at home again in her world, and she knew fully who she was and where she was.

"She's already pregnant," murmured her stepmother from behind the body of one of the sacrifice victims.

Sarai's aunts told her it would take at least a few weeks before she would be properly pregnant. Perhaps, just the fact that she was under the influence of a fertility spell had protected her from being used by the demonic monster. It hadn't wanted the competition.

"*You useless slut,*" Alaric shouted and slapped her across the face, sending her to the floor. She didn't mind as she tasted blood in her mouth. It made her feel... alive. And she had something more to fight for.

"We're going to need to get rid of it. Get new sacrifices. Start over from scratch," he fumed.

Sarai stood. She had to fight back. If not, they were going to destroy what she and her lovers had created. Without a second thought, she lunged for her father, power surging in her good hand.

He screamed in pain and tried to fight back, but she sidestepped and pushed him over her leg, just as Marcelle, Bear, and Angela had taught her once in their training room.

Sarai's hand landed on his neck, spreading darkness across his skin as he struggled.

The force of a truck hit Sarai's side, and she found herself grappled and silvered in Victor's hands.

Alaric stood, shaking with anger and pain. "You turned your gift against me?" he growled. Half his face was distorted from the magic, like she had burned his veins under his skin.

Sarai didn't reply. She was furious at herself for not finishing him off.

"Lock her back in her room," Alaric said. "We have to prepare everything again."

Chapter Thirty: The Graveyard

The hair pin hadn't been enough to pick the lock on Marcelle's collar, but she still had means to escape. She broke her left thumb to get free of the handcuffs and allow her more freedom of movement to pull off her shirt. Once that had been managed, she carefully wrapped it around the silver collar, protecting her skin from contact. With a sign of relief, she took a few minutes to heal, setting her thumb in place. Now she could get out.

Still, while strength could help her break the lid of her coffin, it was difficult to claw her way up through six feet of packed dirt. Brute strength helped, but it was disorientating to be underground in the darkness. Every once in a while, the silver slipped past the cloth and burned her. The first time, she opened her mouth to scream and was rewarded with a mouthful of dirt. It took monumental effort to get her hand back to her neck to try to fix it, and she had never before been so aware of how weak she had been at her moment of her death. The deteriorating death of tuberculosis that left her dying in the gutter meant her strength when silvered was pathetic.

Eventually, and she wasn't sure how long it took, only that it felt like she was incapable of the speed she needed, her hand pushed up through the soil and felt a breeze from the open air. Her heart leapt and, with renewed hope, she dug her way out, spitting out earth from her mouth and wiping it from her eyes.

A loud slurping sound resounded through the graveyard, startling Marcelle. She turned and saw Alma Reinhart sitting in a folding lawn chair sipping lemonade through a straw.

"I told Dad that you were tougher than a coffin," she said and took another sip. "But no one ever listens to me."

Marcelle's fangs dropped and she darted forward to slam into an invisible barrier and broke her nose. She held it in place as it healed and wiped the blood from her nostrils. Alma slurped again, aggravating the vampire.

"Since I'm smarter than him, I put down a little barrier charm," she said.

Marcelle bent down and picked up a rock, flicking it at the barrier, only for it to be blocked. A shame… she couldn't kill Alma with projectiles.

"Are you going to call him back?" Marcelle asked.

"Dad? Oh, fuck no. He's busy summoning a demon to possess Sarai or something."

Marcelle felt colder than the grave she'd just clawed her way out of. "They started the ritual? So soon?"

Alma nodded. "It has been a few hours, you know. You've been in there a while. They've been ready to go since she popped up at Ellis. I didn't want to watch my sister get freaky, so thought my time would be better spent out here waiting for you to break out."

Marcelle paced like a caged lioness in her limited space. "I don't suppose I could convince you to join me in taking them out before they hurt Sarai?"

"Mm, no, not my style. See, I like it when I know I can win a fight. Going up against the whole Reinhart clan, just us chickens? I'd get my ass handed to me. And so would you. Sure, you could take out a few of them. But not enough of them to save your girlfriend."

Marcelle paused. "You sound like you've given this some thought."

Alma smiled. "Don't worry. I won't keep you in that barrier all night."

"Really?"

Alma sipped her lemonade again.

Soon enough, she saw what the wait was for. Setanta stood with his mighty spear in one hand, a disembodied hand that Marcelle instantly knew was Sarai's from the ring it wore in the other, a line of vampire knights behind him. And, surprisingly, both Lochlan and Captain Moretti at his side.

"Marcelle," he said in relief as he saw her, but didn't move past the tree line at the edge of the graveyard.

"I'm okay," Marcelle assured him. "They tried to ground me. It didn't take."

That brought a smile to his lips, which quickly disappeared as Alma gave a long, drawn-out slurp on her straw. Marcelle clenched her fist as she fought the urge to try and shove the straw through Alma's skull.

Alma smiled at the vampires. "Might not want to take another step," she told him. "You'll trip the alarms and defenses."

"You knew we were coming."

"It was just a little obvious. Plus this is the weakest spot in the perimeter because of the graveyard, so your smartest move would be to try to break through here. Of course, that will alert the coven and you'll be attacked."

"That's the plan," Setanta said, planting his focus, the giant spear Gáe Bulg, in the ground with force. "I intend to use the power of their deaths to break through the protective enchantments. We are prepared for battle."

"I see." She eyed his spear. "Compensating for something?"

"No," he snarled. "Is there something you want, Alma?"

"Well, there you go, isn't that the million-dollar question no one fucking asks me around here." She put down her drink and applauded him. "That's the question. What do I want? I know what you need. An invitation. Would be a lot easier than depending on a bunch of idiots to rush out here and get themselves killed for you to break through."

Setanta cocked his head to the side, curious. "I'm listening."

"I want everything," she said, a vicious hunger in her voice Marcelle knew all too well. She'd met too many people thirsty for power and willing to do anything for it. "I want you to go into that mansion and kill my father for me."

How interesting, Marcelle thought. It seemed that it hadn't paid for Alaric to play favorites between his daughters.

"Lucky you, we're here to do exactly that," Setanta said. "What else do you want?"

She smiled. "I want people to fucking respect me for once. I want this estate. And I want money. Ten million dollars."

A bribe? Marcelle almost laughed at the banality of her request. Ten million dollars was nothing. They could spare it. And Marcelle doubted Setanta cared about what became of the Reinhart plantation.

"Five," Setanta countered.

"Seven and a half."

"Done," Setanta said without hesitation.

"Oh, but I'm not done. That's not all I want. I want you to spare my mother, Regina Reinhart, and I want you to swear none of you fine folks are going to retaliate against me for what I did to this one."

Setanta looked down at his lover, the question of her approval in his eyes. They didn't need words. Marcelle knew he could see the grim dissatisfaction in her eyes, but also that she would resign her right to revenge if it helped them. She could put up with tolerating Alma's existence if it meant they could have Sarai returned to them. She mentally added it to the list of things to talk over with her psychologist once the whole affair was concluded.

"I'll renounce my claim on her," Marcelle offered, and Setanta nodded.

"Then that is acceptable," Setanta said. "We will not retaliate for your past crimes and will spare your mother if possible. If that's all?"

"And one more thing," Alma continued, her heterochromatic eyes sparkling. "I want you to turn me into a vampire, CuChulainn of Ulster."

The only noise to be heard was the crickets chiming in the night. Marcelle scowled. Alma was a horrible choice to give eternal life to. She was already a grating individual with a lust for power and an entitlement that meant she would grow to become even more of a nuisance until someone put her down. But… if she were a vampire of Setanta's bloodline, then the vampire king could control her. There were perks to having an enemy under one's thumb. Marcelle had a vibrant fantasy that perhaps she could watch while Setanta ordered Alma to

323

torture herself, though knew he wouldn't if he'd given his word that he wouldn't retaliate.

"I'll allow my subordinate Lilly to turn you," he said. Lilly was a fifth-generation vampire, so her progeny would be weaker than one made by him. It was a good move.

"No, I know how it works. I know you're the big man and the closest I'll get to your power for myself is from you directly," Alma snapped. "I want *you* to turn me. Anyone less and it's no deal."

Setanta's eyes narrowed. Marcelle met his gaze.

"What do you think?" he asked, barely moving his lips, using a tone too low for a human to hear.

"She said they already started the ritual," Marcelle said. "Give her what she wants. We need to find Sarai."

Marcelle could see that he didn't like it, but he'd turned people for less before. Time mattered.

"I will turn you myself," Setanta agreed. "After we take the plantation. If you want my blood, you will fight on our side to prove yourself."

Alma gave him a wicked grin. "Oh, I was hoping you'd say that. I've been practicing."

She knelt and dug her good hand into the earth, closing her eyes. Marcelle could feel a dark power reaching into the earth, corrupting it. The grass around them wilted and withered, the trees creaking as they died and fell into decomposition.

Then, pale, filthy hands began to claw their way out of the ground. Alma stood up, panting as twenty or so risen bodies climbed out of their graves and joined her, standing listlessly behind her, awaiting orders.

"Impressive," Marcelle admitted. She wondered if Sarai was willing and capable of accomplishing such a feat. Alma was a true necromancer. Or at least, she was able to make the corpses she hadn't personally killed respond. It seemed their souls were absent, which was for the best.

"Won't all you lovely assholes please come in?" Alma invited.

Setanta stepped through the protective barrier, meeting no resistance. Immediately, he had Alma by the throat, holding her up off her feet so he could whisper in her ear.

"I'm in a bad mood tonight, Alma Reinhart. If you betray us in any way, I will flay the skin and flesh from your bones and enjoy every second of your screams. You will beg for the mercy of death at my hands before I'm through with you. Is that clear?"

"Crystal clear," she gasped as she tried to pry his iron grip from her neck. He set her on the ground and let go. She stumbled back a little, massaging the finger-shaped bruises he no doubt had given her.

After Alma broke the barrier holding Marcelle prisoner, and the vampire gave her sire a quick hug to assure him all was well as he helped her remove the silver from her neck, they turned to face the plantation, Alma's undead corpses shambling alongside them.

As they approached, Setanta held up a hand to stop. Marcelle followed his gaze. There was a dull light from inside the old buildings that would have been the slave quarters, as if they had subpar electricity, and the unmistakable noises of many human hearts.

"Who lives there?" Marcelle asked.

"Just the help," Alma dismissed.

"Just the 'help'?" the vampire Lilly said in a low, dangerous voice that made the witch girl jump. "I know who used to live in those places."

"Come on," Alma whined. "Aren't you here to kill my dad?"

"We will." Setanta directed the group towards the slave quarters and threw open the door. Dozens of witches stared back at him, many with tear-stained faces, all with silver collars on their necks. Instantly, there was panic and shouts as the captive witches tried to get away from the door and escape the vampires.

"We won't hurt you," Setanta announced, which made some of the witches stop, but not all. He tried again a little louder, "We are not here for you, and you will not be harmed. Please, tell us who you are."

The witches stilled and one of the women with a tear-stained face stood. "If you're not here for us, then you're after the Reinharts, aren't you?"

Setanta nodded.

"They're useless," Alma said. "None of them have powerful gifts, that's why they're here. You think I wouldn't have freed them first if I thought I could use them to take out my dad?"

"A person's use isn't always in how strong they are," Marcelle murmured. "Why are you all crying?"

"They took thirteen of us. To kill for their spell," the woman said.

"Any chance they're still alive?" Marcelle asked Alma.

"Please, at this point?" Alma scoffed. "If you want to save anyone, focus on your precious Sarai."

"I know where they're keeping her," offered one of the men as he stood. "Let us go and I'll help you. We all know every passageway, every hidden room, every inch of that damn house. We know their weakest points, and we can help you take them out if you promise us our freedom."

"I think that is more than a fair arrangement considering your freedom would be yours regardless," Setanta said. He darted forward to the surprised yelps of several witches who jumped back and gripped the silver in his gloved hands, snapping it off the man's neck and discarding it. "Take my Knight Commander Marcelle to Sarai. The rest of you... take us through the servant passages. We will meet your captors and you will have retribution."

After Setanta gave her Sarai's prosthetic hand, Marcelle separated from the group and went with the man, instructing him to point out which window was Sarai's. He did so, and Marcelle leapt up two stories with ease. She bent open the bars on the window and poised on her toes on the windowsill looking in.

The room was empty except for the minimum of a cheap bed. Sarai sat on the edge of the mattress, hugging her knees to her chest, her eyes wide as she saw Marcelle perched like a bird.

"You're not the one we're looking for. But you don't look like you're on their side either," Marcelle said, echoing the very first words she spoke to Sarai when they met at a Vasi stronghold what seemed like a lifetime ago. "It's not working out very well for you."

"Marcelle!" Sarai gasped and the pair threw themselves at each other, kissing passionately as tears streamed down the girl's face. "You got out! I was so worried that... you're covered in dirt. Why are you covered in dirt? Did they hurt you?"

"They tried. I escaped," Marcelle said and kissed her again. "Setanta's here, as are the knights." She could hear the fighting as it began and hear Setanta's fierce war cry as bodies broke against him. The sounds of battle were loud enough that even Sarai with her mortal hearing could perceive it.

Sarai hugged her tight, and Marcelle shouted a little as the silver on Sarai's neck burned her arm on contact.

"Oh shit, I'm sorry," she gasped, pulling back.

"It's all right," Marcelle said as her arm healed. "Let's get that off you, shall we?" She picked up the sheet from the bed and used it to protect her hands as she broke the collar and discarded it. "Much better."

They kissed again. The warmth of Sarai's lips felt so good, and Marcelle held her close, her hand in the witch's soft hair. She smelled so familiar and comforting now. It was funny how someone she'd known for so little time gave her the same comfort as lovers she'd known for decades or even centuries.

"Are you hurt?" Marcelle asked. "I heard... they were going to start the ritual."

Sarai looked away. "They did. They didn't finish. But..." She stared out into the corner of the room, lost in her own mind. Marcelle gripped her hands tight, drawing the girl back to the present. Guilt gnawed at her.

"Did they rape you?" she asked softly.

Sarai shook her head. "He would have. Victor. Honestly, if it had just been that, I think it would have been better. I saw that thing. That, that creature." She shut her eyes and gripped her hair with both fists, pulling on it. "It was... I can't describe it. I can't stop seeing its face. We're so small, Marcelle. You, me, Setanta. It's all so..."

Marcelle knew the vague details of the ritual, but not enough to know what it was Sarai meant to describe.

Only that something mortals might refer to as a demon, a spirit, or even a god was involved. Why did magic have to be so… weird? "It's not here," Marcelle reassured her. "Look at me, Sarai. Just look at me. Focus on me. Do I look small to you?"

Sarai opened her eyes, taking deep breaths as she did. Those beautiful brown eyes looked so full of fright, but they relaxed as the pair looked at each other.

"I don't know," Sarai mumbled.

"To you. Not what the creature thinks. Do you think I'm small?"

Sarai shook her head.

"Then that's what matters right now. You matter to me, and while you're the shortest woman I know, you're not small."

The witch laughed a little, and Marcelle took the chance to lean in and kiss her sweet lips. They were dry, but the kiss wasn't for passion. It was a comfort, and it seemed to work.

They reattached Sarai's prosthetic hand and waited out the sounds of violence until an eerie calm and the sunrise had settled over the plantation home. Then Marcelle broke down the locked door of the room, leading them both through the halls. There were scorch marks from electricity and fire, blood splatter, and bullet holes. The witches of the Reinhart coven had put up a good fight, but it wasn't good enough.

Marcelle and Sarai found the ones that survived, including Alaric Reinhart, bound in their own silver collars with their hands zip-tied, all clustered in a group outside on the yard.

Setanta lorded over the captives, demonic wings spread out from his back, his spear pulsating with the blood of enemies it had drunk. He was covered in blood, his naked torso dripping with it and red hair that was usually so neatly tied back was wild and slick with the liquid. For the first time since World War Two, Marcelle could see the violent Iron Age warlord in his heart, one who reveled in slaughter. Except this time, he'd had the chance to truly enjoy himself killing witches. The man was a monster. But... he was her monster.

He looked up to see the women descend the porch.

"*My queens.*"

Marcelle noticed three heads held by their hair in the hand that didn't hold his spear. Setanta jumped forward, propelled by the wind from a strong beat of his wings, and knelt before them. He laid the heads at their feet, a grin on his face, red eyes bright with enjoyment. His voice was different than usual, reminiscent of when he had shouted down the throne room of vampires, but with less threat. He was prideful and radiated raw power.

"I gift to you the blood of those who would dare harm you. Consider it a wedding present."

Sarai stared at him, and her breath quickened. Yet, she didn't look afraid as most mortals would be at the sight of a fanged and winged monster offering them severed heads. She took a step forward and reached out to brush back the blood-drenched hair from his face, tenderness in her fingertips.

He stood and held Sarai's hand, then reached out to caress her face.

"*Mo cailín álainn,*" he said. "Sarai, are you hurt?"

"I…" Sarai's voice trailed off, and guilt stabbed at Marcelle's dead heart. "I'll be fine." She looked over the remnants of her family. "I can't focus on that right now.

This is more important. What are you going to do with the Reinharts?"

Chapter Thirty-One: The Witches' Fate

"You may not want to stay for this," Marcelle said to Sarai. The witch bit her lip, her head spinning. It was so strange, to watch the sun rise over her imprisoned family. After what they had just done to her, she still felt... she didn't know what she felt. Vindicated? Afraid? And seeing Setanta as he was, covered in blood, so far removed from the groomed and manufactured veneer of civility he always portrayed, was terrifying. Yet, also satisfying in a strange way. As if she had been given the gift of seeing his true self.

"He's going to kill them all, isn't he?" Sarai whispered as she looked at the silvered and tied witches she had once considered family. What was left of them.

"Most. He's likely going to speak to them all to determine who is most at fault by watching their reactions. Then he'll decide what to do with them."

Sarai's eyes widened. "I can help," she said and pulled out Danior's enchanted button from her pocket, grabbing Setanta's free hand. Before giving him a chance to say anything, she blurted, "Danior gave me this. It's enchanted by his gift. It gets warm when a lie is told. You should use it."

Setanta took the button from her and turned it over in his hand. "Interesting. Demonstrate, please. Tell me a lie."

"I, uh, I have pink hair."

Setanta nodded. "Excellent. Yes, this is very useful. Simplifies matters greatly. You may wish to leave. What I intend to do here will make Lochlan's pyre look like child's play."

"Yeah, I saw it already on my way down. I should stay. I feel a little responsible."

"Do you want to kill Alaric Reinhart? You once claimed his life."

Sarai's stomach twisted. She remembered once being faced with the option to kill a Vasi scientist who had tortured other witches. She had declined, letting Marcelle do the deed for her. But now... her father had hurt her in so many ways. The hell he had prepared for her... what father arranged for his daughter's rape by demons? It was disgusting, and the trauma of being connected to the demon even for those few moments was something she wasn't sure she would ever be able to move on from. She had wanted to kill him in the cellar, and his twisted face still bore the scars of her attack. She should want to kill him. He killed her mother. She remembered the cruel look in his eyes from Liora's memories. Yet now, he looked so pathetic.

"I..." Her voice trailed off as she felt the faint, ethereal touch of her mother's hand on her shoulder. "*Ima?*" Mother?

"*Naten li,*" the ghost said in Hebrew. Let me. "*Ani rotza ha ruach shelo.*" I want his breath. His spirit. His soul.

"*Ma sheh at rotza, ani notenet lach,*" Sarai whispered, feeling magic, necromantic power like a spell in her words. What you want, I will give to you.

She felt a strange tingling in her fingertips, like the feeling of her dark gift. The strength of her necromancy surged like she'd never felt before, and Setanta took a step back.

"Liora," he said in surprise.

The transparent figure stepped forward. "Thank you for caring for my daughter," she said to Setanta, then looked to Marcelle. "And to you for loving her."

She stepped towards a shocked Alaric.

"She's dead," he said in disbelief. "I know she's dead, I killed her! What the hell is this?"

"Advanced necromancy," Setanta murmured. "Something's made you stronger than you were."

Liora said nothing, but walked into Alaric, disappearing. He blinked, then his hands went to his throat and he gasped for air, struggling against his own body as the ghost of his murder victim strangled him. Blood vessels in his eyes popped, and his lips turned blue as he tried to breathe. He looked around desperately, his eyes pleading for help.

Alaric fell to his knees, then keeled over, dead. Liora stood up, pulling her spirit free from his body, a look of peace on her face.

"*Todah rabah, yaldati.*" Thank you, my little girl. She faded away, and Sarai knew through her magic that her mother had moved on to whatever "on" was.

"I suppose that solves that problem," Setanta mused. "Will you still stay for the rest? You may not like what you see."

Sarai nodded. This was her coven. People she once was a part of. And while it wasn't her fault that they followed such a dark path that led the vampire attack, she felt some twinge of responsibility for their fate.

Setanta left the main room to the sitting room, where the witches determined to be captives, the servants, and the slaves of the Reinhart coven were waiting. Sarai wasn't surprised at all to see that most of them were women, though there were some men in the mix. And it also didn't surprise her that an uncomfortable number were darker skinned than the Germanic Reinharts.

At first, the gathered mortals were all still terrified of Setanta. But having Sarai next to him, reassuring them, helped, and they opened up. One by one, they told of mistreatment and hell at the hands of the Reinhart family. They named names, and Setanta listened patiently with the truth enchanted button in his hands. Not a single person lied, and that made Sarai's gut twist. She knew her family was responsible for hellish behavior, but to hear such brutal testimony over and over... it was sickening to know their blood was in her veins.

At the end of all the testimony, Setanta had a simple question. "Would any of you like to kill them yourself, or would you like me to do it for you?" His tone was gentle, but the words were shocking to the abused crowd.

It took some debate, but one woman stepped forward.

"I want to kill Victor," she said. "For the last five years he's been... I just want him to feel some fraction of the pain he's put me through. I want him to know I did it."

Sarai bit her lip. She knew Victor was capable of rape. That was the point of the ritual he had agreed to take part, and he didn't care if she wanted to be with him or not. Yet, to be face to face with another woman he had victimized, when she herself had so narrowly escaped that abuse at his hands, felt haunting. She admired the determination in the girl's eyes.

Setanta looked at Sarai, who nodded.

"Then he will die at your hands," Setanta promised.

Several others stepped forward. Two of the few men, and three more women. And then all the rest but two women in the back stepped forward.

"We've suffered for years under their hands," said a middle-aged woman with a scar across her face. "It's their turn. Give them to us."

Returning to the outdoors where the knights held the Reinharts prisoner, Setanta stood before them.

"Victor Hess. Christina Reinhart. Klaus Reinhart. Lukas Reinhart. Ilsa Reinhart. Frederick Reinhart. Oskar Reinhart."

A few whose names were not called backed away from those who were, as if they knew what was coming.

"You have all participated in a ritual meant to create a new pureblood line within my territory. And according to the testimony that was just given to me, this is just the latest of many violent and horrific acts you've all committed. You are not vampires or part of my kingdom, so I do not have jurisdiction over you. However, I think it is just to give your lives to those you imprisoned. May your victims have mercy on you, for I would not."

Setanta stepped back and the mob of witches and humans, who had faced unspeakable cruelty, at the Reinharts' hands, stepped forward. They were offered weapons by the knights near them: knives and daggers. Most accepted, but the crowd hesitated.

Victor Hess stood, shaking in his silver restraints, glaring down the woman he had terrorized for years.

"If you know what's good for you, you'll turn that silver on the vampires," he told them. "They're worse than us. Most of us are innocent: we were just following

Alaric's orders."

"Historically, the phrase 'I was just following orders' has not absolved anyone," Marcelle snapped at him.

The girl who had accused him of rape stepped forward, a knife in her shaking hands. "I've dreamed of this for so long. Every night you dragged me to your room. Every time you told me I wasn't good for anything else."

"Put the knife down, Carla. Before you get hurt."

The girl's eyes flashed with anger, and she was suddenly on top of him, blood bursting from multiple stab wounds in his chest. The rest of the mob took their cue, and Sarai turned away, shutting her eyes to keep out the sounds of her family's dying screams. They earned it, she thought to herself. And she couldn't fault Setanta for allowing their victims the last word. There was poetic justice in vampire law, if nothing else. Though Sarai felt she would be happy to have a break from it for a while.

When they were dead, the vampires ushered the group outside, and did a sweep of the mansion to ensure there were no more living souls inside. On the front lawn, a shrill voice caught Sarai's attention.

"I think you're forgetting something." Alma stood, hand on her hip, tapping her fingers impatiently.

Sarai glared. "*You.*" She looked up at Setanta. "Shouldn't she be in silver?"

"She fought for our side and is part of the reason we were able to rescue you."

"She's also the one who kidnapped me in the first place!" Just because Alma had conveniently switched sides when it suited her didn't mean Sarai forgave her half-sister for all the harm she had caused.

"Oh, get over it," Alma said. "You owe me a debt, hound dog. I want what you promised me."

Sarai was about to protest, but something about the look in Setanta's eye made her take a step back, not wanting to get between the pair. He looked... dangerous. There was cruelty in his eyes and a smile on his lips. Alma's confidence faltered.

"Sarai, if you still care for your sister at all, you may wish to leave now."

"I said I would stay."

Alma looked afraid. "You promised me. You better make good on your promise. I want my payment."

"Ah, yes. Your payment," Setanta said, his fangs extending as he stepped towards her. "As agreed." All the vampires near them gave them a wide berth, waiting in anticipation. Setanta attacked, his teeth deep in Alma's throat as she gave a gurgled cry. He ripped free, Alma's front drenched in dark red as she bled out over them both. Then, before Sarai had a chance to process what was happening, Setanta bit into his own wrist and pressed the wound to Alma's mouth.

"Drink my blood or you will not rise when you die," he warned her.

Alma drank what she could considering half her throat was ripped open, and the vicious wound began to close. Setanta dropped her to the ground, and she looked up, panting.

"Is that it?" Alma asked. "I don't feel any different."

Marcelle stepped forward to hold Setanta's hand. "Darling, you didn't need to be this vindictive. I'm not sure even she deserves this. All for me?"

"Of course, *mo anam cara*."

Sarai frowned. "What am I missing here?" She

remembered what Setanta had told her once, that drinking his blood would kill her. Yet, Alma appeared fine.

No... her expression twitched, then morphed into fear. Alma gripped her throat, then her chest, as if she were trying to claw off her skin.

"It burns," she whispered. Her knees trembled and she fell to the floor, gasping in pain, then in clear agony, screaming through her teeth. "I'm on fire!"

"What did you do?" Sarai asked, unsure how to feel.

"I promised to turn her, in exchange for her assistance. For someone else, I would have broken their neck so they would die before having to endure the full pain of change. It's more, let's say, humane that way. But for her... I don't see a need to."

Alma began to shriek, clawing at herself hard enough to draw blood, only for the scratches to instantly heal. Tears streamed down her face.

"Please," she begged. "Please, just kill me."

"I already have," Setanta said.

It was uncomfortable to watch, and Sarai didn't like how easy it was for Marcelle and Setanta.

"Please stop it," Sarai whispered.

Setanta and Marcelle exchanged looks. The vampire woman sighed, then nodded, darting forward to break Alma's neck and leave her lifeless in the dirt. It was satisfying, but discomforting, and Sarai turned her back on the sight so that she could focus on finding comfort in her lovers.

"If you don't mind, Your Highness," Lilly interrupted. "I would like to return home. I'm not fond of plantations."

"Of course," Setanta said. "Though, you may

appreciate what I have planned. Stay a little while longer?"

Lilly looked at him skeptically and nodded. "If you insist."

"Lochlan," Setanta called to the nearby fire witch.

"Hm?" Lochlan said, jerking his head up from thought. "Yeah, what's up, man?"

"I'd like you to provide a demonstration as to why it is pyromancers are so prized and feared," Setanta said.

Lochlan smiled a bit. "Yeah? I'm always down to let loose. What did you have in mind?"

"You see that plantation mansion?"

Lochlan nodded.

"Burn it to the ground."

The witch grinned. "Hell *yes*."

Lochlan, with the expression of a child in a candy store for the first time, marched up to the front of the mansion. With a shout, he let loose a firestorm that sent waves of heat over the entire property. In less than ten minutes, the mansion was engulfed in flames, and Lochlan stood back, panting. Sarai had never seen any witch perform so much magic with their gift. It was awe-inspiring, and also terrifying that he was capable of such power.

"I don't think I've ever done something that big before," he said, breathing heavily as if he had run a mile. "That was amazing. Moretti never let me off the chain like that. I should have become a knight with you vamps ages ago." Lochlan stumbled back a little.

"Are you feeling unwell?" Marcelle asked.

"I… think I might pass out."

Marcelle darted forward to hold him up from behind. "I've got you," she told him. He blushed, but didn't protest, leaning on her for support as she helped him back towards the group. He stumbled, his eyes drooping, and Marcelle scooped him up into her arms as he closed his eyes and fell unconscious.

"You're right, that was worth waiting for," Lilly said. "Thank you. But didn't you promise the estate to Alma?"

"I never said what condition the estate would be in. She can have what's left. And I'll compel her to be incapable of leaving the grounds. She'll have enough money to be comfortable here for, say, fifty years or so. We can see how she behaves when the time has passed as to whether I'll allow her to leave or not."

"A good call." She exchanged glances with Setanta. "It's a good thing that boy is on our side. Make sure you keep it that way. Though be a little more careful with him."

"I intend to. I only wanted to see what his limits were, what he's capable of. Power like that comes around once or twice in a generation, even among the Tuatha de Danaan." The red glow of the burning plantation illuminated a satisfied look on both the vampires' expressions.

Sarai gave Marcelle a half hug from the side but stopped herself from a kiss. It felt awkward in front of Lochlan, even if he was unconscious.

Marcelle, however, didn't care, and went for Sarai's lips. It was what they both needed, and Sarai closed her eyes. Even though Marcelle was covered in dirt and blood, she was love like Sarai had never had before.

"I suppose I should tell you about the ritual they tried," Sarai said, catching the attention of both Marcelle and Setanta instantly.

Setanta looked crestfallen. "We didn't make it in time for you, did we? I'm so sorry."

"I'm just glad you were able to come at all," Sarai said. Though if they'd been just a little earlier... she shook her head. She couldn't think like that. She had to be grateful for what she had. "The spell they tried to do, it sent me to some other plane. And there was a thing that tried to possess me."

"Tried?" Setanta asked. "You were able to repel it?"

She shook her head. "I didn't need to. It didn't want me because..." Her hand touched her lower abdomen, and she looked up with a slight smile at the stunned looks on Marcelle and Setanta's faces.

"It worked?" Marcelle whispered.

"It worked," Sarai confirmed. "The thing didn't want me because I'm already pregnant. Or at least, already under the fertility spell's effect."

For the first time ever in Sarai's memory, both the vampires looked amazed and terrified. Marcelle thrust Lochlan into Lilly's arms and dropped to her knees in front of Sarai, reaching out a hand towards her.

"May I?" she asked. Sarai nodded, and Marcelle pressed a hand to her belly. "I was so sure the spell wouldn't work. So sure that adding my blood would ruin it and you'd realize I couldn't. That I would ruin everything."

"You could never ruin anything," Sarai said.

Setanta stepped forward like a man entranced and knelt with Marcelle before Sarai, placing his hand over the vampire woman's.

"This is why eternity is worth surviving," he said softly. "Even when you think everything repeats, everything has been seen, there's always something new that comes along and surprises you." He leaned forward and kissed Sarai's abdomen. She felt a wave of happiness as she looked into the eyes of her lovers. "Thank you, Sarai. For making this possible."

She just knelt next to them and allowed them both to embrace her. She didn't need any of the Reinharts. Their loss was no loss. With them gone, she could truly accept she was a Meir witch. Truly find freedom. These two people, Marcelle and Setanta, were her family now. And she couldn't have chosen a better pair.

Chapter Thirty-Two: The Myrk

Sarai wasn't sure how she got back to the palace. She slipped in and out of awareness, and time didn't seem to have the same meaning. When Marcelle or Setanta talked to her, or when she focused on the precious fluttering in her abdomen, she felt whole and present. But when she was alone, or someone else tried to talk to her, she couldn't focus as well. Particularly other vampires, witches like Hannah or Lochlan, or humans like Rosaline. They all were so meaningless. What did anything matter in the face of the creature that haunted her nightmares?

The Midnight Festival ended with a handfasting wedding ceremony between Setanta, Marcelle, and Sarai officiated by Muach the druid and with a coronation that felt like a blur. It was overwhelming, but she knew the importance of being recognized properly before the vampire world so pushed herself through the formalities, allowing Marcelle to lead her through unimportant details such as what to say and what to wear. She felt grounded when she swore an oath to the kingdom of New Ulster as she knelt before Setanta's throne and when he placed a golden circlet on hers and Marcelle's heads, but after the sound of applause drowned out her own mind. The world felt like swimming through molasses, all while that *thing* was close behind her. Waiting for her.

She knew others were trying to help. Bear would tell

her jokes, Rosaline would offer game nights. She had a vague notion of sitting in front of Marcelle's psychologist, whose face blurred in and out of reality. But how could she explain what she had experienced? The raw power that tried to consume her, that she had touched so briefly. She didn't have the words. And it wouldn't leave her mind.

Thankfully, Setanta knew without words. With the excitement of the Reinharts in the past, she could sense something inside him, some part of his power akin to the power of the creature, but on a far smaller scale. He knew. She knew he knew. But that fragment of power frightened her, and it took some time before she could bring herself to be alone with him again, without Marcelle. Or perhaps it didn't take time? She couldn't quite tell. At least, when she finally decided to, it felt good to cuddle with him in front of the fireplace while Marcelle was off at her psychologist appointment. Or was it training with the knights? Or maybe private training with Lochlan? Sarai couldn't remember what day it was, only that Marcelle had something planned that day that kept her away. Sarai rested a hand on her belly. When had it begun to protrude? How long had it been? She looked larger than she remembered, maybe a few months pregnant.

"This is nice," Setanta said, and kissed her forehead. "We should do this more. I've been worried about you."

"Worried?" she parroted.

"Ever since the coven business, you've been avoiding me. I realize that what you saw, how I behaved, might have been frightening."

Sarai looked up at him. She blinked, then burst into laughter. As if Setanta could be frightening compared to the creature!

"You have me at a disadvantage here," he mused. "I missed the joke."

"You're not scary," she scoffed. "I… you know, right? You can feel it? You've felt it?"

"Felt what?"

"The… ritual."

Amusement drained from Setanta's face. He caressed her cheek. "I can't express my regret enough. I'm sorry, Sarai. I know I wasn't fast enough."

"I'm not mad at you. You know about it, right? About," she took a deep breath. "About the thing. The creature. I can feel something like it in you whenever I'm near you. In your magic. Your soul. You can feel it too, right? What is it?"

Setanta sighed. "To tell you the truth, I don't know. There are a number of beings like the one you encountered. Each is a little different. One of them lent a portion of its power to create my bloodline and gave my family its attributes, its magic, and its bloodlust. In my family's case, the being's name is the Morrigan. At least, that's one of her names. I've had some dealings with her before, though she never sought to possess me, to my great relief. She views me as her child the way humans call dogs their babies, I believe. And I know the continued existence of my family's bloodline allows her to travel between her realm and Earth at will, for whatever purposes of amusement she might desire. I know we entertain them. But do I know what she is? I can genuinely say that I hope I never learn more than I already know. Men have gone mad trying to comprehend her true nature."

"The one I saw… was it the Morrigan? A goddess?"

"Unlikely. She wouldn't have an interest in creating a new bloodline when she has one already on earth. The competition would lead to bloodshed. If it touched your mind, you might know its name."

"Its name," Sarai whispered. Yes, she did know. It felt as if some dark instinct had whispered it in the crevices of her mind. "The Myrk. Her name is the Myrk."

Setanta nodded. "I think I know now why you've been so distant and unlike yourself. The Morrigan and the Myrk have minds not meant for people like us to comprehend. I may be able to help."

"How?"

"I'll do a spell to suppress your memory of encountering the Myrk from your conscious mind. If you can't remember her, then she won't be able to haunt you as she does. Would you like that?"

It was such a huge relief, like a thousand bricks had been lifted from her shoulders. "Oh, please, yes," she breathed. "I can't handle any more of this."

The time between their conversation and the spell was a daze. She knew he got his spear for the spell, and some old book. A taste in her mouth and a cup in her hand told her that he had given her a potion to drink. As the fog lifted from her mind, time had meaning again. The memory of the Myrk and how it felt to touch the creature's mind evaporated. Sarai felt as if she had been entrenched in a thunderstorm she hadn't been aware of, and the skies were clear. She could *breathe*. She could *feel*. She could *care*.

"Sarai, focus on me. I need to make sure your mind is intact as it should be," Setanta said. "Do you know where you are?"

Sarai looked around. They were outside, in the circle of stones where he had pronounced her his future queen to the world of vampires. But now it was just them, alone.

"Yes," she said. "The standing stone circle. You announced me as your choice for queen here."

"And you know who I am?"

"You're Setanta. King of New Ulster. A vampire and a witch. And my husband."

He nodded, taking her hands in his. "Who is Marcelle?"

"Knight Commander Marcelle de Sauveterre. Also a vampire. Not a witch. Also my wife. Also your queen. And I love her."

"And do you know who you are?"

"I'm Sarai Reinha… No." She smiled. "I'm Sarai Meir. I'm pregnant with your and Marcelle's baby. Our baby. I am a necromancer and a healer. And I am queen of New Ulster."

A word about the author...

Evelyn Silver graduated from Florida Atlantic University with a BA in English, completed an editorial internship at HCI Books, worked as a freelance editor, and is currently enjoying her experience writing bisexual and polyamorous romance. She won NN Light Book Heaven's award for Best LGBTQ Book of 2022 with her first novel, Witch's Knight, and is hard at work continuing the series.

She lives in Florida with her spouse, their sons, and two cats.

https://eternalevelyn.com/